**Suddenly, the door swung open, and
a shadow moved toward her.**

She recognized Blackmer instantly, and desire ignited inside her. He crouched above Clarissa, breathing hard, his skin still damp and the tight flex of muscles in his shoulders darkly illuminated. The scent of the soap from his bath filled her nostrils. Her pulse raced, her heart near exploding.

"You," he growled deep in his throat. "Are my preference."

A second later, he kissed her, pressing his thumb against the side of her jaw, commanding her lips to part while his tongue boldly entered and teased. She gasped for breath, stunned into half-senselessness...and surrendered, her mouth opening fully to accept each deep, possessing stroke.

His mouth moved to her cheek...her neck, leaving her skin hot and awakened wherever his lips touched. Sensations she'd never experienced before spiraled up from inside her, delicious and achingly sweet, awakening a need in her body and rendering her unexpectedly wild.

God help her, she didn't understand, but she wanted him as well .

appealing. Sophia's pain is very real, and every interaction is fraught with honest emotion. As they struggle to recapture their romance, readers will feel deep sympathy for both characters and hope for them to find happiness."
—*Publishers Weekly* (starred review)

"4½ stars! The first in Dalton's One Scandalous Season series grabs the reader's emotions in an intensely passionate love story, filled with misunderstandings, past indiscretions, trust, and forgiveness. But, for all the intensity, this gifted storyteller also deftly lightens the mood in a very well-written and satisfying read by adding a few zany characters bent on mischief and mayhem."
—*RT Book Reviews*

"*Never Desire a Duke* is a terrific debut novel—it reminded me of Lisa Kleypas' most memorable novels with a to-die-for hero and a lovely but heartbroken heroine. It's an intensely beautiful, moving story (but it does have its funny moments) and you won't be able to help yourself—you'll be rooting for them to get back together."
—EverAfter.com.au

Never Surrender to a Scoundrel

to a Scoundrel

One Scandalous Season

LILY DALTON

FOREVER

NEW YORK   BOSTON

Copyright © 2015 by Kim Ungar
Excerpt from *Never Desire a Duke* copyright © 2013 by Kim Ungar

Forever
Hachette Book Group
1290 Avenue of the Americas
New York, NY 10104
www.HachetteBookGroup.com

Forever is an imprint of Grand Central Publishing.

The Forever name and logo are trademarks of Hachette Book Group, Inc.

The Hachette Speakers Bureau provides a wide range of authors for speaking events. To find out more, go to www.hachettespeakersbureau.com or call (866) 376-6591.

The publisher is not responsible for websites (or their content) that are not owned by the publisher.

Printed in the United States of America

First printing: January 2015

10 9 8 7 6 5 4 3 2 1
OPM

*For Jana,
the bravest heroine ever!*

*And for my brother,
Lt. Col. Master Blaster,
her forever hero*

Acknowledgments

The third book in a trilogy series has a lot of expectations riding on it. As an author, you want to give your reader everything they're hoping for in a "grand finale" and make them yearn for the next adventure. So, reader, this book is for you. Thank you for loving the Bevington sisters as much as I did and for celebrating their Happily Ever Afters alongside me. Thank you for all the e-mails, Facebook posts, and Twitter mentions. But most of all, thank you for loving books and romance!

Thank you also to Kim Lionetti, my spectacular agent! I treasure the encouragement you always provide and the confidence you place in me. Also, the awesome sushi (and handsome waiters) you have such a knack for finding.

Next...I'm not just throwing out words when I say the One Scandalous Season series would not have been possible without Michele Bidelspach, a truly amazing editor who always sees beyond all my tangled, imperfect efforts and helps me transform them into magic on the page and in readers' minds. Thank you, Michele, for your spot-on guidance, for coaxing all those deeply buried emotions out of me, and for helping me learn the beauty of a gentler romantic conflict.

Thank you also to Forever publicist Julie Paulauski for her enthusiasm for each book and for making me feel like a rock star every time we have a new release. Thank you to Megha Parekh for answering so many questions and keeping me on track. Thanks also to the Hachette art department and production team for making these books shine.

I want to also thank all of my family for their support. Jana, I know this has been the toughest year ever, but I'm so proud of you, and of my brother and all our parents, for being the most amazing support system. You inspire me every day, and help me keep things in perspective.

This year marks 20 years that my "hero," Eric, and I have been married. How can that be? And how can we have two fantastic kids who are now both taller than me? It seems to have happened in a blink. I love you all.

Never Surrender to a Scoundrel

Chapter One

"What do you mean, 'it seems Mr. Kincraig isn't our cousin after all'?" Clarissa Bevington asked, shocked, looking between her grandfather, the elderly Earl of Wolverton, and the tall, bearded man in question.

Holding true to his rakish reputation, Mr. Kincraig stared back bleary-eyed, with his jaw-length hair disheveled and wearing rumpled evening clothes. Obviously he had never made it home to his bachelor's residence on Bennet Street the night before, which wasn't at all a surprise.

"Why, Miss Bevington," said Mr. Kincraig, one dark slash of an eyebrow raising higher. "Can it be that you are disappointed?"

"Me, disappointed?" She exhaled. "Certainly not."

For almost two years, after Mr. Kincraig had been presented to the family by the earl's investigators, they had all believed him to be their distant relation and sole heir to Wolverton's title.

Indeed, the entire family stood in the earl's library, having been gathered for what Wolverton had told them would be an important announcement.

The family included the earl's widowed daughter-in-law, who was also Clarissa's mother, Lady Margaretta, and the Duke of Claxton, who stood protectively beside his expectant duchess—Clarissa's oldest sister, Sophia—who sat on a garnet-colored settee. Daphne, their middle sister, occupied the center cushion, her blond hair and bright blue eyes so similar in appearance to Clarissa's that strangers often mistook them to be twins. Lord Blackmer, whom Daphne had married the month before in a thrilling turn of events, lowered himself to the vacant end of the settee beside his new wife, his gray eyes mirroring the same surprise reflected all around the room.

The only members of the family missing were Clarissa's father, Lord Harwick, who had died three years earlier after being thrown from his startled horse, and her brother, Vinson, who had perished shortly after while at sea on a scientific expedition. Their deaths, while a great tragedy on the deepest emotional level, had also brought around the need to designate Wolverton's heir, and that was the impetus that had brought a stranger—Mr. Kincraig—into their midst.

"That's it, my dear girl." He grinned devilishly. "Put on a brave face, so no one will know the heartache you're suffering at hearing this dreadful news."

"Oh, *you*!" she exclaimed, and eased back against the cushion of her chair, a flush rising into her cheeks at being singled out for his teasing. Truly, it never ceased, even in the most serious of moments. "There's not one smidgeon of ache in my heart, I'm—I'm just surprised, that's all."

Surprised that Mr. Kincraig *himself* didn't look more disappointed or heartachey.

After all, if he wasn't Wolverton's heir, he wouldn't be inheriting the fortune and estates and *éclat* the title entailed. What man in his right mind *wouldn't* be disappointed?

Ah, but this was Mr. Kincraig. He'd never embraced the idea of being an erudite gentleman. Not only did he persistently defy any normal expectations of decorum, he only reluctantly joined their ranks for any social or family occasion, usually just when commanded by Wolverton to do so—though more recently she'd believed his attitude toward them had warmed to a certain degree.

"I know this news comes as a shock." The earl leaned forward in his chair, pressing the fingertips of both hands together. He spoke softly and tilted his balding head as if sharing regretful news, but Clarissa saw a brightness in his eyes that might be interpreted as relief. "Mr. Kincraig's family tree is tangled, to say the least, and I don't wish to go into the details—"

"Details most *tawdry*." Mr. Kincraig grimaced, but in a comical way, where his frown wasn't really a frown but a smile-frown, with one corner of his lips turned up. "Prurient, even. It seems my forebears were altogether devoid of moral conscience."

Daphne rolled her eyes. "The apple did not fall far from the—"

"*Daphne,*" Lady Margaretta interrupted sternly.

At this, Clarissa almost giggled, but she subdued the response with a hand to her mouth.

Mr. Kincraig winked at her. "Apparently I did not."

So unrepentantly wicked! There had always been a

tiny—or gargantuan, in some instances—suspicion in the back of many heads that the young man had somehow fabricated his purported relation to Wolverton and that he was an imposter and fortune hunter, but the good humor Clarissa saw in him now put those accusations to rest.

Wolverton's aged eyes crinkled at the corners as he glanced toward the man at his side. "Let us just say the evidence presented by my investigators is sufficient enough to disqualify Mr. Kincraig from being in line to inherit, in any form or fashion, the earldom."

"What a relief," muttered the duke in a cool tone. His Grace had never taken a liking to Mr. Kincraig.

Mr. Kincraig did not shy away from or ignore the comment. He shrugged and crossed his arms over his chest, appearing completely at peace. "For you and I both, Your Grace."

Clarissa stared down at her hands, which lay crossed on her lap. Was she relieved, as Claxton and even Mr. Kincraig declared themselves to be?

Why wouldn't she be? She and Mr. Kincraig had never been particularly close, though since his introduction to the family they had attained a certain ease of familiarity. With Sophia married and Daphne recently wed as well, she had gotten to know him better than the rest, on those occasions when he acted as her and her mother's escort to this function or that. She felt quite certain she was the only one who appreciated his blackguard sense of humor, though she'd tried very hard not to let him or her mother know. Wasn't it only normal that she should feel a little sad?

Also, too, she could not help but suspect he had come into their lives a wounded creature. Her own family had suffered such grief and loss in recent years. Perhaps for that reason she thought she recognized a certain hauntedness in the back of his eyes that no roguish smile or spoken humor could conceal.

Just then Lady Margaretta sighed from where she sat and with sparkling eyes peered up at Mr. Kincraig. "I know we have Michael, so our situation is not as dire as before, but—"

She spoke of Clarissa's little nephew Michael, of whose existence they had only recently become aware along with other surprising secrets; namely, that Vinson, before his death, had entered into a clandestine but legal marriage with Lord Raikes's sister, Laura, who had later died in childbirth. But from those dark tragedies had come great joy and hope, and the little boy was now a much-adored member of both families as well as Wolverton's declared heir.

"—I confess that I, for one, *am* disappointed to hear this news." She frowned, her lovely features darkened by regret. "No matter how you may feel about us, Mr. Kincraig, I've come to think of you as family."

From his chair, Wolverton nodded and smiled warmly. "Indeed."

Mr. Kincraig peered at Her Ladyship for a long moment. "Thank you, my lady. And thank you, Wolverton, as well." He tilted his head in deference to the earl.

He looked about the room and offered a slight bow, which caused a thick lock of his overly long hair to swing down over his forehead, something Clarissa found unexpectedly endearing.

"Thank you all," he said.

Emotion swelled in Clarissa's throat. She didn't think

she'd ever seen him look so sincere, so unguarded by the wry, naughty humor she'd always suspected he wore as armor against the world. If only his cravat did not hang from his neck so inexpertly tied, like...like a grappling octopus! Her fingers itched to repair it, as she had done numerous times before.

Oh, it was true! Clarissa felt a deep stab of sadness that he was no longer part of their family.

Though Mr. Kincraig, since his arrival in London, had kept the family in constant fear that they would be humiliated or scandalized as a result of his love affairs, rakehell ways, and gambling debts, she...well, she actually liked him, and very much so. It had always been such fun to arrive at the party in the company of a pirate—at least that's what she and her sisters had decided he looked like. All the ladies of the *ton* had been equal parts scandalized and enamored of him, a fact that had on more than one occasion turned a dull evening into an exceedingly entertaining one.

As a young lady expected to live her life within the strict dictates of society and rigid rules of decorum, she found it refreshing to know someone who simply didn't care about all of that. Days were just...more *interesting* with Mr. Kincraig in them.

Perhaps, on a deeper level, her unexpected attachment had formed because she had already lost two family members who were very important to her and she did not wish to lose another, even to a less serious circumstance such as this. For his part, beneath Mr. Kincraig's boisterousness and bravado, he seemed alone in the world, a man in need of a home and a family and love. After all this time in their midst he'd remained a mystery to them all...a mystery she'd always assumed they as a family would one day unravel and eventually embrace.

Now she feared they wouldn't have that chance.

"What will you do now?" she asked, truly wanting to know.

He smiled. "That's an easy question to answer. I'll go abroad and seek my next great fortune. And the next, and the next." He made a rolling gesture with his hands.

"There are indeed fortunes to be had," said Lord Raikes.

Her new brother-in-law had himself been a prosperous saltpeter merchant in Bengal in the years before he came into his title.

"How soon will you depart?" inquired the duke, doing very well, Clarissa thought, not to sound overly eager.

"Soon," Mr. Kincraig answered vaguely, nodding.

"You must visit," Lady Margaretta declared, bright eyed. She fumbled in her skirts and dabbed a handkerchief to her eyes. "Every time you are in London."

Clarissa nodded in agreement, even though Mr. Kincraig didn't see.

He tilted his head. "I very much appreciate the invitation."

At hearing his response, Clarissa frowned because he hadn't actually accepted her mother's invitation. Inside her chest, her heart grew heavy. Did that mean they would never see him again? That they would never know how his life turned out?

"I should be going then." Suddenly Mr. Kincraig was taking his leave of them and offering polite good-byes all around.

"Stay for the luncheon," insisted Lady Margaretta. Every Tuesday Her Ladyship hosted an informal luncheon in the small ornamental garden behind the house.

"Thank you, my lady, but I must decline," he answered, bending over her hand.

A moment later, he offered a similar farewell to Clarissa. "Miss Bevington. A wonderful summer day to you."

"To you as well," she answered quietly.

Backing away, he smiled at her before pivoting on his heel and proceeding toward the door.

That was it? That was good-bye?

Was it good-bye, or would they see him again before he left town? She didn't know.

Her pulse gave a little jump of anxiety, one she felt compelled to soothe by speaking to him at least one more time, to say something more sincere, more thoughtful than some decorous comment about a summer day.

She followed everyone else into the corridor, but Lady Margaretta blocked the way, pushing the earl's wheeled wicker chair. By raising up onto her toes, she saw Mr. Kincraig caught in the small crowd of guests who had just then arrived for the luncheon. The elderly Lady Dundalk and Sir Keyes trundled past, arm in arm.

"Dear Clarissa, so good to see you," said Lady Dundalk, reaching out to touch her hand. Today she wore a peacock blue satin toque, with a fan of dyed pink feathers on one side. "Come and tell me all about your week, my dear. The parties and balls and beaus."

"I shall." Clarissa smiled, sweeping past them. "I will join you in the garden in a moment."

Mr. Kincraig...*there*, he strode past a potted palm in a large Chinese pot, in the opposite direction, toward the doors that would take him to the street. Footmen attended guests there, taking hats and walking sticks.

Rushing up behind him, she reached out and touched his sleeve. He half turned toward her, his expression far away, appearing as distracted as if his mind had already gone out the door and into the street. "Miss Bevington, yes? What is it?"

"Mr. Kincraig, you said you were leaving London soon—"

"Yes, soon."

"But not before my come-out ball. You'll be there, won't you?"

"Me?" His eyes widened slightly.

"Yes, you. It's an important night for me." More important than anyone knew, though she couldn't explain that to him or anyone now. Not yet. "I would like for you to be there."

His mouth twisted. "Hmmm."

His reluctance ruffled her. She was trying to do something nice, to reaffirm his welcome at family events, even though he wasn't family anymore.

"You attended Daphne's," she reminded him, shameless in her attempt to make him feel guilty for hesitating for even a moment. "Don't you wish to attend mine as well?"

She smiled brightly.

His lips moved, framed by his beard. "Remind me again of the pertinents, the date and time?"

Could he appear any less interested? Oh, he was so...Mr. Kincraig! Which was why she couldn't truly be angry with him. His lack of concern over social matters was almost charming, in a subversive sort of way.

"It is one week hence on *Thursday*, the final week of the season," she retorted lightly, resisting the urge to give his arm a good pinch. "You should know because you received an invitation last week, though I know for a fact you have not replied your intention to attend."

He chuckled, and his brows came together. "Do you mean to say I'm on a list somewhere and that you've noticed there is not...what, a check or a 'will attend' inscribed beside my name? I'm so pleased you noticed."

She huffed out a breath, exasperated. "Mother mentioned it, that's all."

His eyes widened and he smiled. "I know when your ball is. I am only teasing you, because you are so teaseable and believe everything I say, which by now I would think you would have learned better."

"Mr. Kincraig!" The tension in her shoulders eased. She *should* have known. Yes, he was always teasing, and she believed his silliness every time. Why hadn't she learned? Perhaps because she didn't want to. "Well? Will you attend?"

"There's so much I must do, in such a short amount of time. I must close up my residence, and—"

She scowled menacingly. "*Mr. Kincraig.*"

Already knowing he teased again. Now she teased as well.

His smile broadened into a grin. "Of course I will be there. I wouldn't miss it."

"Wonderful!" She smiled.

Because even though Mr. Kincraig wasn't family after all, she wanted him present with everyone else to share in her good news. To celebrate the announcement.

In just one week, her perfectly wonderful, *spectacular* secret wouldn't be a secret anymore. All of London would share in her joy. Her heart leapt at the thought. Indeed, she doubted her feet had touched the floor for days. Oh, she was bursting with it, but she couldn't tell anyone, despite being terrible at keeping secrets, because she and Lord Quinn had promised each other they wouldn't tell anyone.

At the mere thought of Lord Quinn's bright blue eyes and smiling lips, the earth moved, enough to dizzy her.

Even now, she could hardly believe it was true. London's most eligible and handsome bachelor had fallen madly in love with her, and she with him. *And* he ought to be arriving for the luncheon any moment, with his father, the Duke of Lowther, whom Claxton had invited so that he might persuade him toward his way of thinking on some labor act he wished to introduce in Parliament. Just the thought of his arrival sent her pulse jumping in anticipation.

While at first she'd believed him to be just another attractive face, as consumed by the youthful and sometimes empty pursuits as most young gentlemen of the *ton*, he'd revealed to her the honorable man beneath. Once she knew the truth, there'd been no holding back her heart. They'd kept their romance a secret, wanting to savor their unfolding feelings away from the curious eyes of family and society's gossips and newspapers, but also for the simple enjoyment of romantic subterfuge.

Then, last month in the midnight shadows of Vauxhall Gardens, as the intoxicating scent of jasmine filled the air, the young lord had asked her that *most* important question and she had deliriously and happily said yes.

Yet Quinn, ever the romantic, wanted the memory of their engagement to be perfect for her and suggested that they wait until the night of her ball to make things official, and she had agreed. They'd enjoyed the most exciting game of secrecy ever since.

"Now, what about lunch?" Clarissa asked, taking Mr. Kincraig's arm. "I know very well you've been out all night. You must be hungry."

Now that she'd found such happiness, she didn't want anyone to be lonely. Mr. Kincraig needed a family, and who said he couldn't always be a part of theirs, if not by blood?

At hearing the doors swing open again, her pulse jumped and she glanced over her shoulder toward the vestibule. Disappointingly, Lord Quinn wasn't among the party that entered.

"What I am is exceedingly tired," Mr. Kincraig answered in a gravelly voice, resisting, though he did not remove his arm or step away. "I only want to sleep, that is all, perhaps even in the carriage that carries me away from here. Yes, I think that would do nicely."

"Nonsense, you need sustenance," she chided in a tone that sounded very much like her mother.

"Clarissa..." He held firm.

"Mr. Kincraig." She tilted her head toward the garden and tugged gently at his arm.

He exhaled and pursed his lips. "Why are you always so—"

"Nice to you?" she supplied, laughing, knowing full well "nice" wasn't the word he'd intended to use. He would have said "exasperating" or "bothersome" or "persistent."

Yet his shoulders relaxed, and his expression warmed. "Yes. You are very nice to me. Why?"

The genuineness of his gaze caught her off guard, and

in the moment she could be no less honest. "Because I like you, Mr. Kincraig, and I don't want you to go. I don't want you to be lonely or uncared for—"

"Me, lonely?" He chuckled, looking dismayed. Uncomfortable.

"Yes, you." She saw past his bluster.

"I have plenty of companionship." With the slightest tilt of his lips, his smile went wolfish.

"That's not what I mean," she exclaimed, blushing.

"What *do* you mean?" He grinned, but his eyes were serious.

"Just stay for Mother's luncheon," she urged, knowing several young unmarried ladies would be in attendance.

"Actually..." His gaze drifted to the corridor that led to the back of the house and thence the garden. "I *am* rather ravenous."

She smiled, triumphant. "It's settled then."

Her hand on his arm, they proceeded that way, but she came to a halt, her gaze fluttering over him. The smile dropped from her lips. "Only you can't go out there looking like that. Mr. Kincraig, have you truly never learned how to properly tie a cravat?" How many times had she asked him the very same thing? She reached for his neckcloth and loosened the tangle.

"I don't think it's as terrible as you make it out to be," he said, his dark eyes rolling heavenward.

"Oh, it is," she replied with a playful smirk, tugging the top layer of cloth upward through the hole she'd created and tightening the knot. "Trust me. And why do you insist on keeping that beard? My sisters and I all agree your appearance would be quite improved without it."

He growled good-naturedly, and she laughed, neatly

tucking the linen into his vest. Hooking her arm through his elbow, she led him to the garden.

* * *

The moment a certain young nobleman stepped into the garden, Dominick Arden Blackmer—who for the time being still answered to the name of Mr. Kincraig—noticed the change in the young woman standing beside him. As he expected, Clarissa ever so politely extracted herself from conversation with him and Lord Raikes and made her way across the garden.

"So, Raikes, tell me about Bengal," he said encouragingly to the gray-eyed young man. "I've never had the pleasure of traveling there."

"Bengal." Raikes's gray eyes went distant. "Well, it is nothing at all like England. It's a beautiful, mysterious place. One half of the year, you suffer through hot winds and dust, and the other, monsoons."

"Sounds miserable." Dominick flashed a grin and absently smoothed his hand over his mustache and beard, which he'd worn since presenting himself in London because he knew from experience most people would never look beyond them.

"But it's not miserable. At times, I miss it, but...don't tell Lady Raikes."

They chuckled together.

Dominick actually *had* been to Bengal, though he couldn't tell anyone about that particular adventure. Those six months, much like the last thirteen years of his life, had largely been sworn to secrecy. Still, as far as conversation, Bengal was something to talk about.

He knew Raikes had made his fortune there, and better Raikes talk than him.

He enjoyed the easy conversation between them. Raikes had always been a friendly fellow, but there was a wariness to him, as with all of Wolverton's family, where Mr. Kincraig was concerned, because they'd all entertained, to some degree or another, the suspicion he might be an imposter.

If only the family knew the truth about him, as Wolverton did. He might indeed be an imposter of the most calculated sort, but he wasn't a scoundrel intent on fraud. Rather he was their protector. Even though he'd been informed his assignment here had concluded, he couldn't seem to turn off the instinct.

"Why do you miss it?" he murmured, still watching Clarissa. "I only ask because I'm considering traveling there myself."

Dominick was only talking to talk. He'd go wherever his next set of official orders sent him, whether to Bengal, St. Petersburg—or even Timbuktu. At least that was what he hoped for—and in the deepest, loneliest hours of the night, had *prayed for*—a more challenging assignment abroad, now that his mission in London under the auspices of the Home Office had come to an end. Once he had been a veritable dragon, a legend among the most elite of intelligence operatives. Now, fallen from grace and largely a *persona non grata* to the Foreign Office, he had been consigned to this—a common security mission at home in England, where nearly two years ago he had been put in place to protect the old earl from a vague, unspecified threat of harm. He had done his time, earned the respect of his lower-level peers, and not made a single misstep. Perhaps finally his exile would end and he would be reinstated. Returned to his former life.

"To Bengal, truly?" Raikes leaned forward in his chair, interested. "Why there?"

He shrugged. "Why not?"

Raikes rubbed a hand to his chin. "There are certainly opportunities there aplenty to enrich oneself, but don't undertake the decision lightly." He exhaled, shaking his head. "I faced challenges there such that I'd never faced before—"

Dominick sipped lemonade from a cut crystal cup and watched Clarissa continue her progression across the garden, she a bright spot of pink silk moving between tables that sparkled with china, silver, and crystal.

So as not to be obvious, he knew, she very wisely stopped to engage in conversation with several ladies on the way, but in the end, she positioned herself almost back to back to the gentleman with brilliant blond hair who had entered the garden moments before, the one who looked like a magnificent angel. Dressed in a silver-gray suit, he portrayed the epitome of *au courant* male fashion, with not a seam or fold or buckle out of place.

Dominick wasn't surprised to see them together, though not exactly *together*. On numerous occasions before he'd observed the eye contact, the secret smiles and other wordless communications. One didn't have to be an intelligence agent in service of the Crown to observe that the youngest Bevington sister had fallen head-over-satin-slippers in love with the nauseatingly charming and well-connected Lord Quinn.

A smile turned his lips as he drained the last of the tart liquid from his cup. Who did Clarissa think she was fooling? Everyone, it seemed. Her family and friends appeared oblivious to the young couple's *tendre*. How could they not notice, as he had, that whenever the young man entered the room—or garden, in this instance—Clarissa's skin flushed and her shoulders softened, and she became a degree more beautiful, as women in love tended to be?

Not that he'd noticed for any other reason than society gatherings bored him nearly to tears and he had nothing else but her clandestine romance to entertain his languishing mind...although observing them now, out of the corner of his eye, did make him feel wistful for a time when he too had been in love.

But this wasn't about him, it was about Clarissa and her young man, whom, truth be told, he didn't particularly care for. In his limited exchanges with Lord Quinn, he had not discerned much mental or moral substance. But who was he to judge the choice of her heart? Young men often improved with time.

Raikes continued his informative lecture on Bengal, its bad roads and river crossings and saltpeter. Dominick wearily nodded and said *mmmhmmmmm* at the appropriate intervals, wishing he'd resisted Clarissa's persuasion and returned home to a cold bachelor's supper and his bed. This assignment had been decidedly nocturnal, and his eyes were damnably scratchy from lack of sleep and his stomach growled ferociously.

Just then he noticed Clarissa slip away into the house. Predictably, several moments later, Lord Quinn followed.

His eyebrows raised in surprise. A bold move from Clarissa, and one he had not expected, but who was he to condemn the impetuousness of young love? He remembered a time, not so long ago, when he would have risked anything to be with the woman he loved if only for a fleeting moment and a single breathless kiss. But certainly her mother would notice her absence. Scanning the garden, he found Lady Margaretta surrounded by a chattering wall of ladies. Everyone else in the family was similarly distracted.

Perhaps he ought to go and "accidentally" interrupt?

Or better yet, he should remember his place, mind his own business, and stay where he was. He exhaled, and examined his knuckles. He closed his eyes.

Ah, damn. His conscience forbade inaction.

Curse Clarissa for putting him in such a position, but as she was so young and inexperienced with men, he doubted she realized her allure and the temptation she might present to a weaker man. Though she was far too silly and innocent for his particular taste, he'd have to be blind not to have noticed her attractiveness, with her pale blond curls, bright blue eyes, and seemingly perfect bosoms. Certainly Lord Quinn had been raised a gentleman, but Dominick, out of respect for Wolverton and the family he had protected all this time, could not risk the chance that he would compromise Clarissa, if only with a kiss.

Better he break up their dalliance than someone else, who might not be so discreet.

He waited for a pause in Raikes's dialogue and excused himself. Yet he'd only made it halfway across the garden when Clarissa emerged from the house, radiant and not a bit mussed, which relieved but did not surprise him. His muscles relaxed. Of course, this was Clarissa, an innocent girl who had been raised with the utmost attention and care. He couldn't imagine anything truly untoward taking place. She joined the Countess of Dundalk and her elderly beau, Sir Keyes.

Three, two, one...

And Lord Quinn appeared, looking equally unflustered and polished, and rejoined his father the duke. But not before he flashed a smile in Clarissa's direction.

No doubt there'd be a proposal soon from the young gentleman. Perhaps, even, on the night of her debut ball.

So...good for Clarissa. She was a charming young woman. He liked her very much, and he sincerely wished the same for her as she had wished for him, that she would be happy and never be disappointed in her choice.

Chapter Two

One Week Later,
Thursday

"I can't remember ever being so happy," Clarissa Bevington exclaimed, looking about in flush-faced wonderment. Little Michael, whom she held perched on her hip, clapped his chubby hands.

"Ohhhhh!" he marveled, mirroring her enthusiasm.

Since being discovered, her brother Vinson's young son lived under Wolverton's roof but received regular visits from his other grandparents, who were Raikes's mother and father. They always stayed with the family when they came to town and, indeed, were so well liked they had become part of the family as well. Though Michael received constant attention from his grandparents, aunts, and uncles, they had all agreed upon the importance of him having parents, and Raikes and Daphne had happily assumed that role.

"What a memorable night this shall be!" said Daphne,

throwing them both an affectionate glance. She reached out to Michael, tucking a stray curl behind his ear.

Clarissa had never seen her grandfather's ballroom look more beautiful, nor had she ever felt more special than she did that day. The room had been festooned in flower garlands, and the urns that had been placed before each of the massive Corinthian columns that lined the marble floor overflowed with profuse arrangements of pink and ivory blooms. She inhaled deeply, delighting in the heady scent of roses and delphinium. The fragrance of summer! The fragrance of romance.

At the far end of the cavernous room, the head footman, Mr. Ollister, carefully lowered an enormous crystal punch bowl onto the tea board. The housekeeper, Mrs. Brightmore, perched at the top of a ladder, steadied by two housemaids, having insisted that she'd spied a sneaky bit of dust atop an archway that the rest of them hadn't been able to see. Cook's voice could be heard shouting orders, all the way from the kitchen.

Clarissa felt overcome by gratefulness to the family and staff she loved so dearly. They all, in some way or another, had taken part in the preparations for her come-out ball. Her mother and sisters had helped her choose her gown and flowers and had cheerfully and without complaint devoted hours to addressing invitations. Her grandfather and Lord Raikes had sampled lemonade—which because pink was her favorite color, Cook had successfully endeavored to tint with strawberry pulp—and they'd all eaten various miniature tarts, biscuits, and cakes and judiciously declared their favorites.

Even Sophia's husband, the lofty Duke of Claxton, had taken it upon himself to personally deliver a select few invitations, namely to the Prime Minister and even the Prince Regent himself, which had all but guaranteed their attendance.

They were just days from the close of the London Season, and all these efforts would ensure her ball would be a memorable finale for not just herself and her family but for the dear friends and acquaintances who came to wish her well. The surprise announcement of her engagement to Lord Quinn would ensure the fairy-tale perfection of the night. She had managed to keep their secret one torturously long week more, but tonight as everyone watched from the edges of the ballroom, they would dance their first dance together as a betrothed, and soon-to-be-wed, couple.

"Dance with me, my dear!" Clarissa twirled, taking Daphne by the hands. Together they spun with Michael, secured between them, in wide circles across the ballroom floor, blond curls and skirts flying. At the age of twenty and twenty-one, respectively, and a shade older than most London debutantes, they still sometimes delighted in being utterly silly.

Michael squealed with joy, which inspired her and Daphne to laughter.

"Just like when we were little girls," said Daphne, laughing. "Imagining that we were at one of Mother's parties."

"Only now," Clarissa declared, "we are without a doubt *mature ladies* and won't be sent off to bed with our governess before the guests start to arrive."

"Down!" Michael wiggled to be set free, and she complied. Together she and Daphne stood side by side, watching the boy run up and down the length of the ballroom, as fast as his little legs could carry him. Only, as often occurred, his legs outpaced his body—

"Careful, Michael!" Clarissa called.

He tumbled headlong to the floor.

"Oh, no," cried Daphne.

They rushed toward him, Clarissa scooping him up just as the first outraged bellow emerged from his lips. Turning, his small arms found her neck and she squeezed him, pressing a kiss to his temple. "I know, sweet boy, it's a terrible humiliation to fall."

He inhaled, mouth open.

Daphne examined his legs and patted him on the back. "But you're not broken or bruised, so put your smile back on and—"

He wailed, even louder this time.

"He is tired," Clarissa said, bouncing him gently. "Just look at those droopy eyes."

"It *is* getting late." Daphne cheerfully nudged her toward the stairs. "I'd best take him upstairs and put him down for his nap and you can start preparing for your big night before Mother comes looking for us. You know how cross she gets when we are late."

Indeed she did. Their mother insisted on promptness. Clarissa could hear their mother's voice inside her head now.

"Girls!" Clarissa mimicked, with her free hand balled imperiously on the hip opposite the one that Michael occupied. "I know very well that you both have perfectly accurate timepieces—"

"—because Aunt Vivian gave each of you one for your last birthday," concluded Daphne, in the same familiar voice.

Mrs. Brightmore, descending the ladder, cast them a gently reproving look.

Clarissa flushed and bit her lower lip, abashed at being overheard.

"Oh, Mrs. Brightmore, all in good fun!" Daphne giggled good-naturedly. Looking at Michael, she extended her arms. "Come here, darling. Won't you let Auntie Daphne hold you?"

He peered at her with tearstained eyes, and a smile broadened his lips. Such a sweet child. To think, it wouldn't be long until she had a child of her own. Quinn would make a wonderful father. She couldn't wait until they were a family.

Michael leaned toward her sister, his arms outspread, and Clarissa gave him up. Daphne danced with him toward the door.

Yet Clarissa lingered behind a moment more. She could only stand motionless, savoring the bittersweet immensity of the moment, because just as her sisters' lives had changed as far as finding love and being married, so would hers. By now, Lord Quinn would have concluded discussions with his father, the duke. All matters could proceed and financial arrangements be made and he could approach her grandfather tonight with his suit.

She was almost sorry to see their game of secrecy end, one in which they'd stolen away for every moment and exchanged clandestine notes of the most intimate kind, but for a couple as deeply in love as they were, certainly all that would continue even after they were wed.

A moment later, upstairs on the first-floor landing, Daphne turned to her with Michael already half asleep on her shoulder.

"I'll take him to the nursery," she whispered. "You go on to your room and take a nice long bath."

"It won't be long now," Clarissa replied softly.

"Just a few hours more," answered her sister, continuing toward the next rise of steps. Her white muslin skirt rippled as her legs moved, a picture of Grecian elegance.

Only then Daphne paused...and returned to squeeze Clarissa's hand.

"I'm so very proud to have you as my sister," she murmured, her eyes bright. A moment later, she smiled, as she had done almost constantly since marrying Lord Raikes. Clarissa could only interpret her happiness as a sound endorsement of that venerable state. "It's your turn to find happiness. Next time I see you, you'll be making your entrance on this grand staircase. I've no doubt a score of gentlemen will rush to offer for your hand—"

"A score!" Clarissa laughed quietly, so as not to disturb Michael, who had begun to snuffle and snore. "Certainly not."

Just one. A very special one.

Daphne's expression became serious. "I'm so happy with Raikes. I want you to find the same sort of happiness. Promise me you won't rush into anything. Wait until you know the person and that the moment is right."

Clarissa's family had always believed her to be impetuous. She knew they all worried she would choose recklessly, based on some flash-fire attraction. But the person *was* right, and so was the moment. Quinn. She closed her eyes, savoring the rush of happiness that coursed through her, from head to toe. She could not imagine anything ever being more right.

"I promise," she agreed. "Only when the person and the moment are right."

That moment would be tonight.

* * *

"I shall see you at Miss Bevington's ball tonight, then, Mr. Kincraig?" inquired his companion, Lord Havering, as they exited the doors of White's, the club where they had spent the previous hour reading newspapers and drinking coffee.

"Any chance to reacquaint myself with Wolverton's liquor cabinet is a welcome opportunity indeed," Dominick replied with a wink.

His scant belongings had been packed and his rented town house, largely closed up. He expected to receive his new orders tonight or tomorrow. Why not spend one last evening beneath the glittering chandeliers of a London ballroom? Who knew where tomorrow would take him, or whether the circumstances would be as comfortable?

Havering studied him as he drew on his gloves slowly. "I suspect there's more to it than that, such as that you've grown fond of Wolverton and the ladies, despite yourself."

Havering—or "Fox," as he was called by those who knew him best—had no discernible family of his own and had since childhood been thrown by circumstance into the midst of Wolverton's welcoming brood. While Dominick's circumstances were far different, he too was very much alone in the world. Perhaps for that reason he felt closer to Fox than to the other gentlemen of Wolverton's circle— as close as he could feel to anyone. His occupation was largely a solitary endeavor and did not lend itself to making longtime friends. Sometimes he regretted that.

"They are all very nice people," he conceded.

He looked out over St. James's Street, crowded with carriages and hackneys, uncomfortable with revealing anything more. It had taken him years to perfect the obscurement of his true thoughts and feelings. He wasn't about to start emoting now, here on the pavement, in front of God and Fox and everyone. He kept his manner and tone cool. "Whatever the case, I wouldn't miss it."

He wouldn't miss it. Though it would take a team of horses to pry the sentiment from his tongue, he'd grown *exceedingly* fond of the earl and the ladies who made up the elderly gentleman's surviving family, even though he found the whole idea of a debut ball frivolous and silly, especially when the young lady in question had been out in society for quite some time already—since the marriage of her sister Sophia to Claxton, to be precise.

He didn't have a younger sister, not anymore, but he told himself if he did, he might understand better the wishes of a young lady's heart.

What he did know was that for whatever reason, Clarissa had thought enough of him to insist that he attend, and he would not disappoint her or Lady Margaretta, who just yesterday had pressed Claxton to call on him and confirm he would indeed join them tonight. Even the always-distant duke had seemed more sincere in his manner, just as they all had been since learning he wasn't their relation. Since that day just one week ago, there had been invitations to suppers and parties and rides in the park, some of which he'd accepted and others not. Now that they knew he wasn't an "imposter," it seemed their suspicions about him had eased, as had their minds. Now, on the precipice of his departure, he felt more a part of their family than when he had supposedly been their cousin.

His carriage approached, having come from the nearby livery.

"I will see you tonight, then," he said, tilting his hat in adieu to Fox.

"Until then."

With that, Dominick climbed into the conveyance and settled back for what would be a brief ride to what had been his abode for almost two years.

It was time to leave.

The first rule of subterfuge was that one did not become attached to one's human assignments, which was just as well because life had only ever made sense when he was alone.

Just then, his carriage passed a chapel where a small group crowded the pavement, throwing rose petals high over the heads of a newly wedded couple. All the ladies wore diaphanous summer dresses and fancy bonnets done up with flowers and ribbons, and the gentlemen stood distinguished in their gray morning suits. The idyllic scene momentarily transported Dominick back in time to another wedding.

His own.

All the air left his lungs at remembering. He had been so happy that day. So full of passion and dreams.

But Tryphena was dead for three years now, and even though he still walked and lived and breathed, sometimes he believed he was dead as well. Her passing had forever altered him. Without thinking, he pressed his hand to his heart, which *hurt*, as if a gaping hole existed there. There wasn't a hole, of course, but there might as well have been for the jolt of agony those memories brought.

The sight of a familiar face on the chapel steps jerked him back to present, and his hand fell away.

What? *No.*

He flicked the curtain aside and peered more intently out the window. In an instant he recognized the groom as none other than Lord Quinn, smiling broadly and standing hand in hand with a slender, dark-haired young woman who wore a lace veil and held a white bouquet. If there was any doubt in Dominick's mind as to the event he observed, Quinn put it to rest by seizing his new bride against his chest and pressing an enthusiastic kiss onto her lips.

The carriage traveled farther down the street until, despite straining his eyes and altering his position, he could see no more.

He fell back against the cushion, his jaw clenched tight. How...regretful. Did Clarissa know? The memory of her smiling face flashed in his mind. Certainly she did not. It had been only Tuesday afternoon, at the most recent of Lady Margaretta's garden luncheons, when he'd observed another flirtatious glance between the young couple and the furtive touch of their hands behind the garden column.

No, he had not particularly cared for Quinn as a match for Clarissa, but the news would devastate her. Shatter her innocent heart. Because of that, he could take no pleasure, no satisfaction in what he'd seen. He could think of no honorable explanation for what Quinn had done. His fingers curled into his palms and he resisted the urge to order his driver to turn around so that he might confront the lecher directly, in front of his new bride and their families.

Yet...despite the insistence of his conscience that he call Quinn out in defense of Clarissa's honor, it was not his place. For almost two years he had been the family's protector—but the role had been a professional assignment, he reminded himself, not an obligation of the heart.

So instead he held silent, telling himself she would be grateful to discover the truth of Quinn's faulty character now rather than later. Thank heavens she had enjoyed such a careful upbringing, which only allowed for the most chaste of entanglements. Perhaps, even, the whole incident would teach her a valuable lesson about love and trust, and guarding one's heart a bit more closely.

Once home, he washed and dressed and, as usual, did an intentionally incompetent job with his cravat, and mussed his hair, making sure he looked his usual part. Though he was to have an audience with Wolverton this evening before the ball got under way, he had no wish to arrive too early. He didn't want to cross paths with Clarissa. Despite all his careful training to never reveal his country's secrets even if tortured, he feared one look into her crystalline blue eyes and he would be compelled to inform her of what he had seen.

Why was he even thinking about the chit again? He should be wholly focused on the acceptance of his next assignment.

Yet his conscience chided him for his inaction. He wished Havering had been in the carriage with him when he saw Lord Quinn's wedding. Havering was more like a brother to Clarissa and would know the appropriate thing to do.

Havering, yes, now there was his answer. Knowing Clarissa as long as he had, Fox would know how to best break the unfortunate news, and most important, when— before or after the ball? Fox could comfort her after "Mr. Kincraig" was long gone.

He felt such relief at having arrived at this solution. Once the information was passed to Fox, Dominick would be free of all obligations and ready to depart London on a moment's notice.

Calling the carriage around once again, he traveled directly to Wolverton's house. Upon entering, he observed from a distance a small army of confectioner's assistants in the ballroom setting up some sort of display of little pink cakes or meringues on a table, while at the center of the house workmen finished the installation of a God-awful pink carpet onto the grand staircase, pink being Clarissa's favorite color. The scent of flowers—pink and white flowers, of course—hung everywhere, so strong he fought the urge to sneeze. He marveled at the silly frivolity of it all, most certainly a reflection of Clarissa.

He hated to destroy her happiness with word of her feckless lover's betrayal. Perhaps it would be best she not hear the news until tomorrow? He would leave that decision to Havering. Once the information was passed, his conscience would be troubled no more.

Ah—there, Havering stood just around the corner, speaking to Claxton. Dominick moved toward them, his intention to draw Fox aside for a private conversation—

Only to be intercepted by Mrs. Brightmore, who subtly lifted a hand, indicating he should proceed toward Wolverton's chambers.

"Ah." He paused midstep. "Now?"

"Indeed."

"It's early yet."

She winked. "Some of us have other duties to perform this evening, besides sauntering about in fancy clothes and drinking pink lemonade from a little crystal cup."

His gaze returned to Havering, but in the end duty called. He would find him afterward and discreetly share his concerns for Clarissa then. He changed direction, taking the corridor to Wolverton's chambers as he had so often done over the past two years under the guise of being summoned, or more often *commanded*, by the earl to do so. His role, after all, had been to play a gambler and a drunk. Someone consumed by his own addictions but, more important, inattentive to his surroundings. Though he'd played double duty as a personal guard to Wolverton, his primary assignment had been to lure into the open the man or men whom vague whispers of intelligence said wanted Lord Wolverton and his every living heir dead. The earl's own past in foreign secret service perhaps provided a motive for any number of surviving enemies, known and unknown, at home and abroad. Lady Harwick and the young ladies hadn't been told because the earl had no wish to frighten or burden them with unsubstantiated explanations of past tragedies, namely the deaths of his son and grandson.

Entering the anteroom, Dominick joined his team— O'Connell, His Lordship's valet, Mr. Ollister, the first footman, and Mrs. Brightmore, the housekeeper, the last of whom stepped through a small doorway on the opposite side of the room.

"Reports?" asked Mrs. Brightmore as she briskly circled round to collect a sealed envelope from each man, which she quickly secured inside her apron.

Dominick, aware his next assignment could come any day, had written out his final report the night before. Though he gave no outward indications, his heart beat fast. The ensuing moments might bring him great satisfaction or a devastating blow, in that he might receive his new orders. He closed his eyes, sending up a brief prayer that his superiors would see fit to return him to foreign service, as he so fervently wished.

"How is Wolverton?" he asked O'Connell, his interest sincere.

"Very well today," O'Connell replied succinctly. "His Lordship wishes to see you when we are concluded here."

Mr. Ollister straightened. "Let us finish our business, so we can all return to our posts." He looked to Dominick and nodded cordially. "As we all suspected, the Secretary of State has seen fit to revise the scope of our mission. Now that the earl has a true heir in young Michael, your role, Mr. Kincraig, has been substantially compromised in that you are no longer the assassin's lure you were intended to be."

Even when meeting in private, they used their "character" names to ensure consistency at all times.

They all listened, rapt, as Mr. Ollister continued. "Even though no attempts have been made against Wolverton's life since these indications of endangerment came to light, we will continue to secure the premises and maintain Wolverton's safety as well as that of his family, which now includes the child. Mr. Kincraig, you could certainly remain on indefinitely as security, but no one believes you would look very convincing in a nanny's apron and cap—"

Everyone chuckled.

"As such, the powers that be have seen fit to assign another agent to fulfill the nanny role: Mrs. Hutton."

Yes, Dominick had met Mrs. Hutton before. He agreed with the choice. She would be a formidable protector for the child.

"I believe some of you have worked with her before. You, Mr. Kincraig, will receive new orders." Bending, Mr.

Ollister extracted a folded square of parchment from his ankle boot, which he handed over to Dominick.

Dominick's heart thrummed with excitement. This was the moment he'd been waiting for. He would either be disappointed by another assignment from the Home Office or elated to be assigned abroad once again.

Mrs. Brightmore said quietly, "I hope it is all you wish for."

"Indeed," murmured O'Connell.

They all knew his situation and that this small-scale home assignment, for him, had been intended as a demotion. As professional exile. Perhaps at last his superiors would forgive him for Tryphena's death, though he would never forgive himself.

Breaking the seal, he opened his orders and read.

Chapter Three

A smile broke across his face and he exhaled, his cheeks warmed by a rush of happiness and relief. Hot, fiery pride coursed through his veins.

At last, his superiors had seen fit to return him to foreign secret service. Even more important, his new role was as prestigious as any he had occupied before his fall from grace, proof that he had regained their trust and respect.

Since then he had suffered such self-doubt and, yes, shame over the mistake he would live with for the rest of his life. Perhaps now, at last, he could forgive himself. Perhaps now, at last, he could be free. Tonight, he turned a page.

God, he felt like he was a hundred feet tall.

He felt like a ferocious, swaggering dragon and that if he dared throw open the window to roar his satisfaction to the city of London, the sound just might be accompanied by a blazing stream of flames.

Life, at last, felt bloody good.

"I can see from your reaction that you will be going abroad again. Congratulations are in order. Well deserved!" exclaimed O'Connell, gripping his shoulder.

"Very good." Mrs. Brightmore clasped her hands in front of her apron. "I'm so happy for you, Mr. Kincraig."

They would not, of course, press for further details. As professionals, they knew better than to do so. As required, Dominick tossed his orders into the fire.

"As are we all," said Mr. Ollister, grinning. "But there is little time for celebration. Let us all return to our duties— that is, except for you, Mr. Kincraig. Enjoy your last evening in London before you are returned to the jaws of danger."

"Which, as we all know, is precisely where you wish to be," said O'Connell with a wink. "The earl is waiting."

After confirming his orders had burned to nothing, Dominick continued on to the earl's private chambers.

Wolverton sat in his wheeled bath chair beside the window, dressed in his finest for the ball. Seeing him sitting there so dignified, with his kind eyes twinkling in welcome, Dominick suddenly found himself at a loss for words, and his chest grew tight.

Something about the moment made him think of his own father, from whom he had long ago become estranged. They had never been close—his father always far too busy to trouble himself with the company of children. Then once Dominick had reached a certain age where he could see the world through his own eyes and make his own opinions, everything had truly fallen apart. There had been terrible disagreements over *responsibility*. Endless silences. And always the expectation that he, and only he, should change. Things had only gotten worse after he'd become a man.

Yet he knew he would look back on this time and remember each moment with Wolverton as a treasure. Dominick, who had felt so lowered—so *humiliated*—at being demoted to a security detail had learned so much from the man with whose safety he had been charged, about loyalty, and honor and pride. Looking back on the past two years, he could feel nothing but gratefulness for the time he'd spent with the earl.

He crossed the room and joined Wolverton at the window. The panes had been pushed open and a pleasant breeze wafted through, carrying in the scent of flowers from the window boxes. Below, carriages crowded the street and elegantly turned out guests proceeded to the door.

"And so, it is time for us to say good-bye," said His Lordship.

Dominick bowed his head. "Yes, my lord. I depart tomorrow."

"Very good then." The old man smiled up at him, his eyes warm with admiration. "We have spent a lot of time together, you and I."

"Indeed we have."

"I just want you to know that this old man has enjoyed your company," the earl said quietly. "Our conversations and your humor. I find myself regretting that we must say farewell." He tilted his head forward. "Not because I wish you to remain here in your official capacity. I know you are capable of much greater things. But I have come to consider you as my friend."

On this, his last night in London, there were no words Dominick would rather hear. They bolstered his pride, and he knew he would remember them in the challenging and exciting days to come.

"I am honored, my lord, and feel the same."

The earl smiled. "I know this assignment was not your first choice and that you are eager to return to more exciting pursuits."

"Spy games have always been my true calling." Just speaking the words aloud sent a ripple of excitement through Dominick's blood.

Wolverton chuckled, lifting a wrinkled hand that bore a gold and onyx ring that had once been deeply etched but had been worn smooth by wear and time. "There was a time when I played a few of those games myself."

"So I have been told. You are quite the legend."

The earl chuckled, clearly delighted by the compliment, but then his smile dwindled. "My only regret is if my actions somehow placed my family in any sort of danger, resulting in this need for protection." A deep sadness came into the earl's eyes, and Dominick knew he was thinking about the son and grandson who had died such untimely deaths.

"Yes, my lord, but we don't know that."

The earl nodded. "I just want you to know how very much I have appreciated your devotion to myself and my family. I thank the Lord every day your particular skills were not needed, but I must admit I slept more peacefully at night knowing you, along with O'Connell, Mrs. Brightmore, and Mr. Ollister, were there to protect us."

"Thank you for saying so, my lord."

"Would you care for a parting brandy?" He nodded toward a small cabinet. "Oh, forgive me—I momentarily forgot that despite your very skilled portrayal of a drunkard, you never—"

"Never touch the stuff." Dominick nodded.

"Well, then. Godspeed, young man, and good-bye."

* * *

"Stay there, out of sight!" Sophia instructed over her shoulder, before again looking out over the guests who crowded the cavernous vestibule and beyond, into the wide corridor that led to the ballroom. "Mother will give the signal."

Clarissa stood at the top of the staircase, with her sisters and eight of her dearest friends, each of whom held wreaths covered in flowers. Well, six of her dearest friends and two Aimsley sisters because her mother had quite insisted, even though they were the worst gossips, but their grandfather had been such a dear friend of Lord Wolverton's in earlier times. They all clustered about her, in a happy crush of silk, perfume, and flower petals.

"Everything is so lovely, Clarissa."

"We're having such a wonderful time."

"I can't wait until the dancing starts."

"What a wonderful way to end the season."

Daphne gestured. "Ladies, it's time."

Sophia quickly lined them up into the order they'd agreed upon. In the ballroom, the orchestra began to play. Each of the young ladies held her wreath and made her way toward the stairs, smiling down over an admiring crowd gone suddenly silent. The moment was just as Clarissa had imagined. The first two ladies began their descent.

Clarissa asked Sophia, "Do you think the wreaths and the procession and the carpet are too much?" She looked down under their feet, where the pink carpet radiated pinkness back at her. What a perfect hue. She didn't want to be pretentious, but at the same time, she'd wanted to do something different. The grand finale of the evening would be her engagement.

The duchess chuckled. "Don't be silly. It's your night. Besides, I had twelve attendants, in case you've forgotten, and they were all wearing those ridiculous ostrich plumes." She winked.

Clarissa moved to take her place on the landing, and the crowd, seeing her, murmured in admiration. In response, a flush moved up her neck, into her cheeks. Her mother and grandfather waited at the bottom of the stairs, their faces beaming up at her, and everyone else, but...

She tried to be discreet as she searched the guests' faces, and searched them again.

"Where is Quinn?" she murmured, and she paused on the step. She couldn't very well descend the stairs if her fiancé-to-be was not even in the room to see her. But her sisters urged her to follow her attendants down the steps, and she complied.

"Who did you say you were looking for?" said Daphne, from where she followed just behind.

Again her gaze swept the room. Had he been delayed? Her blush of happiness turned to one of disappointment. Why wasn't he here?

"Did you say Lord Quinn?" said the eldest Aimsley sister, Elspeth, glancing over her shoulder.

"I didn't actually *say* Quinn—" She'd only barely murmured it, more like a whisper to herself. Her chest tightened. She hated fibs, even small ones. They made her feel terribly guilty and like a sneak. "But now that you mention him, why wouldn't he be here when he and all the rest of his family replied that would attend?"

The younger Aimsley, Ancilla, turned and said, "I don't

know about the rest of them, but he won't be coming, of course. He married Emily FitzKnightley this afternoon, and they are already off on their honeymoon."

Clarissa's heart stopped beating.

"That can't be true," she mumbled, her lips numb. She gripped the banister and replayed the words in her head, certain she'd misheard or misunderstood. Blood pounded in her ears, so thunderously she could hardly hear. "Wouldn't we all have known?"

"They married by special license. It came as a surprise to everyone. We ought to know, we are Emily's cousins and served as her bridesmaids."

Elspeth and Ancilla laughed gaily and continued down the stairs, leaving her exposed to the collective attention of the crowd looking up from below. Clarissa's cheeks burned and her face felt locked in its shocked expression.

"Wait," she whispered. "I don't think...I don't think I can..."

"Clarissa, what are you waiting for?" Sophia nudged her from behind. "Everyone's waiting. It's your turn to go down. Straighten up and smile."

Clarissa did stop whispering. Indeed, she stopped everything, as a rush of dizziness pushed through her. That night in the garden. Quinn's kisses...his touch. The words and promises they'd spoken. And now he had married someone else? It couldn't be true.

And yet she knew it was.

The chandelier above the staircase seemed to...twist and spin on its chain. The faces around her veered close, as if magnified with a looking glass, and then—in a blink— became distant. She swallowed and shook her head, attempting to regain control over herself, to no avail.

"I'm so sorry, but suddenly I—" she murmured, swaying forward...then to the side, her arms and legs trembling as if from a sudden fever.

"Clarissa?" inquired Daphne, touching a hand to her elbow.

The world pitched—flipping upside down in an ugly tangle of silk, feminine squeals, and pink.

Dominick read the Aimsley girl's lips and saw Clarissa's face go white. Damn it. That she should find out the news of Quinn, there on the stairs in front of everyone.

He watched, helpless and separated by a sea of people, as Clarissa wavered, then went limp. The room erupted with shouts and screams.

He didn't think twice, he just reacted, pushing through the crowd to where she lay amidst a tangle of flowers and feminine limbs, her face pale and eyes closed. Her sisters, who had been behind her, rushed down the stairs calling her name. Gathering her up in his arms, he lifted her, sweeping her away, past Claxton and Havering and Raikes who had rushed forward as well, down the hall.

Was she hurt? He couldn't tell. If not, she had to be more than humiliated. For a tender girl with such big hopes and dreams to take such a public fall, on such an important night...

Bloody hell, he felt responsible. After meeting with the earl, there'd been no opportunity to speak to Havering, no chance to ensure she would be prepared for the unfortunate news she was bound to hear.

Lady Margaretta followed. "Clarissa?"

"Tell her...I'm fine," Clarissa pleaded against his neck, her voice thick and her words barely discernible. Her gloved hand curled into his coat collar, and she burrowed more tightly against him. He clenched his teeth, wanting only to make the moment and every miserable emotion she must be feeling disappear at once.

"She is well, I believe," he called back, twisting round halfway. "She must have fainted from the excitement."

Her Ladyship nodded and paused midstep with her hands raised. "I shall come straightaway after seeing to the other girls. I pray no one has been injured!"

Dominick carried her into a small sitting room, where he deposited her—or attempted to deposit her—on a small settee. Her arms seized his neck.

"Let go, Clarissa."

"No," she retorted, her voice thick with tears.

"You're strangling me."

She held even tighter and sobbed into his shirt. "For once...j-j-just be a gentleman, please, and suffer through."

Knowing not what else to do, he simply sat with her there clinging to him, trying very hard not to notice how disturbingly soft and warm and perfect she felt, because that would serve absolutely no useful purpose at all.

Fox rushed in. "Is she all right?"

Thank God. He had no intention of being Clarissa's savior. That honor ought to belong to someone else. Someone permanent in her life.

"Take her, please?" Dominick asked, hands raised imploringly behind her back.

Fox took one step toward them, as if intent on complying, but just then Clarissa's sisters and their husbands arrived, pushing the young lord off to the side.

"Oh, Clarissa," exclaimed Daphne, rushing toward them, arms outstretched. "I'm so sorry."

Sophia pressed close as well, touching a gentle hand to her sister's tousled curls, and bending low to murmur near her ear, "Did you slip? Or did you faint? I couldn't see, dear, because I was standing behind you."

"Is she hurt?" inquired Claxton from the door.

"No, no, no," Clarissa cried over his shoulder, toward the wall, still refusing to look at anyone. "I'm fine...only *embarrassed*, and I feel so stupid." She trembled against him and whispered the next words. "How could I have been so stupid?"

Dominick knew, of course, what she meant. She referred to her love for Quinn.

"You're not stupid," assured Sophia. "And you mustn't be embarrassed. You're not the first debutante to faint at the moment of her debut. Remember Elizabeth Malloy? At least you didn't expose your bare bottom to two hundred people the way she did."

Raikes murmured, "Did that truly happen?"

Fox answered quietly, "Oh, yes. I was standing right there, not two feet away."

"I'm sorry to have missed that."

"Gentlemen!" Daphne rebuked.

Clarissa seized Dominick's neck tighter and cried harder. "I am mortified! Humiliated. I just want to be alone."

Lady Margaretta entered the room and, after quickly assessing the situation, said, "I think what would be best is if everyone gave Clarissa a moment alone and returned to the ballroom. You can all help her by telling the guests she is well, that she only fainted from the excitement and she'll be returning to the party as soon as she is recovered."

To Dominick's dismay, everyone left the room, her sisters

throwing glances of concern over their shoulders on the way out and their husbands and Fox dutifully following.

"Are you all right here, Mr. Kincraig?" Her Ladyship asked, touching a comforting hand to Clarissa's back as she still snuffled against his shirt. God, she'd made a handkerchief of him. No doubt his shirt was a mess, and he'd have to go home immediately after.

"I'm certain she would rather be with her mother." He lightly took hold of Clarissa's arms, intending to lift them from his shoulders.

"No." Clarissa held him tighter and shook her head vehemently, pressing her face to his neck. "I can't look at anyone. I can't even move. Not yet. Please."

Lady Margaretta bit her bottom lip. "I really must go and see about Wolverton. He must be very concerned."

Dominick nodded, his hopes of escape dashed. "And so I will...stay with Miss Bevington. If you promise to return." He smiled tightly. "Quickly."

It seemed the appropriate thing to do, although he had no idea how to console an innocent young woman who had gotten her tender heart broken. Truth be told, he wasn't at all comfortable with such an intense display of feelings, having learned years ago to confine and conceal his own. As far as the women in his life, his own dear mother had rarely expressed any emotion other than perfectly controlled placidity, even as the arguments between him and his father had raged. Neither had Tryphena ever needed gentle comforting. She, a demanding Valkyrie of a woman, had only ever required *appeasing*. Usually with sex.

"Thank you, Mr. Kincraig, I'm afraid you don't have any other choice." Lady Margaretta winked, despite the worry still etched around her eyes and mouth. Pausing, she reached to touch his hand. "Do you see, I am not the only one who still thinks of you as family?"

"While I thank you, some might consider me *untrustworthy* where the ladies are concerned." Why not give escape one last try?

"Oh, I shall miss your humor, Mr. Kincraig," Her Ladyship replied. "Clarissa obviously finds your presence very comforting, like that of...well, family." Her eyes misted over as, clearly, she remembered the loss of her son.

"I'm honored," he murmured.

"Thank you for this. I will return momentarily."

And in the next moment, they were alone.

"Oh, Mr. Kincraig," Clarissa moaned, and her body shuddered. "I'm so humiliated."

Hearing her speak his name—even if not his true name—somehow pleased him, as did her insistence on remaining in his arms, but only, he assured himself, because he knew they were the last moments they would ever spend together. Perhaps when he was gone, she would remember him fondly.

"It was that awful pink carpet, wasn't it?" he teased, hoping to cheer her. "You slipped on it, didn't you?"

"You terrible man." She shook her head and drew away enough to glare at him. Both of her hands rested against his chest, balled into small fists. Even with a puffy red nose and tearstained eyes, she was lovely. "To make light of the most miserable moment of my life. You don't understand!"

"I think I do." No, he wasn't a woman, but he'd had his heartaches—life-altering ones that made her present disappointment seem like an afternoon tea party. He pulled a handkerchief from his pocket and pressed it into her hand.

"There is so much more to this moment than meets the

eye," she declared, holding the square of white cloth to hers. "It's not just that I've fallen down a staircase in front of the whole of society, it's...it's..."

She peered at him, and a fresh surge of tears flooded her eyes. Oh, hell. What did he do now? He'd used up his limited repertoire of reassuring phrases. Forthrightness seemed the only way forward.

He cleared his throat. "I know that the young gentleman you had an attachment to has married someone else. I know about Lord Quinn."

She blinked and emitted a small hiccup. "How *could* you know? We were discreet, and we never told anyone. It was a secret."

He shrugged. "The attraction between two people is not difficult to perceive, if one pays attention." He would leave it at that.

She stared back at him. "You were paying attention?"

He scowled. "Not on purpose."

Her eyes narrowed just a bit. *There.* When she looked at him like that, he felt like she saw straight inside him, to his soul, and he didn't like it, not one bit. His walls flew up, and he reminded himself he was "Mr. Kincraig" in this moment, not himself, Dominick Arden Blackmer.

"He was supposed to speak with Grandfather tonight and ask to marry me. It was why we didn't tell anyone. We wanted it to be a happy surprise." Her gaze grew hard. "I'm surprised, all right. Terribly surprised and most miserable."

She held his handkerchief to her mouth, smothering a sob.

"Would you like me to call him out?" Dominick suggested, imposing a dark gleam into his eyes. "You know how fond I am of spectacles, and I'd be happy to make one on your behalf before I leave town."

A superior marksman, he would win any such challenge with ease. But he knew before speaking the words she would refuse, which was just as well. He could not risk losing everything he'd worked for by inflicting a punishing flesh wound—yes, he could be just that precise—on the son of a very important man.

"A duel! No," Clarissa cried, grabbing his shoulders, her eyes wide and appalled. "Everyone would want to know why, and now that he is married you can't tell anyone about us. *Anyone.* Do you understand?"

A little more outraged understanding and his job would be done. She would know someone appreciated her loss, was as offended as she, and then she could return to her party downstairs and hold her head high.

"He betrayed you unforgivably." He raised his clenched fist. "He should be made to reckon for what—"

"*Swear it,* Mr. Kincraig," she insisted, twisting her hands in the front of his coat and yanking him hard, her eyes suddenly wild. "You will tell no one."

Her vehemence startled him. "Your secret is safe with me."

"Good," she whispered, her shoulders slumping.

Her sleeve slipped off her smooth, golden-skinned shoulder, which caused her bodice to sag away from the plump swell of one breast. He snapped his eyes closed, but not before an unsettling stab of desire cut through his gut, and the desire to kiss her, hard and hot, and to make her forget Lord Quinn even existed.

Bloody hell, where had that thought come from? Out of nowhere, and unbidden. Unfortunately, now that he'd thought it, he couldn't stop looking at her plush lips and imagining them pressed against his skin.

She whispered fervently, "Because I must share another secret. If I don't, I fear I will explode."

Dominick's eyes flew open and his fledgling passion extinguished.

"Another secret?" he repeated warily. He did not like the sound of that. He half lifted himself off the settee. "Perhaps I should go for your mother, or one of your sisters—"

She yanked him back down into place beside her.

"It must be you," she insisted, half choking on her words. "A worldly person who won't judge, and who can give me advice without the complication of a heart or feelings."

How she misjudged him. He almost felt stung, but she was an innocent and could never understand the complex emotions of a man who had loved deeply and lost all. Yes, he had a heart. Though damaged and half destroyed, it still beat inside his chest, while hers would no doubt recover quickly and soon assign its affection to someone else.

He could only suppose she'd written some silly, florid letters to Quinn and now wanted them back or some other such nonsense. Left with no gentlemanly avenue of escape until her mother returned, he resigned himself to being her confessor, promising himself that the moment her mother returned, he would say good-bye to Clarissa and this family and this night and disappear into his exciting new tomorrow.

The sooner, the better. "What is it, Miss Bevington?" he queried testily. "What is this secret you have to tell me? Whatever it is, you and I can talk it out and we can—"

He didn't get a chance to finish his sentence before

she exclaimed, "I am with child, Mr. Kincraig. *With child.* What do you suppose *you and I* shall do about that?"

The words rang in his ears, and the horror of what she'd just told him must have reflected on his face, because her face again crumpled into tears and she threw herself into his arms.

He choked out a curse.

Not because of what she'd told him, which indeed had been astonishing enough—but because at that very moment he saw her mother standing in the door, white-faced with shock, having just wheeled Wolverton inside.

Chapter Four

*W*ith child?" gasped someone from the direction of the door.

Clarissa froze. *Someone who sounded very much like her mother.*

Because she'd so unwisely thrown herself against Mr. Kincraig, she felt his every muscle turn to stone. Still half sprawled on his lap, she twisted to see her mother and grandfather open-mouthed, staring at them. The voices of oblivious guests emanated through the open door, carried on a cheerful crescendo of music from the ballroom.

"Clarissa?" said Her Ladyship in a wavering voice, her eyes widening. "Mr. Kincraig?"

"Oh, no," Clarissa whispered, blinking tears from her eyes.

Not Mr. Kincraig. Lord Quinn had betrayed her—

The words jumbled inside her mouth, impossible truths she couldn't yet bring herself to speak. Thoughts spun about her head, dizzying her.

She hadn't told Quinn about the baby. She ought to have. But he had asked her to marry him. She thought she had time. Now he was married to another, and she was alone. How did she tell her mother that? How did she tell Wolverton?

Even now she couldn't believe it.

The man she had loved and who had sworn to love her forever had married someone else. Her heart was shattered, and she was scandalously pregnant and alone.

She trembled in fear. She'd needed more time. Just a moment of delay, of privacy, to compose herself before they all heard the deplorable truth about what a fool she had been.

Yet that moment did not come. Wolverton wrested control of his chair and with his hands turned the wheels until he halted two feet away. Veins protruded from his forehead, and his eyes blazed with temper.

Lifting a shaking hand, he pointed at Mr. Kincraig and thundered, "You!"

"No—" she cried.

"Me?" Mr. Kincraig bellowed, his eyes wide.

A push to her back sent Clarissa tumbling off his lap, onto the floor.

"Oh!" Her teeth *clacked*.

Her second fall of the night. Not nearly as far, but immensely more humiliating.

Clarissa could do nothing but stare up through the tangle of her disarrayed curls at her grandfather and mother, who stared back at her, their eyes round with a mixture of disbelief and anger.

"Damn it all to hell," Mr. Kincraig growled, kneeling behind her and helping her up by the arms. Brows furrowed, he demanded, "Are you all right? I should not have...blast! I didn't intend—it's just that I—"

"Yes, yes!" she choked out. "I'm not injured."

But she was. Her heart was broken, and she wanted to collapse and cry and disappear into the carpet.

Lady Margaretta lifted a hand to her mouth. "Oh, my dear child, is what you said true? Are you...are you...?"

Clarissa nodded and confirmed through tears, "Yes, but not—not—"

Oh, the look in her mother's eyes. She would never forgive herself. She opened her mouth to blurt out the truth, but her stomach pitched suddenly, and she pressed a hand over her mouth. She was going to be sick.

Oblivious, Mr. Kincraig bent, his hand outstretched as if to smooth her rumpled skirts, then halted, as if thinking better of touching her again. "I ought not to have reacted so suddenly, especially given—" His cheeks darkened and his nostrils flared, and he said, "—your...ah—*condition*."

Lord Raikes and Claxton appeared in the door. Things couldn't get any worse than this.

"The ladies are inquiring...whether...you..." Raikes's voice faded and he blinked, as if his mind only just registered what he'd heard. He looked between the two of them, his brows drawn together.

Claxton's eyes went black. In a hushed voice, he demanded, "And what would that condition be?"

Fie! Her brother-in-law! Since he and Sophia had married, he had become very much a protector to them all, with Wolverton's full support. A wonderful thing, except for a time like now. He glowered between the two of them, waiting for an answer. Inside, Clarissa withered, crushed by shame.

"Mr. *Kincraig*—" The earl spat the name. "—has compromised my granddaughter."

Beside her, Mr. Kincraig exhaled through his teeth and closed his eyes. His mouth popped open, as if to speak.

Clarissa flinched and lowered her head, waiting for his denial, for the rush of words that would expose her for the fool that she was, not only for falling in love with a rake who cared so little for her that he had married another, but also for having allowed herself to have been gotten with child by the same lout. She deserved to be exposed for what she was.

She'd done as they'd all feared: chosen impetuously. And now the rest of her life—of all their lives—would suffer grievous effect. Her heart felt like a pincushion, poked and bruised, and she wanted nothing more than to be alone and cry and wail and curse Lord Quinn. But she wasn't alone, and she wouldn't have time to recover from her shock and think of what to do before being forced to provide explanations. To everyone!

The night had turned out so differently than she'd expected. Rather than a celebration, she would break the hearts of all she loved.

Yet...no denial came from Mr. Kincraig.

He stood beside her, unmoving and silent, his face a mask of rigidity, leaving her to no other conclusion but that despite his healthy reputation as a hard-drinking gambler and libertine, he intended to behave as a gentleman by remaining silent on the matter of a young lady's honor.

Which left it to her to set matters aright. Otherwise, how could she live with herself?

She swallowed hard, gathering her courage. "Mr. Kincraig did not seduce me."

"Don't try to protect him," her grandfather barked.

Clarissa flinched. But Wolverton didn't even look at her. Instead, his gaze held Mr. Kincraig's.

"I'd heard talk of scandals in his past," said the earl. "Terrible scandals. But I allowed myself to be deceived as to his character."

"That's not true," replied Mr. Kincraig quietly, the tone of his voice strangely hollow. "I would never have betrayed you."

"No doubt your old life lost its allure, and once you were told you must move on elsewhere, you undertook this desperate scheme to profit from marriage to my granddaughter, to secure a higher place in the world than your *present circumstances* could guarantee."

Mr. Kincraig exhaled a ragged breath and shook his head. "You truly believe this?"

"No!" Clarissa exclaimed, her voice sounding frantic and desperate, in a way she'd never heard herself. "Grandfather, you cannot, because it is not true."

"To think I welcomed you into my home," Wolverton bellowed, leaning forward in his chair. "That I trusted you, that I called you my friend."

Mr. Kincraig remained beside her, rigid. Despite the crushing weight of her present misery, Clarissa felt gratitude toward him for his silence, when so easily he could abandon her and leave her to withstand her humiliation alone. She had confided in him, and still he made no mention of Lord Quinn, an omission she could only guess he left to her to reveal or not, because now that Quinn was married to another, there could be no honorable recourse.

"Bloody hell, when did this seduction even occur?" Claxton strode across the floor, coming to stand nose to nose with the man beside her. He growled, "You played your insouciance well, pretending that the news that your bloodline did not tie you to Wolverton did not matter to you, but you'd already secured a place here by another means, hadn't you? You'd already seduced Clarissa. We all came to trust you, yet you moved among us like a snake in the garden. Raikes, summon the undertaker, and tell him to bring a box. A long one, because I intend to kill Mr. Kincraig. Now."

"I wouldn't attempt that if I were you," Mr. Kincraig murmured in response, staring steadily into the duke's eyes.

"Careful, Claxton," Wolverton warned. "He is dangerous, I know for a fact."

Mr. Kincraig hissed. "I would ask for a moment alone with you, Wolverton—"

"You'll have nothing of the sort," bellowed Claxton.

Clarissa wedged herself between the two of them. "Stop that this instant. You aren't going to kill him, because he has done nothing wrong."

Raikes interjected quietly, "Clarissa, perhaps it is best if you go." He reached for her.

"What's going on here?" Sophia asked from the door. Daphne, too, peered inside, her eyes round.

"If you would all just listen—" Clarissa exclaimed, pressing her hands to her face, wanting to disappear.

Her head pounded harder and louder as each new family member arrived. If she didn't make her confession now, she felt certain she might as well go on into the ballroom and shout the awful truth to everyone.

Her mother extended a hand to her. "Dear, you must come with me and let the gentlemen talk this out."

No, she couldn't leave Mr. Kincraig. She couldn't leave things as they were, all in a confused tangle. "I won't go, not until I tell everyone the—"

"Do as your mother says," the duke commanded, urging her in the direction of the door.

"Oh, my God—" she heard Mr. Kincraig utter, his voice imbued with shock.

Turning, she saw him move very suddenly, lunging toward the earl and kneeling beside him.

The old man exhaled raggedly, clutching a hand to his chest. His mouth worked, as he attempted to speak, but then his eyes closed and he slumped in his chair.

"Grandfather?" Clarissa cried, going down onto her knees beside Mr. Kincraig. "No, please, Grandfather." She clasped his limp hand and squeezed. "What have I done?"

A half hour later, Dominick waited in the corridor outside the earl's chambers, the hair along the back of his neck bristling from a white-hot fury in his blood that wouldn't subside. He prayed Wolverton survived the shock of his unwed granddaughter's announcement that she was with child. He had to know for certain whether the earl truly believed he'd seduced Clarissa, or whether, in his shock, Wolverton had wanted him to take the blame so as to protect her from the deeper shame of naming a married lord of the realm as the child's father.

Whatever the case, through no fault of his own, he'd been dragged into this situation, and by God he wasn't going up in flames over it. Something had to be done. Another resolution had to be set forth, one that did not involve him. He had to believe now that the initial hysteria had passed, clearer minds would prevail.

In the meantime, he hated standing alone in the shadows like some schoolboy waiting to be summoned for punishment. For a brief span of hours, he'd been returned to the full glory of his former self. He'd be damned if he'd return to a place of regret, humiliation, and shame ever again. Though until just an hour ago he'd felt some degree of tenderness toward Clarissa, he would be more than happy now never to see her again.

Nothing had changed. By tomorrow, he would be gone from their lives, and his life would return to its true purpose—his career, and the service to country that satisfied him like nothing else.

Not for the first time, Dominick considered simply walking down the stairs and onto the street, disappearing into the shadows of the night. He remained only because he had no wish to burn bridges with Wolverton. He needed that explanation, and to know Wolverton still held him in high regard.

And damn it all to hell, he wanted an apology for having been thrown to the dogs. Not from Wolverton, of course, who had only reacted out of fear and love for his granddaughter, but from *someone*. He'd settle for one from Clarissa or, better yet, that damned arrogant Duke of Claxton.

Speak of the devil. The duke, having come from the direction of the staircase, swept past without sparing him a glance. Which was worse, being glowered at or dismissively ignored?

To Lady Harwick, who hovered near the door, the duke murmured, "I made an announcement that His Lordship had fallen ill and that out of respect the ball has been cancelled. The guests are leaving now."

"Thank you," Her Ladyship answered quietly, pressing a handkerchief to her eyes, and again disappeared into Wolverton's chambers. Claxton followed her.

O'Connell appeared from the direction of the servants' staircase with a steaming stoneware pitcher, which he held beneath with a thick cloth. Mrs. Brightmore, her expression intense, came from the opposite direction bearing a small stack of folded linens.

The valet glanced sharply at Dominick and made to enter the room, but then he veered toward Dominick, scowling and pressing close. "If he dies, there will be consequences for you. I will see to it."

"You will regret your words," Dominick growled.

"You've brought shame on us all." The shorter, bulldog-faced man hissed, "I have every intention of submitting a report condemning your—"

"Shush!" interrupted Mrs. Brightmore, shouldering between the two of them. She shot a warning glance toward O'Connell. "Mr. Kincraig is no more responsible for Miss Bevington's situation than you are."

"What are you saying?" he demanded quietly, looking between them.

She cast a furtive glance over her shoulder. "That anyone paying any attention at all knows Lord Quinn is the culprit." She looked to Dominick and demanded in a low tone, "Isn't that true?"

"Indeed," he gritted from between clenched teeth, relieved someone else realized the truth.

Mrs. Brightmore returned her gaze to their fellow agent. "You may now apologize."

The tension in O'Connell's shoulders eased, and he exhaled. "Good God, what a mess. I'm sorry, Mr. Kincraig.

It's just that I'm not around the rest of the family as often as the two of you, and she's such a very nice young lady and with His Lordship being so affected by the news... well, I...I just believed the worst of you when I ought to have kept my head."

Dominick glowered at the man, seething. "I am half out of my head as well. I am caught in a terrible spot."

Mrs. Brightmore whispered, "I've no doubt Miss Bevington will do the right thing, given just a little time."

"Will she?" he growled, so angry he could not see straight. "Then why am I still here?"

"Wolverton's health is so precarious. Further revelations would only distress him more." Mrs. Brightmore peered sagely at Dominick. "But I do understand the urgency and must say your silence thus far is admirable. On one hand, I know you're trying to protect the girl and Wolverton, but on the other, such a scandal could threaten your career, even if you are eventually determined to be innocent."

Protect her, yes. Yes, he supposed he was. But at the same time he was also trying to protect himself, and his future. He had to tread carefully. Clarissa was the Earl of Wolverton's granddaughter. The Duke of Claxton's sister-in-law. Those two men had the power to destroy him. Even if he wasn't to blame here, if he spoke out of turn or offended their sensibilities, he would find himself and his professional aspirations ruined.

"But be patient," Mrs. Brightmore urged. "The truth will emerge, and Quinn shall have to marry her."

Dominick closed his eyes and shook his head, his teeth clenched. If only the solution were that simple for Clarissa.

"That, it would seem, is the true scandal at hand and the

sole reason I have held silent. Quinn, you see, is already married."

"No, he isn't," the housekeeper replied, drawing her shoulders up, her eyes wide and shocked as if horrified by the mere suggestion. "Why would you say that?"

He nodded curtly. "It's true, I'm afraid. As of this afternoon, by special license to the FitzKnightley heiress."

"No," she gasped, her shoulders going slack. "Miss Clarissa! The poor girl. What a betrayal."

"Damn," O'Connell hissed, his knuckles whitening on the pitcher's handle.

"No, please!" The sudden cry came from inside the earl's chambers, a young woman's voice that Dominick believed to be Clarissa's. Footsteps sounded on the carpet, making their way toward the door. Mrs. Brightmore and O'Connell broke away and proceeded inside.

Claxton stepped out, his expression distant and grave. "The earl wishes to speak with you."

Dominick nodded, relieved. For a moment he'd feared the old man had expired. If the earl was awake and able to speak, he was moments away from being absolved from this misunderstanding.

Shadows darkened the room. Only one small lamp was lit on a table beside a large state bed draped in gold and black curtains, and a fire in the hearth illuminated the high painted ceiling, wall hangings, and collection of swords that had no doubt been in the family's possession through the centuries.

The windows had been closed, and the curtains drawn against the night and the sounds of London. In the far corner, O'Connell poured water into a basin while Mrs. Brightmore arranged the linens. Dominick approached the bed, which was surrounded by all the members of His Lordship's family and his physician, a tall man with wiry gray hair and spectacles. Solemn-faced and with accusing eyes, they parted for him until he saw the pale pink, silken train of Clarissa's gown.

She knelt beside the bed, clasping her grandfather's hands and pressing her cheek to them.

Claxton frowned. "For a moment he was conscious, and he asked for you. Now . . . I don't know."

Sniffles and quiet sobs broke the silence of the room. All the relief he'd felt just moments before drained out of him on the spot. Ought he remain or retreat?

"You" came a ragged voice from the bed.

The old man struggled to rise. Clarissa attempted to soothe him with low words and gentle hands, but he brushed her away.

"Come here," he commanded, reaching out a shaking hand. The physician took a step nearer, his lips drawn into a thin and disapproving line. Clarissa glanced over her shoulder and through tearstained eyes watched Dominick approach. Was he wrong, or did he see dread there also?

"Yes, my lord," he answered quietly. "I am here."

"Listen to me, now," Wolverton exhaled raggedly before collapsing back onto his pillow.

"No," Clarissa cried quietly, lowering her head on the coverlet.

"You . . . will . . . *marry* her," the earl commanded.

His blood froze at hearing the words, which weren't at all what he'd expected. He had done nothing wrong and did not deserve such a punishing sentence.

"Oh, Mr. Kincraig," Clarissa choked, looking up at him with tear-flooded eyes. "I'm so sorry."

He stared back at her. No, he wouldn't . . . couldn't marry her. Why should he?

"Clarissa, be silent," said her mother from somewhere behind them. Wolverton rested his hand atop her head.

Dominick shook his head. "My lord, I—"

Claxton growled, "By God, Mr. Kincraig, if you do not consent, I will shoot you on the spot."

With that, a round of feminine sobs and sniffles and whispers arose behind him, a heavy cloud of collective female emotion pressing at his back. They were all so disappointed and traumatized at the idea of their darling girl marrying Mr. Kincraig, the scoundrel—a role he simply played, and played very well, as part of his occupation. He had difficulty understanding how he, Blackmer, should be responsible for any sins committed—or in this case, not committed—by Mr. Kincraig. And yet he found himself being threatened with death by the duke if he did not comply. His soul decried the injustice. He had done nothing wrong and did not deserve this condemnation.

"You," Wolverton urged, reaching toward Dominick again. "Come here."

Dominick felt trapped. Smothered. He momentarily closed his eyes, then stared at the earl's hand, knowing if he complied that his freedom might very well be forever lost.

There was only one way out. He would have to tell His Lordship the truth about his granddaughter's indiscretion and pray he survived the shock. But discreetly, and out of hearing of the others. Dominick leaned past Clarissa, into the shadows.

The earl seized his arm and pulled him near. For a moment, two aged eyes held his, bright with tears. The magnitude of hurt and emotion he perceived in them struck him like a battering post to the center of his chest.

"She has confessed...the truth—" Wolverton whispered, in so hushed a voice Dominick could hardly make out the words.

Dominick exhaled, relief coursing through him. God bless Clarissa, he should never have doubted her. The earl knew he was innocent of seducing her, that he had not betrayed anyone's trust, and most important that the child Clarissa carried did not belong to him.

Yet the earl jerked him closer.

"—a truth *no one else* can know. Not her mother. Not the rest of the family. By God, no one. Marry her, Blackmer. Grant this dying man's request. I beg you, as my friend. It must be you."

Chapter Five

Clarissa looked up into Mr. Kincraig's face as he backed away from the shadowed darkness of her grandfather's bed. Pale and scowling, he glanced at her coldly before looking across the room and solemnly addressing her family.

"His Lordship has requested a moment alone with the two of us." His voice was lower and graver than she had ever heard before. He sounded very unlike himself. His jaw twitched, evidence of the emotion he struggled to keep in check.

Her family gathered themselves and filed into the corridor. Tears shone on Daphne's face, and Sophia lingered behind until the duke led her and the bright-eyed Lady Margaretta away. O'Connell and Mrs. Brightmore followed them out last, with the housekeeper turning to give them both one last look before pulling the door closed.

Clarissa remained on her knees beside the bed. Numb and broken by the events of the last hour, she prayed this was all a bad dream and that she would awaken to find her life as it had been before. Mr. Kincraig reached down and assisted her up.

"Come," her grandfather said weakly, reaching for her. She grasped his cool palm, enveloping his aged fingers beneath her own and leaned beneath the canopy, complying when he pulled her down beside him.

"You as well," the earl commanded in a gravelly voice to the silent shadow behind her.

Mr. Kincraig leaned inward, also giving his hand.

Wolverton's eyes met hers, full of love and, yes, hurt. She had hurt him so badly. How could she have made such a terrible mistake?

"Mr. . . . Kincraig—" Wolverton rasped. "—has agreed to marry you. Tomorrow, by special license."

She had already known this and still her heart sank at the words, like a stone to the bottom of the ocean.

"He should not have." She shook her head and looked at Mr. Kincraig, who refused to look back at her, which made her feel even more horrible because he was clearly very unhappy at the prospect of marrying her. Tears spilled over her cheeks. "He should suffer no consequence for merely trying to be kind to me in my moment of need."

"You will . . . do this, Clarissa, for yourself and your dear mother and the rest of this family, but mostly . . . for the child." The earl placed her hand in Mr. Kincraig's, who stared down at their joined hands, stricken, as did she. "You must never tell anyone the truth."

"But I must tell Mother." She blinked. "My sisters. Unless I do they'll all believe he's a . . . a scoundrel who seduced me—"

"Then so be it," growled Mr. Kincraig in a low but forceful voice. "It is the only way I will agree to marry you and to be a father to this child. If the child is to have my name, I will have no one believing that he or she is anything other than my own."

"They would protect my secret."

"Secrets never stay secrets, Clarissa," he argued, his dark eyes blazing like onyx on fire. "If the truth is spoken outside this room, then someone will overhear a whisper here, a sideways comment there, and the talk will start, and it will never stop. I won't have it. *I won't.*"

Wolverton nodded his head wearily. "Do you understand, Clarissa?"

She remained silent, frozen by one thought. As angry as she was with Lord Quinn right now, what if he had been forced into marriage with someone else, perhaps by his father, for political reasons? Yes, he had betrayed her, but didn't he deserve to know about the child?

"But Lord Quinn—"

"Has married another," Wolverton replied in a sharp tone. "It is too late...for recompense. There can be no recourse, no satisfaction without bringing shame and scandal upon us all, not to mention your innocent child. Would you have him or her live under the shadow of illegitimacy for the rest of his life and suffer for the consequences of your actions?"

"No! But neither do I want Mr. Kincraig to suffer the consequences. What if I agree to go away," Clarissa answered, her voice frantic with hope that somehow she could spare him, "and have the child in seclusion?"

"And give the baby away, for strangers to raise?" The earl scowled, his hand seizing atop hers and Mr. Kincraig's, binding them more firmly together. "I won't have it. The child is my blood and will be always and forever part of this family."

His words broke her heart, because they revealed such a depth of love for a child who hadn't even been born yet. Yet the effort of speaking with such vehemence had clearly been too much for His Lordship. The earl gasped and fell back upon the pillow. Clarissa abandoned Mr. Kincraig's hand and reached for her grandfather, embracing him, wanting to soothe his distress.

She could not help but pity herself. Just hours before she'd been the toast of London, with all her dreams laid out before her. Now she must agree to marry a known rakehell, who would most likely despise her forever for chaining him to a dull and respectable life.

She deserved no better, and had no one to blame but herself. She must be grateful to Mr. Kincraig for agreeing to marry her at all.

She rested her head on his chest, tears spilling from her eyes. "I will do as you say, my lord. I will marry Mr. Kincraig."

"I still can't believe this is real, that you'll be marrying Mr. Kincraig." Sophia sighed heavily and hugged Clarissa from behind, squeezing her as tightly as Sophia's six-months-along pregnant belly would allow. "Tell me, Clarissa, how did this come to be?"

All three sisters lay in Clarissa's bed with her in the middle. Last night, they'd simply held her as she cried and said gentle things until she'd pretended to fall asleep so they wouldn't ask her any more questions—questions she couldn't answer, not when her grandfather had urgently sworn her to secrecy, for the sake of her child and the man who had agreed to marry her.

Although she wanted nothing more than to share the truth with Sophia and Daphne, along with all of her anger and her pain, didn't she owe Wolverton and Mr. Kincraig her strictest compliance after all the difficulty she had caused them and everyone else?

"I don't know," she answered numbly, staring into the shadows across the room.

She could just make out the pale pink outline of the dress she had worn last night where Sophia had lain it across her dressing room chair. What a wonderful time she and her mother and sisters had selecting the style of the gown and agonizing over the choice of fabric and trimmings. As she'd endured all the necessary fittings, she'd been filled with such hope for a happy future with the man she loved.

Now the dress had become a symbol of her shattered dreams.

"It just happened," she said in a hollow voice.

But with Lord Quinn, who had told her he loved her, not the bleary-eyed, always disastrous Mr. Kincraig...who had been kind enough not to abandon her.

Why she couldn't have cried on Havering's shoulder? Kind, handsome, generous Havering, so like a brother to them all. She'd much rather be forced into marriage with him.

That wasn't fair of her. It wasn't fair of her at all, not to Havering and most certainly not to Kincraig.

Last night after her sisters had fallen asleep, she'd lain awake alone with her regrets and tears, praying it was all a nightmare she'd wake from in the morning. But now light crept through the curtains, along with the sounds of a stirring city. She simply had to come to terms; she wasn't going to wake up and find it all a bad dream.

She felt tender and bruised, inside and out. Bitterly angry, sad, and betrayed. She wanted nothing more than to confront Quinn, to demand an explanation, but she could not imagine herself playing the part of a cast-off and forgotten little fool. She had her pride.

She could not help but wonder where he was now. Likely honeymooning in the arms of the new Lady Quinn.

Did he think of her? Was he miserable too? She had most certainly made a mistake in not telling him immediately about the baby. It had been three and a half weeks since she'd missed her courses. At first she'd told herself there must be some other explanation, but then she'd started seeing the same bright spots in her vision Sophia had described early in her pregnancy and suffering a vague nausea at various times throughout the day.

And though she had been thrilled, *so thrilled* at the idea of becoming a mother, she hadn't told Quinn because foolishly she'd wanted their lives to follow the prescribed storybook pattern of romance and love, first an engagement and then marriage. Then, and only then, would there be children. The realization she was with child had thrown that "perfect" order all out of balance, so she'd remained silent, believing the news could wait just a little while longer.

Foolish girl. Now her life was anything but a fairy tale.

She felt so dreadfully alone. If she'd told him right away, would he still have married another? The same question had tumbled about in her head all night, unanswered.

One thing she did know of a certain was that she didn't

love him anymore. Quinn had told her he loved her just before he'd taken her innocence—something she could never get back—and then he had married another.

A man like that didn't deserve her love. If he'd loved her, then no matter the circumstances or obstacles, he would have fought to be with her.

She vowed never to speak to him again. Hot tears stung her eyes, fueled by outrage and pain, and her hands curled into fists in the sheets.

Perhaps she would speak to him just once, to find out why he'd married someone else. She wouldn't tell him about the baby, but she wanted to understand and be able to forgive him. She didn't want to despise him for the rest of her life.

"Do you love him?" Sophia asked.

Quinn's handsome face appeared in her mind, to be replaced by Mr. Kincraig's untidy countenance.

She closed her eyes. "No."

"Are you happy to be marrying him?"

"No!" she blurted.

Saying those words made her feel disloyal to Mr. Kincraig. No, she didn't love him and she didn't want to marry him, but given his generous sacrifice, she must in turn give him her loyalty and respect. After all, he had been nothing but a gentleman to her, more so than the man she had loved.

"Then why—"

She closed her eyes. "I don't want to talk about it."

"Clarissa, he didn't . . . he did not—"

"He didn't what?"

"He didn't force himself on you, did he?"

Force himself on her? Of . . . course not.

Her mind returned to that night at the Vauxhall gala, where there had been music and dancing carried on just out of sight, where their kisses had turned suddenly passionate and Quinn had told her he couldn't wait any more, that he loved her so madly he couldn't control his passions.

"*No*," she blurted. "He did not force me."

She'd thought they were in love, and foolishly she'd relented. But they weren't talking about Quinn, were they? They were talking about Mr. Kincraig.

Even though he was the last thing she wanted to think about at the moment, she forced herself to say "Mr. Kincraig has been nothing but a gentleman throughout this entire situation."

"He most certainly has not," Sophia retorted. "If he was any sort of gentleman, you would not be in this predicament."

"I have no one to blame but myself."

Sophia rose onto one elbow and looked down into her face. "You are an innocent young lady. He is far more worldly than you, which makes him a cad. He seduced you. He manipulated your emotions." She squeezed Clarissa's shoulder. "You do realize that, don't you?"

Clarissa's head hurt from so many crisscrossing thoughts. Had Quinn ever intended to marry her? Thinking back, it was he who had insisted on secrecy. Like a fool, she had gamely agreed, believing at the time that love was just a fun and happy game. Whatever the truth about her and Quinn's affair, Mr. Kincraig had not seduced her, and she could not in good conscience allow him to take blame.

"Please don't talk about him like that," Clarissa insisted, and, with a hard wrench of her shoulder, pulled away.

Oh, she was angry. Not at Sophia, but with Quinn. But most of all, with herself.

How Mr. Kincraig must despise her this morning. She could only hope that like many young men, he had aspirations of marrying well to improve his fortune and connections. While she couldn't promise love and passion, she could certainly, with some degree of confidence, guarantee that.

"You feel fondly for him, then, at least," Sophia whispered softly. A moment of silence passed, and then Clarissa felt a hand gently stroke her hair. "It's just that this has all come as such a shock, but I love you. We all love you, don't we, Daphne? That's all that matters."

A snore arose from the tousled heap of hair that was Daphne.

"Daphne—" Sophia pinched Daphne's arm. "*Daphne.* Wake up."

"Ow...what?" Daphne moaned, jerking her arm away and burying her face under the covers.

"I said wake up. It's morning." Sophia sat up and, with her fingers, attempted to comb out her wild mass of dark hair. She had always worn her dark hair longer than her blond sisters and normally slept with it in a braid. They'd forgone their customary bedtime rituals the night before in favor of sisterly commiseration. "Clarissa needs us to be awake and present, to support her through what will most likely be the worst day of her life."

"The worst day of my life," Clarissa exhaled. "Are you trying to make me feel better or worse?"

"You're marrying Mr. Kincraig." Sophia sighed drolly, scooting off the bed. "Unfortunately, I don't believe there is any way to make you feel worse."

She moved slowly and carefully, with a hand resting atop her belly. Clarissa watched, unable to imagine herself in such a state. How she envied her sister. *Both* her sisters, who had married into love matches. She supposed it was too much that three should accomplish such a remarkable feat.

"Oh. My. Heavens," blurted Daphne, pushing the blankets from her face to stare wide-eyed at the pink canopy over Clarissa's bed. "For a moment after waking up I didn't remember, but it is all coming back to me." She covered her face with her hands. "Oh, Clarissa, you always wanted your wedding to be the talk of London, and it seems as if today you shall have your wish."

"Daphne," Clarissa cried, following Sophia out of the bed to thrust her feet into her slippers. No—they were Sophia's slippers! She kicked them off and replaced them with her own. "Don't tease me, not now. It's not funny."

"I'm not teasing." Daphne rolled toward them, resting her head on one hand. "Certainly you know that no matter the degree of discretion around today's ceremony, there's going to be an announcement in the paper, and everyone's going to ask questions about why everything happened so quickly, and why the Duke of Claxton had to exert his influence to obtain a special license so immediately. You're marrying Mr. Kincraig, after all. He is a known drunk and a gambler, and . . . and . . . quite possibly a swindler."

"He is not—" Clarissa blurted.

"Daphne," Sophia warned, her gaze sharp. "It won't be that terrible. It's the end of the season. Half of London has likely already left town as of this morning."

"He's a scoundrel," Daphne accused.

"I won't have you speak ill of him," Clarissa sniffed.

Daphne scowled. "You know all too well we've all thought it at one time or another, as has the rest of the *ton*. There's got to be some reason no one ever heard of him before he arrived on our doorstep two years ago claiming to be a relation, which of course didn't even turn out to be true. That awful beard and mustache, and the way he dresses! He is not at all the sort of man anyone would expect a young lady of your potential to wed—"

Everything Daphne said was true.

"You shush now," Sophia snapped protectively, coming to stand between them.

Daphne pushed into a sitting position, her face puffy from sleep. "Am I the only one who remembers that night when the King's Guards found him swimming in the fountain at Kensington Palace, wearing only a ballerina's tutu?"

"How could any of us forget?" Sophia murmured, then, with an apologetic glance to Clarissa, she said, "Mr. Kincraig has always been a wild cannon."

Clarissa closed her eyes. Yes, by all accounts everything they said *was* true, her savior and future husband was all of those things, a wastrel, a drunk, and a gambler, but he had agreed to marry her, and what other choice did she have? Wolverton hadn't exactly presented her with any other options, and she couldn't very well place a sign in front of the house asking for more desirable volunteers.

"He's insufferable. Irreformable." Daphne rolled from the bed, taking up her robe and pulling the garment onto her arms. "Don't pretend otherwise. We were all quite relieved at hearing he would at last be gone from our lives. I knew there had to be a reason he didn't look more disappointed at learning he wasn't our relation—and it was because he'd already seduced Clarissa."

"That's not true. Please, just stop," Clarissa begged. "There was no plan to seduce me. I assure you with the utmost sincerity that Mr. Kincraig is no villain. He can be very charming and kind. If only you will try to see past all the rest."

The words, even to her own ears, sounded forced, not because her future husband had no redeeming qualities but because she ought not to have to defend Mr. Kincraig. He did not even belong in this story, other than by unfortunate chance.

Daphne peered at her, her eyes damp. "So help me, by all that is holy and good, if he was not the father of your child I would tear him apart with my own hands for the shame he has brought upon you. I shall despise him always for what he has done. Oh, fig! Christmas is ruined forever."

A wave of misery enveloped Clarissa. Christmas! Where would life find her and Mr. Kincraig then, when she could hardly see past the shock of this morning?

"Now you're being cruel," Sophia rebuked.

"I don't mean to be." Daphne's pale hair glinted brightly, touched by a beam of morning sunlight. She swiped her hands at the tears in her eyes. Her demeanor softened then, as did her voice. "It's just that I'm so very worried about grandfather and our dear mother, both of whom I came two inches from scandalizing just weeks ago with all my carrying on with Raikes. And not least of all, I am concerned for my sister, whom I love very much and want to be happy."

In two steps Daphne threw her arms around Clarissa, embracing her tight. "I'm sorry for speaking harshly about the man you love."

Sophia watched them, a sideways smile on her lips.

"She doesn't love him. You missed that all-important revelation when you were asleep."

Daphne pulled back and looked at Clarissa, her expression baffled. "Then how did this happen?"

With both of them looking at her in sympathy and puzzlement, a confession welled up from deep inside Clarissa's chest, threatening to burst from her lips.

But even if she went against her grandfather's wishes and told them the truth, they could do nothing to repair her situation. At least if she held her silence, they would believe she was marrying the father of her child and someone whom she respected enough to defend. If they knew about Lord Quinn's betrayal they would only pity her more, and she didn't want to live with that inglorious badge for the rest of her life, being poor Clarissa, the reckless little fool living a lie. She didn't want to live a lie. She must embrace this new reality.

She inhaled her sister's comforting scent, that of lilacs and sleep.

"There's nothing to be sorry for. I have hurt everyone with my impulsive choice." She gently withdrew from Daphne's embrace and stepped back, straightening her shoulders and holding her head high. "But it is all my doing, and I must live with the consequences. Thank you both for passing this long night with me, but I think I'd like to be alone now."

Her sisters looked at her, looking more traumatized than she felt in their sleeping gowns and rumpled hair and emotion-flushed faces.

"I am a terrible sister!" Daphne exclaimed, reaching for her again. "I shouldn't have said all those things. I've only made you feel worse when I should have just held my tongue and told you Mr. Kincraig is a gem in the rough and that everything will turn out for the best."

Clarissa squeezed her hands and laughed, albeit darkly. "I wouldn't have believed you. Go on. I know you'd both like to see your husbands after a night spent apart."

Sophia moved closer, a frown on her lips. "I don't think you should be alone right now."

Clarissa went to her dressing table and looked at her reflection in the mirror. What a mess she'd made of her eyes, with all the crying last night. What a lovely bride she would make, if indeed they married. If her conscience allowed it.

"Mr. Kincraig is to arrive before eleven. It is my wedding day and I'd like to bathe and dress if you don't mind." She looked over her shoulder at them, doing her best to hold her countenance placid. "Could you send Miss Randolph? And one of you, could you please look in on Grandfather? As I am responsible for the shock that caused his downturn in health, I'd like to know if he is all right."

Sophia nodded, her expression no less worried. "Yes, dear, of course."

A knock sounded on the door, and Sophia looked out and spoke to whomever stood in the corridor. She nodded, and closed the door.

Her shoulders rigid, she looked at Clarissa. "It's Mother, with the physician. I think he is here to confirm the... the..."

"The pregnancy," Clarissa said, nodding bravely. "It's all right. Let them in."

Dominick sat in the same chair, at the same table, staring at the same bottle he'd stared at since returning to his residence some five hours before. He'd removed the cork a score of times—and thrust it back into its berth just as many—daring once, but only once, to lift the opened bottle to his nose.

What a mistake that had been.

Even now, with the bottle securely corked, he smelled whiskey in his nostrils—and his mouth watered.

He closed his eyes and bit his bottom lip. The scent crept inside his head and encircled his brain and kindled a fire inside his chest, already blazing there over the injustice served up to him last night in Lord Wolverton's chambers.

He'd been so careful, meticulously executing each assignment, knowing his superiors watched and judged his every action and reaction. At last, he'd regained everything he'd lost. For a fleeting moment, his world had been returned to right.

But now he feared his dreams were just as charred and destroyed as the perfectly marvelous foreign assignment orders he'd committed to the flames.

He hissed into the darkness. His present predicament was all part of God's curse upon him, brutal and ceaseless. For a brief moment last night, he'd thought his penance paid, but apparently not—

All those nights he'd pretended to be a sotted drunk, he'd never touched a drop. It had all been a well-executed act, designed to draw Wolverton's enemy closer, when in truth he remained clear-headed and alert for any sign of danger.

Of course he'd been tempted, but never enough to surrender, but this thing with Clarissa—

"Put it down, Blackmer."

He blinked, breaking his stare at the bottle, which was tipped against the crystal rummer in his other hand. Exhaling through his nose, he lowered the bottle to the table, but not without regret. His stomach twisted in want, and his mouth went sour, denied.

He'd been one breath away from the pit, the same one that had consumed him within its shadowy blackness for nearly a year after Tryphena's death—until he'd dragged himself out from its depths and decided to live.

"I've been waiting for you to come. What took you so long?" he said to the shadow in the doorway, a man who stood tall and lithe and, like him, still dressed in evening clothes from the night before.

The shadow answered. "As you can imagine, there were others with whom I had to consult."

Always the others. Faceless, powerful men who determined his destiny from behind a veil of anonymity.

"Of course." Dominick held himself rigid, waiting to hear what would come next. A verdict upon his future.

"You're out, I'm afraid."

The words struck him like a bottle smashed to the back of his head. Though his eyes remained open, his vision went black. He could barely muster the breath to emit a response.

"I see."

"Certainly you understand."

He thumbed the base of the whiskey bottle, the urge to bellow in rage almost too strong to bear. He had done nothing wrong, and for that, he had lost the last thing that held any meaning in his life.

"I can't say that I do."

His visitor—his handler in the secret service—emerged

from the deeper shadows of the doorway, and the early light of morning coming in through the window revealed his familiar features. "As might be expected, the earlier tragedy is still fresh in everyone's minds. We took an enormous chance afterward, returning you to duty, and now this."

"*This*," Dominick repeated in a hushed whisper.

He had provided an understanding shoulder to a frightened girl, and for that, his life was ruined? His hands flexed atop the table, his knuckles itching for the satisfaction of a wall.

"You know the standard to which we are held." The man's voice grew hushed with regret. "Really, there could be no other decision."

Dominick's jaw tightened as a tangle of words pressed against the back of his teeth and lips, a denial so hot he felt certain its vehemence would burn the eyebrows and hair off the man standing before him. The degree of self-control he exerted in that moment in order to remain silent about the truth of that night almost sickened him.

He gritted out, "I suppose there could not be."

Only one thing prevented him from speaking: his promise to Wolverton, a misguided attempt to assuage a dying old man's fears for his granddaughter's future and that of her fatherless child. The power of that vow extended even here, between two men who built their lives around secrecy.

His visitor circled round to stand beside the fire. "What are you thinking, Blackmer?"

Black thoughts. Dangerous thoughts. His hands curled into fists. He had worked so hard and so long to get his life back.

"I'm certain you can imagine."

The man murmured, "Aren't you going to tell me it wasn't you who seduced Miss Bevington?" He reached out to touch the silver matchbox on the mantel. "That it was Lord Quinn?"

Chapter Six

At hearing the name spoken, Dominick's pulse leapt. But just as quickly, his mind adjusted a few lopsided pieces of the puzzle that before hadn't quite fit, and he knew nothing had changed.

You're out, I'm afraid. The words had already been said.

"Does everyone on the council know then?" he inquired darkly.

He nodded slowly. "You can thank Mrs. Brightmore for offering her confidential assessment."

Dominick closed his eyes. "And yet the truth makes no difference."

"I'm afraid it doesn't, because you see—"

"Wait, don't tell me." He stood suddenly, grabbing the bottle by the neck and walking toward the liquor cabinet, where he lowered the bottle to the inlaid-leather top with a solid *thunk*. "It's because Quinn's father, the Duke of Lowther, is favored to be the next Prime Minister."

His handler nodded and sank into the chair Dominick

had just vacated. "If Wolverton survives . . . if we don't keep the matter utterly quiet and discreet, a war will break out among England's most powerful men. Other powerful men would join in and choose sides. Given our perpetual state of conflict with France and Spain, any breath of internal upheaval, any weakening of our ranks, must be squelched in the—"

"—best interests of the empire," Dominick announced sardonically, with grand flourish of his hand. "And for those interests, I shall be sacrificed."

How humbling to learn he was nothing more than a pawn in the games of more powerful men and that none of the missions he had accomplished, the valor he had displayed, or the sacrifices he had made for the last decade of his life had meant one damn thing.

He was out. A warm body to be installed into a necessary spot, simply because he'd had the misfortune to be holding Clarissa Bevington in his arms when everything had gone to hell.

He felt grievously slighted. Betrayed by very organization he'd sworn to live and even die for, if necessary. Just like that, the fire in his chest that had burned so bright, fueled by loyalty and pride, wavered . . . and flickered out, leaving nothing but a cold and vacant hole in its place.

Although he was only thirty-four years old, he suddenly felt very old. Insignificant and worst of all, powerless. There was no one to whom he could appeal for reconsideration, because no one of importance gave a whit whether he'd been treated fairly, only that the political foundations of England remained unshaken.

His handler shrugged. "Think of it as a reassignment."

"But it's not a damn reassignment. It's not even a demotion. You said I'm out," he snarled bitterly. "What in the bloody hell about this arrangement benefits me?"

Other than marrying the beautiful but painfully naïve Miss Bevington, who loved another man and even carried that man's child, one he'd now be expected to raise as his own? He might as well go out tonight and leap into the Thames for all the joy that future would bring him. He felt sick about all he had lost. He could not even think beyond the moment to imagine what tomorrow might bring. For so long, service to his country had been his purpose and salvation. Now he had nothing.

"I'll see if I can secure your pension from the Exchequer."

"Oh, that's prime." Dominick let out a bitter laugh. "My country's generosity, after my thirteen years of service and sacrifice, astounds."

"Pardon me for daring to tread on the sanctity of your personal tragedy, but if you don't mind me saying, you're looking at all this in the wrong way." His handler stared at him, his lips drawn into a solemn line.

"How then should I be looking at things?" Dominick answered angrily.

His companion answered quietly. "I understand that you take great pride in your service for England, but any other rational fellow would consider marriage to the Earl of Wolverton's granddaughter to be a magnificent gift."

Dominick laughed bitterly. "I'm so very lucky."

Twin nostrils flared their displeasure. "It's not as if Miss Bevington is a terrible match. For one thing, she's lovely, both inside and out, and I don't have to tell you that's rare. But more important, I'm certain she will come with a respectable marriage settlement. Perhaps not immediately, but at some time in the future when the turmoil has calmed down. You'll have married into one of the most respected families in England."

As simple as it all sounded, spilling from his handler's lips, Dominick knew marriage wasn't that tidy. There were emotions involved. Expectations of love. But he had loved his once-in-a-lifetime love, and she—Tryphena—had nearly destroyed him. His soul was scarred. Incapable of the intimacy. He couldn't fathom the idea of marrying ever again.

Dominick gritted out, "I don't want marriage, or wealth or connections. I want my life back. The one I worked so hard to regain. Is that so difficult to understand?"

"No, it's not. But I hope, given time, you'll change your mind."

Dominick narrowed his eyes. "If she's such a prize, why don't you marry her?"

"I can't."

"Why not?"

He chuckled, without humor. "Because I wasn't fool enough to get caught in your situation. What's done is done. Given the sensitivity of the matter, no one else can be brought in. We can't take the chance someone will talk. It has to be you."

"Hmmm. Clarissa Bevington. Mine, all mine. Lucky me." Dominick steepled his fingers together and, with no small amount of dramatic flair, peered ceiling-ward as if greedily pondering the idea of a grand fortune, then dropped his arms to his side. "Not only have I lost everything, but her family will make me miserable for the rest of my life. They'll forever despise me, believing I betrayed their trust and seduced their angel."

"They'll forgive in time."

"I wouldn't," he bit out. He imagined Quinn's aristocratic features then and thought how nice it would be to smash them with his fist. "Not if she was my daughter."

"No, I don't think you would. One suggestion..."

"A suggestion?"

He shrugged. "Call it a parting order, if you prefer."

Dominick's eyes narrowed. "What's that?"

"Get her away from London as soon as you can, away from the questions and scrutiny. And when I say scrutiny, I mean it is best that people don't have the opportunity to ask questions about you, other than what we will allow them to know. It's for your safety as well as hers and the child's. Live a quiet life, away from here for the first few years. By then any interest will have died down. Do you have somewhere you can go?"

"Perhaps." Dominick paused in front of the fire. "I'll... find somewhere."

Again the anger returned. This had never been part of his plan. He was supposed to be embarking on a thrilling mission tomorrow. Returning to stand shoulder to shoulder with his peers. Not shrinking into obscurity.

"Good."

Dominick looked up at the ceiling, feeling caged, wishing it were the sky and that he could just fly away. "I don't have to go through with this, you know. I could just leave. Disappear forever and make a life for myself on the other side of the world." He crossed his arms over his chest and stared up at the plaster medallion on the ceiling. "I could just leave that chit to suffer her own consequences."

"You could do that, indeed," the man answered quietly. "But I don't believe you will."

* * *

"Who is that gentleman with Claxton and Raikes?" Daphne asked from the drawing room window, where she stood peering out through lace curtains.

"They've invited a friend to come along?" Clarissa started up from the chaise where she'd been sitting with Sophia.

Joining her sister, she peered down to the street where Claxton's black town carriage had arrived. Footmen secured the door, and the three men who had emerged proceeded up the walk toward the house. Claxton led the way, his lips drawn into a scowl that still proclaimed *blast you, Clarissa*, followed by Lord Raikes, who, while less stern of countenance, tugged at the knot of his neck cloth as if it strangled him, as if he'd just suffered through the most unpleasant ride of his life. A third man followed, tall, erect, and solemn. Clarissa's attention lingered on him momentarily, taking note of the figure he cut in his fashionable gray morning coat and the angular set of his jaw above a perfectly executed ivory silk cravat—

Her nerves already a tangle, she jerked the curtain closed. "I can't believe they've brought a stranger, someone I don't even know, to gawk through the ceremony. I thought it was understood that, given the circumstances, there would only be family present. Men can be just as terrible gossips as ladies and I would just like a small bit more time before news of my wedding is bandied around town."

Sophia joined them at the window.

"Certainly they wouldn't have," replied Daphne in a soothing tone, reaching an arm to squeeze her shoulders.

"Perhaps it's the priest, and he's not yet put on his vestments."

Numerous vases filled with flowers brightened the room, sent by well-wishers and more than one hopeful suitor who had attended her short-lived ball. Stacks of notes had arrived by courier, inquiring about Wolverton's health. By all accounts, London remained oblivious to the fact that in less than an hour's time, Clarissa would become Mrs. Kincraig.

The inevitability of scandal weighed like a stone on her chest. Clarissa paced and fretted, wringing her hands.

"What does it matter if they did bring someone? Everyone will know soon enough that I've married the most unlikely candidate, in questionable haste, and wonder about the reason why. Perhaps we ought to have just invited the entire *ton* and gotten the whole sordid announcement over with."

Sophia straightened suddenly, with a sharp intake of breath. "Clarissa, that's no stranger. That's Mr. Kincraig."

Clarissa froze, hearing the words, but then shook her head.

"That's not possible," she replied. "Daphne and I know perfectly well what Mr. Kincraig looks like."

She quickly returned to the window but caught only the briefest glimpse of wide shoulders and top hats as the men moved out of sight.

Which meant they were entering the house. She'd braced herself all morning for this moment, but still, the room spun around her.

If indeed the stranger was Mr. Kincraig, she hadn't even recognized her own husband-to-be! Didn't that only prove the folly of the situation at hand? This morning, after the physician had solemnly confirmed her condition, she'd resolved to marry him. She'd convinced herself that Mr. Kincraig had agreed to the arrangement because he would most certainly benefit from the union, both financially and through the social and political connections he could make by association with her family. Lots of people married for those very same reasons, without ever thinking about love.

But now she doubted everything. Was she only being selfish? Had she and her grandfather imprisoned a man who had so kindly, in her time of need, tried to protect and comfort her?

"I don't think I can marry Mr. Kincraig," she announced quietly, her face and throat going hot and her palms humid. Suddenly the drawing room felt like a furnace.

"I know you're afraid," Sophia assured quietly, a look of pity in her eyes. "But it will all turn out for the best. It must, because, Clarissa, you don't have any other choice. When there's a baby, the father must take responsibility, and you must as well."

She didn't want to punish the baby by denying it a father, but neither did she wish to punish Mr. Kincraig.

"I can't," she said, this time a degree louder and more resolute. "I need to speak with Grandfather."

Footsteps sounded in the corridor and Lady Margaretta appeared, her expression strained. At seeing her, a strong pang struck Clarissa's heart. Her beautiful, loving mother had barely spoken to her since last night, nor had she offered a single word of comfort. No wonder. Clarissa had disappointed her terribly, destroying all the dreams Her Ladyship had held for her since her birth twenty years ago. She'd disappointed them all and shamed her beloved father's memory. Clarissa's only peace came from knowing her mother had found love again with the kind-hearted Mr. Birch, whom she liked very much. He had arrived at the house earlier that morning and had surely offered his support to her mother in his quiet way.

"Mr. Kincraig has arrived," announced the marchioness, her voice tight with emotion.

So the stranger with Claxton and Raikes was indeed Mr. Kincraig. She tried to recall what she'd seen from the window. He'd appeared different, but why?

"We saw them arrive," said Sophia, clasping her hands in front of her waist before throwing Clarissa a rueful glance.

To Clarissa's mortification, Daphne chose that moment to burst into tears.

"I can't believe this is happening," she choked, pressing a hand to her face and fishing a handkerchief out of her pocket. Several fell out and fluttered to the carpet. Dearest Daphne. She must have anticipated a veritable river of tears and come prepared.

In the next moment, Clarissa forgot them both. An imposing shadow appeared behind her mother, a man whose features remained obscured by the half-light of the corridor. Her breath hovered in her throat, suspended in place, as the shadow emerged and transformed into a grim-featured gentleman in a dove gray morning coat and dark trousers. His black gaze swept the room touching momentarily on her sisters before focusing with excruciating exactness on her.

The Mr. Kincraig she'd known before had always kept to the shadows and the farthest corners of the room, rarely drawing undue attention to himself. He'd been reluctant to ever pay formal calls or involve himself in the polite conversations of a Belgravia drawing room. Yet in this moment he stood at the center of the room, the very picture of a gentleman.

"Good morning," he said smoothly, with only the slightest edge of sarcasm.

Her mouth fell open in startlement.

Gone was the unkempt beard and mustache and unfashionable long hair. She felt quite certain she'd never even glimpsed his ears. The man she had come to know for the past nearly two years of her life—but apparently had never truly *seen*—stood proud and calm, his features laid bare for her viewing.

And what a shock it was to find that Mr. Kincraig had very fine features. Broad cheekbones, with down-swept hollows beneath and a Grecian nose that boasted a decidedly aristocratic bump. How had she never noticed that detail before, when certainly his nose had not been covered by his beard?

She'd fussed over his shabby appearance and retied his cravat countless times—a cravat that this morning was tied to perfection. Why did she now feel as if she were looking into the eyes of a stranger?

"It's only me," he growled, sounding very much like himself. His jaw tightened in annoyance. "You needn't look so appalled."

"I'm not appalled," she answered. No, not at all. She couldn't define how she felt at seeing him like this. Relieved? Breathless.

"It's just that I've never seen you look so...so..." Clarissa's voice faded away. Heat rose into her cheeks, and for a moment her hands gestured aimlessly, as if with a mind of their own.

"Clean?" suggested Sophia archly, one eyebrow raised.

"Shaven," added Daphne, from behind her lace-edged handkerchief.

"—turned out." Sophia's gaze descended from his face to his shoes.

Daphne sniffed. "Sober."

No. Handsome *is what Clarissa had thought. Not to the same magnitude as Quinn, but handsome no less.*

"Don't let that fool you," muttered the duke.

"Claxton." Clarissa shot her brother-in-law a pleading glance, before her gaze veered back to Mr. Kincraig.

His eyebrows raised drolly. "Oh, that's nothing. You should have been there for his diatribe in the carriage. Do I even have ears left? They may have melted off."

"He didn't deserve that," Clarissa declared, glaring at her family.

"Quiet, all of you," Lady Margaretta intervened, color rising into her previously pale cheeks.

Claxton and Raikes exchanged a grim glance. Mr. Kincraig stood tall and still, and he held a box. Given the circumstances, she could not help but think him very brave. Remembering herself, she proceeded toward him, determined to salvage the moment.

"Good morning to you," she said in a voice that came out regretfully wane. She cleared her throat. "Thank you for coming."

She supposed that would have to do. She thought to reach for his hands, but no. Although she supposed they were betrothed, she could not bring herself to extend that degree of familiarity, especially now that he was outright glowering at her as if to say *I had no choice.*

He exhaled and closed his eyes.

Opening them again, he said, "I brought you flowers—"

He pressed the box into her hands, his gaze moving over her, as if he too saw her for the first time. She looked down at his swarthy-skinned hands against the ivory box, long-fingered and square at the knuckles, and imagined them touching her. She swallowed, instantly flustered and discomposed.

Unaware, he continued on. "—and a special license, which the duke was generous enough to exert every ounce of his influence to procure." Even his voice, to her, sounded different. Deeper and more serious than the Mr. Kincraig she had known. Polished and clipped. Could the change also be the effect of sobriety? Before he had always appeared in a perpetual state of sottedness, to one degree or another. Now everything about him, from the clarity of his gaze to his dress and movements, spoke of precision and care.

"Thank you," she said, accepting the box from his hands.

Around them, the room remained utterly silent. She knew everyone watched to see what would happen next.

"The least you could do is open them." His jaw twitched, adjacent to a frown. As she held the box, he removed the lid and lifted out a small nosegay of roses, one that represented every possible shade of pink.

Her favorite color. It touched her that he'd noticed at all. Taking the box from her hands, he replaced it with the flowers and set the box aside. She looked up at him, and her heart softened a degree more toward him.

Which was exactly why she couldn't marry him.

Voices sounded in the corridor and in the next moment Havering appeared.

"Good morning, everyone," he said. "I've brought the priest, Mr. Woodcombe."

Her cheeks warmed. Mr. Woodcombe had married both of her sisters to their husbands and had years of history with their family, and would undoubtedly be as perplexed over this marriage as anyone else. Her mother woodenly introduced Mr. Kincraig to the reverend, who only briefly raised questioning eyebrows at Clarissa before politely offering his congratulations.

"Wolverton is waiting, so let us proceed upstairs at once," Lady Margaretta announced, her eyes bright.

Sophia and Daphne joined their husbands. Mr. Birch appeared in the corridor and smiled comfortingly at her mother.

"If you all don't mind," Clarissa said. "I'd like a moment alone with Mr. Kincraig."

All conversation stopped and everyone turned to her. She gripped the ribbon-wrapped stems of her nosegay.

Lady Margaretta looked at her steadily. "We can't keep your grandfather waiting, dear." Her tone was not unkind.

"I understand," Clarissa replied. "I ask for only a moment."

Her Ladyship nodded. "We'll wait for you in the corridor."

Once the door was closed, he turned full on toward her, glowering. "What is it, then?"

He did not approach her. Instead, he seemed to prefer keeping the whole of the room between them, so distancing was his rigid stance and cold demeanor.

"I thought we should talk," she said. "We haven't really had a chance to do so."

He exhaled through his nose, as if struggling for patience.

"Forgive me, but at present I don't want to talk." He bit out each word through his teeth. His eyes scalded her with their heat. "Not to you. Not to anyone. I just want to get this bloody ceremony over with."

She swallowed hard, doing her best not to wither beneath the intensity of his displeasure.

"You're angry," she said. "You've every right to be. I understand."

An angry smile turned his lips. "You understand? Oh, I beg to differ." He did step toward her now, coming so close she smelled his shaving soap. Fury lit his eyes. "I don't think you understand anything. Believe me when I say, my dear Miss Bevington, that it's taking every fraction of my willpower not to break Claxton's nose, or smash that vase of flowers, or throw that table upside down. Or reveal your secret."

"My secret." She nodded, knowing she more than deserved the harsh words. "Yes, you've been very kind. Kinder than I ever expected. Kinder than I deserve. That's why I owe you my thanks, and a way out of this entanglement. Last night it was wrong of me to agree to this marriage, to allow my feelings for my grandfather and my family to keep me from telling everyone the truth."

"You've come to this decision now?" he growled, his eyes widening.

She nodded. "I won't distress them further by revealing Quinn's part in all this." She shrugged ruefully. "He has married another, and nothing can be done. But I'll make certain they understand you have nothing at all to do with my predicament."

How she hated that word. *Predicament.* It sounded so feckless.

"What do you suppose the truth will accomplish now?" he scoffed.

She raised her hands, exasperated, not understanding why he did not rejoice at her offer to make things right. "Your freedom?"

If at all possible, his gaze grew harder and colder.

"Too late," he seethed.

"It can't be," she exclaimed. "Not for you."

"Well, it is," he responded, between clenched teeth, his eyes flashing fire like the Devil's. "You've already bloody well ruined my life, and by God, now you're going to marry me so I can have the pleasure of ruining yours."

"Oh!" she cried, dismayed not only by his vulgar language but his threat.

Without another word, he turned from her and wrenched the door open. With mock graciousness, he tilted his head and crooked his arm in gentlemanly invitation, his features still sharp with anger.

Everyone stood in a cluster, watching from the corridor.

"But—" she said, afraid to take even a single step toward the door, because once she did, she wouldn't turn back.

"Now," he growled.

Sophia's mouth fell open. "What manner of gentleman behaves so to his bride-to-be on their wedding day?"

Daphne cried, "No *true* gentleman would."

They all saw him as a villain, but he wasn't. They didn't know what she'd done to make him behave so. He still wanted to marry her, even after she'd given him the opportunity to escape. Yes, he was angry, but she didn't for one second believe his words about ruining her life. Of course, she still felt a mixture of relief and dread about what they were about to do, but her decision was made and she would not shrink back from it again.

Crossing the carpet, she tucked her gloved hand to his arm.

"We're ready!" she announced to her family, offering them her best smile.

No one in the waiting wedding party appeared convinced, and a sideways glance proved her groom made no effort whatsoever to feign the slightest modicum of joy.

Side by side they followed her mother and the reverend, with her sisters and their husbands following along behind, in utter silence up the stairs, like a procession to the guillotine.

Chapter Seven

Dominick—his mind a maelstrom of conflicted emotions—stood hand in hand with Clarissa beside the bed, along with the clergyman. The curtains remained drawn, and shadows filled the room. Wolverton lay propped on a high embankment of pillows, watching through glazed, half-open eyes.

How different from his first wedding day, which had taken place in sunshine and light with much laughter and optimism for the future. Tryphena had loved him then, in the beginning, of that he had no doubt.

Lady Harwick, at the last moment, came forward to drape what appeared to be an heirloom veil of lace over her daughter's hair and pressed a kiss on her cheek, before returning to Mr. Birch's side.

"Mother," exclaimed Daphne, reaching to take hold of Her Ladyship's hand.

Clarissa stared at the floor, clearly struggling to hold back tears.

Dominick had nothing to do with any of this, so pardon him if he didn't join the funeral. He stood taller and straightened his shoulders, an intentional show of pride.

Mr. Woodcombe peered over the top edge of his prayer book and said, "If you will, my good Mr. Kincraig, repeat after me. I—"

"I," he repeated clearly.

The priest tilted his head and lifted his hand in encouragement. "Say your name, please. Your forename and surname and all illustrious names between."

Mr. Woodcombe chuckled and smiled, as if they were all having a splendid time.

Dominick's young bride already looked half near fainting. Pale and tense, she stared at his chest and gripped both of his hands as if fearful she might at any moment be swept over an imaginary ship's railing into a ravenous and punishing sea.

How utterly opposite she was from Tryphena, who had been radiant on their wedding day and had claimed him like a prize she had won, with smiles and kisses and whispered promises of what she intended to do to him as soon as they returned to their lodgings. Like him, Tryphena had been an agent in the secret service. An equal, she had matched him both in passion and in professional ambition. Clarissa, on the other hand, was just a girl.

Ah, but his name. His real name. Dominick shifted stance. A glance to Wolverton revealed him to be staring steadily back, watching the proceedings in silence. For a brief moment their eyes met.

The earl winked.

Winked, at him? No, that had to be wrong. He'd merely observed a tremor, an involuntary consequence of an old man's failing health. Whatever the case, there could be no more delaying the inevitable. Now he would set them all back on their heels, and with pleasure.

"I...Dominick Arden Blackmer—"

Clarissa's head snapped up. Behind them, the sniffles and sobs went silent.

Oh, he couldn't help it. A satisfied smile curled the corner of his lips.

Mr. Woodcombe's brows gathered in puzzlement, and he referred to the slip of paper tucked into the back of his book, yet after a moment he cleared his throat and continued on. "Take thee..."

"—take thee—" Dominick stopped there, realizing he could proceed no further. To Clarissa, he said, "I'm sorry, my dearest *darling*—" Sarcastic emphasis on the "darling." "—but I've realized I don't know your full name."

"Clarissa Anne Georgina Bevington," she answered in a quiet voice, her blue eyes brightly illuminated with temper, something that heartened him because he supposed he'd prefer angry over hopeless any day. "And what did you just say your name was?"

He chuckled, enjoying the thrill of satisfaction he felt at her confusion, but purposefully did not answer her.

"I take thee, Clarissa Anne Georgina Beving—"

"Pardon me," interrupted a man's imperious voice from behind, one belonging to the Duke of Claxton.

The same one that had made his life hell all morning long, with its lectures and cutting remarks and outright snide aspersions as to his character. Footsteps sounded on the carpet.

"I too would ask that the gentleman repeat his name."

Dominick didn't move. He only looked into Clarissa's

eyes, fighting the urge to laugh outright because the idea of shocking his new family had suddenly became utterly satisfying.

Clarissa answered in a clear voice, "I believe he said...Dominick Arden Blackmer...Kincraig?"

She scrutinized his face.

"Hmmmm, no," he answered coolly.

"No?" Her eyebrows went up. "As to the Kincraig?"

He smiled graciously. "That is correct."

Clarissa's lashes—much darker than her hair—fluttered against her pale cheekbones and she bristled, her gaze brightening and her shoulders going very straight. "Interesting."

Now it was he who gripped her hands, refusing to allow her to snatch them away.

"Is there some problem?" inquired Mr. Woodcombe.

The ladies whispered.

"Did you hear what he said?"

"If he isn't Mr. Kincraig, then, who is he?"

"Isn't that fraud?"

"Can't we do something?"

Yes, God, yes, he prayed one of them or all of them would "do something" and stop this farce of a wedding. Chase him from the house. Throw candlesticks and books at him, insisting that he never show his face in their presence again. Procure a constable to escort him to the edge of town. Anything.

A low growl came from Wolverton in the bed, faint yet imperious. "*Proceed.*"

"But—" started the duke.

"Stand...*down,* Claxton," insisted the earl, the words ragged and labored.

For a moment Claxton fumed, motionless. He pivoted on his heel and strode, with his hand over his mouth, toward Sophia, who reached out to him with a consoling hand.

Dominick bit down a curse, his scant hope at freedom dashed. For a moment they all looked at one another in silence.

Red-faced, the priest hooked a finger into his cravat and tugged, exhaling loudly. He nodded and looked down into his book again. "As His Lordship desires."

Standing before Dominick, Clarissa exhaled and frowned. With a shake of her head, she closed her eyes, and reopened them to sullenly stare down at his boots. Her hands lay completely limp within his.

He tugged her several inches closer and insisted in a low murmur, "I would have you look at me while we speak the vows."

Color rose to her cheeks. Yet after an extended moment, she did look up, her eyes snapping with a blaze of fire.

"Look at you? I don't even know who you *are*," she hissed.

All her girlishness fell away, leaving him hand in hand with a different person than he'd known her to be before. A woman, wide-eyed and lush, and obviously furious at him.

Deep in his chest, a sleeping dragon roused...raised its head and growled out a low, drowsy stream of smoke and cinders.

Dominick exhaled through his teeth, unsettled.

He'd never felt *that* sort of reaction to her before, no sudden appreciation of her as a sensual creature capable of passion. He'd found her lovely, of course, much like one would admire a pretty flower, in a garden full of many other pretty flowers. Never once before had he felt the startling snap-quick drag of flint against steel, deep in his chest, that indicated a deeper awareness of her womanhood.

That he should feel it now, in this most unlikely, most miserable of moments—

Well...he felt tricked. Bamboozled. And he instantly snuffed the fledgling flame.

He didn't want to feel anything for her. Not affection, or attraction, and certainly not need. Especially for a woman who very likely, at this moment, still loved another man.

"Ahem," said Mr. Woodcombe. "Do you need me to repeat the words?"

No. No he didn't.

"I take thee, Clarissa Anne Georgina Bevington," he uttered in a low voice, "to be my wedded wife—"

He had never thought he would say these words to another woman, ever again.

"—to have and to hold from this day forward, for better, for worse, for richer, for poorer, in sickness and in health—"

Clarissa's blue eyes sparkled, full of accusation and mistrust, a delicate, oblivious little creature who didn't understand at all what she was getting herself into, or the sort of damaged man she married.

"—to love and to cherish, till death us do part—"

The first time he'd married, the concept of death hadn't seemed real. Like a fool, he'd believed in forever, in the immortality of his and Tryphena's youth and the sanctity of their love, and yet here he stood not four years later, promising to cherish and protect another woman. Bloody hell, barely a woman. A pretty chit he hardly knew and most certainly did not love.

Nonetheless, he had said his vows. Now she must do the same.

She cleared her throat.

"I, Clarissa Anne Georgina Bevington, take thee—" She paused and swallowed before proceeding. "Dominick... Arden...Blackmer—"

Mr. Woodcombe droned on and on and on saying words he did not hear. At the clergyman's urging, Dominick and Clarissa knelt and joined hands, hers very small and delicate and cool within his. A stranger's hand.

"—and husbands, love your wives, and be not bitter against them."

The words cut through the curtain of Dominick's thoughts and memories. His vision returned to clear. Beside him, Clarissa stared up at him.

He'd lost everything. Everything but her.

Him, bitter? In that moment, he couldn't contain himself. A most inappropriate welling of mirth barreled up from inside him.

He laughed.

"Where has Mr. Kincraig gone?" whispered Daphne, inching closer to Sophia on the striped settee. "I mean Mr. Blackmer—if that is indeed his name."

"Of course that is his name," the Duchess of Claxton responded in a low voice. "A person must speak the truth when taking a vow of matrimony."

"Says who?" hissed the middle sister, with a deep sigh. "What if our sister has been swept up into some outlandish fraud or scheme, just as we suspected all along—"

"Would you please stop saying such things?" Clarissa interrupted—in the most discreet voice possible—from the chair she occupied. "I'm sitting right here. Mr. Blackmer is with Claxton and Wolverton. They remained behind and shut the door."

She plucked at the lace on her skirts, fuming, wondering what the gentlemen were talking about. After all, this was *her* life. It was she who had just married Mr. Blackmer, whoever Mr. Blackmer really was. Shouldn't she be there to hear any explanations as well? For them to have closed-door discussions while she was relegated to the drawing room with the ladies, set her blood to boiling.

After the ceremony, they'd gone to the Jade Room, a small parlor adjacent to the dining room, where they waited to be seated for a wedding breakfast that Cook had fussed and complained about having to so hastily prepare. Like all master cooks, he took special occasions most seriously and had almost made himself ill worrying that her special day be just as special as he'd always imagined it, with only a few hours' notice.

Only the day wasn't all that special, when one had indeed married a scoundrel.

Because Mr. Blackmer was a scoundrel, wasn't he, if he'd been lying to them all this time about his name? To what degree she did not know, nor could she guess his motive, but his intentional misrepresentation, which had been put forth by him for nearly two years, deeply troubled her.

What she couldn't understand was why her grandfather had allowed them to be married.

"Your sister is right," said Lady Harwick, who stood at the center of the carpet. Lord Raikes, for his part, perused the small bookcase filled with books, very obviously trying to pretend he didn't hear any of their conversation.

"Which sister?" asked Daphne, eyebrows raised.

"Your sister *Clarissa,*" the marchioness responded, eyes widening with rare temper. "Be careful of the words and accusations you speak, for you may well regret them later. I'm certain we shall have some answers explaining Mr. Blackmer's use of a different name very soon."

Still, Her Ladyship appeared fretful, and glanced to the door as if waiting for the next scandal to arrive—or perhaps only the tall, dark-haired one that her youngest daughter had just married.

Mr. Birch drew near to Lady Margaretta's side and spoke in assuring tones.

Her brother-in-law, the duke, entered the drawing room. His gaze met Sophia's fleetingly before he nodded to Lady Margaretta and settled his attention with great solemnity on Clarissa. She couldn't help but feel that a hammer was about to fall—right on the top of her head.

"I have spoken with Wolverton and Mr. Blackmer," he said.

"Just say it. Get it over with." She pressed a hand to the center of her abdomen, which *hurt* from hours of anxious churning. "Tell me who he is."

"Perhaps you'd like to hear this in private?" he said.

"Why?" she said, dismayed. "It's not as if everyone won't find out two moments after. Tell us all."

"Very well," he answered gravely. "But I warn you, what I've learned may shock you. What I tell you must never leave this room."

"Would you like me to go?" Mr. Birch asked Lady Margaretta.

"No, please stay." She reached for him, and he moved closer to her side.

Clarissa nodded and swallowed hard, bracing herself for whatever dark revelations His Grace would share about her new husband. Her sisters closed in, each taking one of her arms as if to support her if she should pitch to the floor.

She let them.

She'd believed it punishment enough to be forced into marrying Mr. Kincraig as a price for her romantic foolishness. Apparently not. Mr. Kincraig didn't even exist. What if she'd married a murderer? A villainous felon? A man who kept a harem of mistresses and boasted a score of children as well? She had to be prepared for the truth, no matter how unfortunate it might be.

Claxton glanced over his shoulder toward the door. "Mr. Blackmer, it seems, is an agent of the Crown."

The words rang like a bell inside her head, not at all what she'd expected to hear.

Clarissa's heartbeat took on a different tempo, still wild but...a degree slower. Yes, slower. Mr. Blackmer, the stranger she had just married, wasn't a murderer or a criminal then. She exhaled a shaky sigh of relief.

The duke continued, "A domestic operative, if you will."

Silence held the room as everyone appeared to allow his revelation to sink in. At last Sophia spoke.

"An agent of the Crown," she repeated breathlessly.

"That's not so terrible," murmured Daphne, squeezing Clarissa's arm. "Indeed, it's rather...exciting. He still acted abhorrently, in luring you into a romantic entanglement, but at least we know he is not a fraud."

"But an agent of the Crown? Why was he here?" Clarissa started, her thoughts and her memories now confused.

They were just a family. She couldn't think of a reason why their daily activities would interest anyone or require secret observation.

Her mother looked to Claxton. "Why did he pretend to be Wolverton's heir?"

Sophia tilted her head and moved closer. "Were we all being watched?"

"All this time? Did Wolverton know the truth?" Raikes asked.

"Yes, he did." Claxton looked between the four of them. "His Lordship kept this secret to himself, so that none of us would be unduly concerned, but apparently, some two years ago, home intelligence became aware of a possible threat to Wolverton's person."

"Someone wanted to hurt Grandfather?" Daphne asked, her face transformed in that moment by fear.

"He's elderly! Why?" said Sophia.

He lifted two hands in a calming gesture. "I was as alarmed as you when I first heard. Something to do with old enemies with a grudge from long ago. Perhaps French. But the threat turned out to be no threat at all, which is why Mr. Kincraig, as we had come to know him, had received instructions to depart. He had been reassigned. Received new orders, if you will."

Lady Margaretta looked at Clarissa. "And yet you are married to a stranger in truth. Someone whose true identity even you did not know." Her arm came around Clarissa and she gave her a comforting squeeze. "My dear daughter, you did not know, did you, dear?"

"No," she answered truthfully, her mind still adjusting to this new truth. "I'm as stunned as the rest of you are."

One realization filtered through. Wolverton had known

Mr. Blackmer's true identity when the wedding took place. He had not, then, knowingly married her to a rakehell gambler and drunk but instead to a man who had protected him from harm. A man she could only surmise that he trusted. The dark cloud that hung over the day became less foreboding at realizing that.

Sophia touched Clarissa's arm but looked at her husband. "And now Clarissa will accompany Mr. Blackmer on his new assignment? How thrilling. Perhaps somewhere abroad. An embassy assignment? They have such marvelous parties."

Clarissa's spirit lightened. Traveling abroad. Parties? Oh, she hoped so.

Daphne interjected, "Or better yet, she will remain here with us, while Mr. Blackmer fulfills his duties alone?"

She wouldn't mind that so much either.

Again, Claxton glanced to the door, his expression regretful. "I'm afraid not. Given the circumstances of what has taken place with Clarissa and the trust his behavior has broken, Mr. Blackmer's superiors at the Home Office have released him from service."

"No," exclaimed Clarissa, guilt striking her through. No. No. No.

Not only had she caused his identity as an agent in the household to be revealed, which she could only suppose was a terrible thing, but she had cost him his position as an agent. The anger she had seen in his eyes! It hadn't only been because he'd been impressed into marrying her, but because accepting the blame for her ruination came at a painful personal sacrifice.

"Don't blame yourself, Clarissa," said Lord Raikes from where he stood beside the bookcase. "Espionage agents are by nature calculating. They are fully capable of exerting the utmost in self-control. I suspect Mr. Blackmer knew exactly what he was doing by luring you into this entanglement."

And there was the tragedy. Despite Mr. Blackmer having been revealed as a Crown agent, in their midst for necessary and honorable purposes, they all still considered him her seducer.

The duke nodded. "I'm afraid what Raikes says is true. Mr. Blackmer is no master spy but something far less dazzling. He is a low-level security officer." He shrugged. "One step above a Bow Street Runner. I can only imagine he came from modest circumstances and rather liked playing the part of a gentleman of wealth and connections and sought to secure a more legitimate position within the family by whatever means possible. That means being you, my dear girl."

"That's not true," Clarissa said in a firm voice.

But her vow to her grandfather and Mr. Blackmer kept her silent and more frustrated than ever that she could not speak the truth.

Mrs. Brightmore entered the room and murmured something to Lady Margaretta, who announced, "The meal is ready. Shall we all go in?"

Clarissa answered firmly, "Not without Mr. Blackmer." To Claxton, she said, "Where is he, do you know?"

"When I came here, he went outside," he answered. "Why, I don't know."

"Most likely to escape us." Clarissa frowned reprovingly at them all. "We haven't been very welcoming."

She looked out the window and observed Blackmer speaking to a footman near the street. The servant nodded deferentially and set off to do his bidding, whatever it was. No doubt he was arranging some means of escape. Most likely without her, and she wouldn't blame him.

She saw something then, she hadn't noticed before. Her new husband moved with an air of confidence, his shoulders straight and his chin high. He appeared to be more than comfortable speaking to servants. Masterful, even. A low-level agent working security detail for an elderly earl? A man of little importance? Something in his manner contradicted that. Perhaps it was only her wishful thinking, in wanting to be married to a man of distinction.

Turning back, she saw Daphne cross her arms across her bodice and frown. "I don't want to make you feel any worse than you already do, but did you truly believe we'd make him feel welcome, given the circum—"

Anger, and the fierce need to defend Mr. Blackmer, surged through her in a lightning rush. Clarissa interrupted, pointing a finger at her sister.

"I will hear nothing more of circumstances. Do you hear? Mr. Blackmer and I are married now. He is my husband and I must insist that you extend to him every measure of respect."

Daphne's eyes widened, and a long moment passed where her mouth hung open as if caught on an unspoken word. At last she closed her mouth and blinked.

"Why, of course, you're right," she said, contrite. "All that matters is that you are happy."

Emboldened, Clarissa stood an inch taller.

"That goes for the rest of you as well," she added, leveling a steady glare upon her family. "I might approach some modicum of happiness if you would all stop behaving like savages."

They had always considered her an impetuous child. Now they all looked back at her with expressions of surprise, clearly stunned by her strong words and finger jabbing. Lady Margaretta...smiled. "Oh, Clarissa."

Sophia lifted a hand. "I'm so proud of you. Truly I am. Good for you for calling us out."

Claxton scowled, but the sharpness of his gaze decreased. After a long moment, he nodded in assent.

Suddenly, Raikes stood beside her. "Why don't I go and find him, and bring him here?"

"Thank you, Raikes, but no," Clarissa replied. "He is my husband, and I will go to find him, after which I shall bring him back here, where my hope is that we can enjoy our wedding breakfast together, as a family." Her throat tightened with emotion as she looked into each of their faces. "You are the people I hold most dear. I can look back on this day as a nightmare or a happy memory. It all depends on you."

They all nodded at her. She turned on the heel of her slipper to quit the room. She paused just outside the door, gathering herself so as not to go to Blackmer with tears in her eyes. A happy memory. Was that even possible?

Just then, she heard her mother say, "We must all do as Clarissa says. Out of love for her, we must let go of our grudges, do our best to forgive Mr. Blackmer, and accept him as part of our family."

"I am in complete agreement," Sophia quietly said.

Daphne spoke then. "We shall be nothing but accommodating from this moment on."

There wasn't much to smile about today—but Clarissa smiled in this moment.

She descended the staircase to the ground floor and approached the front doors. She sought out a footman to deliver her request to Blackmer that he rejoin her—

Only she didn't find a footman or her husband. Instead, she came face to face with Lord Quinn, standing on the threshold, as if he'd just stepped inside, with his top hat in hand.

"Quinn—" she gasped, feeling as if the world had opened up underneath her feet.

"Thank God it's you," he murmured fervently, striding toward her, taking her hands while searching the corridor behind her. "I've come under the pretense of seeing Claxton, just hoping for a moment with you. Quickly, my darling, where can we go? I must speak to you alone."

Chapter Eight

From the street, Dominick observed Lord Quinn—
with his distinctive gold Adonis curls glinting beneath the
brim of his top hat—climb out of a town carriage and make
his way up the steps to the front door.

The muscles along the back of his neck tensed, and his
blood went cold. He stood motionless only long enough to
determine, with cool calculation, what his response would
be and then proceeded, following the same path His Lordship had taken just moments before. Once inside, he heard
the voices of Clarissa's family echoing faintly down from
the drawing room upstairs.

However, at just that moment Mr. Ollister crossed his
field of vision, escorting one of the younger, second footmen, to whom he gave quiet instructions.

"—you and the others must prioritize duties amongst
yourselves, so that at all times the front doors remain attended so that visitors are welcomed properly."

Behind the young man's shoulder's, Ollister gave Dominick a hard stare and jerked his chin in the direction of the corridor located just across the rotunda, a silent communiqué Dominick instantly understood.

He nodded his thanks and strode briskly across the polished marble floor into a shadowed space, where he found three doors. It took only a moment to locate the one from behind which voices could be heard. Quiet voices, speaking in urgent tones.

He leaned closer, listening—and didn't feel the slightest bit guilty for it. After all, he wasn't *eavesdropping,* per se, but educating himself about his new bride's feelings toward the man who had so recently compromised and abandoned her.

Because, bloody hell, Clarissa was his wife now and he would not play the cuckold, most especially not on his wedding day, within an hour of speaking the vows.

It wasn't about loving or even possessing her. It was because he was a man, by God, and he damn well had his pride.

He heard Quinn's voice first.

"Blast those Aimsley sisters for telling you before I could do so myself. Yes, I married another. I had no other choice but to do so, but I love *you,*" Quinn murmured ardently. "Forever. That will never change—"

Boots scuffed across the carpet. Then lighter footsteps—Clarissa's. But away, as if in escape. Interesting.

"And as I said, you have my sincerest congratulations," she said.

"Your words offend my ears. You're punishing me, aren't you? You want me to beg. You want me to crawl on my hands and knees."

"What I want is for you to *stand over there.*"

There came the sound of scuffling. Some unseen piece of furniture scooted against the floor, a small chair perhaps.

"Stay where you are," she insisted in a clandestine whisper. "Don't come any closer."

At that moment a footman came round the corner. One sharp glance from Dominick stopped him in his tracks. The servant lowered his gaze before quickly retreating. Dominick turned back to the door, where Quinn's voice could be heard again.

"What choice did I have, except give in to my father's demands? He threatened to place a hold on all my accounts and send me off to Scotland until I was forty if I did not agree to marry that girl for her connections and her fortune, which I regret to say he determined to be a minuscule degree greater than yours, enough to tip the scale. He doesn't care what I want or that I'm happy. It's all a game to him. I'm merely a pawn in his march toward greatness."

Dominick glowered, recalling the look of pleasure on Lord Quinn's face the day before when he'd observed him at the church, moments after having taken the vows. The enthusiastic kiss he'd shared with his new wife. Truly, a pawn in his father's game, or his own?

"It doesn't matter anymore," Clarissa answered tightly. Dominick heard the emotion in her voice, and could tell she struggled to keep control of herself. "Everything's changed. You see—"

"How can you say that? You must be as miserable as I am. Don't deny that you still love me as well," said Quinn. "My dear, there's no reason we can't still be together, if we are discreet—"

Clarissa answered in a shocked voice. "How dare you suggest such a thing!"

"Come here," Quinn commanded imperiously. More masculine steps. "Stop running away."

Dominick's lip curled and he closed his eyes, seething. The lady—his wife—had made herself quite clear that she did not wish for her companion in conversation to approach her. A gentleman would respect that. Apparently His Lordship was no gentleman at all.

But then, Dominick had already known that.

"You shouldn't even be here," Clarissa warned. "Neither of us should be here, not alone in this room. Quinn, no—stay where you are." Clarissa's whispering intensified. "I said *no. Don't touch me.*"

The muscles along Dominick's shoulders clenched, and his hands seized into fists. *Enough.* He turned the door handle and pushed.

His temper flared, finding Clarissa crowded into a corner by Quinn, who had one hand clenched on her shoulder and the other squeezed on her chin, in an obvious attempt to force her face toward his.

Clarissa shoved the flats of her hands against Quinn's shoulders, grappling against him in a valiant attempt to push him away.

"A-*hem*," Dominick said loudly, announcing his presence.

"Oh!" Clarissa exclaimed, her gaze contacting his over Quinn's shoulder.

She shoved again and broke free but only because Quinn released her, pivoting around to slide several feet away, where his top hat conspicuously lay half overturned on the carpet. At first His Lordship's eyes widened in alarm, but then, upon seeing who had interrupted them, they narrowed with suspicion.

"Well, that was an enthusiastic congratulations if ever I saw one," Dominick announced, lightly touching the back of a settee on his way toward them. He left the door open behind him.

"Who are you?" Quinn asked haughtily, straightening his coat sleeves from where they'd bunched at the shoulders during the attempted assault of his former lover. With the heel of his boot, he slyly nudged his errant hat behind an upholstered chair.

Dominic had been introduced to Quinn previously as Mr. Kincraig, and they had subsequently crossed paths on more than one occasion, but as with everyone, Dominick had played a part and played it well. Quinn didn't know it, but he hadn't paid that much attention to the actual details of Mr. Kincraig, only to those superficial details Dominick had wished him and everyone else to see.

Dominick was at least half a foot taller than the other man. He took wicked pleasure in staring down his nose at him. "I am an acquaintance, if you will, of that lovely young lady who you were just embracing, so...very... enthusiastically."

Quinn tilted his head. "An acquaintance, you say."

"You haven't yet heard our happy announcement?"

Dominick took a few steps more. Arriving at the bow window, he pushed aside the curtain to peer out. On the street, servants were strapping several trunks atop the rented carriage he had procured.

"*Our* announcement?" Quinn repeated frostily. "Whose announcement?"

Dominick turned round again.

"Ours. As in hers and mine," Dominick answered succinctly. "But I'm a forgiving sort. Since the news hadn't got out quite yet, I shall try very hard to overlook your most inappropriate—and apparently, from what I heard upon entering, unwelcome—show of affection toward my new bride."

He watched as his words filtered through Quinn's pretty head.

His Lordship exhaled sharply, then smirked nastily, slowly shaking his head as he turned his chin to glare at Clarissa, who didn't even notice because she stared intently at Dominick, a dazed sort of amusement turning up the corners of her pretty lips.

"Darling?" he said, and extended his hand to her.

After a moment's hesitation, she moved toward him, her small hands wrapping around his larger one. He drew her to his side, so close her skirts touched his trouser leg, and the side of her beaded mule aligned with his shoe.

Quinn looked between the two of them, his nostrils flared. "Your...bride, did you say?"

Dominick nodded, and grinned. *Wickedly.*

"I know it's a shock. Everything happened so fast, our feelings for one another—my proposal and her acceptance." He spoke with a deliberate edge of drama to his voice. "Yesterday morning, after she accepted my suit, we pondered a Christmas wedding, but then..." He glanced at Clarissa and lifted her hand to press a kiss to the tops of her fingers. "We both decided we just couldn't wait to start our lives together. Isn't that so, my love?"

Clarissa stared at his lips, clearly fascinated by the untruths they spoke. After a moment's hesitation, she said, "It was all very sudden."

Her gaze lifted another degree, meeting his. For a moment, everything else disappeared as the unexpected brilliance of her eyes dazzled him like a thousand faceted blue diamonds caught in the rays of a summer sun. The room around them became a blur of color and light. The man who stood eight feet away ceased to exist at all.

He had the sudden urge to kiss her.

And by God, she was his wife, so why shouldn't he?

His hand came up under her chin to gently lift her face toward his. His heart skipped a beat—perhaps two—as he bent his head and pressed his mouth to hers.

Her lips parted, emitting a gasp. No...something softer and sweeter.

A sigh.

Delicious. Her breath tasted of fragrant tea, and her skin smelled like...flowers. Clean white flowers and green summer grass. He shifted, opening his mouth ever so slightly against hers, loving the sensation of hers, plush and warm, beneath his.

"Again, who are you?" Quinn demanded, but in a tempered, hollow voice, as if he were doing his best not to sound demanding.

Ah, that voice. It was a reminder of all the things he wished to forget. He dropped his hand from Clarissa's face and straightened, ending the kiss.

Clarissa peered up at him, looking dazed and shocked, her lips a deep shade of rose now.

Claxton entered the room, his expression both annoyed and relieved. "There you are, the both of you. If you would come now, please, Lady Margaretta is asking for you. Your wedding *déjeuner* awaits and you know Cook, he will lose his mind if we don't go into the dining room immediately—"

He paused at seeing their visitor.

"Well, hello there, Quinn. I didn't realize you were here."

Quinn exhaled through his nose, looking very angry. And yet, in the next moment, a warm, gregarious smile spread across his face.

Hmmm. Impressive. Dominick wondered if he'd ever considered a position in the secret service. He was admirably good at faking.

Quinn strode toward the duke. "Ah...Your Grace, I stopped by to speak with you about...something or other, but find I have interrupted a...celebration. My bit of nonsense can certainly wait. I don't wish to intrude."

The duke rested his hand on the carved upper frame of a chair. His ducal ring glinted in the midday light shining through the open window. "Blackmer and I were at the office of the archbishop this morning. We heard something about you having gotten married as well." His cheek drew back in a grin. "Is that true?"

"Lord Quinn had just informed us," Clarissa responded with a nod. "We had not yet even had the opportunity to offer our congratulations before you entered."

Dominick chuckled darkly. Clarissa discreetly pinched the back of his arm, as if to silence him, which only made him chuckle again.

Lord Quinn threw him a sharp look. Claxton, a curious glance.

"I'll walk you out," the duke offered to Quinn, and together they walked toward the door.

"Lord Quinn," called Dominick.

Both he and Claxton turned back. Though the duke couldn't see Quinn from his perspective, the other man's countenance had gone icy cold.

Dominick bent toward the floor. "You...forgot your hat."

"My thanks," Quinn gritted between his teeth. He snatched the hat from Dominick's hand and, turning on the heel of his boot, disappeared into the corridor. Claxton followed.

Dominick offered Clarissa his arm, and she accepted. Together they followed the other two toward the entrance hall.

"Thank you for that," Clarissa whispered confidentially. "I'm eternally grateful. His expression! Priceless. I shall never forget."

"I did it more for me than for you," Dominick murmured in response.

"Will there be a honeymoon?" the duke inquired as they arrived near the front doors of the house.

Lord Quinn nodded curtly, and turned on his heel toward them. Behind him a footman signaled out the door, toward the street, motioning to his lordship's driver. "We were to have departed yesterday after the ceremony, to my family estate in Wilshire, but Lady Quinn is..." A flash of annoyance crossed his countenance. "Well, she is very attached to her mother and needed another day." He looked sharply at Clarissa and Dominick, his jaw tautened and nostrils flared. "And what about the two of you?"

"A honeymoon?" Clarissa said, lifting a hand to her throat.

Dominick answered smoothly. "Why, yes, indeed and we've a long journey ahead of us, so we will depart within the hour."

Clarissa could no longer criticize her family's treatment of her new husband. Indeed, as they had enjoyed Cook's masterfully prepared repast, they had all done their best to be gracious and draw Blackmer into conversation. Only now it was he who persisted in making everyone ill at ease. For the entirety of the meal he remained steadfastly aloof, refusing to engage in all but the briefest exchanges. After a miserable hour confined to the dining room and what quickly became forced small talk, they again adjourned to the drawing room, and everyone scattered to opposite ends of the cavernous chamber.

Clarissa did as she felt proper and remained by her new husband's side. Even so, Mr. Blackmer made no real effort to speak to her, but brooded out the window while she sat in a nearby chair. No further mention had been made of any honeymoon or an immediate departure. She'd been too afraid to even mention the subject, for fear he would repeat his earlier intention. She hoped the mention of their leaving London together, as man and wife, had only been part of the farce he'd been putting on for Quinn.

Because...leave? With him? She didn't even know him. Even though she'd taken vows, she didn't feel like anyone's wife, most especially not the stone-faced stranger at the window.

As if he heard her thoughts, Mr. Blackmer pulled his watch from his waistcoat pocket and, after glancing at its face, quietly said, "The day's getting on. You'll want to say your good-byes now."

"Now?" she answered, stunned. She stood and joined him at the window. "I haven't packed my things. I'll need time to plan and prepare."

He answered in the same even tone. "Your maid, Miss Randolph, has been very helpful in that regard. Everything has been secured onto the carriage."

Her pulse increased. "You had my things packed, without telling me?"

One dark brow lifted higher than the other. "I'm telling you now."

"Where are we going?"

"To my home," he answered distantly.

"To your London house?" she inquired hopefully. That would just be across town, and she could still see her family as often as she liked.

His jaw twitched, and heat flared in his eyes. "I don't have a house anymore. If you will recall, until last night, I'd intended to take my leave of London. I relinquished the lease. The house has been closed up."

Just feet away, her family talked amongst themselves, with only her sisters glancing toward them from time to time.

"I see," she said, anxiety bunching into a tight ball between her shoulders. "Are we going to take a house elsewhere?"

He did look at her now with fire in his eyes. "Clarissa. I have been relieved of my livelihood and have no suitable means of supporting you. That leaves me with little choice but to return, with you, to my family home, where after a time I hope more suitable arrangements can be made."

Her cheeks burned. He didn't blame her for anything. Not with words. But his eyes did.

"Where does your family live?" she asked quietly.

He scowled. "In Northumbria."

Northumbria. That was so far away. She'd never even traveled that far north. There it would always be cloudy and cold, just like Mr. Blackmer's eyes.

"Why don't we just stay here, at least for the time being? There's plenty of room, even if you wished to have your own quarters." Yes, he could have his own quarters, and she would have hers, and they could get to know one another over time and perhaps even grow to like each other.

Not that she didn't like him. But things had been so tense, and she had the distinct feeling he did not like her very much at all. Not anymore. How could she blame him?

"That arrangement will not suffice," he said, his speech clipped.

"But why?" she whispered, not wishing to alert her family to what very well might be their first quarrel. Still, she felt desperate to change his mind. She reached for his hands. "Why the need to rush away?"

In a sudden move he caught her by the wrists instead. Not roughly. Gently, actually, with his palms and fingers just grazing her skin, almost as if he was reluctant to touch her, wary of getting too close. Yet his dark eyes peered down at her, in that moment completely unguarded. She knew in that moment that, while things might be difficult between them, she would never have cause to fear him.

She stared back, unafraid. "Tell me."

He answered in clipped syllables. "Because I refuse to remain under this roof where I am believed by all to be a villain. A seducer and conniver. I have been unfairly maligned and condemned, and there is nothing I can do or say in defense of myself. Please know I *like* your family. I *admire* them, one and all. Do you realize how difficult this is for me to be here, under these circumstances?"

He released her and stepped back, his gaze no less intense.

"Dominick, I'm sorry," she said, opening her palms to him. "I don't know how else to say it."

* * *

Dominick flinched, hearing her speak his given name for the first time, with such emotion in her voice. No matter how angry he was, it wasn't his intention to hurt or punish her.

"I don't want to hear that you're sorry," he said. "I know that you are. At the same time, please understand I have lost everything."

"Because of me."

"Yes, because of you," he muttered. "But I don't despise you for it. I know you didn't intend any of this."

She nodded, her hands coming together in front of her bodice. "We're married now—there's no turning back from it. But perhaps my grandfather was wrong for insisting that we keep everything a secret." She glanced across the room at her family, who were doing their best not to be obvious about being riveted to their heated discussion. "Let me tell them the truth about what you've sacrificed for me. I beg you. My conscience demands it."

He stared into her blue eyes. Dear, foolish girl. He knew her intentions were pure, but how little she understood of a man's honor and his pride when it came to his offspring and the legacy he would one day leave behind.

"Wolverton wasn't wrong," he answered. "He understands, more than anyone, the power of blood. I don't have much control over this situation, but I shall exert control in this. I won't have the child..." He closed his eyes. "*Our* child ever doubting his or her place in the world, nor anyone else challenging their legitimacy."

He did not know this girl he had married. Not well enough to bare his soul to her and tell her that early in his marriage to Tryphena, after months of trying for a baby, a physician had told them she was most likely barren, although by all accounts her health was absolutely perfect. A second physician and then a third professed the same opinion, although strangely they too deemed his wife as being in possession of all the necessary qualities of a fertile woman.

He'd known then the deficiency was somehow his, and he'd seen in Tryphena's eyes that she knew it too, though no doctor would ever dare say it because women, it seemed, were always to blame in such matters, something Dominick found ludicrous. As if the male body were never defective or infertile. In another life, perhaps he would have been a scientist and proved it.

Whatever the truth, the news had crushed them both, him feeling cursed and her devastated to learn she'd likely never be a mother. It was then they'd first begun to grow apart.

He had not wanted to marry Clarissa, but what was done was done. The one blessing he could see in the whole miserable situation was that in a matter of months he would be a father, when he'd long given up hope of ever experiencing that joy. He would have the honor of being there from the child's birth, to its first step and its first spoken word. He would be more of a father than his own had ever been, and like a lion he would protect what belonged to him from any threat of harm.

"Thank you for caring about the baby so much." She nodded, pale and blinking. "I consider myself fortunate to have married you. I admire you for what you've done."

"Well, don't," he muttered. "Not yet. I'm still too bloody furious about this whole situation to be considered anything close to admirable. I have no choice but to remain the villain, seducer, and conniver they believe me to be— and I will do so." The hard look returned to his eyes. "Just don't expect me to stay here."

"I understand." She nodded—and though she trembled with emotion, she offered him a brave smile, which he appreciated more than he could convey at present. "I shall inform everyone that we will be departing shortly."

Chapter Nine

Clarissa approached her family. "Mr. Blackmer and I will be departing soon."

Her mother's eyes widened. "Soon, when?"

"Soon as in now," Clarissa said, forcing a smile. "I shall have the honor of meeting Mr. Blackmer's family. I must go upstairs and change for travel."

"We must leave posthaste to arrive by nightfall at a suitable inn," Blackmer said in a clear voice. "We will travel to my family home in Northumbria."

"So far?" her mother said, her eyes shining with sudden tears. "Why not just stay here tonight and leave in the morning?"

Clarissa's emotions shattered to pieces. There had already been too many tears today.

"It's all right, Mother," she answered. "Truly, I'm ready."

But she wasn't. She'd never passed a single night away from her family and had never really thought about how it would feel to leave them. She'd just assumed that when she married, she'd be deliriously happy and in love and there would be no sadness.

Her mother nodded and, coming closer, pressed a hand to her cheek. "You will need warmer clothes. It's been a cold summer, and will be much colder in Northumbria."

Sophia added, "It will take hours to pack."

"Again, why not delay your departure until tomorrow?" Daphne suggested with cheerful enthusiasm, as if there could be no other answer but hers.

"I'm afraid that's not possible," said Blackmer from where he stood by the window, holding himself removed from the rest of them.

"Ladies, you must respect Mr. Blackmer's decision," Claxton said quietly. "And Clarissa's."

Her wishes. She avoided meeting their eyes, because she feared if she did, they'd all see the truth, that she didn't want to leave.

"Miss Randolph has already packed my belongings," Clarissa announced. "I'll just hurry upstairs and change."

"We'll come with you," said Daphne, tugging at Sophia's arm. Their mother followed. They all three looked over their shoulders at Mr. Blackmer pleadingly, clearly hopeful he would change his mind.

Yet he moved toward the door. "I shall see to the carriage."

He'd already seen to the carriage. Clarissa suspected he simply couldn't bear to remain in the drawing room with Claxton and Raikes and Mr. Birch.

A half hour later, she stood by her grandfather's bedside, with Mr. Blackmer beside her, his expression grim.

"Grandfather, Mr. Blackmer and I are leaving." Her

throat closed as a deep sadness rose up from inside. She'd done so well until now, managing not to cry. But he looked so frail, and she couldn't help but feel responsible and fear she might never see him again. "I'm going to meet his family."

The earl's eyes remained closed and his breathing ragged. She rested her hand on his chest and bent down to press a kiss to his cheek.

His hand covered hers, and he murmured, "Good girl... Mr. Blackmer... is a fine man, who will be a good husband... and father to my grandchild. You will see. Everything will be... all right."

"What did he say?" asked Lady Margaretta in a soft voice.

Clarissa lifted her grandfather's hand and kissed the knuckles. "He wishes Mr. Blackmer and me well. Thank you, Grandfather," she whispered. "I'll see you again very soon."

Mr. Blackmer's hand touched her elbow, and he gently drew her away as her vision blurred. All of a sudden she found herself in the arbor of his strong arm, crying into his chest, which was more comforting than she'd expected. He smelled very nice. Clean and masculine, like soap and leather.

Outdoors, he left her side and proceeded toward the street. A brisk wind met them, and a blanket of clouds in the sky. Having changed into a cambric dress and simple pelisse of cerulean blue, more suitable for travel, Clarissa dabbed a handkerchief at her eyes. Her mother and sisters did the same, while Claxton and Mr. Birch looked on solemnly. Raikes had gone to the nursery and fetched little Michael from his nap, who, seeing the ladies' tears—

oh, the darling boy—took to crying as well. Clarissa squeezed the boy around his small shoulders and gave him a kiss.

"Aunt Clarissa will miss you so much."

She turned and moved from one family member to the next, embracing and kissing them all. "Well, it seems this is good-bye, for now. Not forever, of course." After one final glance to them all, Mr. Blackmer, with a hand to her elbow, helped her up the steps.

Miss Randolph, her lady's maid, already waited inside, dressed in staid traveling clothes. An older woman, with dark hair, now streaked with gray, she looked at Clarissa as she entered and smiled her usual pleasant smile.

Miss Randolph took her profession seriously. Clarissa had never once heard her complain. True to form, the older woman appeared completely content with their present situation, giving no outward hint of what she might be feeling inside. Unlike the close bond shared by Daphne and her lady's maid, Kate, Clarissa and Miss Randolph were not in the practice of confiding in one another or chatting about every little thing. This, at Miss Randolph's quiet insistence. Indeed, the woman already held a book in her hand and a finger holding her place on the page, as if she were already immersed.

Mr. Blackmer reached inside and stowed Clarissa's valise under the seat, then crouched to enter. He lowered his tall, long-legged frame to the center of the bench across from them. Here, in such closed confines, he looked larger and more imposing than before.

Wolverton's footman removed the steps and latched the door, and at once the wheels began to turn. Clarissa peered out the window, waving as the faces of her loved ones grew distant. Mr. Blackmer, tellingly, looked out of the opposite window.

The carriage turned the corner and, despite straining, she could see her family no more. Not even the house she had called home for so many years. She closed her eyes and, with a gloved hand, smothered the sob of anguish that bubbled up from inside her chest. Never before had she felt as alone as in this moment.

She rested her hand on her stomach and remembered the child she carried, and knew she must get used to the idea she wasn't alone at all. Knowing there would be a baby soon to love and care for made everything feel better. She only hoped Mr. Blackmer would allow her, as his wife, to take care of him too. That they could eventually talk to one another and enjoy each other's company.

"Well," Clarissa hiccupped, and attempted to smile through tears. "Just three...or will it be four days, and we'll arrive at your family home. I assume they will be surprised to learn you have wed?"

She could only assume he hadn't written them. There'd been no time.

"Four days. Yes." He brooded, his gaze fixed on the scene passing by outside the window. "They will indeed be surprised."

Silenced filled the carriage. Again, she attempted conversation. "How long today until we arrive at the inn?"

His jaw twitched, and he looked toward the corner of the carriage. "I'm sorry, I—I—"

To her surprise, he reached for the bell pull. Wrapping his gloved hand around the cord, he yanked. The carriage slowed and altered direction, and after a moment came to a stop.

"I apologize," he murmured. "I think I'd prefer to ride up top. I'll leave the two of you to your conversation."

He moved as if to exit the door. She reached for his wrist, and he froze.

"Oh!" Miss Randolph exclaimed softly, her eyes wide with surprise. She looked between them, as if shocked by the dramatic moment unfolding in front of her, before looking pointedly away.

"Don't go, Mr. Blackmer," Clarissa whispered, so that only he could hear. "I want you to stay."

"I'm sorry," he answered, but not unkindly. Indeed, though his gaze did not meet hers, he rested his gloved hand atop hers and briefly squeezed. "But I cannot do *this*. Not now. Not yet."

She nodded, releasing him. "As you wish."

Then he was gone, and she left staring at the closed door, her ears filled with silence. A moment later, the carriage jerked to one side as he climbed atop to join the driver. Then the carriage started and continued on.

Embarrassed, Clarissa glanced at Miss Randolph, who stared fixedly into the pages of her book, but after moment, her gaze fluttered up and she smiled.

"Gentleman," Miss Randolph said in a reassuring tone. "Try as we might to contain them, they always prefer the outdoors."

"Indeed," she said, somewhat soothed by the woman's calm tone.

"It's very nice that you'll be able to meet Mr. Blackmer's family," said Miss Randolph.

"I'm looking forward to doing so." It was the polite thing to say.

Another smile, and Miss Randolph returned to her book.

Clarissa sagged against the seat, thinking it might be nice to indulge in a good, thorough cry right now. Only she wouldn't. She would not succumb to histrionics. She wasn't a child anymore. She dabbed her eyes one last time, then thrust her soggy kerchief into her reticule. Yes, she was done with all that. Every young woman, at some time or another, had to leave her family. Her situation could certainly be worse. She shouldn't have believed all the romantic nonsense in the ladies' magazines and novels anyway.

"What are you reading, Miss Randolph?" she inquired softly, needing to talk about something that didn't have to do with her or Mr. Blackmer.

Miss Randolph looked at her a long time, taking note, she knew, of her red eyes and stained cheeks. If they were at home, she knew her maid would immediately set about pressing a cool compress that smelled of chamomile to her skin. But there was no chamomile here.

At last she answered. "It's a manual for servants. I've read it several times before, but it never hurts to refresh oneself on the finer points."

Clarissa nodded, thinking such reading material didn't sound very interesting. But for the first time she realized that's what made Miss Randolph so pleasant to have around. She behaved with such unerring dignity and always put forth her best effort. Nothing ever got her down. What a wonderful example. One she needed to strive toward herself.

"I'm so very glad you're here with me, Miss Randolph," she said, feeling the need to voice her appreciation, because she felt very certain she'd taken Miss Randolph for granted until now. "If I can't have Mother or my sisters, at least I can have you."

The woman's expression softened. "That's very kind of you to say."

They smiled at one another, and after a moment, Miss Randolph went back to her book.

Sighing, Clarissa realized silence wasn't such a terrible thing. She forced herself to relax. She wondered what Mr. Blackmer's family was like and where the couple would live once they arrived. If she had gauged Mr. Blackmer's demeanor correctly, the prospect of returning to his family in Northumbria did not please him. Why? she wondered. Had there been some sort of disagreement in the past, or was it just that he regretted being forced to leave the secret service?

She resolved in that moment that whatever situation awaited them, she wouldn't complain. There was a little baby to look forward to, and as long as her new husband did not overly begrudge her or the child, the future would not be so terrible.

Across the carriage from her, Miss Randolph turned the page of her book.

A book would take her mind off things. She bent and opened her valise, and instead chose a notebook and pencil and settled into the corner. Her breathing slowed, and she opened the volume to the first page and wrote:

Henry Reginald...
B-l-a-c-k-m-e-r.
Dorothea Marie Blackmer.
Robert Vinson Blackmer.
Elizabeth Willomena Blackmer.

All fine names for a baby. But nothing that struck her as perfect just yet.

"That's a smart girl," Miss Randolph murmured, her tone quiet and comforting. "Just you wait and see. Everything will be fine."

"Wake up, Mrs. Blackmer. We have arrived at the inn."

Mrs. Blackmer? Who was Mrs. Blackmer?

Oh, yes. *She* was Mrs. Blackmer.

Clarissa burrowed further into the cushion, trying to disappear into sleep again.

But a gentle shake to the shoulders awakened her, and she sat up, her vision unfocused from sleep. The inside of the carriage was dim. She could barely make out Miss Randolph beside her.

With a swipe, she brushed away the hair plastered against her cheek, but the dream still lingered in her mind...

A handsome mouth—

Hot kisses.

Her eyes flew open in sudden realization. She'd dreamed of Mr. Blackmer kissing her. Touching her lips, she remembered the moment he'd kissed her after their wedding, as Quinn looked on in shock. She blushed, feeling a rush of excitement as strong as when the kiss had actually happened.

How... unexpected.

"Your eyes are open, my dear, but I'm not certain you're awake," said Miss Randolph, offering an open tin of rose-and-ginger pastilles. She felt quite certain Miss Randolph had never called her "my dear" before, and the endearment pleased her. Clarissa selected one and placed the lozenge in her mouth, appreciating the sweet-hot flavor that exploded on her tongue, awakening her a degree more.

Her lady's maid lowered Clarissa's straw bonnet onto her head, then tied its wide grosgrain bow to one side of her charge's chin, which, as they'd observed in *La Belle Assemblée* ladies' magazine, seemed to be the most flattering compliment to a round-shape face. Normally Clarissa would tend to such personal matters herself, but after such a difficult day she appreciated the tender care.

She lifted the curtain from the window beside her and saw a sturdy two-story structure, with light glowing from its windows. A sudden question came to mind. Were she and Mr. Blackmer going to sleep together?

In the next moment, her fears eased. Certainly not. He hadn't even been able to suffer being in the carriage with her for more than five minutes.

Just as Miss Randolph finished tying on her own hat, the door handle turned. Clarissa froze, her breath caught in her throat. Mr. Blackmer stood there, beside the carriage, his expression shrouded in shadows and inscrutable.

Behind him, two hounds circled and whined with excitement over the newly arrived visitors, their feet caked in the churned-up mud of the inn's yard. Stable-helpers rushed to assist with the horses.

"We'll pass the night here," her husband said quietly.

Chapter Ten

*C*larissa emerged to stand on the metal carriage step and perched there, considering her next move. Several boards lay strewn across the courtyard. She pondered which were closest and which looked stable enough for a foray across the muck.

Yet in the next moment, a strong arm came round her waist and the evening sky turned, as Mr. Blackmer lifted her easily, another arm sweeping up under her knees. By necessity, her arms went round his neck. A whirl of movement followed, then several powerful steps, whereby he deposited her on the wooden platform at the front of the inn. She stood, breathless, not only because he'd squeezed the air from her lungs, but because she hadn't been prepared for his touch.

"Go on inside," he instructed. "A Mrs. Harris will receive you."

He turned back to Miss Randolph, who had already stepped down onto one of the boards and wobbled while considering her next step. He extended his hand to help her across. Clarissa could only stand, watching the way his coat tightened over his back and shoulders when his muscles flexed. But she didn't wish to be caught staring. Admiring. So she turned and went inside, where a low-ceilinged room awaited, filled with shadows except for a fire that burned on the hearth. Once her vision adjusted, she saw several tables against the walls, and at one, a well-dressed older gentleman and two young boys conversed quietly, over a platter of victuals, the specifics of which Clarissa could not discern other than a flavorful aroma that wafted through the air. A young woman polished silver in the corner, and another, beside her, folded linens.

A third woman, older than the others, and wearing a lace cap and apron, stood near the stairs, wearing a polite smile of welcome. Blackmer entered the room and removed his hat and gestured that she should follow.

She did so—but noted that he did not. Admittedly, this relieved her. If they were to share quarters, she would need a moment or two to compose herself. To prepare herself emotionally for the intimacies that might very well follow, even if those intimacies did not involve lovemaking. Simply the thought of lying next to him in a bed, waiting for sleep to come, sent her stomach spiraling with anxiety.

Upstairs, Mrs. Harris led her into a room crowded with a large bed, two chairs, a chaise, and a dressing table. Though small, everything appeared clean and comfortable.

Mrs. Harris lit a second lamp and adjusted its position on the dressing table. "I hope you find your accommodations sufficient, Mrs. Blackmer."

Would it ever feel natural to answer to that name? Before, she had always traveled in the company of her mother, and innkeepers and servants had always addressed Her Ladyship as to whether their comforts were being met. Now she was a married lady, traveling with her husband, and Mrs. Harris welcomed her. There was something very satisfying about that.

"Everything is very nice, thank you," Clarissa answered, her gaze returning to the bed. There were numerous pillows and a rich scarlet coverlet with gold cording. Her cheeks warmed, imagining herself there with Blackmer, tangled in the bedclothes, their bodies intimately entwined.

Two of the young women from belowstairs delivered the smaller of her two trunks, the one packed with sleeping and traveling clothes and other assorted whatnot, which Miss Randolph instructed them to deposit beneath the window. Another appeared with Miss Randolph's large, embroidered valise.

Mrs. Harris opened a door beside the bed. "There is a dressing closet here, where your maid can sleep."

Miss Randolph crossed the room and peered inside assessingly.

"My husband's things—" Clarissa began.

"Have been placed in the room next door. There's another door in the dressing closet that adjoins the two."

So they would not be sharing a room. A rush of relief washed over her, and she exhaled.

"Would you care for a bath, madam?"

Despite her nap in the carriage, she still felt very tired. She thought she might just go to bed and read. "Perhaps just a basin of warm water, if you please."

She removed her hat and set it on the table.

A half hour later, Clarissa sat at the dressing table brushing her hair while Miss Randolph folded the garments she'd worn that day and placed them in the trunk.

A scuffling came from the hallway, along with stifled giggles and the sound of sloshing water.

In the mirror's reflection, Clarissa saw Miss Randolph straighten from where she bent over the trunk. "It sounds as if Mr. Blackmer will be enjoying a bath."

"Hmmm, yes." Clarissa rubbed a dab of fragrant skin cream onto her forehead. "Good for him. He must be very dusty from riding atop the carriage all day long."

Miss Randolph approached her from behind, eclipsing the light from the fire and casting the mirror into shadow. "Pardon my being so bold as to suggest it, but perhaps you should offer to assist him."

"Assist him," Clarissa repeated, taken aback. "With his bath? Why?"

Miss Randolph bent an inch and peered into the glass, meeting her gaze. "Because that is what wives do."

Clarissa pressed the cap on the cream jar. "Perhaps later, when we know each other better. Miss Randolph, I'm not sure what you know about the circumstances, but—"

"I know he is not the man you love."

Clarissa blinked, feeling strangled. "*Loved.*"

"But he is your husband. Did you not see the reaction of those girls downstairs when he entered the room?"

Clarissa paused. She hadn't. "How did they react?"

Something peculiar happened inside her heart. She experienced a pang of dismay, threaded with...jealousy? Perhaps not jealousy, exactly, but Mr. Blackmer was her husband. She didn't know how she felt about another woman "reacting" to him when he walked into a room.

"They took notice. He is a very handsome man. Certainly you noticed as well."

"Yes," Clarissa answered in a distant tone. She rearranged her brush and her hand mirror on the tabletop, setting one down in the other's place. "I've noticed."

Of course she had. What woman wouldn't? Mr. Blackmer was indeed handsome—but in a very different way from Lord Quinn. Lord Quinn had to be at least ten years younger than Mr. Blackmer. Fine-featured and golden-haired, he wore his aristocratic title with ease. He might very well be a model for a gentleman's plate in Ackermann's Depository. He knew his horses, and his manners and never failed to charm everyone in the room.

Was it wrong that those were the sort of young men she'd always found attractive and with whom she'd expected to share her future? They were, she supposed, the sort of man society told her she ought to admire.

Mr. Blackmer, on the other hand, was the opposite side of the coin. His eyes and his hair were as dark and dangerous as the Devil's, and he exuded...

He exuded what?

Masculinity. Where Quinn was barely more than a boy out of university, Mr. Blackmer, was a man with a lifetime of experience in his repertoire. He'd been in the secret service no less. He might very well be dangerous, but not to her—she didn't believe that for one moment. There was something undeniably thrilling in realizing that.

"So what are you saying?" Clarissa asked Miss Randolph, listening now.

"That if you don't offer to assist him with his bath, someone else will." She lowered her voice and murmured, "I don't know if you understand my meaning but—"

"I do understand your meaning." Clarissa looked about, scandalized. "That sort of thing happens here? I believed this to be a respectable inn, not a . . . well, you know. One of those sorts of places."

"It happens everywhere, madam."

"I see. But certainly all men don't . . ."

"Of course not. Only those with inattentive wives."

Footsteps sounded in the corridor, light ones. Most certainly female. And the hollow sound of bumping buckets.

Miss Randolph glared at the door. "That's one leaving now." Her eyes narrowed. "*One.* I'm quite certain there were two."

Clarissa gasped and jumped up from the stool, nearly toppling it.

Miss Randolph pointed toward the dressing closet door. "See for yourself that I am right."

"What? Peek through the door? Barge in and interrupt? No. I can't." She stared at the door. "Mr. Blackmer and I barely know each other, Miss Randolph. What he does is his own affair."

"Very well." Her maid rested her fists on her hips. "Concede nuptial failure on the very eve of your wedding."

"Nuptial failure?" exclaimed Clarissa, pacing the floor. "After only one day? Why are you doing this to me? I just want to go to bed."

She had lost Lord Quinn in a blink. Was she destined to lose her husband too?

"Because I want you to be happy, Mrs. Blackmer, and I believe you can find happiness with the man on the other side of that door. But you must lay out the rules from the start, or else there will be misunderstandings and angry feelings that will only grow out of hand."

"Rules?" she repeated. How could she make any demands whatsoever of Mr. Blackmer, after the sacrifice he had made for her? Whether he'd been willing or not, he'd remained silent and suffered through. Now, to imagine asserting control over his most private moments? His most private desires? She felt torn over what to do. "What makes you so knowledgeable on the state of marriage?"

"Oh, dear girl." Miss Randolph sighed. "I've not always been a lady's maid. We are very different, you and I, but that does not mean you cannot learn from my mistakes."

"Miss Randolph." Clarissa reached to touch her arm. "I'm sorry."

"You will be, if you don't do something, and quickly."

Clarissa remembered the vow she'd made to herself, to try to make a life with Mr. Blackmer. She wanted...she *needed* things to be good between them, if she was going to face the future with any sort of optimism. But most of all, for the baby's sake. She wanted a father for the child. A father in truth. Not just a name.

She stared at the door, wickedly curious but afraid of what she might see.

"Go on," urged Miss Randolph. "What are you waiting for?"

Dominick closed his eyes and eased into the hip bath. Hot water enveloped him to his abdomen. Groaning in pleasure, he raised two handfuls to his face. Four hours of riding atop with the driver, clenching onto the rail at every bounce and turn, had left his muscles sore and his skin covered in dust.

"May I assist you, sir?" said a female voice, husky and sweet.

The inn's servant. He'd almost forgotten about her.

He lowered his hands from his face and shook his head. "My thanks, but no. You may go."

"Are you certain?" she asked seductively, her dark hair draped fetchingly over one shoulder. "I could...rub your back...or anything else you like, with that very nice gentleman's soap on the tray."

"Yes, I'm certain. But thank you again."

"Very well." She pouted. "I'll turn down your bedclothes and be on my way."

She'd watched him undress with unconcealed interest, staring raptly at his shoulders, his chest, and yes, his manhood, until he'd lowered himself into his present position, which at least concealed that part of him from her view. He'd traveled much in his thirty-two years of life and often encountered women eager to earn an extra coin. Some just wanted a man's companionship. He did not know the motivation of the maid who stood smiling at him, her hand on the coverlet of the bed she'd just turned down, but the invitation was clear. Her breasts strained against the bodice of her dress, more so than he'd noticed a moment before, which suggested she'd purposefully adjusted the garment for effect.

Yet her efforts did not have the desired result. Yes, he wanted a woman's hands sliding over his skin, but not hers. He wanted to make love tonight, but not to a nameless servant girl in the inn, who had likely seduced scores of others before him.

As emotionally distant as he felt toward Clarissa, he found that, to his surprise, he wanted her. He wanted his wife. Hell, he'd been forced to marry her. There ought to be some reward.

If only he could let go of his anger and the inner voice that kept reminding him he shouldn't be here at all, that he ought to be on his way to France, where, at last, he would do what he did best, and that was to spy on wicked people who deserved to be spied upon.

He was no good at being a husband. He'd learned that once before.

But he was a husband again, and one who had not made love to a woman in a very long time. Not since Tryphena.

Until today, he'd always somehow considered himself still married, if only to her memory. He'd remained faithful to a ghost, feeling he owed her that. Did his marriage to Clarissa mean that at last he could say good-bye? Perhaps he wished that. Yes, he thought he did, at last.

But it had been a mistake to kiss Clarissa after the wedding, in his quest to provoke Lord Quinn. Indeed, the memory of her lips against his, and the way her body had felt in his arms, had teased and tormented him ever since, which had left him exceedingly ill-tempered, because he didn't want to feel anything too deep for a young woman who didn't love him and likely never would.

How could he begrudge her for loving Quinn? He couldn't. She was young and in love and too trusting. She certainly hadn't imagined the young lord would ever betray her. Just as he'd never imagined Tryphena would betray him.

They'd both been hurt. They were very much equals in that way. But he was old enough and experienced enough to know it wouldn't do either of them any good to rush into anything too quickly or try to force feelings that simply weren't there.

Which was why this lingering desire he felt for Clarissa

after their kiss troubled him so. All afternoon since his mind had buzzed with thoughts of her, and his blood went hot each time she came near. He had gone too long without a woman, and suspected his mind and body simply leapt hungrily at what it had not experienced in so long. Otherwise why the drastic change? Just hours before he'd believed her to be just another pretty face. Which was why he doubted the authenticity of his reaction to her and pulled away, not wanting to hurt or mislead her.

As a result, he feared he'd behaved boorishly after the wedding by scowling at her at every opportunity and then vacating the carriage when he found himself thinking about how brave and pretty she was, instead of how she'd ruined his life.

Still, here he was thinking about her. She was pretty, yes. More so now than yesterday. It was as if by marrying her and realizing they would spend the rest of their lives together in some form or fashion, he saw her through a different lens. Once his thoughts had started down that road, he'd noticed the charming freckles that dappled her nose and the way her hair always looked slightly mussed, but in the loveliest way, no matter how much attention her maid took with styling it. And she had the loveliest figure.

Just knowing his young wife undressed and prepared for bed in the room next to his set his blood on fire. If he had no conscience...

Oh, but he did.

His conscience wouldn't shut up. What sort of man was he to be having desirous thoughts about a young woman who had just had her heart broken by another man? No doubt she was crying into her pillow now over Quinn. He knew, better than anyone, that love didn't just die. He owed her understanding, and time to adjust to his presence in her life. He owed the same to himself.

Just then, in the mirror, he glimpsed something, the movement of the door adjoining his room and Clarissa's. Through a sliver of a crack in the door, two pairs of eyes peered inward, revealing the intrusion of not only one eavesdropper but two: Clarissa and her lady's maid, Miss Randolph.

What a surprise. Clarissa wasn't crying herself to sleep. She was spying on him. That knowledge pleased him so much he chuckled, amused by their attempt at subterfuge, which was no doubt undertaken because of the presence of Her Naughty Maidship, who leaned across the bed, pretending to neaten the bed linens until one round breast broke free of its confines to bounce about unencumbered as she moved.

At this, the door jerked, and he almost laughed out loud—though he strongly suspected Clarissa's interest in his private activities was not inspired by jealousy or a need to claim her territory, but rather in defense of propriety. The Earl of Wolverton's youngest granddaughter would never suffer a husband's adulterous escapades, at least not while she occupied the room next door.

But he wasn't an adulterer. He understood the sting of that betrayal, more than anyone.

"Oh," the dark-haired girl exclaimed with feigned modesty, cupping her breast before slowly tucking it into its proper berth. With wide, innocent eyes, she approached him. "Now, what about that back rub?"

No, he wasn't an adulterer...but he did have a wicked sense of humor, one he felt the sudden inclination to satisfy.

"On second thought, I'm very sore from traveling and I would like one," he answered, smiling.

"I knew you'd change your mind." Taking up a folded cloth from the nearby table, she approached the bath and sank to her knees. Dampening the cloth, she squeezed it free of liquid and rested the heated compress across the upper half of his face. "There, doesn't that feel glorious? Just close your eyes and allow me to do the rest."

He almost felt the air leave the room, as Clarissa and Miss Randolph watched to see what would happen next. He did relax, easing deeper into the water as she rubbed soap over his chest and shoulders, until his skin and muscles were slick beneath her hands.

"God, that feels good," he said, in a voice loud enough for them to hear. "So damn good."

"I could...make you feel even better, if you desire for me to do so." Her hands slid slowly down his stomach... seductively toward his groin.

He hadn't expected her to be so bold so fast. He tensed, his hand poised to stop her—

But the door made the slightest *whoosh*ing sound. Though he couldn't see anything, because of the cloth over his eyes, he heard footsteps cross the carpet, and the maid let out a squeal of dismay. A moment later and he knew she had been dismissed. Now the scent of orange blossoms filled his nose.

"What's that? Did you say something?" he said, a smile turning his lips. His muscles tensed as he waited for what his bride would say or do next.

Chapter Eleven

Clarissa stared down into the tub, at the unexpected wealth of male shoulders and sinewy brawn, and her mouth went dry.

He bore scars. Two, one on his shoulder and a second lower...against the taut skin of his torso, just below his nipple. Both appeared quite neat, as if finished by a surgeon's practiced hand.

But that wasn't all. Her gaze descended...

Light from the fire cast shadow against every swell and indention, painting the athleticism of her husband's body for her inquisitive eyes. Yet even in the dim light, she could see through the water, to his thigh and hip. If the tub wasn't so restrictive and Mr. Blackmer's long limbs so confined she might be able to see—

Well, to see *better*.

A quick glance ensured the cloth remained over Mr. Blackmer's eyes. His chest rose and fell steadily, he seemingly content and relaxed.

Knowing Miss Randolph had closed the door a moment before so that they would have their due privacy, she squinted, shamelessly curious for a glimpse of his manhood, believing that curiosity served her best practical interests and Mr. Blackmer's as well. That night at the Vauxhall gala, she hadn't seen Quinn's body for the jumble of their clothing and the urgency of his passion.

As a newly married woman, she'd rather be shocked now, without Mr. Blackmer's knowledge, than to react with surprise later when faced with her husband's unfamiliar sex. She tilted her head and bit into her lower lip, thwarted. Fie on that floating jumble of bubbles swirling about and obscuring her view.

Of course she'd gone with her mother and sisters to the museums and, like all the other young ladies in the viewing room, pretended very hard not to scrutinize the exposed genitalia of the ancient statues. She feared that in true life the reality of a man's body might prove somewhat off-putting, especially if she wasn't wildly in love with that person.

"Are you still there?" Mr. Blackmer inquired in a silky tone, one that plainly spoke of seduction. Not to her, but to the saucy maid she'd just pinched on the arm and sent out of the room.

And on their wedding day! Mr. Blackmer proved himself to be a scoundrel after all.

"Yes," she peeped, doing her best to sound like the maid, who in her opinion had sounded like a yapping teacup-size dog. "I am here."

She knelt and seized up the cloth from where it floated in the water. For a moment, she considered cramming the soppy rag into his mouth. Instead, hesitantly, she rested the cloth against his skin and rubbed it over his shoulder and across his chest. Her mouth went dry like cotton and her heartbeat quickened. The warm water caught within fell in a sparkling waterfall against his golden skin...

He exhaled through his nose and growled low in his throat.

His white teeth bit into his lower lip.

She stared, there, at his lips. They were nice lips. Masculine lips, with the lower being more generous than the top...

"Well, don't stop just yet," he murmured in a teasing tone.

Leaning forward, so that the vapor from the bath dampened her face, neck, and bosom, she rubbed again, this time in the opposite direction. Only his chest flexed beneath her hand as he placed his atop hers. She froze, paralyzed by the unexpected touch.

"Lower, please," he murmured.

"Lower?" she whisper-squeaked, eyes widening to peer at the surface of the water, which from her perspective showed nothing, only a golden glare of firelight.

"Yes, lower," he drawled, pushing her hand downward.

She jerked free.

"Beast!" she cried, dropping, no, throwing the cloth into the water, which splashed his face.

He pulled the cloth from his eyes.

His eyes widened. "Oh, it's *you*."

But then he smiled, looking amused.

"Oh, yes." Her sleeping gown had tangled about her legs, and she struggled to stand. She gripped the side of the tub for balance. "It is me. *Just me.* Your new wife. So sorry to disappoint you."

He grabbed her arm and tugged her back down. "I knew it was you."

"You did not," she argued, knowing he lied. Didn't he? "If I hadn't arrived, you would have—you would have—"

He grinned. "I would have what?"

Her mouth snapped shut. She wouldn't lower herself by saying the words.

He released her, planting his hands on the sides of the tub.

She only had a moment to brace herself because—

He stood. Water sluiced off his nude body, splashing into the tub. Droplets landed on her face. Startled... shocked...she gasped, falling back onto her bottom, and crawled backward like a crab.

Moving efficiently but unhurriedly, he lifted a folded towel from the washstand and stepped onto the thick rug on which the tub had been placed. He moved toward her, step by purposeful step, catching the cloth behind his hips and holding a corner in each hand. She held his gaze, refusing to retreat further, declining to look lower, but then...

Her eyes defied her wishes, and she looked.

She swallowed a gasp. Were all men that large?

With a jerk of his muscled arms, he covered himself and knotted the towel at his hip.

"Ahem," he said, commanding her attention upward, this time to his smiling lips. "I believe you were about to inform me as to what I would have done if you had not interrupted."

"Something with that girl," she blurted.

He extended a hand to her. After a moment's hesitation, she accepted, and he hoisted her up to stand in his shadow, so close she felt his heat, which for some reason...made her shiver. To her mortification, she felt her nipples harden into peaks, and she knew they jutted against the cambric of her sleeping gown. She prayed he did not take notice. But his gaze dipped. She forced herself to remain unmoving, allowing him to look his fill.

"Would you care if I did?" he asked in a quiet voice.

She hesitated, then told the truth. "Of course I would."

His jaw twitched. "Because we are married."

He spoke the word "married" with an edge of sarcasm.

"We've spoken vows," she answered haughtily. "I don't take them lightly, and neither should you."

He laughed a strange, hollow laugh then shrugged and backed away, toward the bed where behind him his night-shirt had been laid out. "What makes you think I do?"

"I don't know." She sighed, frowning. "That's just it, I suppose, I don't know you. While I admire you for your service to the Crown and for protecting Wolverton, I know less about you now than when you were Mr. Kincraig."

He stared at her for a long moment, and at last he replied.

"I'm the eldest son in my family. I have a younger brother. I had a sister also, but she died, very young." His eyes darkened at saying that.

"I'm sorry to hear that. What about your parents? Are they both still living?"

"As far as I know." His eyebrows went up. "I left home a long time ago after years of quarreling with my father—"

"About what?"

"Many things. I had opinions. Ideas he did not wish to hear. Mostly...I wanted a different life than his. I wanted to see the world beyond England. To experience adventure and to know people who weren't...just like me. My father has never understood that desire, and has always sought to punish me for seeking my own way. Suffice it to say we are estranged. Not hatefully, but disaffected all the same and have been for a very long time, although I have visited from time to time."

Clarissa knew there was much more to the story, but she did not press for more. But one question required answering.

"Will they be happy to see us?" she asked.

"I don't know," he answered, frowning. "We'll find out, won't we?"

His words promised nothing but uncertainty, but at least he'd answered honestly.

"How long were you with the secret service?" she asked.

Another pause. "Almost thirteen years."

Thirteen years was a long time. Since he'd been a very young man.

"Was my grandfather truly ever in danger?"

"I can't answer any questions about that, or any of my assignments. I've sworn not to. Perhaps that's something you might wish to take note of. I keep my vows."

She felt the heat rising to her face. He referred to their marriage vows, of course. The moment suddenly felt very intimate again.

"About that servant girl," he growled.

"Yes?" She frowned, just remembering the curvy temptress.

"I wouldn't have done anything, married or not." He turned and took up his nightshirt. "She is not to my personal preference."

Her gaze moved over his back, and the muscles, and her mouth went dry.

"What is your personal preference?" she dared ask in a whisper.

Not her. She wouldn't be. She wasn't the sort she'd seen him with.

She couldn't deny having noticed Mr. Kincraig's popularity with the ladies, at those events Wolverton commanded him to attend. Beautiful widows and those women of independent means who brazenly sought out intrigues with misbehaving and dangerous men. They'd fluttered round him like thirsty butterflies to nectar, while he'd brooded and scowled and not shown a preference for any one of them. Not in public. But what about in private?

She had not married Mr. Kincraig. She'd married Mr. Blackmer. Could it be that some of their qualities were shared? That sort of magnetism wasn't an act. She couldn't help but wonder how many women there had been. But did she really have any right to know?

He set the nightshirt back on the bed and spoke over his shoulder. "I think it's time you returned to your room."

He spoke the words without passion. She could only assume he'd had enough talking and wanted her to leave. The night air chilled her skin, and she wrapped her arms around her waist for warmth. She felt rebuffed by him. Stung. Her husband, the man with whom she would spend the rest of her days, did not have the slightest interest in spending a moment more in her company.

She knew she ought to calmly say "Very well then, I bid you good night," and quit the room, but she feared with a certainty that if she opened her mouth and attempted to utter a single syllable, her voice would falter and reveal the confused tumult of her emotions.

Not because she cared for him. Of course she didn't. Clearly he did not care for her.

They'd been thrown together, and no amount of wishful thinking or good intentions would create a spark between them, when such a spark was never intended to be. She blinked away tears. Foolish tears! As if he had hurt her, but he hadn't.

It had just been a long day, and a long night before that, and she'd made a terrible mess of everything, and she hated Quinn. And perhaps still loved him. And she was lonely. So very lonely and frightened of what the future held.

So instead she nodded jerkily, her chin outthrust, and turned on her slippered foot to escape into the dark dressing closet, taking care to close the first and the second door firmly behind her. Miss Randolph reclined in her sleeping gown and robe on the chaise with her book open and steepled across her forehead, snoring, which was just as well because Clarissa could not face the woman's questions or her pity.

She doused the lamps and, in darkness, with only the scant light from behind the fire grate to see, crawled into bed and lay on unfamiliar sheets, her mind tangled with thoughts of...Mr. Blackmer.

Suddenly the door swung open and a shadow moved toward her, stealthily and swift, with only the faint white swath across his hips visible in the night. She recognized Blackmer instantly, and desire ignited inside her. He crouched above her, breathing hard, his skin still damp and the tight flex of muscles in his shoulders darkly illuminated. The scent of the soap from his bath filled her nostrils. Her pulse raced, her heart near exploding.

"You," he growled deep in his throat, "are my preference."

A second later, he kissed her hard, pressing his thumb against the side of her jaw, commanding her lips to part while his tongue boldly entered and teased. She gasped for breath, stunned into half senselessness...and surrendered, her mouth opening fully to accept each deep, possessing stroke.

He gave a husky groan. His large hands caught hers by the wrists, pinning her to the mattress. She squirmed beneath him—but with no intent to escape.

Moments before he had dismissed her coldly and made her feel invisible and unwanted, and yet in this moment he revealed his true feelings, ones he'd tried to conceal. She knew without a doubt that her husband desired her. Something about that made her weak, and—

His mouth moved to her cheek...her neck, leaving her skin hot and awakened wherever his lips touched. Sensations she'd never experienced spiraled up from inside her, delicious and achingly sweet, awakening a need in her body and rendering her unexpectedly wild.

God help her, she didn't understand, but she wanted him as well. The moment he released her hands she moaned and seized his shoulders, sliding her hands upward over his neck, finding unexpected appreciation in the powerful contraction and flux of his muscles beneath her palms. He exhaled, filling her mouth with his breath, and sucked her bottom lip—

Only to groan and twist away.

No. She reached, her hands trailing over his shoulders and his arms, desperately wanting more. More of his kiss, and his warm, firm skin. And yes, for him to ravish her so she would forget—

Then nothing.

The bed creaked, relieved of his weight. She heard his sharp exhalation of breath—a laugh, perhaps?

"Good night then, Mrs. Blackmer," he murmured.

Silence filled the room.

"Good night," she answered breathlessly.

He crossed the room, disappearing into the dressing closet, gone the way he had come. She heard the door close.

After a long moment of silence, Miss Randolph's voice came from the direction of the chaise. "Well, *that* was rather thrilling."

Clarissa sat straight up in the bed. How mortifying. Her husband had kissed her so senseless, she'd forgotten Miss Randolph was even there. Her cheeks burned with embarrassment.

"Indeed," answered Clarissa, sinking back onto the pillows and flinging her arms wide. She could not recall ever having experienced anything so exhilarating. No, not even with Lord Quinn—

Her hand rested upon something soft and damp.

Mr. Blackmer's towel.

Two days later, the carriage bounced and rattled, the road having turned into an abomination some four hours ago, so much so that it felt to Clarissa as if her bones were no longer in their proper sockets.

"Are you all right, Mrs. Blackmer?" Miss Randolph peered at her wearily. "Should I ask the driver to slow our pace?"

"No, Miss Randolph, I am well, and would rather arrive at the inn sooner than later."

"I as well, madam. I as well."

Fortunately, her condition thus far had not caused her to suffer any morning or motion sickness, unlike Sophia, whose first weeks *enciente* had been spent with her head bent over a pail.

The air had grown progressively chillier, and though there was no need for warming pans or blankets yet, she and Miss Randolph wore wool dresses beneath lined pelisses instead of muslin. There was nothing to do to pass the time except grit one's teeth and anticipate the next sudden jolt.

Just then a dark blur streaked past the window. She leaned to peer out, her gloved hand on the cool glass. It was Mr. Blackmer, of course, atop the horse he had won in a card game the night before. He looked very fine in the saddle, his cheeks ruddy with vigor and health, despite having passed the night in the common room as the inn had been able to provide only one room to their party.

Miss Randolph watched her from across the carriage, clear-eyed as an eagle. Clarissa stiffened, realizing the obviousness of her actions, and drew away.

"Why, just look at the sky," she said, peering out and upward. "I hope it doesn't rain."

"Hmmm. Rain. Yes, my dear."

Miss Randolph smiled, clearly not fooled by Clarissa's claim of interest in the weather, though it did look like rain.

Why she felt the need to hide her newfound fascination with Dominick from the older woman, she could not precisely explain even to herself. Miss Randolph had already made it clear she wished for them to be happy together. Indeed, this morning her maid had vehemently insisted that if accommodations were limited at the next inn, as they had been the night before, Clarissa must insist her new husband share her bed while she, the servant, would make do with whatever else.

Clarissa knew Miss Randolph was right. She should concern herself with her husband's rest and comfort. They should learn to care for one another. That could only occur as they spent more time together. Which was why she felt so exceedingly relieved that after that first night in the inn, there had been no more passionate exchanges, no visits to each other's rooms...no bone-melting kisses. Yes, relieved. Their relationship would take more than a day or two to build, and she wanted to proceed more slowly, so there would be no disappointments for either one of them and no regrets.

She suspected Mr. Blackmer felt the same because he had ignored her almost completely since. Things weren't unfriendly between them, not by far. They had exchanged pleasantries each morning and each night, and had even shared a meal together, where they'd conversed about nothing much of substance. Which all suited her just as well, because the quiet between them had given her the time she'd needed to *ponder* and *dissect* and, yes, *accept* the events that had occurred in London.

The carriage sprang sideways, creaking and rattling.

"Oh!" exclaimed Miss Randolph, pitching backward into the seat. She snatched for her book and spectacles, which in that moment became airborne.

Clarissa seized hold of the iron door handle and planted her boots against the floor. The carriage bounced and leveled and continued on, as did the train of her thoughts.

If she'd feared she could never feel for another man after Lord Quinn's betrayal, Dominick's kiss had proven that false. For that she could only be grateful to her new husband for helping her understand the capabilities of her heart. Each time she remembered the first night as he'd crouched over her in her bed—

The smell of him...the taste of his mouth and skin...

She closed her eyes.

—her blood went instantly hot, as if from a fever. Every time he appeared at the bottom of the inn stairs, looking up at her, or striding across a muddy courtyard, her heart leapt with interest.

Only one thing troubled her. Just four days ago, that same heart had leapt with interest for Lord Quinn. There was something very uncomfortable about acknowledging that.

At last, when she believed she could endure no more carriage-bound purgatory, they arrived at an inn, which she hoped would be the final lodging on their journey before arriving at Mr. Blackmer's home.

The wind blew so hard, the carriage rocked. Having glanced at the timepiece that hung from the simple chatelaine at the front of her pelisse more times than she would care to acknowledge, she'd anticipated the stop and had gathered her things and waited, hat on and redingote buttoned. The building's stone façade looked much like the one the night before, but gone were the green fields and trees that had softened the landscape. Here, stone and hardscrabble earth spread as far as her eye could see, overshadowed by dark gray skies and the scent of ocean brine intermingled with impending rain.

Her husband did not open the door, but rather the footman, which she noted only because Mr. Blackmer's face had always been the first she saw each time they disembarked for a meal, a roadside pause, or to pass the night. It surprised her how disappointed she felt not to see him. She descended and, followed by Miss Randolph, both women crossed the narrow courtyard against the wind, followed by the footman, who carried their belongings.

Just then she glimpsed Blackmer's tall figure, his broad shoulders and his flapping coattails as he disappeared inside the front door. She noted then what she'd noted countless times since the day of their wedding. Mr. Blackmer was quite simply magnificent, in a way Mr. Kincraig had never been. It was in the way he moved with such purpose, his eyes piercing and so perceptive to everything around him. When he spoke to people, they paid attention. He could indeed be imposing, but not in an arrogant way. Rather, he quietly impressed.

A moment later she passed through the same door just in time to hear an elderly man in a dapper suit, whom she supposed to be the innkeeper, say, "My sincerest apologies, sir, but we have only the one room. Your lady's maid there is welcome to sleep in the storeroom, which is secure and private, and there is a fine pallet. I believe she would find it most comfortable."

Miss Randolph's lips thinned. Clarissa knew her servant had always taken excessive pride in being employed by the Earl of Wolverton and had her standards. Still, the woman closed her eyes and exhaled before nodding in assent. "I would sleep on the floor in the corridor if it meant not getting back in that carriage."

Her maid gestured to the footman to deposit their valises onto the floor beside her, which he did before returning outside.

However, Dominick frowned, his cheeks darkly flushed

from his ride in the elements. Yet dark hollows showed beneath his eyes, evidence of his exhaustion. His hat, now removed, revealed a windswept head of shining dark hair. Clarissa's fingertips throbbed, remembering its thick yet silken texture.

"I'm sorry," he said. "But one room simply will not do. Is there another inn nearby that we might make before nightfall?"

Clarissa's mood fell. Like Miss Randolph, she had no wish to return to the carriage and that terrible road, especially not when the night grew dark and cold and the skies threatened rain.

The innkeeper shook his head sympathetically. "Another hour's travel, at least, and of course there is no way to guarantee empty rooms. My apologies, sir, the week has brought a constant stream of carriages, with so many leaving London at the close of the season."

Clarissa exhaled. An hour? The man may as well have said twelve.

"Please no," Miss Randolph murmured beneath her breath.

They were all road weary and exhausted. Another inn would not do. Clarissa and her exhausted husband would simply pass the night together in the available room.

"Mr. Blackmer, one room will suffice," Clarissa said, stepping nearer to his side.

Speaking the words sent an unexpected thrill fluttering through her. She'd just invited her husband to share her bed. They were both too tired for anything but sleep, but the idea of lying beside him both terrified and excited her. But it would be these sorts of circumstances that would serve to bring them closer together, and that wasn't a terrible thing, being that tomorrow he would introduce her to his family as his wife.

Yet at her words Dominick looked sharply toward her—a distancing and almost angry glance.

"It's too far to the next inn," Clarissa said firmly. "No one wants to travel on."

"Does it seem strange to you that I would like to sleep in a bed tonight?" he retorted.

Her cheeks burned that he would make it so obvious in a public place, before onlookers, that as man and wife they did not make a practice of sharing a bed.

Just then, a man bundled in a coat, hat, and scarf barreled inside, and with him came a gust of frigid air and a spattering of rain. Water drizzled off the brim of his hat and streamed in thick rivulets from his coat onto the wooden floor.

Clarissa shivered as the cold crept beneath her skirt and up her stocking-clad legs.

"The sky is coming down now," the man exclaimed with a smile, shaking his sleeves.

A maid let out a sharp rebuke and rushed toward him with a rag, with which she proceeded to sop up the mess as he trundled past.

Mr. Blackmer muttered a low curse and closed his eyes, as if trying to rein in his temper.

Clarissa stepped closer to him and spoke in a low tone. "There is a bed, and there is no reason why we shouldn't both sleep there. As I said, one room will suffice."

He answered with a curt nod and exhaled through his nose.

With a glance to the innkeeper, he said, "We'll take the room."

Clarissa nodded, satisfied that her husband saw things as rationally as she did. She waited for instruction from the innkeeper.

Dominick, however, took a few steps toward the crowded common room, which was filled with gray tallow smoke and the scent of burned food. His jaw twitched and his eyes narrowed, revealing his dark mood. A sudden blast of thunder shook the walls and windows.

"Sleep well. I will see you in the morning," he said to her, his eyes not even meeting her gaze.

Returning his dusty, wide-brimmed hat to his head, he turned as if to proceed to the door.

The innkeeper looked at Clarissa in bewilderment but then discreetly averted his attention. A surge of embarrassment shot through her at having been so publicly rejected. Yes, she and Dominick had kept their distance for the previous two days, but why should he now reject her offer of a comfortable place to sleep, when he wanted it so badly? Did he find the idea of passing the night with her so abhorrent?

Remembering the passion with which he had kissed her that first night in the dark, she knew he did not. *You are my preference,* he had said in such a seductive tone.

Moving quickly, she placed herself squarely in her husband's path.

"Mr. Blackmer, don't be stubborn. It is cold out there and only getting colder. We've traveled all day, you on horseback. Miss Randolph has already said she is agreeable to sleeping downstairs. There is no reason why you should not share the room with me." She spoke in an even tone, because she wouldn't stoop to beg. "After all, I am your wife."

"Only on paper," he muttered so low that only she could hear. The brim of his hat threw a dark shadow across his face.

The words felt like a slap, despite her knowing them to be true.

"Which makes it seem very real, doesn't it?" she answered. "At least it does to me."

Chapter Twelve

$\mathscr{D}$ominick stared at her a long moment. "You ought not to keep that girl waiting any longer."

A weary-faced servant girl in a white apron and lace cap stood at the landing, a glowing lantern in one hand and Clarissa's valise in the other. "This way, madam."

With a sideways turn of his boot, he angled past her and, after pushing through the door, disappeared into the night. Rainfall and thunder muted his footsteps until the door slammed closed. The innkeeper rummaged in a cabinet, pretending not to have observed their tense exchange.

Clarissa's heart beat like thunder in her ears. Though exhausted, her husband had summarily refused her offer of a comfortable place to pass the night, preferring the dark, wet, and cold to her company. She rejected the hurt in her heart that accompanied his words and her dismay at being so soundly rejected. Things had not been unpleasant between them, so why had he responded so severely? There had to be a reason.

"Miss Randolph," she said, turning back. "You might as well come upstairs with—"

But Miss Randolph was already on the far side of the common room, disappearing toward the kitchens.

Clarissa followed the inn's servant girl upstairs and politely declined all offers of assistance, evening victuals in her room, or a bath, instead asking to be left alone. Once the girl was gone, Clarissa stood in the quiet of the room, shunning the warmth of the fire, listening to the storm rumble and surge outside.

She tried to put herself into Dominick's mind, to imagine what he must be thinking and why he insisted on staying away.

How did he feel toward her? Did he dislike her personality? Did he find her unattractive? Perhaps...perhaps because she carried another man's child?

No. Certainly not, because he'd been compelled to follow her and kiss her so thrillingly that first night, which meant something. He had *wanted* to kiss her, and he had reacted with passion when she kissed him back.

Perhaps, then, the key to understanding his behavior tonight lay in how *he* believed *she* felt toward *him*.

Of course. That was it. He thought she was unhappy. That she saw him as her consequence, not her choice, which, in a way, was true. She wouldn't have chosen him, but she was a different young woman now than even three days ago. She'd grown up and become wiser. She better understood the measure of a man.

She hadn't had a choice in marrying him. But she *did* have a choice now.

Earlier, she'd convinced herself they could learn to care for one another slowly and over time. That their respect and affection for one another would develop over the months and years.

But he'd kissed her with such passion, which meant...Mr. Blackmer was a passionate man.

How naïve she'd been to think it. If she wanted to ensure the future of her marriage, "slowly" would not do at all.

Dominick stood under the overhang of the stables, a gusting wind and downpour at his back, observing as his coachman and the inn ostlers secured the horses for the night. He'd lit a cigar, his first in years, and had just taken the first long nerve-settling draw when his hired footman straightened from where he stacked the ladies' trunks against the wall and peered with sudden interest toward the courtyard. He raised his hand to point.

"Mr. Blackmer," he said. "Your wife—she is there, out in the storm, do you see?"

Dominick glanced over his shoulder and instantly caught sight of Clarissa, a slender shadow in the dark, clutching what he assumed to be her valise against her chest. All the muscles along his shoulders clenched as, slowly, he turned.

Upon arriving at the carriage, she flung open the door and climbed inside.

What in bloody hell was she doing?

For a moment he experienced bewilderment. Ladies— most especially those of her ilk—did not willingly step foot into a downpour, let alone a thunderstorm, yet he could think of no rational answer why she would do such a thing. There, inside the conveyance, she would at this moment be shivering and completely drenched through.

The next moment brought a blast of anger. Had she no

concern for herself or the baby she carried, his only real hope for ever becoming a father—something he did not realize he needed so desperately until now.

Throwing his cigar down, he crossed the yard in long strides, rain driving down upon his hat and his shoulders, his boots splashing in the mud to wrench open the carriage door handle. Only the handle did not turn, because it was locked. He pounded his fist on the door and peered into the window.

Rain saturated his hat so heavily the brim drooped low. A wide rivulet found the crevice between his coat and shirt, and chilled his spine.

"Open the door," he shouted, half enraged.

Her pale face appeared on the other side of the glass, framed by a wet and droopy straw hat and ribbon. Yet her eyes flashed bright with challenge. "If you won't sleep in that perfectly good room, then neither will I. Good night, Mr. Blackmer." She yanked the curtain closed, making it impossible for him to see inside.

"You open this door right now." He pounded again and tested the handle, to no response or avail.

He felt a tap on his shoulder. His coachman stood there, water streaming off the brim of his hat like a waterfall. Bizarrely, the man winked and laughed.

"And why are you so amused, Mr. Smythe?" Dominick half snarled.

"Locked ye out has she?" the man said, rocking back on his heels, which caused a sucking sound in the mud.

Dominick's eyes narrowed and he seethed. "It appears so."

Mr. Smythe made a clicking sound with his tongue. "Can't say that 'asn't 'appened to meself a time or two.

It's this job, y' see." He gestured toward the driver's seat. "Gone weeks at a time, and time apart always seems to lead to misunderstandings with the ladies."

"Time apart," Dominick repeated. "Certainly a difficulty for a traveling man."

Time apart working on different assignments had only made a bad situation worse when he was married to Tryphena.

But he and Clarissa had never been together. Except for one moment in the dark, and for the three days since he had needed time away from her to assert control over himself and his growing desire for a young woman who carried another man's child, and who certainly wouldn't understand.

He'd gone so long, feeling nothing, feeling numb, but that night the desire he'd felt for his lovely new wife, so deliciously innocent in her white sleeping gown, had shocked him with its power and knocked his world half off its axis. Ever since, his every thought and action had been off kilter.

And now she sought to provoke him with childish theatrics. For what purpose? She did not seem the sort. It was damn cold and wet outside. Did she forget that she carried a child?

He glanced downward at his smiling companion. "Mr. Smythe, being such a man of experience, have you any advice for another who finds himself in such circumstances?"

"Oh, yes." Mr. Smythe fished underneath his cape. "Be prepared."

He held up a key between them, and grinned.

A warm rush of satisfaction washed through Dominick, and he nodded. "Ah. Very good. Thank you, good sir."

Taking possession of the key, Dominick squinted and

poked until he found the lock. Once turned, he wrenched the door—

Only to encounter resistance from the other side, so he wrenched it again.

It flew open and he saw her gloved hands—then her body—retreat from the opening.

"I locked that door for a reason," she exclaimed in a high, cool voice from the shadows of the far corner. "The same reason most people lock doors. Because they wish to be alone."

After climbing inside, he brought the door shut and joined her in shadows, lowering himself to the same bench upon which she sat. Water dripped from his coat to the floor. With a thrust of his muddied boots, he slid closer, until their hips almost touched. She gasped, and crowded farther into the corner.

He turned his face to consider her. "Mrs. Blackmer, I'm very tired and have little patience for this sort of foolishness, most especially on a night like this, which means you shall return inside where it is dry and warm, where you belong. Now. Without a moment's delay." He paused. "Do you understand?"

Sitting rigidly, she stared back, her expression blank. "Of course I understand. I'm not an imbecile." Water glistened on her skin and turned her eyelashes into dark spikes. "But I'm not going anywhere. I'll be sleeping here where it's perfectly comfortable." She patted the upholstery upon which they sat. "If you like, you can have the other bench."

She waved in that direction.

He reached for her hand, which she snatched away, to press between her breasts.

He needed only to look at her to remind himself how

young she was. He reminded himself that she must be afraid, having been taken from her family for the first time. He did his best to keep the surly growl from his voice.

"I did not pay for a room so that it would go unoccupied for the night."

She shrugged and answered calmly, "I have already told you it is yours for the taking. I shall not be making use of it."

His gaze slid over her slim figure, buttoned up tight in her wet pelisse, all the way down to her mud-spattered hem and boots. The damp and enclosed space only intensified her perfume. The tantalizing scent filled his nose, dizzying him...distracting him from any hard feelings he may have had.

A flash of light and a subsequent rumble reminded him where they were, and how ridiculous she was being.

"You're weary from the journey," he said.

"You are right, Mr. Blackmer. I think I'll go to sleep now. If you'll just give me my privacy, I can prepare to retire." She reached for her valise on the floor.

He snatched it up.

"You're being irrational," he growled—yes, growled, because, damn it, he was being very pleasant while she persisted in being obstinate.

"Of course I am," she replied in a velvet voice, then leaned toward him in a provoking pose, her blue eyes flashing. "But then so are you."

Her hand came toward him, palm up...

For a moment he thought she would touch his face, but with a flick of her wrist, she—

Tapped her fingertips to the underside of his hat and flipped it off his head to land on the floor near the door.

Dominick blinked in surprise. He stared at her.

Her lips slowly assumed the shape of a smile.

Blood thundered in his ears, more loud and dangerous than any sound coming from the sky. His temper exploded.

"You should not have done that," he uttered gutturally.

Her eyes narrowed. "I'm glad I did."

He reached for her arm.

She bounded away, to sit on the opposite bench, just out of arms' reach. He lunged across, only for her to duck under his arms and take the space he'd just vacated. Oh, she was quick and wily, while in such close confines he felt like a bull in a china shop. He twisted round to find her eyeing him warily.

He hissed through his teeth. "Joy of all joys, I've married a monkey. Does the answer 'no' always make you behave so absurdly?"

"Only since I married you," she replied sweetly—but her eyes flashed blue fire. Breathing heavily, her breasts rose and fell, and her cheeks had taken on the most lovely blush hue.

"I'm not going to argue with you a moment more." He reached again, thinking simply to take her by the wrist, but she scooted to the other end of the bench to glower at him from against the upholstered wall like a surly, wet cat. Except she was prettier than a cat, and her damp pelisse clung so very nicely to her curves, making her look like a disgruntled mermaid. His mouth went dry, wondering what it would be like to peel off all the wet layers. He closed his eyes and anguished, mentally shook away the thought. "I'm no longer losing my patience, it is lost."

"Then you ought to go find it. I'm certain you left it out there." She jerked her head in the direction of the storm.

"Not without you. You're cold and wet, and you're going inside where it's warm."

"I'm warm here," she retorted, between chattering teeth.

"Have you forgotten you are with child?" he accused.

"Me? Forgotten?" She laughed loudly, a lusty yet comical sound he'd never expected to hear from her lips, and one so unexpected and unlike the young woman he thought he knew she almost made him laugh as well.

"Clarissa—"

"*Who-ooo-ooo* among the two of us," she answered exaggeratedly, "could ever forget that I am with child? I might as well wear a sign, one that says 'wed in haste to an innocent man who is not the father of my'—"

He lunged, reaching for her mouth. "*Don't* say it."

Her eyes widened and she ducked—

He caught her around the waist, binding her in his arms, but not too tightly, because he didn't want to hurt her.

"Tyrant!" she exclaimed, her face smushed against his coat.

"Hoyden."

Still, they struggled—

She wiggled and he grasped. Her skirts twisted around them, tangling their legs. She reached up, grabbing a handful of his hair—and he broke free, turning, arms high—

Only to catch her, his entire body coming around her from behind to cage her, with her face toward the opposite seat. Almost in an embrace. Her muscles eased and she exhaled.

She began to shake.

His heart sank. Damn, he'd made her cry. Clearly she suffered some sort of emotional breakdown for having been forced to marry him. But then, bending lower, he glimpsed her profile and the upward turn of her lips, and he realized she was laughing.

All of his anger and exasperation evaporated. Relief bubbled up inside him, and he laughed too. Just a little, but God it felt good, like sunshine after the smothering tension and stress of the past three days. For a long moment, they simply embraced one another, gasping and breathing hard from the exertion of their physical wrangling, laughing into the darkness.

Chuckling, he asked, "If I release you, will you allow me to take you inside?"

She laughed again, emitting a husky sound. "No."

She went to squirming.

"Oh, hell," he muttered.

He wished she wouldn't move like that because he liked it too much.

Damn it, he wasn't even angry anymore, just... relieved to hear her express laughter and humor, things that had been painfully absent between them since the world fell apart. The weight in his chest became not so heavy. With a groan, he lifted her off the bench, his arm coming up beneath her knees, binding her against his chest.

"Put me down," she insisted, but her tone was subdued and... almost playful. She did not mean it. She was weary too, and wanted rest. He could tell now, by her voice.

"No, but you could collect my hat."

He dipped low, and she caught it up with her hand and returned the wet wool to his head.

"And your valise."

He bent again, and she lifted the case by its handle.

He managed to get them out of the carriage and onto the ground. With a kick, he shut the door before making his way across the courtyard, doing his best to shield her from the downpour with his shoulders and his hat. Several yards ahead, Mr. Smythe clambered up the inn's steps and opened the door.

"Thank you, Mr. Smythe," Dominick said darkly, upon passing through.

" 'Tis no trouble at all, sir." With a jovial bow, the man tipped his hat.

Upon their entrance, the same maid who'd sopped up the earlier mess cast him a sharp glare and again stormed across the room, " 'ey there, wot about them boots?"

Only to be silenced by a glance from the innkeeper.

From the direction of the common room, several men shouted bawdy encouragements that, with a quick glance down, he saw inspired Clarissa's cheeks to blush an even deeper hue. Somewhere inside, someone played a violin, and not very well. The haze of smoke blurred the air. Still carrying Clarissa, Dominick climbed the stairs.

"Which room?" he asked.

"As if I'd tell you," she murmured.

But just then, an upstairs maid rushed down the corridor and opened a door, gesturing for him to carry her inside.

"Poor darling," she murmured sympathetically, as they moved past.

"Poor darling, my ass," he murmured beneath his breath, so that only Clarissa could hear— which got him a sharp pinch on his shoulder.

"Pardon me, sir?" inquired the maid from behind, apparently having heard him speak.

"I said I hope this storm doesn't last."

He sensed Clarissa's eyes on him. Glancing down, he saw that she smiled.

"Indeed, it came on suddenly." The servant rushed across the room and turned down the covers, something that made his gut twist tight with discomfort and, yes, arousal, because in that moment, he imagined himself there with his wife.

A fire blazed on the grate, casting light and shadows about the small room.

The maid moved toward the door. "Would you like me to summon madam's maidservant?"

"No," he answered forcefully—

At the same moment Clarissa did the same. "No."

He felt certain, though he could not see for the shadows, that she blushed.

"Supper then, and some nice hot tea?" she inquired as she backed toward the door.

"Yes, please," Clarissa answered softly. "Enough for two. And some Madeira, if you will."

He listened, liking the sound of her making arrangements for the two of them far too much. It had been so long since a woman had concerned herself with his comfort, though, truth be told, many had been willing.

As soon as the girl was gone, Dominick moved closer to the fire and set Clarissa onto her feet.

"Thank you." She extended her hands toward the warmth. "Doesn't that feel delicious?"

"To think you would rather have stayed in that damp, freezing carriage." He removed his gloves and laid them upon the mantel before warming his hands.

Her gaze matched his unwaveringly, as she removed her hat and its droopy silk flowers and set it on a small round-topped table. Her blond hair clung damply to her head and her neck.

"I think you know that's not true," she answered quietly, shivering.

He touched her arm. "This has to come off as well."

She nodded and fumbled with the buttons, chuckling. "Except my hands are so numb from the cold they are useless." In a quieter voice, she said, "Perhaps I ought to call for Miss Randolph."

"Come here."

Her eyes met his, hers open blue pools to her soul. She nodded, and her arms went to her side, a stance that said simply *yes*.

And just like that, a dangerous fire burst to life inside his chest. Without a doubt, he could have her now, if he so wished. He could push her backward on the bed and push up her skirts and rut into her like the starved man he was. All night long, in every position, until his lust was slaked. He could see that in her eyes—she would acquiesce to his every demand, of this he had no doubt.

His fingers moved to the row of shining military buttons at the front of her pelisse, bound by damnable little loops. "May I?"

"Of course."

"You are drenched," he chided softly, plucking the first button loose. "Why did you do such a thing?"

"I couldn't think of any other way to get you here, where I wanted you."

Again, he stared into her eyes and saw nothing but honesty there.

"I do want you here, Mr. Blackmer," she said. "Words didn't seem to be working, so I tried something else."

"You mustn't do such a thing again, be so reckless with your health and that of the child." He focused his attention on the next button.

"I know," she answered quietly. "I shouldn't have. I won't again. But...you *are* here now."

Despite the chill of his wet clothing, the heat from the fire and her words—and the triumph he heard in them—warmed him to his bones, and other parts of his body that were not so sentimental. She wanted him here. As much as his broken soul craved this intimacy, he felt suspicious of it as well. He feared she only encouraged this closeness because they were married, because she, like all well-bred young ladies, had been raised to be accommodating.

The last button unfastened, he pushed open the placket. She made a sound—a little moan, whether because of the intimacy of the moment or the cold, he did not know—but she did not flinch or pull away as he worked the wet pelisse from her arms. The sound only made the fire in his chest burn hotter. Once removed, he hung the garment across a chair near the fire.

"Thank you," she said.

"You're welcome, but I think it's ruined."

"I'm afraid I am as well. I must look a fright." She lifted a hand to her hair.

No, more like a brightly wrapped present he couldn't wait to unwrap.

"Not at all."

He spoke the truth. Her blue dress clung to her body like wet gauze. A straight-edged bodice left not only her throat and shoulders bare but a tantalizing view of the upper swells of her breasts. Several tendrils of hair clung to the side of her neck, reflecting light from the fire. He could not stop himself. His gaze moved over each swell and valley revealed by firelight and shadows. She was delicate but not at all frail. Slender, but blessed with generous curves. If he were allowed only one word to describe her, the word would most certainly be *lush*.

And now she belonged to him.

She blushed beneath his scrutiny but lifted her arms to remove several pins. Then she shook her damp hair free and loose over her shoulders, her eyes bright with...

Anticipation. Nervous anticipation, but anticipation, no less.

Chapter Thirteen

$\mathcal{N}$ow yours as well," she said in a breathless voice, reaching for his wet coat. He allowed her to try, and she did her best to work the tailored seams from where they fit tightly over his shoulders, until he had to assist by wrenching the coat off and dropping it behind him.

"Your dress," he murmured, hearing only the solid *thud* of his heart in his ears, as he caught his thumbs inside the collar, to trace them downward over its dark outline against her pale collarbone, to her bosoms that crowded there, luscious and full, against the pleated bodice.

"Yes," she answered.

At hearing that word, his cock came to life, stiffening in his trousers.

For a long moment, he savored that barest of touch, the damp coolness of her skin under his fingertips. *Luminous, soft, excruciatingly perfect…female skin.* She breathed deeply, causing the most intriguing shadow play between the soft swells and her clothing.

Tryphena had been more voluptuous, with generous breasts and hips, and she'd known how to use her body to excite a man. He had not been her first, nor had he been her last, but he had loved her in that obsessive and possessive sort of way that in the end had felt more like insanity.

He didn't know what to feel for Clarissa. His body, however, did not seem so confused.

"It's all right, Mr. Blackmer," she whispered, her tongue darting out to dampen her lower lip. She covered his hands with her own and gently moved them to the fastening at the center of her breasts.

She did not flinch, or look away, and he understood what she offered, his young and dutiful wife.

He untied the cording at the front of her dress, which was more like a long and fitted vest. He lifted it off her shoulders and down her now-bare arms, pale and gleaming in the firelight, dispatching it to the chair as well. This left her standing in only her simple cambric chemise and over that a short corset, with her shoes and stockings underneath.

Yet he had already made his decision, and in keeping with that he took up a blanket folded over a chair and drew it over her shoulders, covering her.

"Take your valise, and go over there to take off the rest." He indicated the deeper shadows on the far side of the poster bed, which was hung with curtains. "Put on your nightgown, and go to bed."

They stared at one another in silence, eyes locked, until she spoke again.

"I know you are angry...with me, about everything," she murmured. "You have every right to be. But if we can find some way to—"

He caught her face in his hand.

"Yes, I know." Slowly, he dragged the pad of his thumb across her mouth, a pillowy, perfectly pink mouth that reminded him of summer and sweet wine and strawberries.

"Kiss me, then," she said.

"I...can't." He stared at her lips, tortured and needful all at once. "I won't. Because I *am* angry, Clarissa. I'm angry about a lot of things, and it wouldn't be right. Not yet."

"And yet you kissed me before. Why?"

"I wanted to," he answered.

And he wanted to again. Yet his hand fell away and he stepped back, because when he stood so close to her that he could smell her perfume and see the diamond-sparkle flecks in her blue eyes, he couldn't think.

"Why not now?"

He turned away from her. His feelings. He had learned to conceal them so well. It wasn't easy to speak them. "That was in the dark."

"The dark." She paused as if to ponder those words, then nodded slowly, her eyes wide with understanding. "Do you find my appearance so displeasing?"

He chuckled at the ludicrousness of her statement. "On the contrary, I find your appearance utterly pleasing."

In a quieter voice she asked, "Is it because of the baby? You don't find me appealing because—"

"No." He shook his head, though he could not bring himself to say more...he did not allow his mind to think upon the subject further, even now, and he did not wish to shock her by attempting to explain that the knowledge that she carried a child only made her more alluring in his eyes, even while he suffered the deepest regret that the child wasn't his. "That's not it."

"Then why?"

He turned back to her then.

"Tell me," she demanded.

But there, in those same beautiful eyes...he saw something else.

"Because we've been through a lot of unexpected changes these past few days. Because we don't know each other very well. But mostly because there's someone else here, in this room, between us. I see him every time I look in your eyes."

"Quinn?" she said. "You think I still love him."

He flinched and smiled darkly, looking to the carpet. "Don't you?"

The haze of sensuality that had come over her, that she'd welcomed because it would make intimacies with her husband so much easier, all but disappeared the moment she uttered the other man's name.

"No," she whispered. "I despise him."

"That may be true, but hearts are complicated. You need more time. I know you do, because I see those tears that have just come into your eyes. So as much as..." He paused, and his jaw tensed. "As much as I want you right now, Clarissa, I think it would be wrong of me to make love to you. For my own sake, as much as yours."

Clarissa nodded, unable to speak, her throat crowded by emotions she did not want to feel. Loneliness and regret over the choices she'd made and, most of all, a sudden need to be close to Mr. Blackmer. To *Dominick*.

He was wrong. She did not need more time. She wanted to be closer to him, and if that meant making love, she wanted to make love.

But she wouldn't plead with him. Not for that. She couldn't.

She took her valise and did as he told her to do, going behind the bed-curtain. She felt so strange, and confused, wanting nothing more than for him to change his mind and lie beside her in the bed, so she could hear his heart beat and feel safe, and know that everything would be all right.

With shaking hands she untied the ribbons of her short corset. After hanging it on a wall peg, she removed her chemise and for a moment stood naked except for her stockings and boots in the chill, staring down at her body, wondering how Mr. Blackmer saw her. Her breasts ached, feeling tight and swollen and overly constricted by the corset she'd worn that day. They were larger now, she knew as a result of being pregnant, because Sophia had reported much the same, only then they'd all giggled over her revelation, and Clarissa didn't feel like giggling now.

Tentatively she touched them, slowly massaging the soreness away. She squeezed them, plumping them in her hands—

Any tears that had been in her eyes dried as she imagined her hands were Mr. Blackmer's, with his darker skin and long fingers. Her mouth suddenly became parched, and she licked her bottom lip for moisture. Still imagining him there with her in the shadows touching her, she dared graze her palms across her nipples, which tightened responsively into peaks.

A knock came at the door, startling her. She peeked round the curtain to observe as the maid brought in a steaming tray, two mugs, and a sturdy earthenware teapot, and deposited them on the table beside the fire. Once the girl was gone, Mr. Blackmer perused the offerings on the tray and tore off a chunk of bread, which he popped into his mouth, before swinging round toward the fire. He pushed

his suspenders from his shoulders and in one fluid movement twisted his shirt over his head.

If her mouth had gone dry a moment before, at imagining his hands on her breasts, it became a veritable desert
now. She could only stare in fascination at his long, lean,
and muscular back, flexing along his torso and bunching at
the shoulders as he shook out the shirt and draped it on a
screen beside the fire. Her eyes found a scar on his back
that matched the one on his torso. His warrior's body in-
trigued her. She wondered if she would ever learn the story
of how he had received such a terrible wound when he had
already told her he was sworn to secrecy over his past.

She withdrew again to the shadows, her hands returning
to her breasts, which tingled and burned, but in the most
wonderful way. Again she teased her nipples, this time
with her fingertips, enjoying the pleasure of self-touch,
something in which she'd never before indulged.

Strangely, her furtive experimentation created a tight
and urgently needful pull between her legs. A most wicked
and insistent hunger, intriguingly new to her. She skimmed
her hands downward over her torso and her belly, as yet un-
changed by her pregnancy, and dared to stave her fingertips
between her legs, just above the pale tapes of her stockings.
There she found herself very damp and wondrously sensitive to touch. Yet after a few unsatisfying strokes of her
hand, she knew she would need something more to make
the feeling—

What? Go away?

No, to make the feeling become more perfect.

She knew full well what she needed, because she'd
seen it in the light of the fire after Mr. Blackmer had
emerged from his bath that first night after their wedding,

at the inn. The memory of his wet male sex jutting out like a fence post from its dark thicket of hair had provided endless diversion for her mind during long hours of travel when conversation, reading, and needlepoint had not. She'd convinced herself it was wrong for wanting intimacy with him, for craving his touch, when so recently she had loved another. But now that they were alone and she so bewilderingly aroused, she could summon no feelings of restraint.

"Clarissa, the maid brought supper. Come and eat."

"I'll be right there."

She quickly removed her stockings and boots and found her nightgown and pulled it on, wishing it were something finer and more alluring. Made of plain cambric, it boasted no embroidery, trimming, or particular style, other than a pink ribbon at the neck, which she purposefully left untied.

At hearing her approach, he turned from the fire. He'd draped a blanket over his shoulders in place of his shirt. She felt the shadowy heat of his gaze move over her, and her body shivered in response, as she glimpsed the muscles of his chest.

"Don't you have a robe?" he said, his voice noticeably tight. "Even with the fire, the room is still quite chilly."

"I'm not cold," she assured. "Sit down. I'll pour tea."

"Nonsense." He removed the blanket from his shoulders and draped it over hers. "I won't have you catching a chill, now that we're inside and by a perfectly good fire. I...apologize for my own state of disrobement. My clothing is in the stables, and so I shall have to wait for my shirt to dry." He gestured toward his drying shirt.

"Your breeches won't dry at all as long as you're wearing them."

She felt wanton just suggesting that he take them off, but she wasn't the only one in danger of catching her death of cold.

"Later," he answered brusquely. "I'll...take them off later."

How amusing that he had suddenly become modest. He'd all but let her stare at his naked body before. Yet she remembered his words about seeing Quinn in her eyes and knew he was trying to give her time to grow accustomed to him, which she appreciated.

"Whatever you wish," she said.

She poured tea, and pushed the chairs together so that they could share the tray. In silence, they ate their fill of a warm and fragrant stew with buttered bread.

"It's very good," she said.

"It is indeed," he answered.

"So we shall arrive tomorrow at your home?" she inquired lightly, hoping to learn more about his family and what she might expect upon their arrival.

In response to her question, his countenance fell solemn and his eyes shuttered.

"If the road is safe for travel," he answered quietly. "Due to the rains, we may be confined here for another day. Perhaps even two."

She nodded, keeping her tone inquisitive and genial. "You mentioned your father. Is your mother alive still as well?"

"Yes." He looked toward the fire. "Last I heard."

His tone held no malice.

"Were you ever close to her?"

He frowned, and his brows furrowed together. "She wasn't ever that kind of mother. It's not that she was ever cruel or neglectful, but some mothers aren't motherly, if you understand what I'm saying."

"I do understand."

He nodded. "She's not at all like Lady Margaretta. I hope you won't be disappointed."

"I won't be," she assured him. "I'll be fine. Rest assured, if we are to make our lives there with your family, I'll do whatever I must to get along."

"You won't have to for long, because we won't be staying."

She looked at him in surprise. "I assumed we were to take residence with your family."

"And why wouldn't you have?" he said quietly. "We haven't really talked about it, which is my fault, I suppose, but...Clarissa, this visit is not something I look forward to."

"All families have their problems," she answered softly.

His lips turned into a wry smile. "I would vow to say mine has more than most. Long-held disagreements and grudges that I don't wish to trouble you with."

"I wish you would."

"In time," he answered quietly. "When we know each other better. That doesn't hurt you, for me to say that, does it? Such things are difficult to think about, let alone to share."

"I understand." She wouldn't press. Not yet.

He was correct in saying they didn't know one another very well, so how could she demand that he share painful memories? Some men were very private. More than once Sophia had mentioned Claxton's difficulty in sharing painful details from his past. Just as Sophia had been patient with the duke, she must be patient with Mr. Blackmer, and eventually, when the time was right, he would open his heart to her.

"Thank you," he said. "We'll stay just long enough for me to claim my inheritance, a small residence with land for farming. It's nothing grand, like what you're accustomed to—"

An inheritance. A small farming estate. His family was gentry then, which explained the proud bearing she'd observed in him since their marriage.

"I don't need or expect anything grand," she said reassuringly. She didn't need a London palace or a sprawling country home, just a place where they could await the birth of the baby together and become closer and spend the rest of their lives.

"It might require some work to make it livable again, so I don't know if we'll be able to live there immediately, but soon, I hope."

He seemed so concerned for her comfort, for her happiness, and for that her heart opened toward him.

"I can't wait to see the house," she answered warmly. "I know it will be wonderful, and if it's not, we will make it wonderful." She set down her mug, and in doing so the blanket slipped from her shoulders. His attention shifted to fix there on her bare skin—intriguingly intent, so she did not endeavor to cover herself. "One question—does your family know you were an agent for the Crown?"

"No, and please don't tell them. Secret means secret, even from one's family. You only know because my cover was effectively..."

"Destroyed by me."

"Yes." He smiled wryly. "My family knows only that I was attached to the diplomatic service, which is true to a degree before this most recent assignment to Wolverton, I...traveled abroad mostly, under such auspices."

"That sounds much more exciting than a London assignment. Why the change?"

"Well...you see—" He shifted in the chair and straightened, leaning forward suddenly. "Clarissa, there's something else you need to know about me. Perhaps I should have told you earlier, but no time has seemed right."

He spoke in a quieter tone than before.

"What is it?" she asked, leaning toward him as well.

His dark eyes seemed to take on the shadows in the room. "I have been married once before."

Married. Dominick had been married before. It took a moment for the words to sink in, and when they did, something *hurt* deep down inside her, though she knew it shouldn't, because of course he'd had a life before her and because of the way they'd been thrown together, bits and pieces of their pasts would come tumbling out every now and then. This news of a prior marriage was just a big piece, and one she hadn't expected.

Now she understood what Dominick meant when he'd said he saw Quinn in her eyes. Because now she suddenly felt as if there were someone else in the room with them— his memory of another woman.

"What happened to her?" she whispered.

"She died," he answered softly. "Nearly three years ago."

"What was her name?"

He cleared his throat. "Tryphena."

Tryphena. Such a powerful female name.

"And how did she die?"

He hesitated a long moment as if pondering what to say

next. "She was an agent like myself. I shouldn't even tell you that, but it seems like something you should know."

He scrutinized her as if trying to determine whether she was trustworthy and whether he'd made a mistake in sharing something so private and secret with her.

"I won't tell a soul," she assured him. "There are lady agents? I had no idea."

He nodded. "Quite a few of them actually."

"That's very exciting." She felt so dull in comparison. What exciting or dangerous thing had she ever done? She almost felt envious, but no—the poor lady was dead. "I'm certain she was very brave, and good at it."

"She was indeed. All I can tell you is that it happened while she was working an assignment." His voice went hollow, his gaze strangely flat. "I am bound by duty to a certain level of secrecy and can say no more, only that afterward I remained here in England."

"I see."

And she did. There would be some things he could not tell her. Such was the nature of this man she had married. She would have to be satisfied that some mysteries would always remain between them. She looked at him, trying to discern the answers to deeper questions. Had he loved Tryphena? Did he love her still? How deeply had her death affected him? Did he carry the grief of her loss in his heart each day?

Sitting back in the chair, he raked both hands through his hair and stared down his nose at her, a perspective of him she found both distancing and attractive.

"God, that was difficult to say to you," he murmured, exhaling. "I hope you aren't hurt, or angry that I didn't tell you before."

"Not at all," she answered softly. "Given the circumstances, there really hasn't been an opportune time."

"It's late." He nodded. "You should go to bed."

Suddenly she was very tired. She'd had the urge to kiss him and, yes, even seduce her husband just moments before, but this revelation about his prior marriage dampened that impulse. Things felt different now between them, and in a good way, she thought. He'd confided something painful to her, and she could not help but believe it had brought them closer together. Although it seemed his past was filled with difficulties and tragedy, her mind felt more at ease that he'd shared them with her, even though she still had questions and might never have all the answers.

"You'll join me later? I'll take the far side, and you can sleep here. I promise, I keep to my side of the bed, and I don't kick or snore, although Daphne tells me I at times breathe irritatingly loud."

He chuckled at that, and nodded. "That's reassuring to know. Good night, Mrs. Blackmer. I won't be long."

And yet when Clarissa awakened sometime before dawn, he wasn't there.

In the darkness she found him sprawled in the chair, his long legs still clad in his breeches and boots and a thin linen towel draped across his chest. He looked so uncomfortable, the chair too small for his large frame.

Her heart fell.

Rather than sleep with her, he'd passed the night in miserable circumstances, without even a blanket to keep him warm. The fire still burned and so he must have tended it late into the night.

In that moment, she realized she felt something more for him, an affection that now made her fret for his comfort and rest. If not for that feeling, she would not want so desperately for him to leave the chair and come to bed.

There could be no more softly spoken invitations. Instead, she would insist. Starting now. She pushed back the covers and made her way across the carpet. The cool air touched her arms and shoulders, leaving her chilled. When she touched his hand, his eyes opened. Deep shadows scored his face below his eyes, proof of his exhaustion.

"What time is it?" he asked.

"Still night. Come to bed so you can sleep there and not in this uncomfortable chair."

"I wasn't asleep," he growled. "I was just thinking with my eyes closed."

"I don't believe you," she retorted softly, and set to work pulling off his boots. "So just be quiet."

"Don't," he warned, tugging his leg back.

She held on to the heel. "I said shush."

Setting the boots aside, she knelt and, with all efficiency, reached for the placket at the front of his breeches. Wives assisted their husband in such ways, and she wasn't going to shrink away any longer like a frightened child.

His hand seized her wrist. "Clarissa."

"*Dominick,*" she replied in kind, firmly. "Let me do this."

She needed to take care of him. She needed to be his wife.

A moment of silence passed. His grip relaxed. "Go on, then."

Her hands shook—only she knew, because of the

shadows. The leather was still damp, but she easily un-
buttoned the four buttons at the upper edge of the top
flap. Without hesitation she dropped the flap free to unbutton above and at the center of his waist. Even in
the shadows she saw through the remaining triangle of
leather, his sex lying flat against his stomach, larger than
she remembered.

All moisture left her mouth and she closed her eyes,
realizing she had to make him stand and help her, else
she'd never get his breeches off. She reached then for the
towel, thinking to remove it from his chest before assist-
ing him up—

Only to have her wrist seized again and her body pulled
atop him into his sudden embrace. She gasped, her breasts
crushed against his bare chest and her thighs aligned with
his, as his strong hands held her there. He exhaled raggedly
through his nose and hungrily kissed her while rearranging
her limbs so that she straddled him.

In that moment she experienced more exhilaration,
more anticipation than any moment ever before with
Quinn, whose face she could hardly remember because her
mind was filled with Dominick, the heat coming off his
body against her palms, and the spicy-male smell of his
skin, and the inevitability of what was about to happen between them.

Oh, his lips, and his kiss, and the growling sound he
made deep in his throat. She had never experienced anything so thrilling. His hands pulled her knees around his
hips, deeper into the cushion of the chair so that her
sex settled on top of his, which felt stone hard, but hot
and shockingly thick against her now-aching and needful
flesh.

She'd never felt true desire like this before. She hadn't understood until now what Sophia had once told her and Daphne, that if they were lucky and waited for the right man, they would want and even need intimacies as much as their husbands did.

She wasn't a wanton—she was a wife—and she wanted more of this man, her husband. His kisses, his touch. She wanted him to be inside her.

"You—" He breathed against her cheek, his hands moving up the bare skin of her back beneath her gown. "—make it difficult for a man to get any sleep."

"Is it sleep you want?" she whispered, feeling a wicked excitement at just speaking the words.

"No."

"Neither do I."

"I have tried my best to stay away, to give you time." Fisting his hand in the sleeve of her gown, he dragged the garment off her shoulder, kissing her there and along her collarbone, making her squirm from the pleasure of it. "To give myself time."

Clarissa felt his sex move against her thigh, and she complied with the demands of her body, readjusting so that they aligned more intimately and sinking more fully against him. He emitted a rough grunt in response, and his hands seized tightly on her arms.

"I don't want time," she said. "I just need you."

"I don't love you, Clarissa," he murmured against her skin. "I wouldn't want you to misunderstand. I'm not there yet."

Feverish, she answered, "I don't love you either. That's all right though, isn't it?"

She leaned forward, cupping his face in her hands. She

memorized his features in the firelight before leaning in to press her mouth to his. He responded with passion, turning his face and deepening the kiss.

"I don't know what's right anymore," he murmured. "But I know I can't...resist this."

With a groan, he tugged the cambric lower...yes, oh, yes, lower, to her waist, leaving her breasts and torso exposed. The cool air touched her skin, and she shivered and then quaked from the sensation of his mouth on her skin as he gripped her firmly under the arms and lifted her several inches higher, kissing her rib cage and the underside of her breast.

"You're beautiful. Lovely. I want to eat you alive."

There was something deeply pleasurable in being handled so gently, and yet so brutishly, by such powerful hands and arms.

"Dominick," she heard herself say, and then his mouth closed on her nipple.

Stars exploded inside her mind, and she moaned in pleasure, her arms coming around his neck as she inhaled the scent of his hair. He lowered her, and she again felt the power of him between her thighs. Nothing, in all her life, had ever felt like this. Her fingers scored through his hair. His tongue swirled and laved, while his mouth, in concert, kissed and sucked.

She surrendered to instinct, arching her back and rocking against him, feeling him become harder and more prominent as she became slick and ready—

He turned his face aside, and he breathed against her collarbone.

"I can't wait," he said urgently.

"I don't want you to."

"Here in the chair." He gripped her thigh and, reaching between them—

"Yes." Her excitement grew, anticipating their joining, because it was something she wanted, for her marriage to be real. To be closer to Dominick.

He moved, and she felt the sudden pressure of his member prodding against her, impossibly large. Too large?

She gripped his shoulders.

"Damn," she heard him mutter. "Damn, *damn*. You're so lovely."

He thrust his hips upward and, in the same moment, with his hands on her waist, guided her down.

She cried out, feeling torn from the inside. Though no longer a virgin, their joining sent such an unexpected frisson of pain deep into her abdomen, her body still unused to penetration. It had hurt her first time, but not like this. She hadn't realized two men could be so different and could only surmise Dominick was bigger. He thrust again, and she seized against him, frozen and overwhelmed, unable to proceed.

"Are you all right?" he asked raggedly.

"I don't know." Her hands rested on his shoulders, palms open.

He stilled for a long moment...and then he pulled her closer, his mouth closed gently on hers.

"I went too fast. I shouldn't have. I'm sorry." His hands moved up her back and shoulders, kneading her skin and into her hair. "Slower now. I don't want to hurt you."

"Just please don't stop."

He moved beneath her, slower now, guiding her hips into a similar movement, very akin to riding a horse at a low canter. The discomfort remained, but lessened. His hands slid down the column of her body, to close firmly on her buttocks, which he squeezed.

One hand did not remain there, but came round to splay across her belly, the thumb dipping down to press firmly against the place where their bodies joined, directly at the center of her sensitive pearl. Nothing hurt anymore. Everything felt right.

"There," he said thickly.

He rubbed in a circular motion, in rhythm with the motion of his hips, something that felt so good, she bore down against him, wanting more, taking pleasure now in his sex and the heated friction between their bodies. Her nipples tightened, feeling as hard as diamonds.

"*Yes.*"

"Oh, my . . . ahhh—" He gasped. "Your sex is so tight."

"I'm sorry." Her hands squeezed his shoulders.

"God, no, it's good. Beyond good. Perfect." He chuckled. "But I might die from it."

"Don't die." She kissed his jaw.

"I need this," he murmured, his head falling back. "Clarissa, I need you."

His every thrust brought her closer . . . closer . . . closer to something she couldn't define. Something that felt more and more like paradise.

"*Dominick.*"

Something she had not felt before with Quinn.

He groaned. "This damn chair is both heaven and torment. I can't get deep enough."

"The bed . . ."

Binding her tightly against him, he stood, wrapping her legs around his waist. The movement drove him deeper inside her. She gasped in pleasure, embracing him. He carried her to the bed, where they fell together in the center of the mattress, dark shadows formed of muscle and sinew.

"Do you see?" she murmured, pulling him into her arms. "It's not so bad here that it should take such effort to convince you to join me."

"I'm convinced." He pulled the covers atop them and dipped his head to kiss her breasts and her neck and face before his hands slid to her thighs, spreading her. He lowered his hips between her legs, and his chest crushed her breasts.

"It seems strange," he murmured against her temple. "To be like this with you."

"Does it feel wrong?" She stared up at the bed canopy.

"No."

"Not for me either. I'm glad."

He kissed her face. Her mouth, his tongue driving deep inside. Gently, he pulled her arms above her head and, at the same time, entered her again.

"You're beautiful," he murmured. "Thank you."

"Dominick," she moaned.

The pleasure. It came over her in waves, so intense she feared she might not survive the inevitable end.

"I'm hardly inside you," he said. "I need to be deeper."

Suddenly...the room wavered...and everything felt smotheringly close...and he, too heavy and hot. What had happened so suddenly to make her feel this way, when only moments before she'd been squarely at the center of heaven?

Her stomach—felt so unsettled. Her skin, clammy.

Oh, no.

"Get off me. Please!" She gripped his arms.

He stiffened against her.

"Now, oh hurry."

His eyes wide and glassy, he rolled off, looking stunned. "What is it?"

She tore free of his limbs and the bed sheets and stumbled across the room. There she found an empty basin and, leaning over it, retched.

Chapter Fourteen

Two days later, Dominick stood outside Clarissa's door, dressed in his coat and hat.

"You're certain she can travel?" he asked Miss Randolph again.

"Yes, sir, I vow she's much better today." She smiled hopefully. "I've even managed to get some broth down her."

"It's true, I'm much better today," Clarissa called weakly from the bed, sounding valiant, if somewhat muffled.

He peered inside and saw her lying atop the coverlet fully clothed for travel, her boots on. Her bonnet rested on her face.

"Much better today..." she repeated faintly, her voice trailing off.

"If you say so," he said to Miss Randolph, unconvinced, but he could only smile at Clarissa's efforts.

His pregnant wife's morning sickness had chosen the

most inopportune time to come to life and had interrupted their lovemaking in the most unfortunate way. He could not begrudge her. Of course he couldn't. She'd been so miserable since, and he felt terrible for her and helpless to make her feel better. Not knowing what else to do, he'd left her to Miss Randolph's expert care. Dominick spent the next two days and nights in the common room with all the other travelers who had crowded the inn, watching the rain pour from the sky and, yes...thinking of her.

Clarissa. His wife.

Even though their lovemaking had ended awkwardly, they *had* made love. He could hardly believe it still. He hadn't intended for things between them to move so quickly, but when she'd come to him in the dark, looking so desirable with her pale hair loose around her shoulders, and touched him so gently, his exhausted psyche had simply reacted, wanting comfort and finding it in her. She had seemed more than willing, and touching her felt natural. Exhilarating. He hoped she felt the same way too and that when she emerged from her illness she wouldn't regret what had happened, because he didn't, and he wanted it to happen again.

Her kiss, her body, and her touch had made a miserable situation not so miserable. Even with the rain, and too many people crowded into the inn, his mood had held since then, lightened because of her. But yesterday, at last, the rain had stopped, leaving behind cold, wind, and dark skies—setting a perfectly dreary mood for his return home.

"I'll be downstairs in the common room having breakfast," he said to Miss Randolph. "If Mrs. Blackmer is indeed well enough, we'll depart within the half hour and

arrive at a place outside Ashington by nightfall. Summon
me if you'd like me to help her down."

Downstairs, he avoided eye contact with the attractive,
ginger-haired young woman who placed a platter of bacon
and eggs before him, having firmly fended off her advances
for two nights in a row.

"I 'ope your missus feels better," she said in a feather-
soft voice, imbued with false sympathy. "Been a bad few
days for 'er, poor thing. 'ope you don't have to stay another
night."

Unfortunately, the inn servants talked, so this one knew
more than he would have liked about them.

"She is doing much better, thank you," he answered
with a curt nod. "We'll be leaving this morning."

With a sigh of disappointment, she pivoted on her heel
and retreated, her skirts swishing to and fro as she went,
drawing the admiration of several other men, young and
old. He was ready to be gone from this place that smelled
of grease and burned tallow and too many human bodies.

But was he ready to go home? It had been some three
and a half years since the last time, when between assignments he'd gone only to dutifully introduce Tryphena to
his family, at their insistence. The visit had not gone well.
Tryphena, never one to soften her manners or to curb her
tongue, had not gotten on with his parents at all, while she
had gotten on all too well with his younger brother, Colin.
He closed his eyes, remembering, and still not understanding why she'd seemed so determined to hurt him.

What a miserable time that had been, the true beginning
of their end. Later he had written his parents informing
them of her death and had received a polite reply in his
mother's handwriting, offering condolences. In it he could

practically hear her and his father's unified sigh of relief that he was no longer attached to such an unsuitable woman—and their expectation that might come to his senses and at last return home. Viewed by his family as a prodigal son, his father wanted him returned to the fold. And yet he couldn't return home.

He didn't hate his family. He loved them, but in a very different, more complicated way than Clarissa loved hers. He just couldn't live with them, and they knew why—he had never shied away from making that clear.

As a young man, he'd craved adventure and had no other choice but to make his own way in the world. He'd been proud of his independence and that he'd supported himself every step of the way. Returning home now, after so long, with his tail between his legs—or so it felt—and asking any favor of his father would be difficult to stomach, but he would do it for Clarissa and the child.

Just then, the common room grew silent. Looking up, his heartbeat arrested. Clarissa made her way toward him, dressed in a simple blue traveling pelisse. Behind her, Miss Randolph waited near the vestibule with their valises.

He stood, forgetting his family troubles, forgetting his breakfast. Forgetting everything but her. Because even ill, with her skin pallid and her features drawn, his wife was heart-stoppingly lovely. God help him, despite everything that had happened with Tryphena, despite all his efforts to guard his heart against his new young wife, he was smitten.

He strode toward her, extending his hand, into which she placed her gloved one. Leading her to his table, he lowered her onto the bench beside him, because, yes—he wanted her near. Looking at his plate, she quickly glanced away. Her skin, he felt quite positive, went several shades paler.

"Good morning," she said weakly.

"And a good morning to you," he said with a chuckle.

Clarissa looked into Dominick's eyes, doing her best to ignore the plate of half-consumed eggs beside him. "I'm sorry to have caused such a delay."

"You did not," he replied easily, seeming very large and masculine beside her. His dark eyes peered into hers, bold and interested, and she blushed, remembering the intensity of their lovemaking before she had suddenly become ill. "The roads have been impassable until today."

His smile broadened a degree—just a small, teasing turn at the corners of his lips—and he slid the plate to the distant end of the table. Bless him. He'd realized how miserable the presence of his plate had made her. Perhaps she could indeed fall in love with this man.

Perhaps she already had, just a little.

Her gaze skimmed over the strong line of his jaw, and his lips.

Perhaps more than just a little.

She remembered the urgent way he had kissed her, and touched her, as if he needed to be close to her, just as she needed to be close to him. She exhaled, feeling shaky just being near him again. She didn't know why her heart had opened to him so quickly, but it had. Though she was grateful that he'd married her to spare her and her child from scandal, the feelings she experienced went much deeper than that.

The weather. They'd been talking about the weather, hadn't they?

"I'm afraid I have been so confined by my ailment that even if Miss Randolph told me about the rain, I don't remember."

"I'm sorry you feel so badly. I fear that once we resume our travel, you'll only feel worse again. Are you certain you don't wish to stay here and rest another day?"

There was an intimacy to his tone that hadn't been there before, one that made her feel as if she belonged here sitting by his side, not as an obligation but because he wanted her there.

"No, let's go on," she said resolutely. "Are you ready to see your family? Are you ready to go home?"

"As ready as I can be," he answered wryly.

"Maybe things will be very different than you expect."

"They won't be. Clarissa, just—"

"Just what?"

Dominick closed his hand over hers and squeezed. "Just know that my family does not define me. They haven't for a very long time now. Don't...judge me by them."

"I won't."

"The house...everything might be...startling. I just don't want you to be overwhelmed when we arrive. They aren't like your family at all."

He had mentioned difficulties with his parents. Disagreements and old grudges, he'd said. But...was he also embarrassed of them? Did he fear that his new wife, the granddaughter of a wealthy earl, would find his country gentry family too simple in manners or dress or their dwelling too crude? She truly hoped not. She hoped she already realized she was not the sort of young lady to look down on someone because of a difference in social standings.

Just then, a redheaded kitchen maid approached the table and, with a saucy, intentional smile at Clarissa, very deliberately placed a steaming plate onto the table in front of her, one containing an oozing mass of beans and kidneys in red gravy. The smell filled her mouth and nose.

"Enjoy breaking your fast, madam," the girl said cheerfully, before winking at Dominick and flouncing off again.

"Did she just wink at you?" Clarissa choked out, barely able to breathe for the smell of the food pressing into her nose.

"Did she?" He shrugged. "I did not notice."

"I'm sorry." She lifted a hand to her nose and mouth. "I can't stay here. It's the smell."

He grinned. "I understand. Go on then, and wait with Miss Randolph. I'll be out momentarily after settling the bill."

She nodded and stood, as did he. But then she observed the redheaded girl peek out from the kitchen wearing a big smile, unabashedly jubilant at seeing her flee the common room.

Clarissa turned back, touching his forearms.

"Dominick."

Speaking his given name sent a jolt through her.

"Yes?" he answered in a low voice. His hands came up to rest familiarly underneath her elbows and their eyes met. "What is it?"

In a rush, all the heat and passion that had taken place between them two nights before and the memory of his body against hers returned clear and exciting, as if the room full of people around them did not exist.

"I'm very sorry for what happened the other night. The way things ended."

Did he blush? She thought so. Just a little.

"You needn't be," he replied. "It's not as if you could help it."

"I wish it wouldn't have happened. Everything was lovely until then." She smiled ruefully. She reached between them to touch the buttons at the front of his greatcoat. He stared down at her hands while she did this. "More than lovely, it was perfect."

In the next moment, his gaze snapped up, meeting hers. "You'll feel better soon, I hope."

A fire burned in his eyes, one she understood without needing explanation.

"Miss Randolph says I will. Sophia's difficulties lasted only a week or two, and I pray for the same, because, Mr. Blackmer..."

His eyebrows went up. "Yes, Mrs. Blackmer?"

"I should like to resume where we left off."

How bold. Had she truly said it? Her cheeks flooded with color. To her great pleasure, his did as well.

"As would I," he replied, his eyebrows raised and his tone a degree huskier than before.

Oh, but she wasn't finished.

"One more thing." She leaned closer.

"Yes?" His head bent, bringing his ear nearer to her lips.

Quite intentionally, she turned her placid smile upside down into a scowl.

"That girl over there *did* wink at you, and I suspect she brought me that horrid plate of muck on purpose, to make me feel worse. Why would she do something like that unless she has developed an inappropriate fascination with you?"

His eyes widened in surprise. "You're...jealous?"

"Jealous, no," Clarissa answered firmly. "Attentive, yes."

"Attentive is...*good*. But as for that girl, I...ah..." He stammered and shifted stance. "*No.* Of course not. I haven't encouraged any such thing."

"And yet she is standing there watching us right now. Smiling even. Not a friendly sort of smile, I must say." Clarissa looked at the girl and narrowed her eyes. "Do you know, I think I'd feel better if I spoke to her at once."

She turned on her heel and set off across the room. The girl straightened and her eyes widened, as she scooted backward toward the kitchen.

He followed her on long legs, chuckling. "No, I—ah, don't think that's a good idea."

She turned back to him, her eyes wide. "Why not? Is there some reason why you don't want me to talk to her? Did you carry on a flirtation—"

"Certainly not." His hand found the small of her back, and he led her to the door. "Why would I, when it seems I am on my way to being a very happily married man?"

Unfortunately, Dominick had been right. No sooner had they embarked a mile down the road when Clarissa's sickness returned with a terrible vengeance. Yet she had stayed Miss Randolph's hand away from the bell cord, because she wanted nothing more than to reach their journey's end.

"Please, try to eat the biscuit. Just a bite," pleaded Miss Randolph.

"I can't," Clarissa moaned, closing her eyes against the utterly disgusting sight of the hard square of shortbread in her maid's hand, something she knew to be completely bland and tasteless under any other circumstances.

"What about some tea?" Miss Randolph lifted up a corked jug.

"Ugh." Her stomach roiled in response. She pressed both hands over her nose and mouth and burrowed face-down into the bench. Miss Randolph tucked a blanket around her.

For hours, Clarissa hovered somewhere between sleep and awareness, her mind crowded with a thousand jumbled thoughts. She missed her family. Most especially her mother. When would she see them again? Whatever the answer—it would be too long! She wished Dominick was here inside the carriage. His presence was so comforting. But she didn't want him to see her like this. All she wanted now was privacy and for the world to not bounce each time a wheel went over a stone or rut.

At last, feeling restive, she pushed up and pressed her head against the cold glass, finding the chill soothing, and stared dully outside.

Here the climate was colder and harsher than London and the southern regions of England. She had never traveled this far north. Sophia had honeymooned north of the border with Claxton at his Scottish estate, and spoke of the wild beauty of the landscape and charm of the local people. But looking out her window now, Clarissa saw only wild, and not so much beauty. Cold crept into the cracks of the carriage and seeped through her traveling clothes. She shivered and pulled the wool traveling blanket over her nose.

"What time is it?" she mumbled at Miss Randolph, knowing that any attempt to look at her own pocket watch would just make her dizzy.

"Nearly four o'clock," the woman answered. She too

sat beneath a blanket and had wrapped a thick, gray wool scarf around her neck. "I do believe we may be getting close."

"I pray so," said Clarissa, though she felt so poorly the announcement roused only the barest excitement.

Dominick suddenly appeared, cantering alongside the carriage, his shoulders rigid. His greatcoat billowed out behind him as he urged his mount to go faster, and he traveled out of view. Clarissa sagged again into her seat.

Soon she took note of a high stone wall that ran alongside the road and continued on for what seemed an eternity until at last the carriage slowed before an ornate iron gate, with large lanterns affixed to columns at either side as well as at the center, four bright orange spots at the twilight of a dark and dreary day. Two liveried servants stood vigil—and immediately leapt from their posts to open the gates.

Which seemed to indicate they recognized someone, that someone most certainly being Dominick. Through the haze of her discomfort, Clarissa struggled to sit higher, and Miss Randolph bolstered her up. Once the carriage passed through, the gates were closed again, and they traveled up a long drive, at the end of which stood a sprawling fortress of ancient stone, against a barren, sea-swept ridge.

"Blackmer has brought us to a castle," she said, gripping the window frame. "I don't understand why."

"This must be his family home," Miss Randolph suggested in a hushed voice.

"It...can't be." Certainly his family simply lived somewhere else on the grounds.

Yet the conveyance traveled down a long curving drive and rolled to a stop directly in front of the towering pile.

Window curtains moved and faces appeared. Doors opened and servants spilled out.

Reality sunk in. "I do believe we are going in there."

"I do believe you are right."

"Oh, Miss Randolph. We should have...repinned my hair," Clarissa whispered, suddenly panicked, her heartbeat jumping like a startled frog. "I ought to have worn something finer. Where is my tooth powder?"

She reached for her valise but Miss Randolph pushed her back against the seat.

"It's too late for any of that." Popping the lid off a tin of peppermints, Miss Randolph frantically pressed several between Clarissa's lips before producing a lint wand, which she brushed over the sleeves and lapels of her mistress's pelisse.

"I look like a bumpkin and I most certainly...*smell bad*."

With a jab of her elbow, Miss Randolph knocked open the window beside her and, in the next moment, dabbed Clarissa generously with perfume.

Clarissa pushed her maid's hands away. "Oh—that smells horrid." One of the peppermints popped out of her mouth to roll across the floor.

"Whatever you do, my dear, don't retch on the stairs."

Retch! Oh, she just might. Clarissa's heartbeat increased, for there out the window she saw her husband dismount—with the reverential assistance of two liveried footmen, no less—and turn on his heel toward her. With his face a mask of intensity, he strode toward the carriage. His coattails snapped in the wind.

Her eyes widened. Her heartbeat stalled.

He looked *different* than before. But why? He had always carried himself just so, with confidence and masculine grace.

And yet here in this setting, with that palatial house behind him, she saw *something* she hadn't seen before.

Something, she now realized, that had been there all along.

Chapter Fifteen

Dominick walked toward the carriage. Behind him, a murmur rippled through the gathered servants. He heard boots on stone as one of them set off at a run toward the house. Darthaven loomed above him, as magnificent as in his dreams, its shining windows looking at him like expectant eyes.

One of the footmen rushed ahead of him, pivoting smartly on polished boots to open the door. Inside Dominick saw Clarissa's pale face.

"What is this place?" she asked quietly from where she sat on the bench.

"It's Darthaven, my family's home."

"I see," she whispered.

Looking closer, he saw she looked fragile. Even... distressed.

"Clarissa, are you all right?" he inquired, leaning inward. With a sharp glance to Miss Randolph, he said, "You should have informed me she was this ill. We would have stopped."

"I forbade her from doing so," Clarissa answered plainly, peering at him, intent. "Tell me...tell me who you are."

He knew what she meant.

"I'm your husband," he responded. "Dominick."

Miss Randolph diverted her gaze. Normally he wouldn't speak with such intimacy in front of a servant, but he felt the need to reassure Clarissa that he was the same person he'd been before, just hours ago at the inn and in London.

"Nothing has changed," he added.

The wind gusted strongly, causing the carriage to sway and creak. His gaze dropped to where Clarissa's gloved hands gripped the seat, as if she might topple over at any moment.

"Darling?" He reached for her, the endearment slipping from his lips before he could stop it, startling him, because it revealed his heart's devotion to her, something he wasn't yet ready to confess, even to himself. She appeared not to have even noticed, which relieved him.

"Come with me," he urged. "Let's get you inside where it is warm."

She nodded jerkily and stood, placing her hand in his. Again she peered up at the house.

"Don't look so shocked," he murmured. "It's just an old pile of stones."

"You said I might find it overwhelming...this is not what I expected," she whispered, looking up at his family home.

At that moment there came the sound of boots crunching upon the pathway.

"Lord Blackmer," a deep voice boomed from behind. "Darthaven welcomes you home."

He did not have to turn to recognize the voice of Guthrie, his father's butler—or *majordomo*—as his appearance-minded mother had always preferred to title him.

Clarissa looked into his eyes. "Lord Blackmer."

"I'm afraid so," he replied. "My father is the Marquess of Stade."

"You are an earl." She stared at him, confusion dimming her blue eyes. "Why didn't you tell me?"

Why hadn't he told her? Perhaps because he'd feared that like so many she would fall under the spell of Darthaven's magnificence, and he wanted to delay the moment it drove a wedge between them? Because he feared that, once they arrived, she wouldn't understand why he couldn't stay?

"I did tell you. I told you my family and this place don't define me," he answered. "And because you are married to me, neither can they define you. Please understand that. We won't be staying."

"You've brought someone with you, I see," came a different voice, female, and as smooth as silk. His mother's.

His hand closed firmly on Clarissa's, he turned to introduce her.

Lady Stade stood there, dark haired and striking, looking as if time had not touched her in the years since he had last seen her. Indeed, since he had been a boy. The tails of her fox fur cape flew on the wind behind her.

"Mother," he said.

She frowned, as she always did when he or his brother called her that.

"Lady Stade," he amended.

The frown eased.

"It pleases me to introduce you to Lady Blackmer."

"You've married again," she answered in a quiet voice, her countenance expressionless. "What a surprise. Oh, Blackmer, you might have written to let us know."

"I'm so pleased to meet you," Clarissa said in a clear if not completely steady voice. Her hand tightened on his, a small vise.

"And I you, dear." His mother scrutinized Clarissa, and if he knew anything about his mother, he knew she was analyzing every detail of his new wife, from the embroidery on her cuff to the inflection of her voice to deduce where in the echelon of society her new daughter-in-law belonged and whether she ranked higher than herself.

"Lady Blackmer," said the marchioness, taking a step closer. "Are you feeling unwell?"

Guthrie too stepped forward.

"Quick!" warned Miss Randolph from the carriage. "She's falling."

"Oh, catch her," urged his mother, her hand coming to her lips.

Guthrie and two footmen lunged, but Dominick was closer.

He turned just in time to catch Clarissa in his arms. He braced his boot against the carriage step, adjusting her against his shoulder, while Miss Randolph reached out to neaten her skirts over her boots.

A sudden fear struck him that she might be more ill than he believed, and in danger of losing the child. He would never forgive himself, because it had been he who had insisted they travel. Carrying her, he strode past his mother, who gathered her fur against her throat and peered into his face.

Guthrie shouted at the servants who had gathered. "Make way."

"Please summon a physician," Dominick said to him as he swept by.

"Yes, my lord, immediately."

He climbed the endless rise of stairs to the front doors, which were held open on either side by servants anticipating their passage. Inside, more servants lined the entry hall, having assembled in mere moments to greet him.

"Thank you, all of you," he said quietly, moving past them. He received a nearly in-unison reply of nodding heads as well as politely murmured words of greeting and concern for the lady in his arms.

High above, illuminated by blazing torchères, an immense gallery greeted him, hung with portraits of his ancestors and family, each face a window to the past. And just like that, the past pressed into his nostrils, his mouth and ears, smothering him, seeking to be the air he breathed when he had worked so hard to expel it from the man he was. In that moment it was as if he had never left.

He looked down into Clarissa's face, and she became his anchor, reminding him why he had come home and of the man he had to be.

Two male servants appeared at the base of the staircase with a chair, into which he reluctantly surrendered his wife, and they conveyed her up the stairs.

"I shall allow you some privacy," called his mother from below, her voice echoing up. "Come to greet me properly, Blackmer, when you can."

He followed them up two floors. Guthrie sped past to lead the way, followed by Miss Randolph.

Halfway down the corridor, Guthrie pushed open two

doors, and they proceeded inside a large bedchamber decorated in hues of green. Two maids who on first glance bore matched features appeared as if from thin air, which did not surprise Dominick. That was how his mother kept house, with an army of perfectly trained servants who moved like silent and invisible spirits from place to place. One turned down the bed, while the other poured water into a basin. As in all of the rooms at Darthaven, the furniture was ages old, yet perfectly polished. However, the curtains and carpet and bedding were of the most current colors and style, so the place smelled not like an old musty castle but fresh, despite the ancient wall hangings and art that covered the walls. He lay Clarissa down on the bed, and Miss Randolph rushed to unbutton her pelisse and loosen her boots.

With relief, he saw that his wife's bosom rose and fell with regular breath.

"What do you need, ma'am?" Guthrie asked Miss Randolph, his eyes politely averted from the young woman in the bed.

Dominick had always liked Guthrie, a deep-voiced giant of a man who looked at everyone, noble or common, with kind eyes.

Miss Randolph answered with brisk authority. "A rich beef broth, if you will, and butter and hearty brown bread."

Guthrie caught the eye of one of the maids. Wordlessly, she disappeared from the room. The butler then assisted Dominick in removing his greatcoat and passed it off to another maid, who disappeared with it into the corridor.

Miss Randolph turned to Dominick and urged, "Leave us, my lord. Greet your family, and I shall tend to Her Ladyship and soon enough she will be well enough to join you." She untied Clarissa's bonnet and set it aside.

"You're certain she's all right?"

He was reluctant to leave Clarissa, even though he knew she was in capable hands. It was almost as if now that he was here at Darthaven, he realized the strength of his attachment to her, and feared the moment he left her, she would be torn away. This place had only driven himself and Tryphena farther apart. What if the same thing happened with Clarissa?

The impulse was too great. Caring not that anyone watched, he leaned beneath the canopy and, taking her hand, pressed a kiss to her temple.

"Rest," he murmured.

Miss Randolph touched his shoulder lightly. "She and the baby will be fine, my lord. I vow the physician, when he arrives, will confirm what I say. Just you wait and see."

Her voice held a reverence he'd not heard before. *My lord.* How could he explain that he would forever prefer "Mr. Blackmer," as she'd addressed him before?

"Please summon me when she awakens."

With one final look over his shoulder toward Clarissa, he descended the stairs to the first floor and for a moment stood outside the wide-open double doors of the King's Room, preparing for whatever might await him. Inside, the high wood-paneled walls appeared to waver in the glow of not one fire but two oversized hearths at either end of the long gallery. High windows along the north wall, every other one of them bearing stained glass family insignia, overlooked the ocean.

There, beside the farthest hearth, sat his mother, her fur cape having been exchanged for a long India shawl, which she wore artfully draped across one shoulder. She always took care with her appearance, and he couldn't recall ever having seen her wear the same dress more than twice. Several books lay strewn on a settee behind her, and a large needlework frame. At seeing him, she stood and waited for him to approach her.

"My lady." He bent to accept her kiss on his cheek. Her fragrance scented the air, expensive and complex. She returned to her seat, while he remained standing.

He loved his mother, but things had never been warm or affectionate between them. She had always been the beautiful, distant lady who had left his and his brother's care to nannies and their minding to a cadre of governesses and tutors. His relationship had been much the same with his father, an aloof, sharp-eyed man who existed either behind closed doors with land stewards and advisors or off hunting with titled, wealthy friends.

Dominick's life had not been terrible, not by far. He had been raised much like any son of the aristocracy, with the very clear expectation that he should grow up and behave and look and dress like the rest of them. Yet his grandfather, the elder Lord Stade, who lived on a much smaller estate known as Frost End and who had once been a brave naval officer on the high seas, had shared stories of adventure with him and given him his first inkling there was something *more* to life than this. After university, Dominick had set off to find it and had never really come back home.

"Blackmer," she said in her elegant, cool tone. "Again, what a happy surprise to have you home. You were assigned to Constantinople last we heard. Your duties have at last allowed you to return?"

"Indeed." His throat closed on any further explanation. They'd never developed a confiding sort of relationship, and it would be awkward to confess to her now, so soon after arriving, that his dreams had been destroyed—but that in smoldering cinders of loss, he'd found another. How he wished Clarissa was standing beside him now.

"And you bring us another bride." Her smile faltered. "Was her father or...guardian also in Constantinople?"

"We met in London, actually."

"You were there for the season?" Her voice thinned.

"Unexpectedly," he said. "Briefly."

"If we'd known, we might have come down. When was the wedding? You know I don't read the London papers and would not have seen the announcement."

Indeed, Dominick knew she hated to read about the fashionable world in distant London and the lives of her girlhood friends, now grown women, going on without her.

Lord and Lady Stade did go down to London from time to time, but rarely, because his father complained about the bad air and crowds and despised travel. He had actually glimpsed them two years ago inside the well-heeled society crowd at the Royal Gallery, where he had accompanied Wolverton to view a showing of Dutch masters, but because he was Mr. Kincraig on secret assignment, he could make no effort to speak to them.

"The wedding took place recently."

"How recently?"

"Last week."

His mother's gaze sharpened. "And she is already *enciente*?"

Had she made that assessment herself, or had the news been discreetly conveyed from one of the servants in Clarissa's bedroom? He would not be surprised.

"It would seem so."

Her expression did not change.

"Who are the young lady's relations?" she asked coolly. "Would I know of them?"

It had vexed his mother and father greatly that he'd married Tryphena without consulting them first and that his wife had never offered anything more than murky explanations of her family's lineage and whereabouts. Even he, as her husband, had learned not to pry for details about her past, but being that they were both spies, secrets had seemed natural...for a time.

It was a relief to know exactly who he had married in Clarissa.

"Lady Blackmer is the Earl of Wolverton's youngest granddaughter."

"The Earl of Wolverton." The tension in his mother's features eased. She relaxed and looked at the ceiling, as if trying to recall something. "A man of great power in his day. If I remember correctly, his heir died some years ago. A riding accident."

He nodded. "Yes, Lady Blackmer's father. His son died as well, but with issue, a young son."

"You've married well then." She let out a dismissive little laugh. "A marked improvement over your first effort."

He agreed—but still, her comment did not sit well with him. Indeed, it sparked his anger. "Tryphena is dead, Mother. There is no need to speak ill of her now."

She smiled, as if she hadn't heard him. "I'm just so glad you've come home."

"Where is His Lordship?" he inquired.

Likely out with his brother Colin, whom he dreaded seeing more than anyone.

Her brows gathered and, for a brief second, she bit her

lower lip. "His Lordship...well, he was here when the footman announced your arrival." She drifted to the window and peered out over the ocean. "Now I'm afraid I don't know."

He swallowed down the unexpected slice of hurt that came with her announcement. His father had left upon hearing of his arrival. Yet he supposed His Lordship was justified in holding hard feelings toward him, being that he'd been gone so long.

"I've just prattled on," said his mother. "You must be exhausted from your journey, and chilled through. Come and sit by the fire, and I'll ring for tea."

She reached for a silver bell on the table beside her.

"No, Mother. Thank you but don't."

"You'd like to rest until dinner. Of course."

"I'd like to find His Lordship. I've matters to discuss with him."

She nodded, her gaze dimming, as if she already realized what those matters might be. She said quietly, "I shall see you at dinner then."

He turned to the door.

"Dominick," she called.

"Yes, my lady?"

Her tone seemed softer now, as did her gaze. "He may have gone to the falcon house. That is usually where he goes when he is—"

Troubled.

"...thinking." She looked down at her hands, which were clasped on her lap.

Even without her direction, the falcon house was the first place he would have looked. In the entry hall, a servant appeared with his hat and his coat, both immaculately brushed clean. At the stables, he insisted on taking out his own travel-weary horse rather than riding one from Darthaven. A short ride brought him to the falcon house, which was just a small stone shed, where he found the gate locked. Peering through the small window, he saw his father's falcon on its perch, its feathers dull and sparse with old age, but the marquess was nowhere to be seen.

His gaze scanning the landscape for another rider, Dominick rode across the sweeping plain over which Darthaven presided, inhaling the briny scent of the ocean and listening to the crash of the waves against the stones. He continued up the incline, which led to a wide plateau upon which stood an ornamental domed folly, its marble columns strikingly white against a small forest of trees.

From that high perch, he took in the impressive sight of the house, with the sea spread out behind it like a backdrop of dark blue silk.

Just then he heard the sound of horses' hooves on the earth behind him.

Chapter Sixteen

So you've come home," said his father.

Only then did Dominick turn his horse around. In the three and a half years that had passed since he'd last seen him, his father had aged. Though sitting in his saddle as elegantly as ever, streaks of gray threaded through his dark hair, and he looked weary and somehow smaller than what Dominick remembered. Dark clouds lumbered across the sky behind him.

"Home?" said Colin, who sat on a horse beside Lord Stade. "When did Blackmer ever consider Darthaven home?"

Dominick ignored him.

"Greetings, my lord," he answered with a tilt of his hat. "Colin."

Strange, but he thought he would feel more anger at seeing his brother now, considering the ugly terms upon which they had last parted, but he felt mostly regret. Once they had been brothers. They had been friends.

His brother's eyes did not waver from his own. "Dominick."

"What brings you to Darthaven?" his father asked, his gaze wary.

"I have married again," answered Dominick.

His Lordship nodded, his countenance reflecting no change. "We shall meet her at dinner then."

"Perhaps not tonight," said Dominick. "She is ill."

Lord Stade's eyebrows drew together, and Dominick perceived a flash of genuine concern. "Nothing serious, I hope."

"She is with child," he answered. "And did not make the trip well."

"A child, you say? Did you summon the physician?" The rigidity of Lord Stade's shoulders eased a degree. In his heart Dominick knew he had just made his father very happy, at least to some degree. The marquess had never made secret his wish for grandchildren—but, more specifically, for his sons to propagate a healthy line of heirs.

"Yes, my lord. I'm assured she will recover to full health in due time."

"You must inform Guthrie if anything more can be done to make her more comfortable."

"If she is in such a delicate state of health, perhaps you shouldn't have come at all," Colin suggested darkly. "But you weren't thinking about her, were you? Only yourself, apparently. Still the same old Dominick, I see."

"Perhaps that's true," he answered calmly, refusing to be goaded. "But we are here."

"Why?" his brother demanded, his eyes flashing. "Why come back now after all this time? Not for the purpose of a simple introduction, I venture to guess."

"Colin—" warned their father, lifting a staying hand.

"What?" Colin scowled. "Duty requires him to introduce another wife to us, but nothing else? He is only to travel the world at his whim and marry, hopefully better this time than the last, but not share in any of the responsibilities here at home—"

His brother dared speak of Tryphena to him in such a manner? Dominick's anger, which he'd held in check, exploded.

"Watch your tongue, brother," he growled. "Else I'll meet you on the ground."

"Dismount then, because I'll say it again," Colin spat. "Your first wife was a—"

"*Now.*" Dominick unhooked one boot from his stirrup, his thighs and shoulders tensing.

"Silence!" barked the marquess. The horses, startled, shifted and pranced in place, their harnesses jangling.

Dominick and his brother eased back into their saddles.

"Why have you returned, Blackmer?" asked his father gruffly.

"I've left the consular service."

"Oh?" his father asked warily. Hopefully. "Permanently?"

"It seems that way."

"So you've come back here," his brother chided. "After all this time. Because you've nowhere else to go?"

"I've come to ask for Frost End," Dominick said, ignoring Colin and speaking directly to his father.

"Frost End?" said his father, dismayed, as if he'd asked to live in the barn. "Whatever for?"

Frost End—not Darthaven—was Lord Stade's ancestral home, a modest domain when compared to the grandeur of the unentailed estate willed to him by Lady Stade's father—the last Earl of Aveling—whose title had lapsed after he died without an heir to continue his line. As a boy, Dominick had spent several summers there with his grandsire, fishing, running through fields, and tending sheep. He remembered those days as the finest, freest times of his life. It seemed a hopeful place for him and Clarissa to start their lives together.

He nodded. "It's been empty for years, I know, and is certainly in need of repair. I'd like to take residence there and work the estate. Draw back the tenants. Make it profitable again."

His father stared at him coldly.

With a kick of his heel, Colin's mount lumbered forward, coming almost nose to nose with Dominick's.

Colin ground out, "You've been gone for more than thirteen years. Thirteen long years, brother. Leaving me with no choice but to take your place in all but name. No, I'm not the first son, but I've earned a say. Don't think you can just come back and start making demands."

"Frost End is my birthright." Dominick sidled his horse alongside his brother's, forcing the other animal to canter aside. "Grandfather intended it for me."

"Grandfather didn't know you'd betray your family." Colin pointed at him with his gloved hand.

In a rush, the old anger returned, and Dominick struggled against the urge to knock his brother from his saddle into the dirt.

"I've never betrayed this family. Or you, brother. Can you say the same thing to me?"

His brother's eyes hardened.

"I'd rather burn Frost End down," Colin muttered, "than see you have it."

"You want me back here at Darthaven that badly?" Dominick goaded, and narrowed his eyes. "I missed you too."

"Why Frost End and not here?" asked his father, whose lips had taken on a deeper frown. The nostrils of his aristocratic nose flared. "Are we that offensive to you, even after all this time?"

Dominick held his tongue, refusing to dredge up old disagreements. Old transgressions—namely Colin's dalliance with Tryphena, which he'd never revealed to his parents because as difficult as things had been between them, he hadn't wanted to hurt them in that way. He did not need to. Like a dark cloud it hung between him and his brother, tangled up in all the other difficult family memories. On the precipice of this new life with Clarissa and the baby, he preferred to look to the future.

"It's important for me to have something that belongs to me. That I prove my worth, in my own way, by my own efforts and no one else's."

"That old man filled your head with nonsense," said the marquess, his lip curling.

That old man. His father. Dominick's grandfather.

That old man had been Dominick's hero, and he had challenged him to do more with his life than to live inside the confining box of wealth and privilege. Dominick had done so in the secret service and intended to do so now, just in a different way, building a meaningful life for him and his new family.

"No, my lord," he answered steadily. "It isn't nonsense at all. It's what I want."

His father looked to the ground, as if digesting the words, then into Dominick's eyes again. "I've no obligation to convey Frost End to you, not until I'm cold in the grave."

"Frost End is not, and has never been, of consequence to you—yet it means very much to me, and I'm asking you to give it to me now."

His father's gloved hand tightened on the reins, and his lips thinned. "What if I refuse?"

"Then I leave again, Father," he answered quietly. "And I don't come back."

The words weren't intended as an ultimatum. They were just true. He would take Clarissa and they would leave here and he would find another way. He had been gone too long, become too independent. Though Darthaven—and the family who lived there—had been the bedrock of his past and had formed him as a man in so many ways, for that same reason, they could not be his future. He would make his own way, with Frost End or without it.

"So be it," Lord Stade answered bitterly. "If you're so determined to *spurn* your family and your obligations here, then go, but please know I've waited long enough for you to return here. My patience is spent. You may have Frost End, but not without consequences."

Consequences. He'd known there would be.

"Such as?"

"If you want Frost End now, then you forfeit the rest, any claim to the unentailed fortune you would have received upon my death."

Dominick nodded and without hesitation answered, "I'll agree to that."

He'd lived this long without benefit of his family's largesse. Fortunes were nice to have, but he would take pride in building his own.

"I will...speak with my advisors, and have the papers drawn."

"Thank you, my lord," Dominick answered with all sincerity.

He meant it. He did not despise his father. He loved him. They just weren't alike enough to live together. He directed his horse to turn, and he looked out over the ocean again, appreciating the brace of cold air that swept over his skin.

He heard the sound of a horse's hooves on stone. A glance over his shoulder found Colin nearer, glaring at him.

"If that was all you wanted, you could have just written. Why come back at all?"

Dominick realized their father wasn't in their presence anymore. He'd turned his mount and had already begun to make his way back to the house.

"For one thing, I wanted to see you, Colin. We never spoke of what happened with Tryphena. I was too angry then, but it's important now that I forgive you."

"I'm not sorry," Colin muttered. "So don't trouble yourself."

With a pull of the reins and a jab of his heels, Colin whirled his horse toward the house as well.

Clarissa awakened to what were now-familiar surroundings, a green-wallpapered room darkened by night. In the distance, ocean waves crashed and grew silent, only to crash again. After having been confined to her bed and this room for more than a week, her body ached and she felt vexingly pathetic, but the overwhelming nausea she'd battled since arriving at Darthaven had at last subsided yesterday, and since then she'd slept. At some point in the afternoon, Miss Randolph had helped her into a hot bath, and after a walk around the room, she'd slept again. Now, with her days and nights out of order, she had fallen wide awake.

Restless, she climbed down from the bed, enjoying the luxurious softness of the carpet beneath her toes. Her legs were weak from lack of use, but grew stronger with each step. Pulling the heavy drapery away, she peered out the window into the darkness beyond, but saw only a black bank of fog pressing against the pane. Feeling smothered, she released the curtain and turned again toward the room.

After finding her robe and slippers, she lit a lantern, which she took with her, peeking into the adjacent dressing closet, only ten feet away from where she'd lain for days, but she'd not felt well enough to explore. The lamp illuminated a spacious and expensively appointed room, with a rococo-style dressing table accented with gilt paint and drawer pulls. Oils in ornate frames covered the walls all the way up to the high ceiling, which was thickly framed with carved molding. Her rooms here at Darthaven were far more luxurious than anything she had ever enjoyed at home.

A rustle of movement in the opposite corner alerted her to Miss Randolph, who slept there on a narrow bed. Behind her stood the door that led to Dominick's chamber.

Over the previous days as she'd lain suffering in bed, he'd visited her numerous times, and urged her to eat and drink and rest. It chafed her vanity sorely that her new husband had seen her in such an unattractive state, when she only wanted him to see her at her best. Just knowing he was on the other side of the door sent a tremor of anticipation through her. The shadows brought to mind memories of the night at the inn when he'd made love to her.

His kisses had shattered her. His touch had awakened every inch of her body.

But at present she was angry at him. Furious, actually, and she had to let him know. He'd been an earl all along. It was one shock she shouldn't have had to suffer, especially not in front of Miss Randolph, his mother, and everyone else.

She wasn't a child, plying him with bothersome questions. She was his wife. The person with whom he would share his life, and for that she deserved some measure of respect and consideration. If he wouldn't give it to her outright, then she would demand it.

She withdrew again to her room, where Miss Randolph had left a small basin in close proximity to her bed. She scrubbed her skin, cleaned her teeth, and tidied the sleeping braids that encircled her head, then settled a white lace cap atop them.

Without the lamp, she returned to the dressing closet and passed through, careful not to bump the corner of Miss Randolph's bed. After turning the handle, she entered Dominick's room and secured the door behind her. A small fire burned on the andirons, providing enough light to see. She peered toward the bed, the interior of which was concealed by shadows and dark curtains that hung from decorative cornices on the ceiling.

"Dominick," she called quietly.

Silence.

"*My lord,*" she added with a touch of impishness. "It is I, Clarissa."

She found his bedclothes rumpled and thrown back and her husband gone. Finding the outside corridor dimly lit by wall sconces, she descended into a cavernous entry hall, cluttered with settees, chairs, and carpets and all manner of family artifacts and portraiture. Two footmen dozed on a bench and did not awaken as she passed by.

Downstairs, she discovered a drawing room with a vaulted ceiling and, next, a dining room that could have seated the House of Lords, each room darkened by night. As for the next room, she noticed that light shone from around the door, which was slightly ajar. Considering those rooms she'd already seen, she deduced this one might be a library. Perhaps Dominick, unable to sleep, had gone there and found a book or newspaper to read. She lifted her hand to knock on the door—

But then whispers and smothered laughter met her ears, a man's and a woman's.

Silently, she pushed the door open and stepped inside. She spied a flash of white linen—a man's shirt—and recognized Dominick's shoulders and his dark hair, but also a woman's pale arms gripping him tight, her long copper hair streaming. The two kissed and grappled, their bodies sliding against the wall.

Clarissa could only stand paralyzed, stunned by the pain.

Tears rose to her eyes, and she felt as if she couldn't breathe. Had it taken this to realize she had very real feelings for him? To find herself betrayed a second time by a man she'd believed she could trust.

In the next moment, fury replaced the hurt. She wasn't just going to leave and pretend that she hadn't seen them. She was far too outraged for that.

"Pardon me," she announced loudly, storming toward them, needing to see Dominick's face when he realized she was there. "I don't mean to interrupt, but I've a few words to say to my husband."

* * *

The young woman—whoever she was—gave a little shriek, while Dominick stiffened and turned, shielding the woman from Clarissa's view.

"What the hell?" he snarled.

Only it wasn't Dominick at all, but a man who looked very much like him, only younger.

Clarissa gasped, going from furious to horrified in one second. Dominick *had* mentioned a brother. This had to be him. She had wrongly jumped to the worst conclusion and made the worst sort of fool out of herself.

"I'm so very sorry," she blurted, her cheeks ablaze. "I thought you were someone else."

"I think that's obvious," he retorted, his expression furious and strained.

"I'll just go back to my room." She retreated toward the door.

His eyes narrowed. "You must be wife number two." And then moved over her in slow appreciation. "Aren't you a pretty thing?"

Behind him the girl struggled to return her clothing into place and in doing so provided glimpses of elbows and tousled hair.

"Wife number two?" she repeated.

His eyes widened. "You do know about wife number one, don't you?"

How unfriendly of him to phrase things in such a tactless manner. "Of course I do."

"But you don't know everything about her. No, I'm certain you don't...or else you wouldn't have married him."

"Shut up, Colin. She's not your plaything."

Tension struck through Clarissa's shoulders at hearing Dominick's voice behind her. She turned. He stood in the doorway wearing a coat and a thick gray scarf. His cheeks were deeply flushed and his hair tousled, as if he had been outside in the cold. He stared at the man before them, his expression formidable.

The young woman chose that moment to escape the room, her head low and her face turned aside.

Despite his lover's departure, Colin's gaze did not break from Clarissa. "Thank you, Blackmer, for that heartfelt introduction. Oh, look at you, you must have been outside for hours brooding over the sea, thinking about how miserable you are to be home with your family. You're chilled to the bone. Come inside by the fire, where it's warm. Oh, wait—I forgot. You can't. That would be far too dull and *smothering* for you, and without the necessary adventure you require. How wrong of me to even suggest that you *stay*."

Dominick leveled a dark gaze on his brother, looking much like an annoyed lion dealing with a bothersome cub. "Obviously, we've matters to discuss, you and I, but we aren't going to do it now. Not like this." He pointed a finger to the ground between them. "So why don't you go and sleep off some of that bitterness, not to mention whatever you've been drinking, and we will talk in the morning."

Dominick's hand touched the small of Clarissa's back and he led her out the door.

"What? Leaving so soon?" Colin glibly called after them. "I had hoped we could all stay up late together and talk about old memories and such. I'm certain Lady Blackmer Number Two would like to hear them all."

The footmen wakened and stood, attempting to look aware. Clarissa and Dominick continued on past them toward the staircase.

"That *is* your brother, I presume?" Clarissa asked.

"That, my dear, is an ass," gritted Dominick in response.

"I do believe in *this* circumstance, the ass, my dear prodigal brother, is you," the other man called in a voice roughened with spite. He leaned his shoulder to the wall and, in an artificially light tone, called, "See you both at breakfast, then?"

Blackmer led her away. His head thundered with anger, but as they neared the staircase, Clarissa suddenly broke away from him and rushed up several steps above him, her pink dressing gown sweeping behind her, skirts rustling against the marble. Her hand on the banister, she stood glaring at him, her blue eyes bright with accusation and hurt.

"Clarissa, it's very late, and you've been unwell." He closed the distance between them, taking the first stair—

"Don't," she said, holding her hand up to halt his advance, to reject his touch.

He did as she asked. "What is it?"

"*Do* I know everything there is to know about Tryphena? Or is there more?" she demanded, glaring at him. "Tell me, Mr. Blackmer...oh, wait, it's actually *Lord* Blackmer, isn't it?"

Displeasure curled his lip. He disliked the taunting tone of her voice—and her unfortunate choice of repeating Colin's words, because even if she did not intend to do so, by speaking them she placed herself on his brother's side. Just as Tryphena had done.

Clarissa wasn't Tryphena.

He knew that. He did. But after nearly a week spent apart while she recovered from her illness, he felt distant from her now, especially when she spoke to him as she did. He glanced over his shoulder to be certain the footmen did not overhear.

"Go on," he said darkly. "It's obvious you have something to say, so say it."

She exhaled. "You should have told me everything after we married. I understand that we were strangers and that I have been ill, but most certainly before we arrived here at your family home."

Indeed, even after making love, they were strangers still. She was a beautiful, vivacious creature he wanted to claim and touch and seduce until she stopped asking him so many damn questions.

"I *did* tell you everything," he replied, doing his best to keep the edge from his voice. "Everything you needed to know to understand who you'd married when you married me."

"Who *did* I marry?" She ascended several steps, putting more distance between them. She looked so slight in her pale pink dressing gown. Her breasts, high and shapely, rose and fell each time she took a breath. "Tell me please, I don't think I know."

"Not this." He gestured at the room around them.

"I don't care about *this*." She waved her hand as well. "I care about us."

His heartbeat jumped at her words. He had missed her. To see her standing in front of him, the vibrancy returned to her cheeks, filled him with relief. He wanted to be close to her again. Holding her. In bed with her. Not arguing. Stepping higher, he caught her hand and tugged her off the step, so that she stood beside him in his shadow. She peered up at him warily.

"I care about us too," he murmured.

Lowering his head...holding his breath...he dared to kiss her, softly at first, his lips just grazing hers, testing their pillowy softness. She smelled like soap and peppermint. When she sighed and leaned into him, he opened his mouth and tasted her, his tongue touching hers, sliding against her teeth in languid exploration, instantly lost to desire and wanting more. Her hands curled into the front of his coat.

Suddenly she pressed against his chest and broke away, *again* climbing several steps to stand out of his reach. He clenched his teeth, biting back a growl of disappointment.

"I can't think when we do that," she whispered, her eyes bright and aroused.

"That's what I was hoping for," he muttered.

"Dominick, there can be no more secrets between us," she said. "Is there anything else you haven't told me?"

He rested his hand on the banister. A cold numbness spread through his veins, slowing his heartbeat. She didn't realize what she asked. Her innocent mind couldn't even imagine the things he held inside, nor would he ever want her to.

"Secrets," he answered quietly. "Oh, yes, I've got more of them."

In his prior life, he had worn them with pride, like jewels in a crown. He was tired of apologizing for them.

"You married an agent in the bloody secret service, Clarissa," he replied, standing taller...and *prouder*. "Do you truly believe that by marrying me, you're entitled to hear them all?"

There was so much he couldn't reveal to her or to his family. Not to anyone. Things he had accomplished and survived that made him *proud*. Things that he'd witnessed that still *hurt* and haunted him. Most especially, the night Tryphena had died.

She swept higher, to the landing, and turned to look down at him. "Claxton said you were a security agent, describing you as—as...well, he said you were just a step above a Bow Street Runner. What sort of secrets would such a lower-echelon agent have?"

His eyebrows went up. "Is that what he said?"

He'd known Wolverton had understated his role in the service so as to downplay the ongoing mission in his household and to squelch questions. Still, the words pricked. They were an offense against his years of sacrifice for England and the many times he had faced danger, risking his life on his country's behalf.

He smiled, but without humor. "Well, by all means, believe him, if you like."

His innocent wife stared at him, her cheeks flushed. "Blackmer, you *were* a lower-level agent, weren't you? Or were you...something else?"

Something dangerous. That's what she wanted to know. Something else—yes, that would be him.

"I'm your husband now." He approached her, his palm skimming over the banister, wishing it was her bare skin. "That's all that matters."

"You *are* my husband." Her eyes widened, glazing over with tears. "And yet I feel as if I don't even know who you are."

He halted, her words echoing inside his head. A long moment of silence passed between them.

"I don't know if that will ever change," he said.

She shook her head. "Well, it must. Please understand, I don't want or need to know England's secrets—but I won't be kept in the dark about you. I need you to be my friend. My husband. My confidant. Not immediately, of course, but I should have some hope of your becoming so. Is it so wrong to want to be the same to you?"

He stared at her solemnly. "I understand that's what you want."

"But you don't know if you can give it to me," she whispered.

He did not answer, because he wouldn't ever be able to confide the one secret that bled from his past into their present, tainting each moment between them, so much so that last night he'd lain awake almost until dawn, certain he'd seen a ghost outside his window. All for the better. If she knew the truth, it would only tear them further apart.

"It's obvious, what you think about me," she said, her eyes going hard but sparkling with tears.

"What's that?"

"Not very much," she alleged. "That's what."

"That's not true—" he countered, stepping higher.

She gathered her skirts in her hands and backed away. "That I'm some silly child that you've been saddled with, unworthy of your thoughts and cares because most certainly they are too deep and complex for simpleminded little *me* to understand."

He stepped onto the landing and exhaled through his nose. "You're wrong."

She stood with the shadows of the long corridor at her back, untouchable, but so beautiful his fingertips throbbed from the desire to touch her.

"That a spoiled young woman like me is only good for shopping on Bond Street—" Her voice was thick with equal parts emotion and sarcasm. "—and going to parties and gossiping and wearing pink. Not to mention kissing and petting and sleeping with, now that we're married of course."

"Why would you say such a thing?" he demanded, furious and dismayed that she should perceive his feelings toward her in such a negative light.

Her shoulders stiffened. "Well, you can sleep alone. Forever, for all I care."

His gut twisted, hating that he'd made her so miserable and feeling as if he couldn't do anything about it. She turned away from him and escaped down the corridor toward her room. He wasn't about to let her go. He followed, only to find her door shutting in his face. He flattened his hand against the wood, holding it open.

"Clarissa..." he gritted out, between his teeth.

She pushed back, her face pale and her eyes bright. "You can't have it both ways, Dominick. Now let go of the door. Please."

He lifted his hand away and stepped back, and immediately she shut the door. He stood in the shadowed corridor for a long moment, tormented by her rejection, before proceeding to his room alone. There, a sea gale rattled the windows, a lonely sound.

He unwrapped the scarf from his neck and threw it aside before pacing in front of the fire. Did she truly believe the things she'd said? Had he made her feel that inconsequential?

He removed his coat and his cravat. Sleep alone forever? No. That simply wouldn't do. He wanted more from his marriage than separate rooms and a lonely bed.

Bloody hell, he wanted Clarissa.

He would...apologize in the morning. While he could not promise that everything would be perfect between them, he would do his best to reassure her of his intention to be a good husband and father and hope that eventually...that would be enough. He had been so impatient for her health to improve, knowing days would be better at Darthaven once he could see and talk to her again. Brighter for her presence.

Earlier tonight, dinner had been a silent, miserable affair, with only his mother prattling on about nothing in particular to fill the awkward silence. Afterward, restless, he'd walked the shore, allowing the cold and scent of brine to clear his mind. He looked toward the bed, with its fine linens and coverlet and hangings. Its comfort called to him, but he wasn't sleepy. What the hell time was it? He went to the table where he'd left his watch—

But it wasn't there. Instead, he found it on the windowsill. Odd, because he didn't recall leaving it there. Indeed, he *knew* he had not left it there. As an agent, it was a habit he'd developed over the years, knowing with a certainty where his belongings were at all times. Had someone been in his room?

Just the maid, he assured himself. Or even Clarissa, before they'd found one another downstairs. Why would they have touched his watch?

The temptation to escape Darthaven's walls called to him again, but he satisfied himself with the window. Unlatching the pane, he pushed it open and looked into the night.

A movement at the corner of the house drew his attention, an out-of-place shadow that on second glance he realized wasn't a shadow at all. A tall figure stood in a long cloak and wide cowl.

The muscles in Dominick's shoulders and his stomach clenched. Because of the distance, he could only discern a pale blur where the face should be. Yet he recognized something familiar.

Tryphena, his mind choked out.

No—it couldn't be. Tryphena was dead. He knew that without a doubt, because he had been there when she died and held her for hours after, refusing to believe.

The night and the fog played tricks, because in the next moment he blinked, and saw her no more.

Chapter Seventeen

The next morning, Clarissa sat in her chemise at her dressing table brushing out her hair. Nearby a fragrant bath steamed, one she hoped would sweep away the lingering effects of fatigue before she went downstairs for breakfast to formally meet Lord and Lady Stade.

In addition to making the best impression possible, she had every intention of being pleasant to Dominick. She'd lain awake for hours the night before...eventually coming to the realization she'd overreacted. Just a little.

It was just that she had always wanted a loving marriage and her own family. Her ideal had always been her parents' seemingly perfect romance and their happy, boisterous family, which had been changed forever by her father's death when she was just fifteen. Perhaps somehow she sought to re-create that happy picture for herself. But it was wrong to place such expectations so soon on a marriage that had started so dubiously. Trust took time, and she reminded herself she must not be overeager or make unrealistic demands on a man who still, by all accounts, remained a stranger to her.

She opened the wooden trunk against the wall and peered inside where her dresses had been carefully stored between layers of scented tissue. From the first moment, something didn't look right. She reached inside and, a moment later, let out an exclamation of bewilderment.

"What is it?" called Miss Randolph, rushing to her side.

Clarissa lifted the gown, which had been torn all to shreds.

Miss Randolph gasped. "Oh, my lady. What could have happened to it?"

It pained her to see the garment ruined. Her mother had chosen the dress pattern for her, with its pale pink tambour work on the bodice, sleeves, and hem, a month before her debut ball. Neither of her sisters had been invited along, because her mother had wanted them to have a special day together, just the two of them. In that way, each time she wore the dress, she relived that happy memory.

"I can think of only one explanation." Miss Randolph's lip curled with disgust. "*Rats.*"

"Rats?" Clarissa looked toward the corner of the room, almost expecting to see a swarm of furry backs and long tails scuttling to and fro. But would rats have gotten inside her trunk? While it wasn't locked, the latches and lid were very sturdy and secure.

Miss Randolph scrutinized the destroyed silk. "Given the age of Darthaven, I suppose we ought not to be surprised...although it makes no sense, seeing the obvious attention Lady Stade gives her household. Nonetheless, I shall inform the upstairs maid in charge, so that the rat catcher can be summoned forthwith."

Briskly she moved toward the bell pull.

Clarissa frowned. "But if it was rats, wouldn't the rest of the dresses be disturbed? Wouldn't there be signs of the creatures nesting inside the trunk and..." Her nose curled. "Other disgusting proof that they'd gotten inside? There is none of that."

Miss Randolph drew her hand away from the bell pull without having touched it.

"You're correct, of course." Miss Randolph appeared doubtful. Again she took up the remnants of the dress and held them up to the light. "But what else could have done this? It almost looks as if a blade cut the fabric."

Clarissa spoke her fear aloud. "It had to be a person, Miss Randolph. Someone did this deliberately. But the only people other than ourselves who have been in the room are Dominick and the maids. Why would any of them have destroyed my dress?"

Dominick wouldn't have. She'd tried his patience more than once, but she couldn't believe for even a second that he'd have done something so hateful. So disturbing.

"His Lordship should be made aware." Miss Randolph removed the destroyed dress and folded it carefully on a nearby table. "I'll have it here if he should wish to see it."

"I'll mention it to him this morning." Clarissa looked into the trunk and considered the dresses remaining inside. "Hopefully I have something else to wear in there. Something warm. It's so chilly here."

"Let us see what we have." Miss Randolph steered her by the shoulders to the dressing table and urged her to sit. Returning to the trunk, she removed several dresses and draped them over the nearby screen. "There is no damage to these. How very strange."

"I can't wear that one, I'm afraid," said Clarissa, pointing to a white Grecian-styled morning gown. "The skirt is so slender. Perhaps that one, with the higher waist."

Miss Randolph smiled at her dotingly. "I thought the same thing. We're seeing the first subtle changes, aren't we? Someone is already making himself known."

Clarissa touched her abdomen, where a small yet distinct change had transformed her shape—a small but obvious swell of her belly, where despite her being so repulsed by all food and drink for days, the child apparently thrived. "Indeed, I've started to show."

Her voice faltered with emotion. The baby that had turned her life upside down was very real now, and she couldn't be more excited about its impending arrival, though she wondered how she would feel... and how Dominick would feel if the child looked like Lord Quinn. She put the thought out of her mind. None of that mattered. She would love him—or her—unconditionally. She wished her mother and sisters were here to share in her happiness, especially Sophia, who would be giving birth to her baby soon. But that just wasn't possible, so instead she'd settle for writing them all letters this afternoon.

Miss Randolph's eyes twinkled back in the mirror at her. "His Lordship will be so proud."

"I hope he will be," Clarissa replied wistfully.

"Do you know I heard him just this morning in the corridor speaking with Mr. Guthrie?"

"What did he say?" Clarissa tensed, waiting to hear.

"Mr. Guthrie was going on and on about how exciting it would be if the child was a boy, and therefore an heir, but His Lordship said he didn't care if the child was a boy or a girl, that he would welcome either with equal enthusiasm because all children were treasures. You should have heard him, my lady, speaking so earnestly. I must confess it brought tear to my eyes."

And to Clarissa's as well. She could hardly speak for the emotions crowding her throat. Dominick had said those things this morning, even after they'd parted on less-than-ideal terms the night before. Miss Randolph lifted another dress from inside the trunk. "Why not wear the lavender today?"

She nodded. "The lavender will do nicely."

Once bathed and dressed, she went downstairs. Wan sunlight illuminated the vestibule, enabling her to see the intriguing room in far more detail than she had the night before. Her nose caught the alluring scent of toasted bread and bacon, and she followed it past the large dining hall, to a more intimate room at the farthest corner of the house. For days, the slightest aroma of food had turned her stomach, but this morning she was ravenous. Tall windows, dressed in scarlet curtains, overlooked the craggy cliffs and the ocean beyond, but she barely had a moment to appreciate the view. Hearing a raised voice, she paused outside the open door.

"Belgium," scoffed Colin. "Constantinople. How exciting and exotic. But all the while you should have been here. Home. Instead you shirked your duty to your family, leaving the full burden to Father and me."

"And a slew of stewards and land managers," Dominick answered calmly. "Duty to one's country is just as important."

A deeper, sharper voice responded now, most certainly belonging to Lord Stade. "For five years, yes. Seven, perhaps. But fifteen? No, I wouldn't agree with that."

Colin muttered, "It would be different if you were someone actually important, but I've not seen a single mention of your name in any of the papers. No treaties bear your signature. You never ascended to an ambassadorship. You just collected do-nothing appointments, as so many privileged elite do, and refused to come home."

Clarissa bit her lower lip, waiting to hear Dominick's angry response. How difficult it had to be for him to remain silent about his role in the secret service and not make them aware their assumptions weren't true.

Yet Dominick responded just as calmly as before. "I think you're just angry because you wish you'd done the same thing."

Clarissa smiled, relieved he remained unprovoked.

"It never bloody hell mattered what I wanted, did it?" growled Colin.

"You will mind your language in Her Ladyship's presence," Dominick's father warned.

"Please," begged Lady Stade. "All of you. Not in front of the servants."

"I won't be silenced," Colin responded in anger. "After all this time, I've earned a say."

Clarissa supposed that now was as good a time as any to enter the room. Besides, she was *very* hungry. Perhaps they'd all calm down once she entered.

"Good morning," she said brightly, announcing her presence.

For a moment they all stared at her in surprise. Then Dominick leapt up from his chair and proceeded toward her, looking freshly shaved and handsome. Behind him, the elegantly dressed, gray-haired gentleman at the head of the table also stood. Colin rose more slowly, his lips never relinquishing their scowl. Lady Stade, whom she had only glimpsed on the day of her arrival, smiled reservedly and reached for her teacup.

"I'm so glad to see you are improved." Dominick stepped closer, where he murmured more intimately, "Can you ever forgive me for last night?"

"Perhaps," she answered in a quiet voice, smiling...just a little, relieved that he cared enough to say the words, because it meant hers had been taken seriously the night before. "But I might require some convincing."

He exhaled, as if relieved by her words, and a heart-stopping, boyish grin turned his lips. Only he wasn't a boy. Her husband was a full-grown, virile man. "Convincing. Yes, I owe you that much, don't I, after being so—"

"Obtuse." She lifted her eyebrows.

He bit his lower lip, but his eyes shone with humor. "Obtuse. Yes, I can certainly be that."

"As can I," she murmured.

"Then we are two of a kind."

"A-*hem*," interrupted Lord Stade.

"Oh." Dominick's eyes widened. "For a moment I forgot they were here. Imagine that."

His smile turned decidedly devilish, and she smiled back at him—relieved that things could be good between them again, but knowing instinctively nothing had changed. Dominick could smile and laugh and be attentive, but the same guardedness hung in the back of his dark eyes. Would he always be a mystery to her?

Taking her hand, Dominick turned round to face his father. "My lord, after much delay, it pleases me to introduce you to my wife, Clarissa, Lady Blackmer."

The pride that warmed his voice did not escape her, and

for the first time she imagined how they must look to everyone else. She thought they made quite the handsome pair.

Lord Stade strode forward. "Clarissa. What a lovely name. How happy I am to meet you." He kissed her hand then rose up to scrutinize her face, but not unkindly.

"And you as well," she said.

"Come, come and sit at the table." Sweeping her away from Dominick, he tucked her hand into his elbow and escorted her to a chair.

"I am sorry to have arrived in such a sad state," she said. "Such was not my intention."

"We are all relieved to hear you are better. Come, sit," Lord Stade insisted, peering at her through dark eyes so like Dominick's. "I'm so glad you came down for breakfast. Perhaps now, in the presence of a young lady who is not their long-suffering mother, these boys will stop with their bickering."

Lady Stade spoke from her place across the table from Clarissa. "Are you feeling well enough to enjoy a bite of something?"

Though she smiled serenely, the strain from the ongoing argument at the table remained evident in her eyes.

While Clarissa was curious to learn more about the difficulties between her husband and his family, she hoped more than anything they would reconcile. She loved her own family so much, she could not help but want the same for her husband.

"A bit, yes," Clarissa answered lightly. "In fact, after days without eating anything of substance, I think I could enjoy a very large bite. Thank you."

Lord Stade chuckled, amused.

Lady Stade nodded—an almost imperceptible movement—to the footmen. A moment later, Clarissa sat in possession of a steaming plate piled embarrassingly high and a full cup of tea.

They were all being very nice, yet despite all the smiles and graciousness, a palpable undercurrent of tension weighted the air in the room.

"For someone who has been feeling poorly, I can't say I can tell," said her new father-in-law, returning to his seat. "What a bright spot you are on this dreary morning. A vision of health. It's apparent already that motherhood will suit you."

Lady Stade nodded, and adjusted a bracelet on her wrist.

"Indeed, she's ravishing," Colin said, one eyebrow going up as he stared at her admiringly, which she knew he did for the sole purpose of provoking her husband. "But then Blackmer's women always are."

Dominick's fist curled on the table beside his plate, and the wool of his coat tightened over his muscular shoulder. "Colin, I'd like to speak to you in the corridor."

Though his expression remained calm and controlled, there was something dangerous in the back of his eyes.

"I'd like to punch you in the nose in the corridor." Colin bit off a point from his toast and smiled, his gaze darting to meet hers.

Clarissa frowned at her brother-in-law. For a fleeting moment something changed and his smile faltered, but then with a sharp turn of his chin, the obdurate expression returned to his face.

Lord Stade shook his head at them both, before shifting his gaze to her. "Dear girl, forgive me if I don't apologize for their behavior. It's just very likely that I'd only be repeating myself five minutes from now when they do it again."

Dominick and Colin glowered like two loaded cannons pointed at each other.

Colin stood suddenly, and dropped his napkin to the table. "Well, I for one have had enough of this pretense of happy domestic life."

"What if it isn't pretense?" Dominick tersely replied. "What if some of us can have a real conversation, despite our differences, without mean-spirited hectoring and back-biting?"

Lord Stade stood, his attitude brisk as he glanced down at the large gold timepiece in his hand. "Actually, we've a standing appointment with the steward to review the tenant ledgers."

Dominick stood. "I'll join you."

His Lordship looked at his eldest son in surprise and, Clarissa thought, with hopefulness.

Colin bristled visibly, and suspicion clouded his gaze. "You weren't invited."

Her husband shrugged. "Until the attorneys have completed their vetting of the agreement for the transfer of Frost End, I find my schedule woefully uncluttered and myself in need of diversion."

Clarissa lifted her teacup and sipped. So that was how Dominick intended to speed things along. By imposing himself into territory his brother had long held, and in which he clearly took deep pride.

And just as she anticipated, Colin inquired of his father, "Did your attorneys say when the agreement would be finished?"

"Soon." His Lordship moved toward the door.

"Soon?" Colin repeated dourly, clearly dissatisfied with the vagueness of the response.

"If Blackmer wishes to attend our meeting with Mr. Kline, he is more than welcome."

"Wonderful," muttered Colin, who bowed curtly to the ladies and took his leave.

"I will find you later." Dominick bent and pressed a kiss to the top of Clarissa's head, an affectionate gesture that surprised and pleased her.

"Please do."

He followed his father out the door.

Clarissa looked at Dominick's mother. The older woman peered back, her lovely features drawn. At last, she smiled the sort of smile one smiled when one did not know what to say.

Clarissa ventured to break the silence. "I'm certain those three gentlemen will have a most enjoyable morning together."

At first, her ladyship appeared taken aback by Clarissa's reference to this morning's unpleasantness—but then she laughed in response. "Indeed, I must admit that I for one am grateful to have been left behind."

Clarissa smiled warmly. "Just because the gentleman aren't getting along at the moment, there is no reason why things should be awkward between the two of us."

Chapter Eighteen

Her Ladyship's gaze lifted. "No, there isn't. Lady Blackmer, would you like more toast? The footman can bring more from the kitchen."

"Thank you but no, I've quite enough here."

As soon as their voices quieted, silence filled the room. A delicate frown turned Lady Stade's lips, as she appeared to wrack her brain for something more to say now that the subject of toast had been thoroughly expended. Clarissa got the feeling Her Ladyship existed in an isolated state at Darthaven and did not have that many female friends. Certainly no sisters.

The marchioness spoke suddenly. "I intended to tell you, I wrote your mother, Lady Harwick, and let her know you were feeling poorly."

"Did you?" Clarissa responded in surprise, her heart already warming toward the woman.

She nodded. "I let her know the physician had visited

and pronounced you completely healthy, and assured her that until you recovered, you would be made comfortable and be well attended."

"I appreciate that very much."

Her mother would be very surprised, receiving a letter from a marchioness, and would very quickly deduce, if she hadn't learned already, that Clarissa had married an earl. While Clarissa knew Dominick cared little for the title and the respect it commanded, no doubt her mother would feel some measure of relief that her daughter had married more respectably than anyone had believed at the time.

"As a mother, I would want to know. I had a daughter, once." She smiled sadly. "Abigail. She died from a fever when she was fourteen."

"Blackmer told me. I'm very sorry for your loss."

"She was a happy, gentle spirit and I miss her still."

"I'm not a mother yet, but I think I understand. I have a brother who died, and none of us have ever truly gotten over the loss, most especially my mother."

"We never do, do we? When Abigail was alive...for that brief time in my life, I felt like I had purpose. To be honest, I've never known what to do with boys, other than to tell them to behave and...send them back to the nursery. Now sometimes I wish I could do the same." She chuckled ruefully.

"I can see why," said Clarissa, in an effort to be understanding though she thought being a mother to a passel of rambunctious boys would be a delight.

Her Ladyship nodded, her dark, perfectly upswept hair gleaming in the light. "Do you know, Blackmer's first wife and I never warmed to one another, which is something I always regretted. For my son's sake."

Clarissa traced her finger over the handle of her teacup. "I must confess, I don't know the first thing about her."

"Perhaps that is best. She was most...a most provoking creature."

Clarissa wanted to know more, but it seemed wrong to ply her new mother-in-law for information about her husband's first wife, when any revelations should come from him.

But wasn't it natural to be curious? She could not help but perceive Tryphena as her rival of sorts. If she and Dominick were so fortunate as to one day fall in love, would he ever be able to give her his love completely? Or had Tryphena, who remained faceless in Clarissa's mind, taken some part of his heart with her to the grave?

"Let's talk about something more diverting," said Her Ladyship. "I had intended to travel into town this morning to visit the modiste, who has sent word that she has received the latest style plates, from *Paris*, no less! Might you feel recovered enough to accompany me?"

"As a matter of fact, I find myself in need of some new dresses." Her body was changing, and soon even the loosest and most forgiving of her dresses would no longer fit.

She remembered the destroyed dress she'd discovered in her trunk that morning and considered mentioning it to Her Ladyship, but something kept her silent. She didn't want to throw the house into an uproar without discussing the matter with Dominick first.

An hour later, Clarissa peered out the window, taking in the sight of Ashington and its tidy thoroughfares and bustling streets. The Stade carriage, immense and black, drawn by a matching team of six and accompanied by liveried outriders, attracted the interest of pedestrians all along the way. Across from her, Lady Stade sat resplendently dressed in a wide-brimmed hat gleaming with purple satin ribbons and a perfectly matched fur-trimmed wool pelisse.

Within moments they arrived at the dressmaker's storefront and waited in the carriage until a shop assistant in a dark yet elegant green dress emerged to greet them and escort them inside. There, in a showroom decorated in the finest style, with marble busts, potted palms, and tasseled draperies, a statuesque older woman awaited them. Upon their crossing the threshold, she breezed toward them, her hands extended in welcome.

"Lady Stade. Welcome."

Several parties consisting of fashionably dressed ladies already occupied the room, sitting in large upholstered chairs beside tables strewn with patterns. Teams of assistants scurried about helping them make selections from all manner of fabric and trim. All faces turned toward them, but Her Ladyship acted as if she didn't notice. Instead she posed like a fashion plate, her head tilted at an attractive angle, her polished expression of greeting perfectly executed and distinctly haughty.

Lady Stade, it appeared, was in her element, but Clarissa understood immediately why she wouldn't attract many lady friends. In contrast, her mother and sisters would already be drawn into those other parties, asking about new engagements or babies, and sharing their discoveries of the perfect haberdashery shops.

"Mrs. Waite," said her mother-in-law. "Please be introduced to Lady Blackmer."

Mrs. Waite bent forward. "How thrilled I am to meet you. I received my latest packet of London papers just this morning and read of your wedding announcement with delight."

At Mrs. Waite's mention of the London papers, Clarissa's heartbeat staggered. She couldn't help but think of the questions and gossip her wedding announcement had inspired at home. Her catastrophic entrance to her ball. Her grandfather's illness. And the next day—she'd wed a man no one in her circle had ever heard of and immediately taken her leave of London. Together those series of events were a certain recipe for scandal. My, but how quickly her grand season had come to a shattering end. Thankfully, this morning London seemed very far away, as did anyone's opinion on her marriage. Here people congratulated her and life seemed almost normal. For that she was very grateful.

Mrs. Waite clasped her hands together. "Perhaps Lady Blackmer would like to keep the announcement as a memento?"

"That's very generous," she said. "Thank you."

The modiste disappeared through a door, and returned a moment later. Clarissa prepared herself to express disappointment to Dominick's mother that his title had been excluded from the wording of the announcement due to some inexplicable confusion. She knew, but could not explain to Her Ladyship, that at the time Blackmer had been very stubborn about telling anyone who he truly was because as an agent of the Crown, he hadn't wanted to draw undue attention to himself.

A moment later, she held a neatly cut square of paper in her hand, one that, to her surprise—and yes, her great pleasure—very properly announced the marriage of Miss Clarissa Bevington to the Earl of Blackmer.

She could only surmise that Dominick had taken it upon himself to ensure the correct details were printed for all of London to see. Apparently he did have some pride in his bloodline, or perhaps he had done it out of kindness to her, to spare her and her family scandal in the aftermath of their hasty marriage. Whatever the explanation, she welcomed it.

"How wonderful that you and Lord Blackmer have returned to Darthaven to make your home." Mrs. Waite smiled.

Clarissa carefully tucked the announcement in her reticule. "Thank you, but we're here only temporarily."

Lady Blackmer frowned and muttered beneath her breath, "Not if I can help it."

Clarissa looked at her inquiringly.

"I want you both to stay here, and for the baby to be born among family."

"That's very kind of you to say."

Just then, a young lady in a puce pelisse and hat, with shining dark curls peeking out all around, broke from the table beside the street-side window, a handkerchief raised to her eyes. She paused only to glare bright-eyed at Clarissa, before storming past and leaving the shop. A woman who appeared by similar coloring and features to be her mother followed after her, nodding politely to Lady Stade and to Clarissa as well before pursuing the young woman into the street.

In the awkward silence that followed, Mrs. Waite quietly said, "Poor Miss Brookfield. I'm afraid, my dear, you've broken her heart for the second time."

"Me?" said Clarissa, dismayed.

Lady Stade offered a tired smile, one that indicated her

to be half regretful and half amused. "Miss Brookfield declared when she was nine years old that Blackmer would be her husband one day, and I'm afraid, despite his lack of interest, she's never altered course."

Mrs. Waite added in a discreet voice, "She held out hope all this time, since hearing of the first Lady Blackmer's passing, and waited very patiently for his return."

"That's terrible," said Clarissa, knowing the pain of having one's heart broken. "How sad."

"Don't feel sorry for her," Her Ladyship said. "She was more in love with the idea of Darthaven than Blackmer. He realized that long ago."

Mrs. Waite nodded. "It's her own fault she's without a husband. A pretty, *spoiled* girl, but she waited too long."

In the next moment Clarissa and Lady Stade were swept behind a sumptuous velvet curtain to a more intimate and private room, where an array of exceptional textiles and trim had been laid out. There were also several stacks of cards bearing colorful fashion plates, organized into evening dresses, morning dresses, riding and travel, and, last, afternoon.

"I think this one for you," Lady Stade exclaimed to Clarissa, holding up a card that portrayed an evening dress of pink satin, trimmed with brilliant green cording. "I do believe pink is your perfect color."

"It is my *favorite* color," she answered with a smile.

"As it should be," declared Mrs. Waite. "I've the perfect pink lustring to show you, and a luxurious jade green velvet as well, which I believe would be the ideal complement, in the form of a spencer."

"Select whatever you like, dear," urged Lady Stade. "The dresses will be His Lordship's and my treat."

A gift from her new family—how kind. She was having such fun. The only thing that would make it better was if her mother and sisters were here. And maybe Dominick too. The idea of dressing not only to please herself but to please him held a certain allure. As she looked at the designs, she could not help but wonder which ones her handsome husband would find most pleasing. Before their marriage he had not pursued her, and they'd enjoyed no romantic courtship. They'd had only a few days of getting to know one another—and one brief experience of very passionate lovemaking—to carry them forward. After she gained weight and increased in size, would he still find her attractive?

A half hour later, Lady Stade disappeared into a fitting room to try on several gowns she'd ordered on a previous visit, and likewise, Clarissa was led behind another curtain where assistants helped her to disrobe. Now she stood wearing only her chemise and a loose velvet robe draped over her shoulders to protect her from chill. The style plates she'd chosen, at Lady Stade's insistence, were displayed on a small stand, to which the seamstress glanced from time to time as she took Clarissa's measurements— which were to be approximated and adjusted to some degree, in anticipation of the child she carried.

Someone pushed aside the curtain and entered, startlingly taller than anyone she might expect—Dominick, who held his hat in his hand, and his cheeks were flushed as if he'd been riding out-of-doors against the cold wind.

"There you are," he said, his expression guarded.

Without a word, the seamstress discreetly slipped from the room.

Her husband's eyes moved to the mirror and took in the

sight of her from head to toe, before settling hotly on her breasts. "I need to speak with you. Is that all right?"

"Of course you may," Clarissa said, flustered by his sudden appearance. Heat rose up her throat, into her face. She'd never had a man visit her fitting room before, but this was her husband.

"I came to town to purchase a curricle and two horses, so that we could get around without hiring from the livery or asking favors of my father, but saw the carriage outside and suspected Mother might have brought you here. I may already be too late to—" He flashed a brief yet heart-stopping smile. "—stop the damage."

"I'm happy to see you."

"Are you?" he answered quietly, moving to stand behind her, so close his heat warmed her back. Her pulse increased, seeing the look in his eyes. His gloved hand ascended the column of her throat and cupped her cheek. The leather, still cold from outside, made her shiver.

"I am," she said, turning her cheek into his hand, craving his touch.

"I didn't like what happened between us last night."

"Neither did I."

"Tonight will be different, I hope."

The intimate tone of his voice made her shiver.

"I do as well," she murmured, blushing, knowing what he was really saying was that he intended to make love to her again.

He bit his lower lip, smiling.

"Mrs. Waite gave me our wedding announcement from the London paper."

"Did she?" His thumb grazed her jaw.

"Are you the one responsible for its accuracy?"

"I am."

"Why?"

His eyes stared into hers in the reflection of the mirror. "I was still so angry then, but I suppose I had the foresight to understand it might be an important record one day for the child. And for you."

"Thank you."

His arm, covered by his dark sleeve, came round her, diagonal across the pale curtain of her chemise. His gloved hand spread over her hip, banding her tight against him in a pose of possession. Clarissa's heart beat faster, seeing his looming reflection, so much larger than hers. His body felt powerful and hard against her back, in thrilling contrast to her feminine softness.

"I didn't have a chance this morning to properly apologize," he murmured into her ear. His damp, warm breath teased her skin, sending a shiver through her. "I was angry with Colin for speaking with you the way he did and for goading me about Tryphena. I shouldn't have punished you for it, and I won't again. God, you smell good." He inhaled deeply, his nose behind her ear. "Your hair. Your beautiful skin."

At hearing his words, pleasure rippled through her, a fever heating her skin. "And then I goaded you about keeping secrets and about who you were before. I should not have. I'm sorry. I just want us to trust each other. For everything to be good between us."

"Good?" he whispered, pressing his mouth to the side of her neck. Opening his lips, he touched his tongue to the sensitive skin there, inciting a divine sensation that reverberated *everywhere*. She shivered. His hand spread over her hip, and he shifted against her. Still bound by his trousers, the hard ridge of his sex nestled between her buttocks. "Like this?"

The intimate tone of his voice thrilled her. Her body came alive. Her already swollen breasts tightened against the fine cambric. Between her legs, she ached, suddenly needful. With a backward tilt of her hips, she pressed against him, praying he wouldn't stop. He seized her closer, pressing an impassioned kiss on her neck.

"Yes," she whispered. "Like that."

The velvet drape slipped to the floor. Voices came near, women talking about gold plaiting to be used as decoration on a spencer. Clarissa held her breath, but Dominick did not flinch or break away, he only stared into the mirror, his gaze burning into her eyes, looking handsome and dangerous.

The voices grew distant again. His hand skimmed up over her rib cage to spread over her breast, caging her there.

"Trust this, Clarissa."

Through the thin fabric, his thumb stroked her nipple and she arched, her hands spreading against his thighs, in ecstasy, gripping him there.

"I will," she whispered. "Yes, I do."

He turned her around and, with a low growl, his mouth claimed hers, his hand coming up to brace her chin. Backing her against the wall, his thigh came between her legs, muscular and intimate, causing her to gasp. In one magical stroke his hands skimmed downward over her breasts and waist and hips to seize upward beneath her bare buttocks, his splayed hands lifting her firmly against him. She moaned.

"I want to make love to you," he murmured, kissing her neck.

"Here?" she said shakily, tilting her head back in surrender.

"*Now.*" His voice reverberated deep in his chest.

She wasn't certain how they would manage without discovery, but at the moment she didn't care. "All right, but we should hurry, I think."

With a hard kiss to her lips, he broke away, leaving her dazed against the wall. A chuckle rumbled from deep in his throat, and for a moment he closed his eyes and covered his mouth with his gloved hand before dropping it away to reveal a grin.

"I was rather counting on you to say no."

"Well, I didn't," she answered, her cheeks flushed.

"I know that," he answered, adjusting his coat. "You surprise me."

"Is that a bad thing?" she asked.

"Not at all." His gaze slid over her, hotly appreciative. Bending low, he snared the drape and, straightening, settled it over her shoulders. Using it as a snare, he fisted his hands in both ends and pulled her closer for another thrilling kiss. "But I shall leave you now, oh...so... reluctantly...so we don't cause a scandal. I just wanted to confirm with Mrs. Waite that I will settle the account for the dresses."

Another kiss, and he moved to the door.

"Actually, your mother has offered them as a welcome gift."

He paused midstep.

"I'm afraid I can't allow that." He came closer. "I hope you understand. Being that I've made such a stand for independence and self-sufficiency for the past fifteen years of my life, accepting such expensive gifts from her would be a contradiction and would not come without expectations in return. I will pay for your gowns."

"Nonsense," said Lady Stade, entering the room just then, followed by Mrs. Waite and two assistants bearing patterns and fabric, which they set out on the table. "Mrs. Waite is very expensive—"

"I can afford the dresses, thank you," he answered tersely, clearly offended at the suggestion he could not. "I know it's difficult for you to understand, but I have my own money that I have earned."

"—and there's one gown we've insisted on having done up exceedingly fast so Lady Blackmer will have it in time for the ball I'm throwing next Thursday in your honor."

"It's satisfying to know one is being listened to," he muttered, his dark eyes flaring.

Clarissa stepped behind the partition and dressed quickly with the help of an assistant, all the while listening to their voices on the other side.

"Don't be so dour, Blackmer. Consider the dresses a welcome gift to my new daughter. My dressmaking bill has always been paid by the estate."

"We both appreciate the gesture, but try to understand and respect my wishes. Mrs. Waite, do you understand, all of Lady Blackmer's accounts will be settled by me."

"Yes, my lord," the modiste answered.

Clarissa again emerged into their midst, buttoning the front of her pelisse.

Lady Stade said in a cool tone, "You know very well Mrs. Waite is going to do whatever I ask once you leave."

"I insist that she not."

The modiste efficiently gathered the slips of paper upon which Clarissa's measurements had been recorded and quit the room along with her assistants, leaving them to an awkward silence.

Lady Stade lifted her chin. "Thank you, Blackmer, for thoroughly embarrassing me."

He turned, crossing his arms over his chest and looking at her. "It is you who placed me in a situation where I was forced to respond."

"Is it so wrong that we want you to come home? That we want you to stay?"

"You want me to *submit*. This is no different than His Lordship's present tactic to delay his attorneys' progress in the conveyance documents for Frost End, so we'll be forced to stay." Dominick leveled a look on his mother. "And I'm sorry, did you say something about a ball?"

"Indeed, to be held next Thursday." Lady Stade lifted a swath of yellow silk and held it underneath her face, looking in the mirror as if judging its cast upon her skin. Frowning, she returned it to the table, clearly not finding it to her liking.

He replied testily. "You should have asked first."

"Where else would you be?" Her ladyship widened her eyes in dismay.

"At Frost End. I must travel there and assess the work that must be done before Lady Blackmer and I can take residence."

"Frost End. I hate even the mention of that place. I wish that old house would fall down! Why must you be so stubborn?" his mother said, her voice choked. She fished a handkerchief from her valise and pressed it to her eyes. "We were having such a lovely day until you arrived."

Clarissa hated conflict. And now Dominick had made his mother cry.

"Blackmer," Clarissa said softly. "Can't you let it go, just this once?"

He stared at her a long moment, his jaw tight and his expression regretful. "And to think I thought you understood."

"Wait—"

Returning his hat to his head, he nodded to them both. "Good day to you both."

He swept from the room.

Clarissa felt torn in two. She looked at Lady Stade. "I've got to go after him."

Lady Stade nodded, her eyes sad. "Do as you must."

Clarissa quickly tied her bonnet and rushed to the street where she found him already atop his dark horse, looking impressive in his saddle. She stood at the edge of the pavement, where he drew alongside, his expression grave and intent.

She reached up for his arm. "I want to understand. Please help me understand."

Reaching down, he lifted her up onto the horse, perching her on the saddle before him before tugging the reins and turning the animal around. Customers watched from the windows, as did Lady Stade and Mrs. Waite. As they rode away, he pressed his lips to the side of her temple, and she wrapped her hand around his elbow.

Two streets more, and he pulled alongside a livery stable where a simple black curricle waited, harnessed to two horses. He helped her across to the seat and dismounted before tying his mount to the back and climbing inside to take up the reins.

Moments later, they had left the streets of town and entered the countryside. They rode in silence, but the silence did not feel awkward. Indeed, they sat very close to one another on the bench, their hips and legs and shoulders touching, and he glanced at her often as they traveled down the road.

The air was chilly, but not uncomfortable with a blanket across her lap. Eventually they arrived at Darthaven, but instead of going to the house, he veered off in another direction, until he stopped the curricle on an overlook beside the ocean. Darthaven could be seen in the distance through a small stand of trees.

It was then she saw the lichen-covered stonework folly, nearly concealed, its rotunda suspended on six sturdy Grecian columns.

"I want to talk to you," he said. "And this is as good a place as any."

Chapter Nineteen

It's charming." After climbing down from the carriage, Clarissa walked toward it.

Dominick followed. Glancing over her shoulder, she saw he carried a carriage blanket—and a bottle of wine. "Where did you get that?"

"The carriage maker gave it to me as thanks for purchasing the curricle. I'm certain it's terrible." He grinned.

"Well, I for one am willing to give it a try."

She circled the folly. He set down the blanket and bottle and followed.

"It's beautiful here," she said, looking out over the ocean.

"It's my favorite place. I could always come here and forget everything else for a while, and just enjoy the beauty every direction I looked."

Taking her hand, he led her just inside the folly and picked up the blanket to spread it over the flagstones, interspersed with tufts of grass, and they lowered themselves to sit. He removed his gloves and, with his penknife, pried the cork off the wine. After lifting the bottle to his lips, he offered it to her.

"Not so terrible," he said. "More like berries than wine."

She removed her gloves as well and, taking the bottle, drank.

"But much better than expected," she answered softly, licking the sweet liquid from her lips. "Just like marriage to you has been. We do have a real marriage, don't we, Blackmer?"

"It's what I want." He stared at her evenly, in a way that made her heart skip more than one beat. Indeed, it seemed to stop altogether.

"I'm glad to hear you say it. But I want to know you better. To understand your misgivings toward your family. They aren't perfect, but neither are they ogres. They want you here. Why can't you stay, if just for a while?"

Resting his elbows on his knees, he clasped his hands together. "My father blames it on my grandfather. His father. For filling my head with what he calls nonsense. The old man and I had so much in common. More than my father and I ever did. He had so many stories from when he was a younger man, of life in the Navy and visits to foreign lands. He inspired my wish for a life of adventure."

"He sounds like a wonderful man."

"He was. But the instinct has always been there, inside me. As much as I love Darthaven, as a boy it smothered me. The rules and the walls and the lessons."

She touched his hand. "There's nothing wrong with wanting to live your own life. I admire you for that."

He looked at her lips and smiled. "Once I left for university, I never really came back, which infuriated my father, who expected me to return home and show an interest in ledgers and estate finances. For a time, I took work as a common sailor on several sailing vessels and visited the places my grandfather had told me about. I loved it. Being free. Going wherever I wished, with no one knowing who I was—until one day a diplomat whose son I'd gone to school with recognized me in a market in St. Domingo and recruited me into a different kind of adventure, one in the secret service."

"So that's how it happened. I wondered but didn't wish to pry."

"It was an exciting life while it lasted, but eventually I did feel it was time to come home and to make amends. I brought Tryphena here to introduce her to my family and suggested settling down and starting a family, which to me meant an end to our days as agents. To my surprise, she hated the idea and insisted we return to London, but I thought I could change her mind. Her personality changed then, with her behaving terribly, doing anything to provoke my parents, which only angered me and made me more determined that we would stay. The more time I spent with my father, discussing plans...the more time she spent with Colin."

"More time with Colin," Clarissa repeated, looking deeper into his eyes. "What are you saying?"

"I think you know."

"They carried on an affair."

He nodded. "To what extent, I don't know. But I caught them together, in a linen closet, kissing. Their clothing out of place."

The revelation stunned her. "I'm so sorry."

"I was too. And caught completely unaware. I knew she

was unhappy but always believed she loved me, and very passionately at that. Sometimes, it seemed, to the point of obsession. Her betrayal made no sense to me. It still doesn't."

"And Colin's?" she asked incredulously.

"Just as is now, he was angry then that I'd stayed away so long."

"But to betray his brother in such a way."

"It's why I left and I haven't come back. Until now, and only to ask for Frost End."

"You never told your parents."

He shook his head.

"Why not?"

"Because he's my brother. It would have destroyed them. And because Tryphena begged me to leave this place and return to London with her, where we reconciled...for a time."

She closed her hand over his, squeezing. "Now I understand."

Far below them, the ocean's waves curled and crashed.

"You don't ever talk about the baby," he said quietly. "Why not?"

"I don't want to make you feel awkward."

"Why would it?" He again reached for her hand and ran his thumb across her knuckles. "When I have accepted him—or her—as mine."

"Do you truly mean that?"

"To my soul." He pressed her hand to his chest.

Clarissa nodded, unable to speak for the emotion tightening her throat. "I suppose it's just so difficult for me to believe, that I should be so lucky. Another man would not feel the same."

"I want children. I would welcome a child into this marriage regardless of the situation. He or she is innocent and blameless and worthy of being loved without condition. But there's something more I must tell you."

"What is it?"

He picked up a stone and tossed it a short distance away. "I may not be able to father more children."

"Why do you say that?"

"Tryphena and I were never able to conceive. When we returned to London after leaving Darthaven, we saw a physician about it, who pronounced her barren." He shook his head. "Yet the realities did not support that diagnosis, and I came to believe the problem was mine."

In that moment, Clarissa felt very sad—which made her grasp on to hope. "But perhaps you are wrong."

"Perhaps I am wrong," he agreed solemnly. "But I don't think so. I'm sorry. I've upset you," he said, reaching to touch her face. "You want more children. Lots of them?"

"It's not that," she said with a shake of her head. "But I would want yours."

"Thank you for saying that." He leaned toward her and kissed her gently, consolingly.

Desire, tangled up with emotion, welled up inside her, and she kissed him back, sighing, needing him and wanting his touch with an urgency she hadn't expected.

His lips moved, and he let out a sound as his hand cupped her chin and he widened his mouth on hers, probing with his tongue. He gently pushed the straw bonnet from her head, running his fingers through her hair.

She sighed, leaning toward him as well, pressing her hand to the center of his chest. He turned his face aside and breathed near her ear. "Am I a savage for wanting to make love to you here, where I can breathe, instead of within those walls, where I cannot?"

His words thrilled her, and the idea of making love with him on a blanket in the out-of-doors thrilled her more.

"Then make love to me now." In anticipation, her breasts swelled inside the confines of her corset and she shifted closer to him, aware of a hunger between her thighs. His tongue traced her earlobe and, for a moment, his lips closed on it, sucking, as he eased her backward onto the soft blanket, his hands moving to her breasts, smoothing over them through her pelisse. She closed her eyes, surrendering to the paradise of his touch.

He murmured, "It's all I've thought of since that night at the inn, being with you again."

He unfastened her buttons, one by one, bending to kiss her as he undid the ones on her dress underneath. He gently tugged the soft, pleated cups down, baring her breasts, which grew fuller every day. Light and cool air tantalized skin that had always been kept covered, a sensual pleasure in itself.

"Dominick," she whispered, feeling as if he laid bare not only her body but her soul as well. He stared admiringly, his gaze burning so hot it took her breath away.

"I've never seen anything more beautiful. Except for your face, of course."

He bent his dark head to kiss her mouth, sweetly urgent as his palms grazed her nipples. She moaned in reaction, startled by the pleasure his touch inspired. His hand closed over a breast and squeezed.

"You're like that wine. Rich and sweet."

She sighed, his touch giving her such pleasure she

couldn't remain still. His words—private words, sensual words spoken between lovers—pleased her.

His fingertips smoothed over her face, her jawline, her mouth, making her feel adored and beautiful. Her lips opened, and she touched her tongue to the pad of his center finger. He exhaled raggedly and slowly . . . gently . . . slipped the fingertip into her mouth. Her lips closed around it, and she sucked, tasting his skin. A gust of wind swept through the trees.

"I want to see you. All of you."

His palms traveled up her stockings, over her calves, to flatten behind her knees. Her legs shifted and slid, one against the other, squeezing tight around the center of her swollen and needful sex, and the tapes of her stockings rubbed together. Her skirts made a soft, rustling sound.

"You're like a present I don't deserve," he murmured. "You do deserve me. And I deserve you."

His fingertips gently scored up her legs . . . lifting her petticoat and skirts . . . gathering them above her waist, leaving her thighs, stomach, and sex exposed. Cool air tantalized, in marked contrast with his heated touch between her legs.

"I love looking at you," he said, lowering himself onto his elbow beside her, still completely dressed.

That simply had to change, and quickly. She untied his cravat and, enticed by the smooth male skin she saw at the opening of his shirt, touched her lips there. His thumbs stroked between her legs, upward, over her swollen sex that felt torturously damp and tight.

"Dominick, please," she begged softly.

At that, he left her, quickly removing his coat. His hands returned to her hips, holding her, sweeping his hands up her legs and between her knees to press them aside, wider. She had never felt more vulnerable or exposed. His hand swept over her belly, over the gentle swell of her pregnancy that had become apparent there.

"You're beautiful."

His head lowered, and she tensed. His hair brushed against her thighs, and his mouth, open and hungry, fell on her *there*. She cried out in shock. In *pleasure*. The sound echoed off the stone canopy above them. He responded with a firm stroke of his tongue, and his hands gripped securely on her hips. She writhed, shattered by the sensual sensations his wicked kiss inspired, and reached for his head, his shoulders. Unable to reach him, she seized fistfuls of the blanket instead.

His shadow fell across her, and she watched as he dispatched the placket of his breeches.

"My cock is an impatient tyrant," he said huskily. "I can't wait any longer."

His *cock*, as he called it, jutted out from his body, darkly flushed and stiff like a cannon ready to fire.

"Then hurry," she said, wanting him.

She rose up to half sitting, feeling dazed and intoxicated, her breasts bared and her skirts at her waist, helping him tug the fitted breeches down his hips, sliding her hands over the heavily sculpted muscles there and along his abdomen. His shirt hung over his hips, his sex tented the linen. She pushed the garment up and instinctively wrapped her hand around his arousal.

He froze and groaned raggedly.

Then he closed his hand around hers, for a moment guiding her hand, showing her how to squeeze and stroke him to greater pleasure, the proof of which she saw when his hips moved and his head fell back in apparent ecstasy. Wanting only to please him more, the way he had pleased her so unselfishly, she kissed the swollen head and he jerked.

He bit out a curse. "Clarissa."

Wanting to deepen their intimacy, she dared even further, opening her mouth and taking him inside her lips.

"You slay me," he growled.

His hands came down against her hair, and he stroked her face, his thumb firm against her jaw, gently urging her to open her mouth wider, to accept him more deeply, which she did as best she could, still holding him at the base.

"I swear to you, I'm dying." Again he urged her to tighten her hand on him. "You can't understand how good that feels."

She slid her tongue along the length of him, testing the velvet-over-steel texture. The soles of his boots crunched against the stone floor.

"No more." His thumb pressed gently against her lower lip, urging release. "I'm going to lose control."

As he pulled away, his hands came down on her shoulders and he pressed her back onto the blanket again, then lowered himself on powerful arms so that his hips came down between her thighs.

Fascinated, she watched as he reached between them, stroking her between the white slash of her garters, while his sex hung heavy between them.

"Take me, darling," he commanded. "Take me inside you."

The afternoon light and the shadows inside the folly played erotically on their bare skin. There were no night shadows to hide their love play as she took hold of his rigid staff and guided him, pressing the swollen plum head to the place where her body begged for him most—

He let out a guttural sound and thrust, *hard*.

She arched, stunned as he filled her...stretching her, and with another sudden push of his hips—*deeper*...yes, more.

"So tight," he groaned.

"So...big," she whispered, her toes curling inside her boots. She squeezed his shoulders, and felt his muscles bunch beneath her palms.

He chuckled and groaned, and as he began to move inside her, he made other, deeper, more wolfish sounds. He grasped her thighs, her knees...brought her ankles behind his hips.

"Is that...good?" he asked, sinking deeper.

"Yes!"

The inside of the folly echoed with their voices and the sounds of their clothing and bodies shifting and sliding together. As his weight settled onto her, he pushed more deeply and she shifted in her efforts to accommodate.

"Ahh." He growled deep in his chest and stopped moving...only to dig the toes of his boots against the stone floor and rock into her more urgently until she cried out, stunned by pleasure.

"My wife," he whispered, his hands finding hers and stretching her arms above their heads, kissing her sweetly. "My beautiful wife."

His hips moved, slowly at first, then faster, delivering waves of pleasure through her womb with each advance and retreat of his sex. She tightened her thighs, pulling his powerful body closer, wanting to bewitch him and keep him there forever. Here there were no arguments, no secrets, and no past, only the now.

"Clarissa," he moaned.

Looking up, she found his eyes glazed and his cheeks deeply flushed. The same fever claimed her, as her body strove for some greater gratification, a paradise she instinctively knew existed just out of reach. He rutted into her, she clutching at his shoulders, learning she brought them both more pleasure when she matched his every thrust for thrust.

"Now." Above her his expression went stricken, yet in the next moment his lips spread...slowly...into a shocked sort of smile. Under his shirt, his muscles seized beneath her hands.

"Dominick!"

"Agh—" he groaned, his head going back.

She froze as a beautiful, throbbing heat flooded her womb—

And quickly transformed into something else, sweeping her into a soaring delirium. Her body clenched and pulsed around his member, finding its release.

She clung to him, startled and amazed, feeling that her spirit hovered high above the earth, tangled up with his. Slowly the sensations ebbed, and she floated like a feather, languid and spent, able to breathe again.

Dominick gathered her in his arms and held her tightly, breathing hard into her hair, his heart pounding against her breasts.

Then he rolled away, falling onto his back on the blanket beside her.

"Clarissa," he said, sounding amazed. "That was... indescribable."

"I did not know it could be like that." The breath rushed from her lungs and she lowered her head against his chest, listening to the heavy *thud* of his heart, never having felt this close to anyone ever before.

"Neither did I," he answered quietly.

His words made her happy. Deliriously so.

She sighed, wrapping her arms around him, and kissed his face—the hard planes of his cheeks. His masculine nose. His eyes. He had just confessed that something truly earth-shattering had taken place between them. She did not harbor ill feelings toward his dead wife but selfishly needed to know their lovemaking pleased him more.

"I can't wait to do it again," she whispered.

He laughed, deep in his throat, and she savored the rich sound in her ear. Reaching up, his hand touched her hair. "I for one am all for an early evening tonight."

She laughed as well. He rolled her onto her back and kissed her, urgently sweet, and then broke away to stand. She watched from the blanket as he fastened his breeches and tucked his shirt in.

Looking down at her, he tied his cravat. "You lying there like that . . . you're the most lovely thing I've ever seen."

She'd been so entranced watching him, she still lay like a wanton, tangled in her clothes, her breasts and thighs naked and exposed.

His eyes burning with renewed heat, he reached down and pulled her to her feet. His palms framed her face and he kissed her tenderly—then passionately, backing her against a column. His hands fell to her shoulders, holding her captive against the cool stone as his hot mouth descended her neck, and then her collarbone, finally devouring her breasts. She arched in response, surrendering willingly.

Catching her hand, he pressed her palm against the ridge of his arousal.

"Look what you do to me," he growled, returning to her mouth.

She did not pull away but boldly measured his size—which increased as she touched him.

"I could have you now, again. Here against this column," Dominick murmured.

"Why don't you?" she asked.

"Wicked minx," he teased as his hands deftly buttoned her dress. "It's getting colder and there are clouds rolling in."

"I hadn't noticed."

Just then a sharp gust of air swept through the folly, blowing leaves across the blanket. Clarissa shivered.

"Ah, see there?" Dominick pulled the open flaps of her pelisse together and buttoned those as well. He smiled, his hands settling on her belly, and his expression became serious. "So stop tempting me, and let me take care of you and the baby."

The day they'd married, he'd never expected to feel such desire and affection for her, along with the overwhelming wish to protect her and the baby.

Clarissa peered up at him. "Just as long as you let me take care of you as well."

He retrieved her hat, lowered it onto her head, and tied the ribbon the best he could. "There. If you don't take it off, no one can tell you've been ravished."

She laughed. But then he heard something. He turned his face to the side and listened. Horses' hooves on the road.

"Someone's coming."

Clarissa quickly pulled her gloves on and gave him a dazzling smile. "Thank heavens they didn't arrive ten minutes ago. We'd have given them quite the shock."

He left her to fold the blanket and pour the unfinished bottle of wine into the grass.

The rider appeared. It was Colin, and he rode close enough to speak.

"Hello, Colin," Dominick said.

Colin gripped the reins of his mount with his gloved hands. "Lady Blackmer has visitors waiting at the house. The Duke of Claxton. Also, a man he has introduced as his brother, Lord Haden."

Dominick's mood turned instantly dark. Claxton, here? Why?

Dominick saw Clarissa's face go white.

"Oh, no," she whispered. "The only reason they would have come so soon after we left London is if they bear bad news. Is it Wolverton?"

She rushed toward the curricle and Dominick followed.

Chapter Twenty

$\mathcal{Y}$our Grace," she said, rushing into the drawing room, fearing the worst. "Lord Haden. Tell me what has happened. Is Sophia all right?"

Sophia had miscarried their first child, but her sister's current pregnancy had seemed healthy from the start.

Claxton turned from where he stood beside the fire. He looked weary and travel worn. "On the contrary. Everyone is well."

"Even Wolverton?"

"He is actually very much improved," Claxton assured in a soothing voice.

Clarissa exhaled, relieved, and threw herself into his arms. "I'm so glad to see you. It feels like forever since Blackmer and I departed London."

"Am I invisible?" Haden asked, drolly.

"Of course not." Euphoric now to see them, she embraced him warmly as well.

Lord Haden was Claxton's younger brother, and while

he'd once collected scandals like Beau Brummell collected snuffboxes, he'd grown more serious of late and traveled much, after receiving an attaché appointment where he acted as a proxy for the duke in matters of foreign policy.

Lady Stade watched raptly from her chair. She had changed for dinner and looked fashionable and elegant in dark blue, thrilled to have a duke standing in her parlor. Lord Stade stood near the window, his expression one of interest.

"How long will the two of you be staying?" Clarissa inquired.

"We won't, I'm afraid." The duke tilted his head toward Lady Stade. "Although Lady Stade has already extended a very gracious invitation."

Lady Stade effused, "Unless you can convince them otherwise."

"I'm afraid that won't be possible," Haden added in a teasing voice, "being that he can't stand to be parted from the duchess for more than five minutes anymore."

Claxton threw him a barbed look. To Clarissa, he smiled. "It's true, of course. He just isn't supposed to say it here in front of everyone."

Clarissa smiled. "Why not stay the night and leave early tomorrow?"

"Of course you will stay the night," said Blackmer from the direction of the door, where he'd remained since they'd arrived. While his expression wasn't exactly welcoming, Clarissa took heart in his insistence that the duke and his younger brother remain. "It's already late and you won't make appreciable distance before it gets dark. I'll tell the footmen to bring in your things."

With one final look toward Clarissa, he quit the room.

Haden drifted toward the door, looking after Blackmer. "That longsword I saw on the way through the vestibule, is it Norman?"

Clarissa wasn't a fool. She recognized his obvious attempt to draw her in-laws away.

Lord Stade's expression brightened. "Indeed. It has been in her ladyship's family...well, since her Norman forebears invaded this fair isle alongside William."

"May I have a look?"

"Allow me to accompany you," His Lordship answered. "There are several other very ancient weapons you might also like to see. I can show them to you."

Claxton said to her, "Clarissa, is there somewhere I could speak with you alone?"

"Should I summon Blackmer?" asked Lady Stade, standing.

Claxton answered politely. "Just my sister-in-law, if you will. Family talk."

"Certainly," answered her ladyship graciously, moving to the door. "Take all the time you need. I must inform Cook we will have guests for dinner and ensure your rooms are prepared."

She left but did not close the doors, something that Claxton quickly remedied. When he turned toward Clarissa, she couldn't remain quiet any longer.

"Why have you come?" she asked.

"Are you well here, Clarissa?" he inquired, his expression intent, and reading her face.

"Yes."

"Are you happy?"

"Things were difficult at first." And still were, between

Dominick and his family. But she thought of the passion that had transpired between them just a half hour ago and answered, "But yes, I am happy."

Claxton moved to the center of the carpet. "I don't know if you were aware, but Blackmer made clear at the time of your marriage that he declined any marriage settlement that Wolverton might offer. At the time, I just thought he was making a show of his pride and trying to prove he wasn't a fortune hunter." He looked about the room. "I suppose now I understand why he could afford to make such a dramatic refusal."

"Pride, yes. He has a lot of that." Clarissa remained otherwise silent, not wanting to explain Dominick's complicated conflict with his family and his refusal to accept the privilege of his family's wealth.

"Even so, Wolverton insists on you receiving a settlement equal to that which your sisters received upon their marriages, to include an income-earning property that for now will remain under Wolverton's stewardship, until such time you decide to transfer that responsibility to your husband or manage those duties yourself." Claxton removed a thick leather packet from his inside coat pocket and placed it in her hands. "You'll find the particulars here, as well as any necessary bank letters. They are yours to do with as you wish."

Things were different between her and Blackmer now, and as soon as they were alone she intended to share the news of her settlement with her husband. Perhaps he would agree to use the funds to improve Frost End.

"Thank you for all you've done for me. It is so good to see a familiar face, but...you came all the way just to bring me this, when you could have sent a letter or other representative instead? Last month you ceased all official travel, to remain with Sophia as the time of the baby's birth grows near. And yet you are here."

"There is something more," he answered, his expression grave.

"Tell me then outright."

His gaze moved to the carpet. "Clarissa, the moment I heard the name Blackmer, I thought I recognized it, but I couldn't place it at the time. Not until after you were gone, and I made some discreet inquiries."

Inquiries. Given her husband's past with the secret service, and his wish to keep the more sensitive details of his role as an agent undiscovered, Clarissa felt immediately wary on his behalf.

"What sort of inquiries? Is Wolverton aware? Did he send you here?"

"He knows nothing of this. I feared the revelation of what I discovered and am about to impart to you would take a toll on his health. And please know Haden knows nothing as well, nor Sophia, nor anyone else. This conversation must remain between you and me."

He seemed so grave; she didn't like it.

"I know all I need to know about Dominick," she assured him. "For whatever reason, Grandfather trusted him, and so do I."

"I have learned something deeply troubling, and I must share what I know with you."

"He was married before. I know that."

"Just listen to me, Clarissa," he insisted, with an edge of command to his voice.

She sighed, anxious. Wishing Blackmer was there. "Go on."

"I was wrong about his role in the service, that he was a lowly security agent."

"I—I know that too, although he has not shared any of the confidential details."

"Well, I will—at least some of them, because you as his wife deserve to know."

"This doesn't feel right without him here." She glanced at the door, wishing Dominick would return.

"Once I have my say you are more than welcome to reveal whatever you wish about our conversation to him."

She exhaled, exasperated, and nodded. "Go on then."

He did not hesitate a moment more. "Clarissa, Blackmer's assignment to protect Wolverton was a demotion for him of sorts."

A demotion? She frowned. The revelation ruffled her own pride for some reason, on behalf of her husband, who instinct told her was highly competent in all things related to his intelligence service.

"How so?"

"Blackmer was once a member of a small but very elite company of foreign service agents who acted abroad, under a veil of utmost secrecy, on the direct orders of the Security Council—and the Crown."

"You are saying that he was a spy," she replied. She rubbed her arms and moved to stand closer to the fire, feeling a surge of pride rather than concern. "I surmised as much, but those matters are confidential, and he very much honors his vows of silence. Perhaps, Claxton, as I said before, we shouldn't even be discussing them here when he is not even in the room."

"He was not just a spy." He stared at her. "The group to which he belonged was a very small and clandestine one, much feared by England's enemies. But I'm afraid you're right, and that's all I can say as far as specifics."

"So why are you telling me this, with such a grave look on your face?"

"Because by nature these men are dangerous, Clarissa. Ruthless, and capable of following any directive without qualm or question."

She read between the lines of what he tried to say without actually saying it.

"You're telling me he was an assassin?"

"I'm telling you, he would have carried out any order." He continued, in a hushed tone, speaking of someone else: the man Dominick had been before they married. A cold and distant stranger, not the man she had come to know. She did not care what he had done in his prior life. He had acted out of duty, and for that she could only respect him more.

She closed her eyes, remembering the husband she'd made love to on an overlook by the ocean. A husband to whom she had given not only her body but her heart. She couldn't deny the truth.

She'd fallen in love with him. Completely. Consumingly.

"None of this makes any difference to me," she said.

If there was more she needed to know, then it must be Blackmer who told her. These were his secrets to share.

"Because you haven't heard everything. Clarissa, it's only right that you know what happened to bring about Blackmer's fall from grace. Something troubling that I wish we had all known before."

She reacted angrily. "So you could foist me on someone else? It's too late for that. I'm happy with Blackmer. More than happy, so you can just stop right there. I don't want to hear anything else you have to say."

"Foist you on someone else?" His eyes narrowed at that, discerning.

Only then did she realize her misstep. Claxton still believed she and Dominick had carried on an affair and that he was the father of her child.

She recovered as best she could. "I only meant if you'd known about Blackmer's past, you would have somehow found someone else to marry me. I wouldn't want that. As I said before, I'm happy with my husband, so just stop there and don't say anything else."

"My conscience demands that I must," insisted Claxton. "I'm gravely concerned because I fear this marriage has placed you in a position of danger."

She shook her head. "In danger, from Blackmer? That isn't possible."

That afternoon, he had bared his soul to her. He looked forward to the baby's birth with such joy and wanted to be a father. No. Whatever Claxton thought he had discovered, it meant nothing to her.

Claxton responded with a degree of emotion he rarely displayed to anyone other than her sister. "It *is* possible, I'm afraid. You must hear me out and then decide whether to leave here with me tomorrow or to stay. Your sister and everyone else are going to Camellia House to await the birth of the baby. It's a short distance, so Wolverton is traveling there as well. You can state that as your explanation to leave."

"To *escape*. That's what you mean to say." She gasped, taken back. "And then what?"

"And then you don't have to see him ever again."

"There is nothing that would make me want to leave him."

"His first wife—"

"Tryphena," she whispered. "Yes, I know, she died. I also know she was an agent as well."

"Someone killed her."

Killed. The word meant something very different than "died," as if by an accident or unfortunate misstep. "Killed" suggested an untimely death. And violence, she feared.

"Just tell me," she whispered. "Tell me whatever it is you have to say, so we can be done with this."

Claxton's lips thinned. "The whole matter is shrouded in secrecy, and I can locate no one willing to reveal the truth of the details, but, Clarissa, Blackmer most certainly had something to do with it. They were estranged at the time and, by all accounts, on very poor terms. I could not remain in London knowing you were possibly in danger."

"You're saying that Blackmer killed her."

She recoiled, angrier now at Claxton for all but accusing her husband of murder. It wasn't true. She didn't believe it for one moment.

Claxton's cheeks tightened with tension. "What I'm saying is that you have married a very dangerous man."

At that moment, the door opened and Blackmer entered the room, tall, lithe, and silent, his eyes dark with shadows.

"Pardon the intrusion," he said, entering a few steps more. "But I do believe I should be included in any closed-door discussions you might have with my wife."

Clarissa looked at him, clearly startled by his entrance. Startled. Why?

"These are private family matters," Claxton replied haughtily.

Dominick raised an eyebrow. "That's interesting. I thought *I* was Clarissa's family."

"That remains to be seen," the duke replied, his voice bearing a distinct edge.

The muscles along Dominick's shoulders tensed and his lips parted to let loose a blistering response—

"*Claxton,*" Clarissa intervened, with a sharp glance to her brother-in-law. "Blackmer is my husband. He is indeed my family."

She looked at Dominick with a smile that didn't reach her eyes, clearly attempting to instill a more conciliatory tone into the conversation. "His Grace brings news that Wolverton's health improves."

"I'm relieved to hear that," he answered, his sentiment sincere.

"As am I," answered Clarissa.

But something wasn't right here. He'd interrupted something tense and suspicious that still hung in the air, weighting the mood.

He pinned his gaze on Claxton. "You left the duchess, in her advanced condition, and traveled four days to deliver news that could have been sent in a letter? And delivered such happy news behind closed doors, no less, ensuring no one in my family overheard?"

Clarissa crossed the room, coming to stand at his side. She touched his arm. "He's also delivered the details of my marriage settlement."

Blackmer's gaze fixed on the duke's. "I already told you, I don't want Wolverton's money. Nothing has changed."

The duke answered, "You made it clear last time we spoke that you recused yourself from such matters, which is why the bestowals are in Lady Blackmer's name."

Blackmer sensed Clarissa's torment. For her benefit, he quelled the demands of his pride. "That is an acceptable arrangement for me."

Clarissa looked relieved at his words.

"Thank you." She squeezed his arm.

She was trying so hard to keep things friendly between him and the duke, but something had changed in the way she looked at him. He saw wariness in her eyes, and perhaps even fear.

Blackmer addressed the duke. "Your Grace, your chamber is ready if you would like to rest from your journey before the evening meal. My mother is waiting with Mr. Guthrie, our butler, to show you up."

"I would indeed like some time to recover," Claxton said. He proceeded toward the door and said to Clarissa in a quiet voice, "Haden and I will depart in the morning. You have until then to decide."

With that Claxton left the room, to be met by Lady Stade and Mr. Guthrie in the corridor. From where she stood, Dominick heard his father explaining the significance of a wall hanging to Lord Haden.

Blackmer closed the doors again, committing himself and Clarissa to silence.

She pressed a hand to her chest, as if to calm a rapidly beating heart. Her eyes were wide and fixed on him.

"You have until tomorrow to decide what?" Dominick asked.

"He asked if I would like to return to Camellia House with him and Lord Haden. Sophia and everyone else are going there for the next month to await the baby's birth."

No. His Grace had come here to tell her something. Something that had upset her. There was only one thing it could be. Why drag this miserable conversation out? Why not tear the bandage from the wound quickly, so he could get on with bleeding to death?

"He told you I killed Tryphena, did he not?"

Clearly, the bluntly spoken words shocked her. Her lips parted on a gasp, and she blinked away tears. His heartbeat faltered. He had no wish to hurt her. These dark tragedies were not her own, but his.

"I don't believe him." Clarissa touched his forearm, trying to draw it from where it crossed over his chest, as if trying to uncover his heart. "You could never have done such a thing."

He couldn't bear her touch—not when he craved her so much. He jerked away.

"That's where you're wrong." His gaze went flat and his voice, hollow. "Because I did."

He didn't want to see the horror in her eyes. Turning, he threw open the doors and exited into the corridor. Clarissa's footsteps followed him and she caught his arm.

"You can't just say something like that to me and walk away," she choked out.

He laughed, low in his throat, an ugly sound. "No, I think that quite does it. There is really nothing more to say."

Everyone stopped where they were in the vestibule and stared at them. His mother and father with expressions of concern. The duke only stared, not bothering to conceal his disdain and suspicion.

"Blackmer," said Clarissa. "Please come back and talk to me."

Talk? He couldn't talk. He couldn't tell her what had happened that night. About the blood. About Tryphena's screams. Of how the instincts that had advanced him to the highest levels of the foreign service had, in one pivotal moment, failed him so shatteringly.

He glared down at her hand on his arm until she released him and stepped away.

Stopping only momentarily to claim his coat and gloves, he walked out the front doors of Darthaven, onto the grass and to the stables. There he commanded that his horse be saddled, his temper so dark the stablemen stumbled over each other to do his bidding. At last, he rode.

He rode away from Darthaven, his mind as numb and dark as the night that fell over the earth. Not knowing where else to go, but knowing he couldn't go back, he returned to the folly where he had made love to Clarissa, and dismounted. After tying his horse to a column, he collapsed onto a bench and stared out over the sea. In the distance, he saw Darthaven's windows lit with firelight. His family and their guests would be having dinner now. How awkward the conversation must be, without him there, but not as awkward as if he were.

He'd known he wasn't suited for marriage, not after Tryphena had destroyed him. Yet when he'd looked into Clarissa's blue eyes, he'd started to believe that at last the past could be forgotten. That he could care for someone— *love* someone—again.

He should never have brought her here. He should never have married her in the first place. He should have slipped away that first night and forced them to marry her off to Havering or some other trusted family friend.

He closed his eyes, knowing it was better to let her go. To release her from the darkness that would never let him go. He would grant her a formal separation. Returned to her family, she could have the baby in a place of support and love, and find some measure of happiness that she would never be able to have with him.

The wind blew colder, and he welcomed its numbing effect. Perhaps he would stay there all night, because tomorrow morning how could he watch her climb into the carriage with Claxton and Haden and leave him forever? He couldn't. Hours passed, and a deeper cold crept inward from the sea.

The hell with sleeping there all night, on a cold hard bench. Everyone would be abed by now. No, he wouldn't go to his chambers. It would be torment to be that close to her. In a residence the size of Darthaven, he could find a room or at least a corner in which to pass the night. He mounted his horse and rode toward the house. He stared at her darkened window, knowing she would be asleep now. And yet something drew his eye to the side, to his window. A movement or a shadow. His heart struck a dark chord, remembering another evening when he'd seen something he could not explain. Tryphena. But of course he had *not* seen her. Perhaps just like that night, though, the darkness played tricks on him, because as hard as he stared, he perceived nothing more.

Why did his mind react so suspiciously? No doubt he had seen a servant stoking his fire before bed, or . . . perhaps Clarissa waiting for his return.

Inside, he passed through the kitchens, snaring a piece of cold chicken from the larder and devouring it as he strode down the darkened corridor. Seeing the staircase, dimly illuminated by light of a night lantern in the vestibule, he paused. He hadn't intended to go upstairs, but . . . there had been that movement in his room. His curious nature . . . his intuition couldn't let it go.

After dropping the bones into the footmen's trash receptacle, he climbed the stairs. Opening his door, he slipped silently inside. Just as any other night, the maid had left a small fire burning on the grate and laid out his nightshirt. Everything appeared in place. So, yes, perhaps it had only been a servant he'd seen from outside.

He crossed the carpet, going to the window. Pushing aside the drapery, he scanned the dark landscape and then the space closer to the house.

His heartbeat staggered to a halt, seeing her.

Her. Whoever she was.

She stood in the same place as the time before, her cloak rippling in the wind. He turned and ran, throwing the door open and racing down the stairs. Outside, he took the corner, his boots thudding over the ground, his muscles straining.

She wasn't there now, but he spied her in the distance, near the trees where she disappeared into the sheltering darkness. He pursued her, but a pale flash caught his eye. Something tumbled across the grass toward him, carried by the wind. He slowed, retrieving a piece of folded parchment.

He stared down and made out the words on the page as best he could in the dim moonlight.

They were familiar, long-forgotten words, written in Tryphena's hand. How could that be? A love letter she'd written to him in the early days of their marriage, in the most passionate terms.

. . . a love so strong, even death couldn't part us.

Nothing made sense. Who had he seen, and how had they gotten this letter? His past and his present twisted into one. Just as Wolverton had feared his own valiant past as an agent decades ago had brought about a retribution plot by an old adversary and a death sentence for his heirs, Dominick now wondered which enemy—or friend— sought revenge against him.

He felt sick. He felt...afraid. But not for himself.

Why now? The answer came to him clearly.

Because at last he had moved on from the tragedy, or at least so it would appear to an outsider looking in. He had remarried and returned home to start a new life.

But he wasn't one to be terrorized by "ghosts" in the night and reminders of his past. If someone wanted to torment him about Tryphena's death...to hurt him...to demand he forfeit something he loved...

The only way to truly destroy him would be to—

His heart seized and his blood ran cold.

It would be to hurt Clarissa.

Turning, he strode toward Darthaven, crushing the letter into his coat pocket. Then he ran.

After entering the house again, he climbed the stairs and raced down the corridor and found Clarissa's door locked. Heart pounding, he entered his own chamber and cut through the dressing room. Miss Randolph wasn't there. Perhaps, as he'd suggested to Clarissa, she had taken to sleeping in her own room in the attic.

Clarissa would be alone.

Alone and unprotected.

The goddamn letter. That woman in the night.

If someone had hurt Clarissa—

Chapter Twenty-One

*C*larissa awakened to large hands seizing her. She saw only darkness, and the blur of the bed canopy. She cried out, afraid—

But then saw his face.

"Blackmer?"

He held her by the shoulders, breathing hard, as if he'd been running. Releasing her, he tore the covers away. The cool air of the chamber chilled her skin. His hands—so cold!—moved over her, everywhere, too roughly. She gasped, shocked by the touch. It was as if he were searching for something. Searching her neck and breasts and torso for any sign of...what?

"What are you doing?" she demanded, near tears, her emotions both angry and relieved. "Where have you been all night?"

After coldly telling her he'd killed his first wife, he'd left without explanation and hadn't returned. Dinner had been a miserable affair, with Claxton and Colin remaining largely silent and Lord Haden doing his best to entertain them with stories from abroad, while Lord and Lady Stade stared at the door and out the windows. As had she.

And now here he was, tearing at her clothes—but not in passion. In some sort of desperate rage. Had he gone mad?

He stilled above her.

"I'm sorry," he muttered. He exhaled and closed his eyes as if in relief. "Go to sleep." Rolling, he collapsed onto his back, his head on the pillow beside hers. He stared up at the canopy. "Go back to sleep."

Turning on her shoulder, away from him, she lay rigid and awake, listening to his breath grow calm. But she couldn't just go to sleep.

"Did you love her?" she asked. "Blackmer, I need to know."

"Yes," he said quietly.

"Did you mean to kill her?"

A long pause filled the space between them.

"No."

"Then I'm sorry," she whispered, unsettled that she could not even imagine the lost woman's face. "I'm sorry, Blackmer, that she is dead."

"I don't know how to answer that," he said. "If she was still here, I wouldn't have you."

She lay awake a long time, torturously aware of him beside her. Eventually she slept. Sometime before dawn she awakened to see him still there, lying atop the coverlet still clothed in his breeches and shirt, his eyes closed and his breathing even.

Did he sleep? She did not know. She didn't care. Even angry as she was at him for leaving her without answers, she wanted him there.

* * *

Early the next morning, Clarissa stood on the front steps of Darthaven, bundled against the chill. A pale fog spread across the grounds, obscuring the overlook and the high stone wall that encircled the estate. The side lamps on the carriage glowed orange in the hazy blue light, and the duke's liveried outrider climbed into his saddle and urged his mount to a place in front of the six horses snorting and stamping in their harnesses.

"I don't want to leave you here." Claxton stood on the step beside her, looking down, his expression stern. "If Sophia knew the situation, she would insist that I bring you home."

"Then I appreciate that you at least understand that I am a full-grown woman, and capable of making my own decisions."

She'd be lying to herself to say a part of her didn't want to go with him. To be with Sophia when the baby arrived, to take part in her sister's joy but also to learn more about what the very near future held in store for her as an expectant mother. But to leave Darthaven now would only weaken an already challenged marriage to Dominick. She had to remain and try to learn the truth of what happened with Tryphena, so she could understand the tragedy of his past that threatened to tear them apart.

"If you change your mind, send word and I will come posthaste to bring you home."

"I *am* home, Claxton," she assured him, and herself. "Home is here at Darthaven, or wherever Blackmer may be. Please give everyone my love."

At that, he nodded, still looking regretful, and bent to

press a brotherly kiss to her cheek. Haden, who had been standing at the bottom of the stairs, ascended, hat in hand, and did the same.

"Good-bye, Lady Blackmer." He smiled handsomely.

"Good-bye, Haden." Just then a cold gust of wind struck, and she gathered her thick wool shawl more closely around her. Beneath the warm covering, her hand instinctively rested over the baby. "Truly, I can't believe some beautiful girl hasn't stolen your heart. I scour every letter from Sophia, always certain that I will see that news."

He tapped his hat against his leg. "When the time is right, I suppose."

"Sometimes love happens even when the time is not right." She smiled, despite the heavy weight in her chest.

"He's lucky to have you." Hayden lifted his hat in adieu and descended to the carriage, where Claxton waited. A movement out of the corner of her eye caught her attention—Dominick descending the stairs. After Haden climbed inside, he said something to Claxton she couldn't hear. Whatever it was, she determined it wasn't an apology. Her husband stood tall and broad-shouldered, eye to eye with the duke.

Claxton listened, intent, and responded in a similar fashion, after which time he too climbed onto the folding metal step and, with a final look over his shoulder at Clarissa, disappeared inside. The carriage rolled to a start, and set off through the fog and eventually through the gates.

Blackmer climbed the stairs to stand beside her. "Why didn't you go with them?"

Looking toward the house, she saw Lord and Lady Stade return inside, as did the servants.

"Because I *didn't*," she answered earnestly.

"Perhaps you should have," he said in a cold tone.

"Dominick," she cried. "Don't push me away. Not now. Not after yesterday at the folly."

"Now that you know about Tryphena, how can you stay?" He grasped her by the arms and backed her against the stone banister. "Tell me, because I don't understand."

She tilted her face, looking up into his eyes. "Because you told me you didn't intend to kill her, and I believe you. And because I know you would never hurt me or the baby. Dominick, I trust you and I belong here with you—"

He seized her close, one hand coming up into her hair, and kissed her. She made a sound against his lips and brought her arms around his shoulders, pulling him tight, cleaving against him. The wind gusted powerfully, tugging her shawl free to ripple around them.

"I don't deserve you," he whispered, pressing a kiss to her hair.

"I'm ready to go to Frost End," she said, resting her cheek against his chest. "For it just to be you and me, away from all of this, where we can start new."

The sound of approaching horse's hooves brought the doors swinging open and a footman to the stairs. Clarissa tore her attention from Dominick long enough to see a man in a beaver cap and belted wool coat and boots cantering up the drive.

"Speaking of Frost End," Dominick murmured as the man dismounted. "With everything that's happened, I forgot to inform you Mr. Galbraith, one of Father's land agents, would be here this morning. He's come to inform us as to the condition of the house and the estate."

* * *

"I'll just lay out the drawing so you can follow along as I provide details," said Mr. Galbraith as he unfolded a large square of parchment.

Dominick's gaze swept across the images on the paper, only to rise and find Clarissa at the other side of the table. She peered down, helping Mr. Galbraith spread the drawing flat, oblivious to his attention.

Mr. Galbraith continued, pointing at the drawing. "The barns...the large one here, and the smaller one just beside it, are in surprisingly sturdy shape. They will require a bit of work on the roofing, and fresh dirt and hay, but that is all to start."

"That's good news," Dominick said quietly, with another look at Clarissa, who appeared radiant and hopeful. Light from the window bathed her profile, painting her tresses gold.

"Which brings me to the house itself." Mr. Galbraith's voice dipped noticeably, and he winced. "The roof is compromised here, and here, with sagging frame and shingles, which means there has been some degree of intrusion by the weather, various fowl nesting in the rafters, and other creatures."

Clarissa threw him a worried glance.

Mr. Galbraith added, "Before I can recommend occupying the premises, there would need to be repair to the roof and ceilings and the plasterwork. And, of course, everything would need to be painted, and the floors refinished. Draperies, furniture, and whatnot."

Dominick inquired, "Given the necessary repairs, how soon do you think until we could take residence?"

He didn't have the papers conveying possession yet but wanted to proceed with repairs regardless.

"Given the approach of winter, it might be spring before all the work can be completed."

Clarissa pointed at the drawing. "Could we not make ready the smaller wing of the house and the kitchen, and simply patch the other until springtime arrives?"

Mr. Galbraith pondered her suggestion for a moment before nodding. "That's certainly a possibility. I would urge you, my lord, to visit Frost End and see for yourself the conditions I describe, and that way we can discuss which work should take priority."

"I could come along as well," Clarissa offered. "I'd like to see for myself."

Mr. Galbraith looked between the two of them. "As the house stands now, it's not at all hospitable for a lady, and unfortunately there are no suitable lodgings in the village. His Lordship and I would more than likely pass the night in the barn."

Dominick saw Clarissa's disappointment at the prospect of being left behind.

"I've no particular aversions to barns," she answered with a shrug.

"No," Dominick said, though he admired her resolve. "Most emphatically no. I won't allow it. Most especially not while you're carrying our child. I could be back in three days."

"Perhaps four, sir," suggested Mr. Galbraith, his tone apologetic.

Clarissa nodded, and sighed. "Just so you're back in time for your mother's ball."

* * *

That evening they supped in Dominick's chamber. He looked across the small table at her. She had come *en dishabille*, her hair pinned up loosely and wearing a tantalizingly sheer dressing gown. Likewise he wore linen trousers and a loose shirt. It seemed all it took for him to be aroused was to be alone with her, and knowing they would pass the next four days apart only inflamed his desire.

"I've asked Miss Randolph to sleep in your room while I'm gone."

"In my room?"

"Yes, and to lock your doors at night."

"Why?" Her brows gathered.

"I don't want to alarm you, but there've been several strange occurrences that make me believe someone holds a grudge against me about Tryphena and may be trying to...I don't know, send me some sort of message."

Her expression grew serious. "What kind of message?"

"I'm not sure. But someone has been inside my room and moved things." He stood and pulled the letter from his desk. "And twice I've seen a woman outside my window, wearing a long cloak and hood. Clarissa, I know it wasn't Tryphena, but in the dark it looked like her. I went to investigate and found his left behind." He handed her the letter.

Clarissa read a few words and blushed. "A love letter."

"From a long time ago. I don't know why anyone would have it."

Her heart beat faster. "Why would someone do this?"

"I've been trying to decide that. I think perhaps it's just a servant who may have known her when we were here before and taken the letter from our things, or perhaps even Colin trying to cause trouble. While there is no reason to suspect danger, I'd like you and Miss Randolph to be mindful while I'm gone."

"I need to show you something." Clarissa stood and went into the dressing closet between their rooms. After a moment she emerged holding something pink in her hands, which she lifted up and released so that it could fall open for his viewing. A dress. A destroyed dress, ripped into shreds.

"What happened to it?" Dominick stood, taking possession of the garment and examining it more closely.

"I don't know and neither does Miss Randolph," she answered quietly, moving to stand beside the fire. "At first we blamed rats, but it was secured inside my trunk and nothing else was disturbed so that explanation doesn't make sense."

"When did this happen?" He set the dress down.

Clarissa looked into his eyes. "We noticed it yesterday morning. But I've been ill, and hadn't been wearing any of my dresses, so I suppose it could have happened before then, any time after our arrival. I don't know."

"I'm going to speak with Mr. Guthrie in the morning before I go and let him know about the dress. You'll have a footman in the corridor outside your door at night and to escort you wherever else you may go."

She returned to the table and sat. "You needn't make such a fuss. Nothing else has occurred. As you said, it's likely just a servant who felt some attachment to her, or Colin acting out in anger."

Moving closer, Dominick tilted her face up to look at him. "Just while I'm gone. Otherwise I wouldn't be able to leave you. The thought of someone touching your things...of someone touching you...makes me feel—"

"Protective?" she said.

"That's a nicer word than I'd have used," he growled, low in his throat.

She reached up and rested her hands on either side of his hips...and slid them beneath his shirt, over the hard plane of his stomach. In response to the sensual touch, his sex grew large and apparent against the linen of his trousers.

"I might need persuading."

He bent and kissed her, his hand beneath her chin while his tongue thrust deep into her mouth. She tugged at the tie at his waist until the garment fell to his ankles. He closed his eyes, breathless, as both of her hands closed on his member.

He let out a deep-throated groan. "I can do that."

Before dawn the next morning, Clarissa helped Dominick dress. At his insistence, she went no further than the threshold of his chamber.

"Go back to bed," he murmured, kissing her one last time before he closed the door.

She drew away, somehow unsettled to have seen the shadowed outline of a footman standing watch in the corridor outside her room. Only then did she realize Dominick must have slipped away from her at some time in the night to make arrangements for her increased protection.

Later that afternoon, she returned from a dress fitting in town with Lady Stade and climbed the stairs. Her faithful footman, a burly lad by the name of Philip, following some distance behind. His protection had been so discreet throughout the day that her ladyship hadn't noticed him. For that Clarissa felt grateful, because she didn't feel like explaining him when it might be her ladyship's younger son who made his attendance upon her necessary.

Miss Randolph met her at the door, and took her hat and gloves.

"I don't remember dress fittings ever being this tiring," Clarissa laughed.

"It will be the same every day, for a time, I venture, regardless of whatever activities you undertake, and we both know why."

"Yes, the baby. Which makes the tiredness no bother at all."

"Perhaps tonight, forgo the evening meal with His Lordship's family. Take your meal here in your room and retire early."

"I think I will."

Besides, she had no real wish to be in Colin's presence after hearing how he'd betrayed Dominick.

Miss Randolph slipped her pelisse from her shoulders and whisked it away to her dressing closet.

Something out of place caught Clarissa's eye, at the center of the bed, but the canopy's shadows did not allow her to discern the specifics. Moving closer, she saw a small frame—and within it a pale face surrounded by dark hair.

Her pulse increased. Hand trembling, she lifted it up from the coverlet and stared into the face of a beautiful woman with green eyes who stared boldly out of the miniature, her eyes flashing with sensuality.

"Tryphena," she whispered. It could be no one else.

Miss Randolph returned to the room.

"Do you know where this came from?" She held the portrait for her maid to see.

Miss Randolph's eyes widened. "Oh, my lady. Is that who I think it is? I arrived in your room just as you did, after taking afternoon tea in the servants' dining hall. Someone must have come inside and left it."

In the next moment, anger crashed through her with such force she could hardly think. What sort of person would play such cruel games?

Storming toward the door, she threw it open and swept past Philip, who started in surprise and followed as she descended the stairs and passed, room to room, until she found Colin inside the library.

He looked up from his newspaper and watched her approach without saying a word.

She thrust the miniature in front of his face. "If you think this frightens me, then you're wrong."

Chapter Twenty-Two

$\mathcal{I}$f I think *what* frightens you?" he said, looking dismayed. "Why would I want to frighten you?"

He took hold of her wrist. She snatched her hand away.

"You know what this is." She held the portrait higher, beside her head. Her eyes narrowed on him, assessing his response.

He tossed the newspaper aside and stood. "Not until you let me see it."

The beating of her heart calmed. He looked sincerely perplexed by her accusation.

"Did you put this in my room?" she asked in a low voice, pressing the frame into his palm before stepping back. "Or have someone else do it for you, such as that maid you are carrying on with, perhaps?"

He stared down at the picture in his hand and his face paled. "God, no. I wouldn't."

"Tell me the truth," she insisted.

He met her gaze. "I *am* telling the truth, I swear it.

Where did you find it? In a drawer? Perhaps it was left behind after their last visit and has remained there until then."

"I returned from town just fifteen minutes ago to find it in the middle of my bed."

His brows drew together. "I'm not responsible. I know things are quarrelsome between Dominick and me, but I wouldn't do such a thing. I'm not vindictive or devious, and I certainly wouldn't want to terrorize you."

"I want to believe that," she said. "But you're the only person who had an attachment to her."

He covered his mouth and exhaled. "Blackmer told you that Tryphena and I carried on an affair."

"Yes."

He closed his eyes. "God, I made a terrible mistake."

"If you feel that way, you should talk to him," she suggested softly. "And apologize."

He looked at her sharply, his eyes shining with tears.

"How does one apologize for kissing one's brother's wife?" He returned to the chair and sank down, pressing both hands to his face before running them through his hair. "There can be no forgiveness for such a betrayal. No going back. I heard they separated after that, and then she died. I feel responsible for it all. I despise myself."

She sat in the chair beside his. "Why did you do it at all, if you knew it was wrong?"

He looked at her for a long moment. "I was so angry at him for leaving Darthaven and so envious of his freedom and for being strong enough to venture out on his own. I have never been so fearless although I've always wished to be. Then he came home with her, suddenly wanting to be part of the family again, and Mother and Father were so happy. They forgave him everything, and, at the time, I didn't understand and it angered me."

"It's not unreasonable that you'd have felt that way. But to betray your brother by carrying on an affair with his wife?"

"Tryphena," he said. "She was just so beautiful and...overwhelming. I knew it was wrong, but it was flattering to believe, if only for a moment, she wanted something in me that she did not find with him. But she loved him. Why she pretended otherwise, I'll never understand. As soon as Dominick discovered us—she was... devastated, and finished with me. He despises me, as he should. And I've tried very hard, for so long, to despise him back just so I can live with myself."

"It might be easier to live with yourself if you just talked to him and told him what you just told me."

"He won't want to hear what I have to say."

"How do you know, if you don't try?"

A long moment of silence passed between them.

"I will," he said evenly. "I want him to come home to stay. I want us to be brothers again."

But then he sat rigidly straight in his seat and held up the miniature. "That still leaves this. Who would have left it in your room?"

"It's not just the picture, Colin."

"What are you saying?" He scowled. "There's more?"

Dominick stared into the leaping orange flames of a small fire built near the barn door, where he'd been sleeping for the past three nights.

"I think the house will be very fine when it is finished." Mr. Gilbraith lay back upon his bundled-up coat, which he had made into a pillow for his head. "Finer even than when your grandsire lived here. And I know many among the local villagers are eager for paying positions, so you'll won't go without good help."

Dominick and Mr. Galbraith had just finished their evening meal, which consisted of a cold chicken, a few equally cold baked potatoes, some bread and cheese, and a bottle of wine. It was late, and getting colder with wind sweeping through the cracks in the barn. Their horses stood quietly in the far corner, near a patch of fresh hay. It had been such a long day, meeting with various tradesmen from the village, Dominick welcomed even the thin pallet on the cold ground behind him. Though he'd certainly prefer a bed, especially one with Clarissa in it. God, he ached for her. He wondered what she was doing and hoped she was well.

He stood and went to the open door of the barn, peering across the field toward the house. Moonlight illuminated the manse, making it look more magical than real. Frost End wasn't a grand house when compared to a place like Darthaven, but he found it beautiful still.

He secured the heavy door, barring it from inside. Already Mr. Galbraith snored.

Dominick too lay down, and closed his eyes on the thought that in two days he would see Clarissa. He dozed. He slept.

Only to be roused by Mr. Galbraith's terrible snoring.

Dominick's throat constricted and, despite gasping for his next breath, he found none. His blanket smothered him. Damn, such *heat*.

Which didn't make any sense. When he'd fallen asleep, the air had been so cold.

A horse whinnied and stamped, distressed.

Dominick sat up, eyes wide and scratchy, attempting to shake off his mental fugue. The barn was black...more black than night. Impenetrable—other than a strange, wavering orange light coming from...where? He had no sense of direction. He glanced to the small fire beside him for guidance—the one he had purposefully built for warmth—and saw its embers only dimly, as if his eyes were thickly veiled.

Smoke already filled his nose, throat, and lungs. The horses neighed loudly, and he heard a solid *thud* as one of them kicked the wall.

The barn was on fire.

His heart beat wildly, yet he forced calm on himself and remembered that when he'd gone to sleep, he'd done so with the soles of his boots facing the barn door. Leaping up, he stumbled in that direction, his arms outstretched in the darkness until he felt wood. Finding the bolt, he cast the door open.

He collapsed outward, into fresh air, smoke billowing out and over him in a thick blanket. He rose up again...stumbled and fell, and scrabbling away saw orange flames leaping from the side of the structure.

But Mr. Galbraith and the horses...

After clearing his lungs and filling them with fresh air again, Dominick dove back into the dark until his boots touched something substantial. He reached down, seizing hold of a leg.

He dragged the man backward, in the same direction from which he'd come.

Outside, he gasped for breath and roused Mr. Galbraith, whose eyes opened with a start, after which he fell into a fit of coughing. Dominick returned inside and shoved open the stall doors, freeing the terrified horses, and they raced past him. He followed, coughing raggedly, his eyes streaming and urged his companion to stand, and together they removed themselves to a distance farther away.

"The fire . . . we built, did it get out of hand?" gasped Mr. Galbraith.

Dominick remembered the fire as he'd seen it upon first awakening, its low-burning embers still neat and tidy in its shallow pit.

"No," he answered, his eyes going to the walls of the barn and the flames that consumed them—not just from one place but from all four walls and, by all appearances, from the outside in. There had been no overturned lantern, no stray ember on dry hay. There was no question in Dominick's mind that someone had started the blaze intentionally.

Just then Dominick felt a wet drop strike his face, and then another. Another moment, and rain fell from the sky.

"Did we sleep though a lightning strike?" murmured Mr. Galbraith, looking at the sky, bemused.

Lightning, no. Dominick turned away from the barn, scanning the darkness and looking toward the house. Was that someone here, even now? He saw nothing. No trace of movement other than the horses, who had ended their panicked streak and now paced spiritedly in the paddock just beyond, two dark shadows illuminated by moonlight.

Mr. Galbraith backed away, his eyes staring out wide from his sooty face at the fire, which had overtaken the roof. "There's no way to save it. What a shame. What a shame! But thank the Lord above that it wasn't the house."

But why *not* the house? Why the smaller of the two

barns? Dominick thought he knew the answer to that as well: *Because he'd been inside.*

His heart seized, thinking of Clarissa so far away at Darthaven, and his mind became a tumble of images—torn dresses and old letters and her sweet face. Was she in danger as well?

"We've hours left until dawn," Mr. Galbraith said. "I suppose there is nothing left to do but retrieve those horses and pass the remainder of the night in the big barn."

Dominick knew, of a certainty, he would not sleep at all. And though the roads were dark and perilous, he could not remain there until morning, tortured by thoughts of Clarissa's safety.

"No, Mr. Galbraith. I'm afraid I must leave you and immediately depart for home."

That Thursday night, Clarissa stood in the midst of the crowd, as a six-musician band played lively provincial tunes. As Lady Stade had promised, she'd planned a party to welcome Lord Blackmer and his new wife home. Only Dominick still hadn't returned from Frost End. Clarissa had been forced to face nearly fifty curious faces without him there.

Still, she had always enjoyed a social nature and had welcomed the break in monotony. It seemed that each day since Blackmer had left had been filled with too much silence—and there was also the rain, which she feared had prevented his timely return for the ball in their honor. Her new gown had been delivered today, and none too soon. She could no longer hide the apparent bump beneath her high-waisted skirts—nor would she want to. The pink lustring fitted perfectly. She'd enjoy the new gown and feeling so pretty more if her husband was there. She fretted over his absence, hoping he was safe and would return very soon.

Almost everyone had been very nice and eager to welcome her. But there'd also been numerous very specific questions about how she and Blackmer had met and come to be married—especially from Miss Brookfield, the young lady who had become so emotional about her presence that day at the dressmaker's shop, and her small group of young lady friends. Clarissa hadn't enjoyed answering them alone.

But this evening, as Lord and Lady Stade dutifully spoke with guests, her brother-in-law had stepped in to ease the awkwardness of the conversations that followed.

"Here you are, my lady. I brought you some lemonade." Colin presented her with a glass.

He had been her salvation tonight, and on those days when she'd languished inside Darthaven, the rain striking endlessly against the panes. After that conversation in which he'd confided his feelings about his brother, they'd warmed to one another, playing chess and talking for hours.

Nearby, Miss Brookfield stood with three other young ladies, and they all looked at Clarissa with wide blinking eyes. Because she was a woman, she knew exactly what *that* look meant—they were talking about her, and perhaps not in a complimentary way. While she had every determined intention to win their friendship—including Miss Brookfield's—she wished her sisters or any of her London friends were here, just to ease the moment. In all her days, she could not recall ever having been the unwelcome outsider at a gathering, and the feeling didn't set well with her at all.

Taking note of Miss Brookfield, Colin leaned closer. "I hesitate to tell you what she's saying."

"I'd rather know than wonder," she replied beneath her breath.

He answered in a confidential tone, but with a shine of humor to his eyes. "It seems Miss Brookfield has deduced from the London scandal rags that you and Blackmer married in shocking haste, to the great surprise of society onlookers, and that my brother was a virtual unknown. There was also something about a disaster of come-out ball, and your grandfather, the earl, being so mortified by the sudden nuptials that he took grievously ill."

Clarissa's cheeks burned with heat and she bit her bottom lip. "Things didn't happen in precisely that order."

"None of it matters now. He's obviously smitten with you."

"And I with him," she answered earnestly. Her heart ached from missing him.

"Miss Brookfield's ordinarily a nice young lady. She's just fancied herself in love with Blackmer forever."

"If she's such a nice girl, then why don't you court her? As a matter of fact, you could go talk to her this moment, and—" Clarissa lifted her lemonade and, taking a sip, peered over the edge at him. She giggled. "Break up that little conversation they are having about me."

He shook his head and smiled, albeit a bit morosely. "And forever stand in his shadow? To settle for being second best? No, thank you, my dearest Lady Blackmer. That said, I do know how to break that little gathering." After taking her glass and setting it aside on a tray, he extended his hand. "Care to dance?"

"Lady Stade should announce when she wishes for dancing to begin."

"She's distracted by her friends." His hand at her back invited her to accompany him. "I know all these people. They've been pent up inside for days, just as we have, and they want to have a good time."

"Don't we need more couples?"

He shook his head, smiling. "Others will fall in, just you wait and see." When the music paused, Colin led her toward a wide space on the floor, where carpets had been rolled away. Sure enough, the room fell silent as they proceeded to take their places for a quadrille—but only for a half second as, with a flurry of movement, others rushed with smiling faces to fill the spaces. With a wild trill from the musicians' instruments and numerous raucous shouts from the gentlemen in the crowd, the dance began.

Clarissa danced for an hour at least, partnering with Colin and then a dozen other gentlemen and ladies. She laughed and learned their names and made new friends, several of whom indicated they would be sending invitations to her and Blackmer to come for dinner or tea.

As the ongoing song neared its end, she swung round to return to her original partner, Colin again. The moment they joined hands, a sudden jolt of awareness made the hair on her arms stand on end.

Blackmer was there. She knew it even before she turned to see him standing tall and elegant beside his mother, clean-shaven and with his hair still damp, dressed in evening clothes. Yet when his gaze met hers, it snapped with displeasure.

Beside her, Colin murmured, "He's not happy and it's because you're dancing with me."

Clarissa made her way through the crowd toward Dominick.

Only then did she realize Colin had followed.

"Why am I not surprised?" Blackmer said, his eyes fixed on his brother and his voice almost a growl.

She forced herself to imagine the scene from his view.

Of course he was chagrined. He'd just found his new wife enjoying herself immensely in the arms of the brother who had once betrayed him. What man wouldn't be bothered?

Just a few feet away, Miss Brookfield and her friends watched with interest. Clarissa didn't even care. Dominick was home, and things were going to be set right.

"Stop glaring at me, Blackmer," she said, moving closer to his side and resting her hand on his arm.

"I'd like to have a word with you in private." Dominick peered down his nose at her imperiously.

She straightened her shoulders and smiled. "I'd like to have word with you as well."

Chapter Twenty-Three

Shutting the door of the library behind them, he turned to her and opened his mouth to speak.

"I missed you," she said, her eyes bright and shining. "I know why you are angry, but don't be."

He closed his eyes and seethed. "How can you imagine that I wouldn't be, finding you and him having the time of your lives together?"

He was tired, and his muscles were sore. He had not slept in two nights. He'd been so worried about her, all those long hours riding back to Darthaven and the even more torturous ones at night, when the roads had been too dark and treacherous for travel. Knowing the fire had been intentionally set had put all sorts of wild fears into his mind. He'd been so relieved to find she was safe. He'd rushed, washing and changing, wanting nothing more but to see her, only to find her with Colin.

"No, we weren't having the time of our lives. I only do

that with you. We were dancing and enjoying ourselves.
That is all."

"And *smiling*," he growled. "At *each other*."

He sounded so jealous, and he hated it, while Clarissa
didn't look apologetic at all—because she had *nothing* to
apologize for. He knew that. How could he not, seeing the
amusement—and love—reflected in her eyes?

"Clarissa, I'm—" he began.

"Don't apologize," she said softly. "Just listen to what I
say. That's all I ask."

Her voice calmed him. Reassured him. Told him everything was all right. A sudden rush of emotion moved
through him, one that came from deep in his heart.

"All right," he said, wholly repentant and wanting nothing more than to gather her in his arms and kiss the sweet
lips that insisted on speaking sense while he persisted in
behaving like an idiot. Instead, he held himself in check
and listened, because she had asked him to.

"Colin is very sorry, Blackmer, about what happened
with Tryphena. More than sorry. He said they kissed but
nothing more. There's more that he wants to tell you himself, but just know he's never forgiven himself and remains
deeply tormented. It's why he acts so abominably. He
doesn't know what to do or say." Clarissa sighed, moving
closer.

Dominick tensed, almost unable to bear her closeness
because he wanted her so much. But the words she spoke
were too important, and he wanted to hear them all.

"I know he's sincere. He told me that all this time, all
he's ever wanted is for you to come home."

"Why couldn't he tell me this himself?" he asked in a
low voice.

"Because he's a man. And it seems he's a lot like you...and your parents. You are all hiding behind your pride and your fears and are too afraid to say the words you need to say."

She was right. She read them all like a book.

"Dominick?" she said.

"Yes?"

Firelight gleamed off her hair and the silk of her dress. His gaze dipped to her breasts, which crushed against the bodice—and lower, to the sight of her now-apparent pregnancy. She looked like a goddess in the night. He had never seen anything more breathtaking.

"Say something," she urged in a soft voice. "I don't know what you're thinking."

To believe her heart could be his, now and forever, rocked him to his core.

In that moment he could only speak his heart.

"I missed you too."

She rushed toward him. He opened his arms, and she threw herself against his chest.

And he was complete again.

Her face came up. "It's what I needed to hear you say."

Seizing her within his arms, he kissed her long and sweet, before pressing his face to her hair.

"I'm so glad you're home," she murmured against his skin.

She felt so good. Everything seemed so perfect. Yet one dark cloud continued to loom above them.

"I need to tell you everything," he said.

She pulled away and looked up into his face. "Everything?"

"About Tryphena." He released her and stepped back.

"I understand why you can't."

"Because of my vow of silence to the secret service, yes. It is a very real thing, one I don't break lightly. There's so much I'll carry to the grave, but not this, Clarissa. I can't be with you unless you know it all. I can't..." He exhaled. "Because I love you."

"I love you too," she whispered, her eyes shining.

"But I can't accept your love—"

"What?" she said, dismayed.

"Not unless you know it all and still look at me...the same way you are looking at me now."

"Then tell me."

He nodded, and closed his eyes. Opening them again, he turned from her, walking the length of the mantel, before at last turning to her once more.

"I didn't intend to kill her—"

She nodded. "I know you didn't."

"Even though I rather hated her, by then. We had been estranged for weeks, but still living and working together."

"Because of what happened between her and Colin?"

"It goes back farther than that. As you know, we were both agents. We crossed paths for years, encountering one another on various assignments, and at first were...casual lovers. I knew there were others, and at the time, that didn't bother me. She was untamed and free-spirited and we never demanded exclusivity from each other. Then one night in Paris that all changed. We married impulsively, and though part of me knew we weren't suited, I was so proud she'd chosen me over the others. After we married we became partners of a sort, traveling about as a married couple pretending to be on honeymoon or attending an embassy ball, whatever the assignment required."

Clarissa nodded. "Yes, go on."

"After we left Darthaven and returned to London, things were good for a short time. But after we learned there might never be children, she became secretive and would disappear for days on end. When I asked for an explanation, I received either screaming or silence in response. At last, I asked her if she wanted her freedom and she said yes."

"You separated."

"We agreed we would, after the Prince Regent's birthday celebration, to which we'd both been assigned. Though assigned to the foreign service, I sometimes worked domestic assignments because of my expertise and personal knowledge of the foreign parties who would be in attendance—both by invitation and infiltration—and because I understood the possible dangers involved."

"This, at the Royal Pavilion."

He nodded. "There was such a crowd there that night, all wearing Venetian masks, just to make things more challenging. Given the immensity of the event, there would have been scores of lower-level agents in place all about the palace, posing as guests and servants, who would watch for any signs of trouble and assist if the night grew out of control. Tryphena was there, in the crowd, taking part as a guest. I, on the other hand, had been assigned to the Prince Regent's personal detail. As you likely know, he has always been notoriously difficult to mind."

Clarissa chuckled. "We've coaxed Claxton to tell a few stories, when Mother isn't around."

"Prinnie was always sneaking off for secret meetings or assignations and doing his best to thwart our efforts to protect him." He smiled, as if remembering. "Sometimes it was laughable the lengths he went to for privacy. That night, things changed so quickly. In a crush of people, I momentarily lost sight of him. Then several things happened to raise my alarm."

"Like what?" she asked.

"A kitchen assistant 'accidentally' knocked over a stack of apple boxes in front of me, which delayed me from pursuing him—and then a young woman slipped and twisted her ankle, which demanded two more minutes of my time. Again, I was aware there were other agents in the crowd providing cover, but they were nowhere to be seen."

"You believed his life was in danger."

"It was just that…something felt very wrong. I rushed into the garden, that being my inclination of where he had gone. There were lanterns there and other guests, but I knew his favorite places to go where he had less chances of being seen. It was midnight, and fireworks burst overhead. All I can tell you, Clarissa, is that I saw him in the shadows, waiting for someone, and that when a figure came rushing out of the dark holding what I felt certain was a pistol overhead, I, having already drawn my own weapon, fired."

Clarissa stood with her hands over her mouth, knowing what he would tell her.

"Everything after that was a blur. Other agents suddenly were there, as if from nowhere, and I was taken to the ground, wounded as well. One of them, thinking I was an assassin, shot me. But Tryphena was dead before she hit the ground. I killed her quite skillfully with just that one shot. Except she wasn't holding a pistol, she was holding her Venetian mask."

Clarissa gasped. "Her mask…"

"Yes. It seems Colin was not, by far, my wife's most impressive conquest. She wasn't there in the garden to protect the Prince Regent. They were there for an assignation."

"And your fellow agents—by employing the kitchen assistant with the apples and the girl who turned her ankle—had tried to prevent you from discovering it."

"Everyone knew but me."

"You didn't shoot her on purpose."

"I made a terrible mistake and, in doing so, killed my wife."

"An *understandable* mistake."

"There can be no mistakes at that level."

"You've punished yourself enough."

"I want to believe that. I want to leave this behind."

"It's all right to do so. You loved her, even then. Dominick, it's all right to love her even now."

His heartbeat staggered in his chest. For the first time he acknowledged that perhaps he did love Tryphena, at least a little—for the good times they had shared.

He exhaled unevenly. "But I also despised her, and no more in those moments after I fired that shot, when the truth of what had just occurred became clear."

"I can't imagine how you'd feel any other way."

"You're too good for me," Dominick murmured, his heart painfully full of love and relief, because, yes, she did still look at him with the same admiring gaze as before.

"What happened afterward?" she asked quietly.

"It was determined that in a moment of...*panic*—" He spoke the word with distaste. "—I reacted unwisely. The whole thing caused the Prince Regent great embarrassment, and the secret service as well. It was even insinuated by some—whom I know were among Tryphena's former lovers—that I shot her intentionally because I was out of my mind with jealousy. There was an investigation. The shooting was determined to be accidental, but as a consequence I was demoted to a domestic service assignment. God, it was awful. My pride was so wounded."

"And you received an assignment to watch over Wolverton."

"Where I bided my time and executed every order with care. I had just received orders to be returned to service abroad when I—"

"Very gallantly let a brokenhearted and terrified young woman cry on your shoulder." Crossing the carpet, Clarissa threw herself against him for a long embrace. Reaching up, she pulled him down for a kiss. "I loved you before, and now I only love you more." She kissed him again, her breath feathering across his lips. "Kiss me, Blackmer. Hold me forever. Don't ever leave me again."

"I missed you so much," he said, kissing her mouth.

"I want you to make love to me."

Together—still kissing—they circled toward the settee and, tangled in one another's arms, sank onto it. Pillows fell onto the floor.

Just then a knock came against the door.

"Don't stop, please," she whispered, her cheeks deeply flushed. "The door is locked."

He was lost in her. Drowning in pleasure. "I won't argue with you."

His lips moved over her skin. Had she always smelled this good? He wished they were naked, but there was something equally arousing about the prospect of making love urgently in one's clothes. The silk of her dress hissed against the wool of his coat and trousers.

Vaguely, he again heard the knocking on the door, but

Clarissa's soft lips on his throat sent the blood rushing into his ears, and his hand came up to cup her breast. Bending, he pressed an urgent kiss against the center of her décolletage as his hand found the hem of her skirts, which he lifted higher, to her knees—

The knocking repeated, terse and insistent.

"Oh, good God." He broke away. "They're not going to leave."

He laughed, his voice tight with arousal. He peered down into Clarissa's flushed face and she laughed too. "It seems not."

He wanted her so badly.

"Make yourself decent. I'm going to answer the door."

Chapter Twenty-Four

After Clarissa straightened her dress, Dominick unlocked and opened the door. Colin stood there, his hand raised in preparation for the next knock.

"Is everything all right?" he asked, his features taut with concern.

"Splendid, actually," Dominick answered, leading Clarissa into the corridor.

His brother's expression relaxed. "I just didn't want you to punish her because of me. We were only dancing."

"No, I...I wasn't punishing her." He looked at Clarissa and raised his eyebrows.

She flushed scarlet and clasped a hand to cover her mouth. Her eyes sparkled in amusement. Her hand fell away. "I was giving my husband a proper welcome home."

Dominick fought the urge to laugh.

Colin appeared oblivious to their mischief. His expression remained grave. "Blackmer, you and I need to—"

"Go back to Mother's party." Dominick smiled at his brother. "We've already been gone too long, and we both know her ladyship has taken notice."

"No doubt she has," Colin agreed quietly.

"Let's talk tomorrow." He clapped his hand on Colin's shoulder and turned him toward the ballroom. "There is much to be said. Let's go back inside. Together."

"There's a lot of people who've been waiting to welcome you home," Colin said. "Myself included."

"You're a very good dancer," Clarissa exclaimed, falling into Dominick's arms, exhausted at the end of the quadrille. "To think I didn't know."

He held her close, his hand coming to rest affectionately on her stomach. "Let's find a place to sit."

"Here!" called Lord Stade, pointing at a comfortable armchair. "Dear daughter, we don't want you getting overly fatigued. Perhaps no more dancing tonight."

Making his way through the guests, he insisted she take his arm and he escorted her there, as Dominick followed behind looking mildly bemused. When she was seated, her father-in-law bent to press a kiss to her forehead.

The show of affection both startled and pleased Clarissa. Watching his father, a smile turned Dominick's lips.

Just then, a flash of pale blue appeared at her side. Looking up, she saw Miss Brookfield, who indicated the chair beside hers. "May I?"

Clarissa smiled. "Of course."

The dark-haired young woman looked toward Blackmer. "I saw the two of you dancing and had to come tell you what an attractive couple you are."

"Thank you," she answered, but not without wariness.

"His Lordship is obviously smitten with you."

"And I with him."

Miss Brookfield sighed and crossed her hands in her lap. "As it should be."

And just like that, they were friends. When the announcement came for the midnight buffet, Dominick came to escort her, and Colin, proving himself a gentleman, extended his arm to Miss Brookfield. Some two hours later, standing alongside Lord and Lady Stade, they saw many of their guests out the door, while others retired to the rooms where they would stay as overnight guests. Only then did Clarissa and Dominick climb the stairs and at last come to stand outside their chamber doors.

"Your room or mine?" he asked huskily.

"I propose we start in yours and end in mine," she teased, a deep rose flush rising into her cheeks.

He swept her up in his arms and carried her into his room, where he stripped her to her chemise and urged her into bed. Moments later he joined her, wearing loose linen drawers, and gathered her in his arms.

Propped on one elbow, he planted a soft kiss on her nose and another on her lips. "Do you know what I want?"

"You want to make love to me again."

He chuckled. "I do, but do you know what I want more?"

"Tell me."

"I want you to go to sleep," he softly urged.

She sighed, happily. "It's been a long night, hasn't it?"

"You're very tired. I can see it in those beautiful blue eyes of yours." He kissed her forehead, then each of her eyelids. "So instead of slaking my incessant lusts on you—"

She giggled.

"I want you to fall asleep." He smoothed her hair across the pillow. "Here in my arms. That would be just as satisfying."

He was so handsome, looking down at her in the firelight.

"I love you," she said. So much it made her heart hurt.

"I love you too, Clarissa." His hand moved beneath the covers and under her chemise to splay across the bare skin of her stomach. "I have loved you almost from the start, I think. And this baby of ours."

He kissed her once more, before pulling her closer, against his shoulder, and stretching beside her, so that their bodies were entwined. She never felt more loved or protected. Never more at peace.

Her last thought before fading was that she wanted each night for the rest of her life to end like this.

Dominick stood by the bed, cleanly shaven, a towel slung low around his hips, looking down at his sleepy-eyed, tousle-haired wife. He loved the way her gaze slid over his chest and torso, shining with unconcealed appreciation.

"Let's go for a ride," he said, his hand sliding beneath the covers to encircle her ankle. "Up to the folly. I'll tell you about Frost End."

He'd let her sleep until he heard her rustling and caught her peering at him from the shadowed recesses of their bed. They'd slept late, arms and legs entwined, and already noon approached. He needed to tell her about the fire at Frost End, and his concern that it had been intentionally set and that perhaps...perhaps they didn't need to take residence there so soon but instead remain at

Darthaven with the family at least until after the birth of the baby.

With each other's assistance they dressed—playfully, their hands and mouths causing several delays. When he went in search of his coat, Clarissa sat down in a chair by the fire to lace her boots.

"Dominick, now that I'm awake and can think clearly, I have something to tell you too," she said. "Something that happened while you were gone." Her eyes darkened.

"Anything I should be concerned about?" he asked, instantly alert and listening.

A quiet knock came at the door, and at Dominick's response, Miss Randolph entered carrying a tea tray with rolls and pastries.

Clarissa looked at Dominick. "It can wait until we're at the folly."

After saying good morning to Miss Randolph, Clarissa stood and went directly into her dressing closet. He watched her go.

"Good morning, my lord." The older woman diverted her eyes. "Since everyone is sleeping so late after the party, they seem to be forgoing breakfast in the dining room, and I thought you might do the same."

Clarissa emerged from the closet, still tucking something into her pocket.

"Actually," said Blackmer, "we were going for a ride, up to the overlook. We'll take them with us and enjoy them there."

Miss Randolph dutifully transferred several pastries from the plate to the center of a napkin.

"What about the tea?" asked Miss Randolph.

"You sit and enjoy a cup with one of those pastries," encouraged Clarissa. "If I know you, you haven't eaten yet."

"You know me too well, my lady. Enjoy your morning," the woman replied, pressing the small, still-warm bundle into Clarissa's hands.

Dominick and Clarissa went on to the stables and waited for the curricle to be brought out. A cold wind swept across the grass, rippling the edges of her skirts. Dominick rearranged her scarf, so that it covered her throat more fully. She held their breakfast between them, and the aroma of fresh-baked bread filled his nostrils.

He still wondered what she'd been about to tell him in her room, but he'd wait until they were at the overlook to remind her.

"It's a bit gloomier today," she observed, looking at the sky. She'd chosen to wear gray, which only made her blue eyes appear brighter. A low thrum of excitement coursed through his veins, just from the mere act of standing beside her, of touching her so familiarly. He didn't think he'd ever get used to it. He'd never get enough of her.

"Winter comes early here and seems to last forever. It won't be long before the first snow."

"How terrible," she teased. "That I shall have to depend on you to keep me warm."

He raised a brow as a slow tug of desire tightened his groin. "Perhaps we *should* have stayed in."

He moved so that he stood behind her, his hand affectionately on her stomach, and she rested her hands atop his.

Suddenly she gave a little gasp and smiled, holding his hands more tightly where they were.

"What is it?" he inquired, looking downward over her shoulder, where she held his hand more tightly against her.

"Did you feel it?" she exclaimed.

"Feel what?"

"The baby moved. I'm certain of it."

"I didn't. Oh, that's not fair." He scowled, but in the next moment he smiled. Enchanted. Thrilled.

She turned in his arms and rose up on her toes to kiss his lips. "Next time. It will happen often now."

"Next time hopefully we won't be wearing leather gloves. Or clothes." He grinned.

The sound of wheels and horses' hooves on earth interrupted their flirtation, and the curricle rolled into view. The groom dismounted and held the door while Dominick led her to the step.

But just then a footman emerged from the back of the house, raising a hand and shouting for them. They waited until he made his way across the grass.

"What is it?" Dominick asked.

The man wheezed, red-faced from exertion. "It is Lady Blackmer's maid, Miss Randolph. The upstairs maid just found her collapsed on the floor. I'm told she is ill and in terrible distress."

"Poisoned?" Clarissa gasped, perched on the edge of the settee where Miss Randolph lay. Perspiration dappled her maid's upper lip, and she drifted in and out of consciousness. Fear struck through her. "You are certain?"

Blackmer stood at the tea tray. He had already poured and tasted the tea. Now he sampled the pastry, touching his tongue to a fragment he had pinched off. He grimaced and spat. "It's in the pastry. That's hemlock."

Her heart beat frantically, and she grasped the woman's hands. "Is she going to die?"

Miss Randolph mumbled, "It tasted strange. I . . . I spat it out."

"Thank God," muttered Blackmer. "She will be ill for a day or two, but I believe she'll be all right."

"Did you hear that, Miss Randolph?" Clarissa squeezed the woman's hand. "You're going to be all right."

Yet Blackmer didn't look relieved. Indeed, as the moments passed, he looked more troubled, more stricken than before.

"Hell, bloody hell," he cursed, his face stricken. "When I think of what could have happened. The tray was intended for you."

He strode to the door and directed the maid who waited in the corridor to summon the cook, Lord and Lady Stade, and a physician.

"This is my fault," said Clarissa, her heart racing. "I should have said something before now about the miniature."

"The miniature?" he said, returning to her side.

"The day you left for Frost End, I found this on my bed." She pulled the small portrait from her pocket and handed it to him.

Staring down at the frame in his hand, Blackmer's jaw tightened. He closed his eyes and cursed. "It is not your fault what happened to Miss Randolph but mine. Your torn dress...the letter. That woman I saw."

"You didn't tell me you saw a woman," she answered, turning toward him.

"It was foggy, and late. That she should be there seemed so bizarre. So unbelievable."

"Is it Tryphena?" cried Clarissa, her eyes bright and afraid. "Could she be alive? Blackmer, if she is, we aren't married."

She wouldn't be able to bear it if their marriage wasn't legal.

"No," he answered firmly. "That's not possible. I know,

without question, she is dead. I also don't believe in ghosts, but I do believe in revenge. I am certain someone wants it against me."

She exhaled. She had to believe him.

"Did she have family? Or perhaps it could be another officer?" She said no more, knowing she could not reveal his connection to the secret service in front of anyone, even the very ill Miss Randolph. "A...lover?"

"Family, I don't believe so." He paced, frowning. "She told me everyone who had ever meant anything to her was dead, unless she wasn't telling me the truth, which would not surprise me. The other possibilities you mentioned might be possible."

"It wasn't Colin," she announced firmly.

"I know that."

"What are we going to do?" said Clarissa.

"Firstly," he murmured, deep in thought, "I'm getting you far from here, that's what."

She nodded, standing. "Is Frost End livable? Can we go there?"

"No," he answered. "There was a fire there, in one of the barns, I feel was intentionally set. That's what I was going to tell you this morning. Mr. Gilbraith and I were sleeping inside at the time—"

Clarissa gasped. "You could have died?" She stood from the bed, more frightened now than before.

Dominick closed his eyes. "Whatever the case, it's not safe there either. I will stay here, while you go to Camellia House to be with your family, where you and the baby will be safe. I will write Wolverton a letter which you will deliver to him only. There is an agent in the household who'll know what to do."

"An agent in the household?" Clarissa's eyes widened. "Still protecting him?"

"Yes."

"I thought he wasn't in danger any longer."

He lifted his hand. "It's just a precaution. Just as this is precautionary."

"Then why aren't you coming with me?"

She didn't want to be separated from him, even to see her family. Just the thought of being parted from him under such circumstances made her feel unsettled and anxious.

"Because I'm going to find out who is responsible for this." Dominick spoke in a calm voice. "And I'm certain whoever is doing this is acting alone."

"How can you be certain?"

"I do have some expertise in these matters." He gave her a pointed look. "That said, I can't be absolutely certain, but nothing further of concern occurred after you found the portrait?"

"No."

He nodded. "I strongly suspect that after they left the miniature here for you, they set off directly to follow me. And now that I've returned, don't you see, this has occurred. This person wants to hurt me, and if you are here, they will hurt you as well to cause me pain."

"I don't want to be separated from you," Clarissa said firmly.

"It won't be for long, I promise," he said. "I'll come for you as soon as I know there's no danger."

She knew he would not change his mind. She paced back and forth beside the window. "When must I go?"

He went to stand behind her, wrapping his strong arms around her. "Tomorrow morning, very early. There's a regular post chaise scheduled to London then, and I shall arrange for them to stop at the posting inn in Lacenfleet, if not Camellia House's doorstep. I'd ask my father for use of the carriage but don't want to make a show of your departure, in the event that all of this is part of something bigger I don't yet understand. Indeed, don't mention your leaving to anyone. We'll do this quietly, so there's a delay before anyone even realizes you've gone."

She nodded. "I'll be ready."

"I'm sworn to secrecy," Miss Randolph said, moaning. "I shall try to be better by then."

Dominick turned toward the bed. "I'm afraid not, Miss Randolph. You're staying here until you're fully recovered."

"Mistress's orders," Clarissa added.

After the doctor visited and confirmed Dominick's assessment, the couple spent the afternoon making Miss Randolph comfortable and packing Clarissa's things. Blackmer quietly investigated the source of the tainted pastries, which he felt certain was in some way related to the scores of additional hands hired from town to assist with the party. All had been vetted for the appropriate recommendations and experience, but still, someone could have misrepresented themselves while the house was in the midst of preparations and gone unnoticed.

Although Miss Randolph's condition improved, Clarissa insisted her lady's maid sleep in the dressing room so she would be close enough to hear if the older woman called out for help or assistance. The servant's proximity made no difference to Dominick, who coaxed Clarissa into making love, at first discreetly, with many whispers and muffled laughter, and then passionately, until the bed creaked and swayed. The next morning, they were much more quiet and discreet.

But then it was time to go. Though she still did not want to leave Dominick, she understood why she must go. He drove her in the curricle to Ashington, along with the young footman Philip, whom Dominick had recruited to attend her. After a short wait and several shameless kisses on the street, Dominick assisted Clarissa up into the coach, to join a gray-haired older woman accompanied by a young boy. Philip climbed up to sit on the perch at the back of the carriage, bundled in a heavy coat and scarf.

Clarissa managed not to cry when the coach pulled away. Blackmer waved from where he stood beside the curricle, looking as morose as she to be separated. When he was out of sight, she did shed tears, but only briefly, because she knew he would find out who was behind the disturbances at Darthaven and join her soon.

Just then the carriage changed direction and rolled to a stop. A moment later and voices sounded outside and the door opened. A pretty young woman in a straw bonnet and serviceable dress climbed inside, and smiled shyly between Clarissa and the other occupants.

"I'm so sorry," she said, taking the seat next to Clarissa and resting her valise on her lap. "Very sorry to cause any delay. It seems I'm always five minutes too late. Thank heavens the driver saw me and stopped."

Dominick returned to Darthaven in a sullen mood. He hated to send Clarissa away, but she would be safe at Camellia House with her family. In addition to writing the letter to Wolverton, on the same coach that conveyed his wife, he had dispatched a sealed letter to Mr. O'Connell,

Wolverton's personal valet and protector, informing his former fellow agent of his present concerns.

Inside, Colin waited in the vestibule.

"Blackmer, there you are. I was hoping we could talk," said Colin. He looked at his brother, and much of the tension within him eased. While they hadn't had a chance to talk out the past and officially reconcile the night before, it had been clear at the party that the conflict between them had all but disappeared. He had his little diplomat Clarissa to thank for that. "Let's go into the library."

Once inside, the brothers looked at one another for a long time, each without words.

Colin looked at him steadily, his eyes filled with emotion, and after a long moment rubbed his hands over his face. "I had such an eloquent speech planned, and now it has all gone from my mind. I should remember the words easily. I've been writing them in my head for years."

Dominick smiled. "It's all right. I don't need a speech."

"I'm sorry, Blackmer."

"I am too. And that's all that matters. Let's start over. Let's start new."

"All right." Colin stepped back, letting out a great sigh of relief. "I'll start by asking what you've done with your wife. I saw you leave in the curricle this morning, and you've returned without her. Where is she? There's nothing wrong, is there?"

"Actually, there is."

"Does it have to do with that miniature being left in Clarissa's room and her destroyed dress? Who could have done such a thing?"

While he could not reveal his past as an agent to Colin, nor the circumstances of Tryphena's death, he told Colin about the fire and the poisoned pastries and expressed his concern that someone was trying to torment him in some way about his first wife's death.

Dominick turned toward the opposite wall, trying to clear his head of emotion. Trying to understand. "I have no idea who is doing these things, whether it's a servant who developed some attachment to her when we visited Darthaven, or perhaps...perhaps a former lover."

"Well, it's not me." Colin pressed a hand over his chest, looking earnest.

"I know that."

"Dominick, I want to be honest."

"Please do."

"But I don't want to offend you."

"You won't. Tell me anything."

"I've had a lot of time to think about the past. Looking back now, I can see that her attentions toward me were very precise and intentional. They weren't about attraction or desire, but it felt more like something she *had* to do."

"What are you trying to say?"

"It's just an instinct, but I can't help but feel I was just a convenient ploy for Tryphena to...perhaps to end her marriage to you. Does that make any sense?"

Memories flowed into his mind, an overwhelming flood. Tryphena had done her best to make him miserable before they separated.

For so long he'd forbidden himself from thinking of their last day together as man and wife, the day he'd told her to go. She'd said such provoking things and behaved so hatefully. Yet the last moment before she walked out the door to travel to Brighton, he'd thought he'd seen something. He closed his eyes, remembering—

Her eyes had shone with tears and regret and something else.

Love?

Dominick had told himself he was only seeing what he wanted to see. That he'd been wrong. As an agent in the secret service, she had always been competitive, wanting the most prestigious, most dangerous assignments. He'd always harbored in the back of his mind the belief she'd married him to get there and that, once there, her use for him was done. But if she'd loved him, none of that made sense.

If she'd loved him, why would she have seduced his brother—if only for a kiss?

Because if he hated Colin, he wouldn't stay at Darthaven. He'd return to London, and his life as an agent . . . and she with him.

Why would she want him to hate her, to push her away?

Because if they hated one another, it would be easier for her to betray him.

To kill him.

For him to kill her.

Shock jolted through him. The answer had come out of nowhere, a gift of instincts, of his deepest psyche. Without context, what did it mean?

"Blackmer, are you all right?" asked Colin, his brows drawn together. "You look like you've seen a ghost."

"No." As Dominick had told Clarissa, he didn't believe in them. "Just thinking."

"Speaking of ghosts," his brother said softly. "Do you know . . . I thought I saw her yesterday."

A slow curl of awareness rippled through Dominick, starting in his stomach and spreading out through his shoulders. "Who?" The word emitted from his lips as a whisper. But already he knew the answer that would come.

"Tryphena. In Ashington, walking along the street." Colin rubbed a hand over his forehead, and frowned. "I knew it was impossible. That it couldn't be her, but I... I even tried to follow her—that is, the woman who looked like her—but when I rounded the corner she was gone."

"That's interesting," Blackmer said.

Interesting indeed.

Chapter Twenty-Five

Clarissa glanced out the window and smiled as Camellia House came into view atop the hill overlooking the village of Lacenfleet. In just moments she would see her family. It was the only thing that made leaving Blackmer less painful. She prayed he and everyone else at Darthaven were safe and that he would determine who was behind the disturbing events that had taken place over the previous weeks. She had no doubt he would because she suspected he had been a very formidable agent, before Tryphena's death had changed his circumstances.

She turned back to the young woman sitting beside her, who had been such a pleasant companion for the duration of the trip. Miss Joyce had recently lost her position as a companion after the elderly lady with whom she spent her days had passed away. Miss Joyce had originally traveled back to London.

"Nonsense, Miss Joyce, you'll come with me. It's a temporary position, but perhaps by the time Miss Randolph returns to serve as my lady's maid, we'll have found something permanent for you as well."

Miss Joyce's face brightened. "Truly? You're willing to take a chance on me? How very generous. Thank you. I'm grateful for even a temporary position. Time spent in the service of the Earl of Wolverton will be quite the feather in my cap and would improve the quality of positions I can attract in the future." The woman relaxed back into her seat and sighed. "What a relief it would be not to have to present myself to my poor father for support. He has such a small pension and can barely tend to himself. I do have a letter of recommendation from my deceased employer's son, which I can give to the housekeeper."

"Then the matter is settled."

The driver kindly delivered them to Camellia House's door. Outside the carriage, Philip took possession of her small bag, advising the Duke of Claxton's footmen he would deliver it personally to her room.

Miss Joyce inquired of the footmen as to the location of the servants' entrance and set off right away, after indicating she would follow proper protocol and introduce herself to the housekeeper, Mrs. Branigan.

Clarissa entered the house and removed her bonnet.

"You're here! What an unexpected and wonderful surprise," Sophia exclaimed, rushing into the vestibule, her arms wide. They embraced, and Clarissa gave her sister's very round stomach an affectionate pat. "Claxton told us there was no hope of you coming whatsoever. I'm so glad he was wrong."

"Look at you!" cried Clarissa.

Sophia did the same. "Look at *you*. You're increasing as well."

Daphne joined them, her expression transforming from lively to crestfallen in an instant. "Oh, Clarissa. I'm so sorry. What did that blackguard do to you? Come, let's go inside, somewhere private, and you can tell us all about it."

Lady Margaretta swept out from the great room to embrace her. "She doesn't have to tell you or any of us anything if she doesn't want to. Give her some privacy and some time."

Clarissa pulled back to smile at them. "I don't need any time or privacy. Blackmer and I are very happy. I've just come for a visit. He'll join me as soon as he can."

Her mother exhaled in relief. "That's wonderful to hear."

"Come inside." Sophia led her into the cavernous great room, which Clarissa was surprised to find full of people she knew. "Everyone, look who has arrived. My sister, Lady Blackmer."

"What's the occasion?" Clarissa asked, delighted to see so many familiar faces.

Sophia answered. "I'll be confined soon, so I decided to throw a small house party before then so everyone could see the house now that it's been repaired. Some guests are just here for the day, while others have yet to arrive."

"It's lovely." Camellia House, though built in the time of Elizabeth, smelled clean and fresh and new. After a fire last Christmas nearly destroyed a third of the sprawling manse, the Duke and Duchess of Claxton had undertaken measures to return the property to all its prior glory.

Daphne touched Clarissa's arm. "Claxton and Raikes are in the garden with some of the gentlemen, talking seeds and hybrids and such. I'm going to go and let them know you're here. They'll want to come inside to greet you as well. You stay here and give Grandfather a kiss. He's sitting just over there. Do you see? He's missed you terribly."

She looked in the direction her sister indicated, toward a small alcove on the far side of the large room, and saw Lord Raikes's mother and father sitting with Wolverton, who appeared even thinner than before—but well, with robust color in his cheeks. All read books or newspapers and remained oblivious to her arrival. Little Michael sat between them, dressed in a suit like a little man, playing with a pair of soldiers.

Her grandfather. Yes! She could not wait to see him, and tell him how well her marriage to Blackmer had turned out, and to thank him for his part in ensuring her happiness. But as she approached, Michael leapt up and barreled toward her.

"Michael!" Clarissa called to him, opening her arms.

How he'd grown, in just their brief time apart! Vinson and Laura would have been so proud. He climbed down and ran to her.

"Auntie!" he cried.

She caught him up and squeezed him, pressing a kiss on his cheek. He smelled so good, like little-boy skin and soap and, yes, a recent peppermint.

Wolverton reached a wrinkled hand for her. "Come and give me a kiss too, my dear."

Clarissa did so, relieved that he looked at her with the same old unabashed affection he always had, even after the circumstances in which they had last parted.

She bent to kiss him. "I'm so glad to see you well. I've been so worried about you."

"I am feeling so much better. My dear, where is Blackmer?" His gray eyebrows raised. "I must speak privately with him. With you both."

Michael wiggled to be set down, and after went to the windowsill where he scrutinized several toy soldiers and cannons there, and repositioned them.

"He did not come with me. It will only be a week before he joins us, I hope."

"Are you well?" the old man asked, his eyes intent and concerned.

"Better than well, Grandfather. I'm very happy."

He closed his eyes and smiled, clasping her hands in his. "He is a...*good* man."

"He is more than I could ever have hoped."

"I'm glad to hear that. I...acted as best I could, given the situation, though even I did not realize the marriage would come at so great a personal expense for him."

"Yes, he lost his...diplomatic assignment. It was difficult for a time, but I think he has recovered from that disappointment."

"I pray so."

"Grandfather, he did ask that I give you a letter." Clarissa opened her reticule and presented him with the folded parchment.

Wolverton stared down at the letter in his hand and traced his finger over the wax seal. Clarissa saw him break the seal after Sophia appeared again to steal her away so that she could say hello to additional guests.

Everyone greeted her and wished her well on her recent wedding. In the vestibule, there came the sounds of additional guests arriving. Sophia broke away to welcome them.

"Where is this Lord Blackmer?" asked Sir Keyes, her

grandfather's longtime and equally elderly friend. "I'd like to meet him."

His affianced, the tiny but always smiling dowager Countess of Dundalk, looked behind her. "Don't tell me he didn't accompany you."

Clarissa feared she would have to answer the question a thousand times. "He did not. He has business to attend to and will join me later."

Sophia returned in the company of the new arrivals. "I believe everyone here knows Lady Quinn—"

Clarissa's eyes flew open in shock, seeing the former Emily FitzKnightley. She felt not one bit of ill will or jealousy toward the young lady, but she realized her presence might also come with that of her husband, someone Clarissa would be happy never to see again.

"And her mother, Mrs. FitzKnightley."

A glance across the room showed Wolverton's lips turned into a deep scowl, his eyes ablaze with fury. As discreetly as possible, Clarissa lifted a calming hand to him.

Sophia returned to her side, murmuring out of the side of her mouth, "I don't know them very well, but Claxton's trying to convince the Duke of Lowther to change his way of thinking about a few things before Parliament goes back into session. They can't seem to agree on anything."

Clarissa didn't have to wait long to confirm her fear about Lord Quinn's presence because he entered the room at precisely that moment. Her heart sank, and she struggled to keep her expression blasé. Dominick had proven himself to be the most honorable of men. Quinn, in contrast, made her skin crawl.

"Ah, Miss Bevington," Quinn said, his eyes fixed warmly on her. "What a wonderful surprise to see you."

"Lady *Blackmer*," she corrected him. "I am Lady Blackmer now, if you will recall."

"That's right. I forgot. The Earl of Blackmer. Where is he?" He surveyed the room. "Not here? That's too bad."

The heat in his eyes intensified, and her blood went cold.

"It is very nice seeing you," she replied coolly. To Sophia, she said, "I'm very weary. Would you mind if I went to my room?"

"Of course you are weary. I recall in the early days of my pregnancy I was so tired all the time. Now I'm full of energy. Mother says I'm nesting. You'll do it too!"

Sophia led Clarissa toward the staircase. In the distance, away from everyone, she spied Wolverton speaking to his valet, O'Connell.

"What was that your sister said?" inquired Lord Quinn, following along behind. Clarissa cringed, hearing his voice. "Are congratulations in order for you as well?"

Sophia paused and, turning, replied, "My apologies, Lord Quinn, I should not have spoken so familiarly in the presence of those who are not family, but I suppose it is no secret. My sister, like me, is happily expecting."

His gaze fell to her stomach. "That's . . . wonderful news. Your husband must be thrilled."

"He is indeed."

"Well, then." He paused, staring into her eyes far too probingly. "Emily and I extend our congratulations. Hopefully she and I will be able to share the same happy news soon as well."

Upstairs, Clarissa spied Philip positioned at the far end of the corridor, wearing the distinctive red Stade livery.

To Sophia, she said, "I hope you don't mind. Blackmer sent Philip to attend to me."

"I appreciate that. I'm afraid I've stretched our small staff to their limits with this number of guests."

"I've also a lady's maid, Miss Joyce."

"We've rooms for them both in the attic. I'll speak with Mrs. Branigan to ensure they're included in the staff count."

In the privacy of her room, Clarissa did her best to put Quinn from her mind, praying his stay at Camellia House would not be long. She napped and dreamed of Blackmer, a dream so pleasant she did not want to awaken when Daphne shook her gently and told her it was time to dress for supper.

Clarissa considered claiming weariness, so that she might pass the evening in her room. But she would not allow Lord Quinn to ruin this time with her family. Miss Joyce appeared, along with servants carrying water for a bath, and did a fine job of dressing her and styling her hair before she returned downstairs.

She might as well have stayed in her room. Despite her efforts to discreetly rebuff him, her former lover constantly gravitated to her side. Supper turned out to be a two-hour-long miserable affair, with her seated between Quinn and his father the duke—and Wolverton scowling at all of them.

After dinner she stayed close to Lady Quinn because it was the only place where Quinn seemed reluctant to follow her. She wasn't surprised to learn she liked Emily. She could only feel sympathy that the girl had married such a lout. Thank heavens she had not. She missed Blackmer so much.

At last, she excused herself and made her way to her room, only to see a door open to the chamber next door, and Philip inside, crouched beside the bed and reaching under.

Sir Keyes crouched there too—as well as his aged legs would allow.

"Do you see them?" he said.

"Have you lost something?" she inquired from the door, drawing Sir Keyes's attention.

"Hello, Daphne," he replied cheerfully.

She corrected him, with a smile. "It's Clarissa."

"My apologies, dear." He chuckled and tapped his cheek. "Just my spectacles."

"I see them, sir," said Philip, flattening himself against the floor.

"I'm so glad. Good night then," she said, and went onto her room.

She had only just shut her door behind her when the door opened again.

Quinn entered and quickly shut the door, turning the key.

"What are you doing here?" Clarissa backed away, alarm spearing up inside her. "Get out of my room this instant."

"I needed to see you alone and tell you I've been so miserable with Emily. It's because I'm still in love with you." He moved toward her.

His words only annoyed her. "You never loved me. If you did, you wouldn't have married someone else after— after—" She gritted her teeth. "It doesn't matter anymore because I'm married now, and I'm very happy. Please leave."

Quinn's smile turned cruel. "You're putting on a good show about being a sweet and dutiful wife, but there's no need. I know you. You're just like me. Adventurous. If you weren't, I wouldn't have had your innocence on that garden bench."

Clarissa gasped in outrage, hating him in that instant. "I was innocent and believed you loved me. It would never have happened otherwise."

"I did love you," he replied angrily. "And I love you still. If only you'd let me show you."

"I said, get out of my room," Clarissa insisted, pointing to the door.

He slowly shook his head. "Not until you kiss me, and then look in my eyes and say you don't feel anything."

He stalked toward her.

"I'm going to scream," she threatened. "Everyone will come."

"I don't think you will," he said, his gaze growing sharper and his lips turning into a snarl. "Because if you do, I'll tell them all that the baby you're carrying is—"

"*Mine,*" a man's voice interrupted.

Whirling around, Clarissa saw the figure of a man in the shadows at the far corner of the room. Blackmer emerged, wearing boots and breeches and a white linen shirt, open at the throat. His hair was tousled, and his skin looked flushed from hours of riding.

She got chills just from looking at him. He had never been more handsome, or more commanding. She rushed to his side, and he pulled her to stand just behind him, in the shelter of his shoulder. She clasped his arm, binding her hands around the muscle. Closing her eyes, she inhaled, savoring his scent through his shirt.

Quinn laughed sharply. His eyes gleamed with displeasure. "I suppose you will...want to call me out now, or challenge me to a duel and bring scandal down upon us all?"

"Sorry to say, Quinn, I play a dirtier game than that," Dominick said matter-of-factly. "You've threatened the wrong man's wife."

"You're just talk."

"Be assured I'm not," Blackmer answered, his voice hushed. "Do you know who I am?"

Quinn sneered. "No one knows anything about you, which says a lot because if I and my friends don't know you...you're no one."

Dominick shrugged. "And yet I know a lot of things about you. I also know a lot about your father."

Quinn's eyes narrowed. "What do you mean, you know things?"

"Delicious, wicked things." He smiled dangerously. "For instance, I know what happened in Italy last summer."

Lord Quinn went rigid, and his face paled.

Blackmer said, "Would you like me to tell you what I know?"

"That's blackmail," he growled.

"Blackmail? No, I'd call it what you deserve."

"I'm going to go now." Quinn backed toward the door.

"So soon?" Blackmer teased darkly. Dangerously. "You only just arrived, and we have so much to talk about. In fact, why don't we summon your father, the duke, as well, and perhaps the Duke of Claxton? Wolverton also might wish to hear what I have to say."

Quinn froze, and shook his head. "I don't agree. We have nothing to talk about. Nothing at all."

"Quinn?"

"Yes."

"Don't ever speak to my wife again. Don't even look at her. If she tells me you have, I'll find you, and I'll do far more than talk. I'll make you sorry to be alive. Do you understand?"

Quinn's head jerked in a nod. He unlocked the door, tore it open then escaped into the corridor as if the hounds of hell snapped at his heels.

Clarissa spun away from Blackmer and stared at him.

He blinked, but an impenetrable blackness lingered, something she'd never seen in his eyes before. It was a weapon, she realized, just as deadly as a pistol or knife, and one that he'd been competent using in his former life. "I'm sorry if I frightened you."

"You did frighten me for a moment." She bit her bottom lip. "But I liked it."

His lip turned up at the corner. "You did?"

She bit her lip and giggled. "Am I a terrible woman for being entertained by that? I've don't think I've ever seen anything more impressive." She moved toward him, taking one of his hands in hers. "Seeing you like that was very...revealing. Breathtaking, actually."

"How so?"

"I find I like being married to a very dangerous man."

The tautness of his shoulders eased. The blackness in his gaze faded, to be replaced by gentleness.

"I'm only dangerous where you are concerned." He touched her chin and drew his thumb along her cheek. "And our child."

Emotion swept through her, overpowering and sweet.

"I missed you so much." She went up on her toes, kissing him on the mouth, before asking, "What happened in Italy?"

He drew away to look down into her face. "O'Connell knows about Quinn. He shared a bit of intelligence with me before I came upstairs. I had no idea at the time it would become so valuable."

"I'm so glad he betrayed me. Or else I wouldn't have you."

They indulged in another long, lingering kiss.

"I want to take you downstairs and share you with everyone," she said, tugging at his hands.

"I want to keep you here and share you with no one."

"Blackmer." Clarissa stepped back, still holding his hands. "Why are you even here? You had to have departed Darthaven just hours after I left."

He stared at her steadily. "I fear you are in danger."

"From whom?"

"I don't know," he answered. "It is only a feeling. My instincts. I only know that after you left Darthaven, I immediately questioned my judgment in sending you away, and have not slept since. I can't tell you how relieved I am to find you safe."

"Nothing has happened." She smiled, wishing he would do the same. "I'm safe. But what instincts are you talking about?"

"I might be wrong." Yet his expression remained grave.

"Tell me," Clarissa urged.

He pulled away from her, and turned toward the fire. "I fear that Tryphena was a double agent of sorts. Working for the English intelligence but also someone else."

"Why do you think that?" she asked.

Dominick faced her again. "When I met her,

Tryphena was a low-level agent, much like Claxton originally described me to be, while I was in a far more selective and highly trusted group of operatives. Once we married, she . . . expanded her circle of contacts. Charmed my superiors. So much so that they began to offer us assignments as husband and wife. I . . . suspect she may have married me for the sole purpose of getting inside."

A terrifying realization washed over Clarissa. "You think she was sent to kill the Prince Regent that night."

Dominick nodded. "It's possible. Some two decades ago, there was a French spy by the name of St. Guerlain. During the war he employed beautiful women to learn British secrets. Troop movements, battle plans, and so on. They were known as the *Violons Noir*."

"The black violins?" she repeated. "As in the instrument?"

"No, like the spider. A single bite can be fatal. St. Guerlain has been silent for years and presumed dead, but . . ."

He crossed the room and pulled something from his coat pocket.

Returning, he said, "Look."

It was the miniature. In the lower corner of the frame, nestled among the carved flourishes and leaves, was a small violin, barely discernible because it had been painted black just like the rest of the frame.

"A violin," she whispered.

"It could be just coincidence. But if it's not, I'm not certain who I'm dealing with, and I'm not letting you out of my sight until I do."

"You'll find out the truth. I know you will," Clarissa said.

An urgent rapping came on the door. Dominick groaned and released her. Crossing the floor, he opened it.

Daphne stood there, her eyes wide and her face pale. "Blackmer, I didn't know you'd arrived."

"What is it, Daphne?" asked Clarissa, going closer.

"Perchance is Michael here with the two of you?"

"Michael? No, why?" she replied.

"Because he isn't in his room, and neither is his nanny. We don't know where they are."

Chapter Twenty-Six

$\mathcal{I}$'m coming with you," Clarissa said, buttoning her pelisse, following him.

"No, you aren't," he said, striding across the lawn, lantern in hand. "It's too dark. Go back to the house. We will find him."

In the distance, the light of lanterns could be seen moving toward the stables and barns and into the gardens. Then Daphne and Sophia emerged from the house, doing the same as their younger sister, pulling on warmer outer garments and adjusting lamps for more light. They set off toward the front lawn.

"Michael!" they shouted, just as many others did.

Clarissa glared at Dominick. "I'm coming. You've never been to Camellia House and don't know the grounds, and I do."

He bit his tongue as she accompanied him deeper into the darkness. All the while he tamped down a different sort of fear, one that whispered *danger*. Instinct told him that this wasn't just a little boy who had wandered into the night, whose nanny—whom he knew to also be a secret service agent—had gone in pursuit without informing anyone.

He had seen the same look of concern on the face of Mr. O'Connell. In accordance with prior plans, as His Lordship's valet, he had secured the very worried Earl of Wolverton in his room until the boy could be found, in the event someone attempted to harm His Lordship as well.

Protocol. But necessary? Were the earl and his grandson in danger? Only the coming minutes and perhaps hours would tell.

"Where would the boy go? Is there a place he liked to play?"

"If I were to guess, I'd say the stables, because he loves horses, or the gardens to hide and play. But he would never go to those places alone. Someone is always with him. He's just a little boy."

"Those places are already being searched by the others. Is there anyplace on the grounds that's more obscure where—" His voice cut off suddenly.

"Where someone might have taken him?" A sharper fear tripped down her spine. She searched her memories of previous visits to Camellia House for an answer. "Perhaps...perhaps the Huntsman's Lodge, but it will be difficult to get to in the dark."

"Take me there," he said.

"I'll try to remember the path. Everything looks so different at night."

Though it was difficult for him to do, he allowed her to lead.

"This way," she said. "No...over here."

"Quiet," he urged in a soft voice.

"Why?"

He hesitated before answering. "If someone has taken Michael, I would not want them to hear our voices as we approach."

"You think someone has taken Michael?"

"No," he answered, reluctant to explain. "I don't know. Clarissa, while I was assigned to protect your grandfather, there was protection in the house for Michael too. You cannot tell anyone, do you understand?"

"Yes."

"His nanny is an agent, placed in the house to protect him."

"But why?" Dominick heard Clarissa's breath catch in her throat. "Does this have something to do with my brother and father's deaths?"

"Possibly."

Her eyes widened in the night. "Blackmer, we have to find him." She scrambled over a fallen tree, heedless of the small limbs that snagged her skirts, and then rushed ahead. Eventually, the dark outline of an old cottage rose before them, an eerie sight in the night.

He pushed her into the shelter of a tree. "Stay here. I'm going to look inside."

She nodded.

He moved forward silently to stand in the deeper shadows created by the cottage walls. He listened for a long moment, hearing nothing.

Then... the creak of a floorboard.

Carefully, he edged closer to the open window and peered inside. A shadowy figure stood against the opposite wall.

He heard a small voice say something. A child's voice.

The hair on his neck stood on end, and all his instincts went arrow sharp—

A hand closed on his arm.

God damn it, Clarissa, he thought but did not say as he yanked his wife down beside him on the ground, thrusting a hand over her mouth.

Her eyes stared at him, wide and frightened. She pointed at the cottage and he nodded.

He pressed his mouth to her ear. "Stay here."

"I know you're out there, Blackmer," a voice said from inside the cottage. "Why don't you come inside?"

A chill raked down his spine. It was a woman's voice.

Not just any woman's, but Tryphena's.

Clarissa stood, moving as close to the open window as she dared. The voice belonged to Miss Joyce. Or whomever Miss Joyce *really* was. And she, Clarissa, had brought her here, into her family's midst. The realization made her feel sick at her stomach.

"Who are you?" Dominick asked. He'd moved to stand just inside the front door of the cottage. The woman gauged his position by the creak and groan of the floorboards.

"Don't you see the resemblance?" she answered.

"You're Tryphena's sister. May I see the boy?"

Michael! Clarissa had never experienced such fear. She shook with it. She felt responsible. If he had been harmed—

"I think not," the woman answered. "He's sleeping."

"What did you give him?" he said quietly, yet angry concern thundered just below the surface.

"Nothing that will harm him," she said. "Not yet."

Clarissa's blood turned to ice and she covered her mouth with her hands to keep from making a sound. Just then she spied three figures creeping through the darkness. She considered screaming to alert Blackmer, but then recognized them as Claxton, Raikes, and Havering. They did not see her, apparently, and continued on as if to the back entrance of the cottage.

"It was you at Darthaven," he said.

"I wanted to have a little fun with you before your demise. Make you believe you were mad, and watch helplessly as my poison killed your pretty wife."

"As punishment for killing Tryphena."

"Revenge, yes, for my sister," she said, emotion thickening her voice. "For making her fall in love with you, which made her distracted and careless. If she wasn't dead, then I wouldn't be here finishing the job. Her death wasn't part of the plan. Yours was. Only she wouldn't kill you."

"What plan?"

The woman hesitated. "I only tell you this so you'll know just how wrongly life has treated you. You didn't accidentally kill your wife. You saved England."

"Tryphena was an assassin, sent to kill the Prince Regent."

"Now you know."

"Afterward, where did her weapon go?"

"You don't truly believe she acted alone, do you? There are others in your ranks, and that night they concealed the evidence of her failure. It took years to get everything in place. She seduced and married you. Earned the trust of your superiors. Caught the Prince Regent's attention. And then you ruined it."

"If you want revenge against me, then why did you leave me at Darthaven and come here?"

"You've heard the phrase 'killing two birds with one stone'?" she said. "After Tryphena's death, you disappeared. I couldn't find you. Imagine my pleasure at learning you had been assigned to Wolverton's detail, a man whom my employer has held a long-standing grudge."

"You are part of the assassination plot against him as well."

"I have learned from my sister's mistakes, and my services are in high demand. But just as I found you, you were gone again. Imagine my surprise when I discovered the announcement of your marriage to Wolverton's granddaughter. So I followed you to Darthaven and had my fun. After that, things only got better. By your sending Lady Blackmer away, you gave me the perfect opportunity to get past the wall of protection Wolverton enjoyed and get close to the others. Now, instead of two birds with one stone, I and my accomplices will kill four: Wolverton and Michael, Lady Blackmer and you. Needless to say, this night will be quite a feather in my cap."

"Who is your employer?"

"I'm done talking. As much as I'd like for you to see me kill the others, I'm afraid you must be first."

In the silence, there came the sound of a pistol being cocked. Terror tore through Clarissa.

"No," she screamed, unable to contain her fear.

Inside, the darkness churned with movement. Three hulking shapes hurtled into the room: Claxton and the others. A shot blasted—a blaze of fire in the night. Clarissa ran to the door, desperate to see that Dominick and Michael and the others were all right. She had only just stepped inside when Dominick leapt to shield her with his body, shoving her aside.

Lithe and quick moving, the dark-haired woman seized a sleeping Michael and backed into the corner of the room, her pistol held to his small head.

Clarissa cried out in horror. "No."

Yet...something in the way the assassin held Michael so carefully...so gently...gave her away.

Dominick stormed toward Tryphena's sister, who whipped her arm straight, pointing the pistol at him. The others leapt on her from the side. Clarissa screamed. Another shot ripped through the dark as the woman disappeared beneath a heap of male assailants.

Blackmer turned, his arms now cradling Michael. Clarissa rushed forward, took the boy in her arms, and ran with him outside.

"How does it feel to be married to a hero?" asked the Duke of Claxton later that night, smiling at Clarissa, then Blackmer.

"I realized he was a hero long before tonight," answered Clarissa, squeezing her husband's hand.

The entire family gathered in the library, behind closed doors.

Michael, awake and cranky, had been returned to the care of his aunts and grandmother, while his nanny recovered from the sleeping narcotics that had been employed to prevent her interference with the boy's abduction. The house had been secured for the night. Tryphena's sister, whose name was still not yet known, remained under guard, as did her two accomplices, who had been captured earlier by Mr. O'Connell after they had climbed through a window into Wolverton's unoccupied bed-chamber. They would be transferred to London that night by Havering and numerous others who had been appointed to go along for the brief trip.

Wolverton leaned forward in his chair. "My grandson-in-law saved the Prince Regent from assassination. Not only that, but he saved the lives of my dear granddaughter and great-grandson."

"Thank you, Blackmer," said Lady Margaretta, resting her hand on Michael's tousled head, where he laid sleeping on her lap. "From the bottom of my heart."

The entire family toasted Dominick then, with brandy all around. Dominick lifted his glass but did not drink.

"Thank you. All of you. But now I think we should get Michael to bed. And the duchess and my wife as well."

Clarissa looked up at him, her eyes sparkling.

A moment later, he led her down the corridor to their room.

Havering followed. "Blackmer. Might I have a moment with you before I go?"

Dominick urged Clarissa toward their door. "I'll join you shortly."

Turning back, he met Havering—the man who had been his former handler in the service.

"You know they're going to want you back," Havering said with a teasing smile.

"Flattering, but I'm done with the service."

"Hmmm." Havering smiled ruefully. "I see Claxton has already gotten to you with his talk of diplomatic appointments."

Dominick raised his eyebrows at that. "No, he hasn't."

Havering flashed a smile. "He will."

He wouldn't deny it. It felt good to be admired. Celebrated. Returned to the good graces of all those whom he so deeply respected. But something else felt better—and that was the idea of Clarissa and family—and home.

Domnick grinned. "I think I should like to settle down for a while and have a normal life with Clarissa, and enjoy being there as my children are born."

"Sounds wonderful," Havering answered wistfully.

"You should try it."

"You know that's not possible."

"I hope it will be for you one day."

Havering nodded. "I envy you."

Blackmer chuckled. "You should."

Havering pulled on his gloves and backed away. "What I should do is to convey these villains to London, where we can question them properly."

"Godspeed, Havering."

"Good night, Blackmer."

Inside the room, Clarissa waited for him in their bed.

"I'm so proud of you," she said, pulling the covers back, revealing her unclothed body in the candlelight. Her body was changing now, becoming more voluptuous.

Desire burned in his belly. He stood by the bed, stripping as fast as his hands and clothing would allow.

"You're lucky I don't murder you here myself. How could you risk your life like that, and the baby's, rushing into the cottage tonight?" he murmured.

She reached for him as he climbed in beside him, enveloping him in her arms. "I didn't think. All I knew is I couldn't face a moment without you or let Michael be hurt."

She clung to him. Kissing her, he rolled her onto her back.

"I love you, Blackmer," she said, looking up. "I choose you. Forever, you."

His heartbeat increased as he heard the words because he knew without a doubt they were true. He buried his face in her neck, kissing her there. Inhaling her scent.

"I choose you forever too."

Epilogue

Samuel fussed, rousing Clarissa from her sleep. She stretched, breaking free of her dream—a very nice and sensual dream about Dominick that she regretted ending—but what a happy reality to wake up to.

Groggily she lifted onto one elbow and peered at the baby's tiny face.

"Hello there, sweet boy." She smiled, love rushing up like a burbling fountain, straight from her heart.

He fisted his hands, closed his blue eyes, and let out a squawk in response. His arms and legs went to moving.

"I know," she murmured soothingly, and gently rubbed his chest and stomach until he calmed. At nearly two months old, he was a very easy child who slept well and ate healthily. She drew her fingertip along his robust cheek, and he grinned.

"What a smile," she murmured. "So handsome. Just like your father."

His father—Dominick, whom she'd just dreamed of kissing until her toes curled. Until she saw stars.

She sighed. Since the baby's birth, there'd been only that: kissing. Well...a bit more than that. She blushed, just thinking about the way she'd pleasured him the night before. But it had been nearly eight weeks, and she felt that, at last, she was ready to return to more mutually satisfying intimacies.

Miss Randolph appeared beside the bed, bestowing an affectionate glance on the child. Clarissa often teased that when Samuel was present, she could have a caterpillar on her nose and her lady's maid wouldn't even notice, because the older woman so doted on the baby.

"It's almost time to dress for dinner," said Miss Randolph. Hearing her voice, Samuel's gaze darted toward her. "Would you like me to summon the nanny to take the young viscount to the nursery?"

Clarissa sat up and gathered Samuel in his blanket. "I'd like to take him up myself. If you could just hold him for a moment while I tidy up?"

"I might be persuaded to do that." Her smile broadening, Miss Randolph reached for the baby, lifting him into her arms with the blanket trailing over. Peering down, she gazed into his face, smiling. "The things I do for you, Master Samuel."

He let out a bellow. Miss Randolph lifted him to her shoulder and rubbed his back, drifting toward the window, where afternoon light streamed through. "Some letters arrived. From your mother and sisters."

Clarissa's heart jumped. Letters! She couldn't get enough of them. While the repairs to Frost End had been made, she and Blackmer had remained at Darthaven for the birth of their firstborn and thereafter, and had been very happy with their decision to stay. She had grown so much closer to Lord and Lady Stade, and Colin, and now truly thought of them as her family. She had also made many new friends, both in Ashington and on the surrounding estates. Still, she missed her family, and looked forward to next spring. Samuel would be old enough to travel, and Dominick had promised her they could go to London for the season. She couldn't wait to introduce her husband and children to all her friends.

"I'll read them when I return, when you try to make sense of my hair."

Miss Randolph nodded, her cheek resting atop Samuel's downy head. "I'll place them on the dressing table."

Clarissa washed at the basin and, with a quick glance in the mirror, did her best to repair her crushed hair. In the closet, she found her shoes.

A moment later, she climbed the stairs, Samuel snuggled in her arms. Clarissa could only smile now, thinking back on the difficulties that had once so divided her husband's family. Those same difficulties had, in the end, brought them closer together. They had all come so far, and it seemed the high walls they had built up against one another had never existed at all.

As for Colin, every now and then he broached the subject of marrying and taking residence at Frost End, but thus far he had shown no preference for any particular young lady and seemed content working together with Dominick to manage the family's estates.

Once upstairs, Clarissa neared the nursery and to her surprise saw her brother-in-law Colin standing in the shadows outside the open half-door, smiling, his eyes bright

with humor. Seeing her, he pressed a finger to his lips—
then extended his hand, urging her to join him.

Only when she stood very close did he whisper, "The
footman told me I could find Blackmer here. Just look what
I found."

From inside the room, she heard a small voice say
"You, sit."

"I am sitting, sweetheart," said Dominick. Then more
quietly, "If you can call it that."

He chuckled, and other voices laughed, those of Lord
and Lady Stade.

Clarissa's eyes widened at the scene inside. She bit her
lower lip, so as not to laugh and reveal herself.

Inside the nursery, Dominick sat on a miniature chair, at
a miniature table, the tops of his knees almost level with
his chin. A miniature tiara with paste diamonds sparkled
in his dark hair. He smiled down, clearly smitten by his
tiny, almost-two-year-old hostess, who held out her hands to
him—one holding a small teacup and in the other, its matching saucer, and pressing them into his hands.

"Thank you, my dear," he said, righting the upside-
down cup onto the saucer and cradling them on his palm.

Clarissa's heart warmed, so full of love and pride she
felt dizzied by it.

Gold ringlets bobbed as the little girl toddled around the
table in a yellow dress, unceremoniously pressing a cup
and saucer into each guest's waiting hands—for across the
table from her father sat her grandparents, also perched on
tiny chairs and wearing tiaras.

"Thank you, Lady Abigail," her ladyship exclaimed, her
eyes warm with affection.

"Such a sweet child." Lord Stade chuckled.

His tiara slid off his bald pate and thunked onto the floor. Abigail immediately took note and pattered to his side. Bending, she retrieved the fallen crown and returned it to her grandpapa's tilted head. He held it there, balancing it as she waddled away.

Abigail's smiling nanny stepped forward holding a wooden tray upon which sat a tiny teapot. The child reached for the pot with both chubby hands. Swinging it toward her visitors, "Teeeeeaaaaa?" she offered.

"Why, yes, thank you," Dominick said.

Clarissa couldn't help but sigh. Her husband had never been so charming or looked as handsome as he did now, doting on their daughter.

Abigail clanked the pot against her father's teacup, nearly toppling it from the saucer, then paused...her eyes focusing on the doorway. "Mama?" She smiled, dropped the pot to the carpet, and clasped her hands, fingers spread wide against her cheeks. "Baby?"

Dominick's gaze redirected toward the door to meet Clarissa's. In that moment, his cheeks warmed ruddily and he grinned. Carefully, he unfolded his long legs and tall frame from the small chair to stand like a Titan at the center of the nursery in white shirt, breeches, and boots as the little girl rushed to the door. He followed, while the nursemaid did her best to assist Lord and Lady Stade up from their chairs.

"Hello, Abigail," Clarissa called.

"We didn't want to interrupt your tea party," Colin added, reaching over the door and plucking up his niece. "Give Uncle a kiss."

She dutifully bussed his cheek—then reached for Clarissa, leaning sideways with her arms wide. "Mama!"

Dominick opened the door, his gaze on Samuel. "Give me the ruffian."

He took Samuel from Clarissa, and she in turn accepted Abigail from Colin, who appeared unabashedly dismayed at being so quickly cast off by his favorite—and only—niece. He let out an exaggerated growl. "I've got to get some little people of my own."

"I'm in complete agreement," answered Clarissa. "Would you like me to invite that pretty Miss Grayson for tea? Or perhaps Lady Barrington—"

His gaze narrowed warily and he answered, "No, thank you. I can do very well on my own."

But then he smiled—looking at Clarissa and his brother, holding their two children. "What a fine family you are."

He strode off toward his parents.

Clarissa looked up at Dominick. "I agree."

He bent to press a quick kiss to her forehead, his voice soft. "As do I."

His tiara slipped off, falling between them. Clarissa caught it with one hand, and they laughed.

"Would you like to put it back on?" said Clarissa, offering its return.

He shook his head and chuckled. "I've rather had my fill of such frippery, at least for the afternoon. Perhaps I'll wear diamonds for dinner."

"Mine," said Abigail, grinning, taking the crown and wiggling to be freed. Set down, she trundled toward Colin.

Her uncle's eyes lit up. "I get to wear the crown now. I'm so lucky."

Looking at them, he winked, before allowing himself to be directed by his hostess to one of the small chairs. Lord and Lady Stade, despite their complaints about aging bones, also returned to their places at the table. The nurse-maid approached and offered to take Samuel, at which time she and the baby were also led away, the little girl tugging at her skirts. Soon she too was seated, Samuel in her arms, a tiara being perched ever so gently on his small head by his doting sister.

"It appears they are all having a wonderful time," Dominick observed.

"As am I, just watching them," replied Clarissa, delighted.

He bent to murmur in her ear. "I haven't seen you all day. I was…hoping I might persuade you into the corridor."

Her cheeks warmed at the flirtatious tone of his voice. He slipped his hand into hers and, lifting it, pressed his mouth to her fingers.

"I don't think you'd have to do much as far as persuasion," she murmured, allowing him to lead her out of the room.

He led her to the end of the corridor, into a shadowed alcove where a small window overlooked the lawn, including the long drive that led to Darthaven. Dark clouds rippled across the sky, casting them both in dim blue light.

She shivered. "It already looks like winter out there."

"It won't be long." He pulled her into his arms, holding her close.

"Are you happy here?"

"Wildly so," he said. His warmth made her shiver, in the nicest possible way. From the nursery came the sound of laughter, and a happy squeal from Abigail.

They smiled at one another, Clarissa peering up at him. "It was a day much like this when we arrived at Darthaven, a little more than two years ago. Can you believe it?"

"I couldn't be happier." His head lowered and kissed her nose. "I mean that. I couldn't imagine being more content and fulfilled as a man, as a husband and a father, than I am now. It's all because of you."

"I feel the same," she murmured. Yet her smile faded. "There's only the one dark spot."

"Mmm," he answered. "St. Guerlain."

"And his Black Violins," she murmured.

"It hasn't been so bad, has it?"

"No, it hasn't." The security agents who protected the house and grounds were largely unnoticeable. "But wouldn't it be nice to wake up one day and know there wasn't anything to worry about? To know that everyone was safe, at last, with no fears for the future?"

"It would be," he replied.

"Do you think that will ever happen?"

"I do. In fact, I feel very strongly that very soon we'll have resolution."

"I pray you're right. Look there, a carriage just came through the gates," said Clarissa, her face turned to the window. "So late in the day. I wonder who it could be."

Dominick chuckled, looking down with affection into Clarissa's unsuspecting face. What perfect timing—he could not have hoped for better. Though certainly not on the level of his work with the secret service, this bit of subterfuge had been infinitely more satisfying than any mission he could recall.

"Why are you laughing?" She smiled. Then her eyes narrowed in playful suspicion. "Dominick! Do you know who it is?"

They hadn't made love in what felt like an epoch. Standing this close to her...smelling her floral perfume, mixed all up with *her*, he could hardly keep his thoughts straight. But he'd kept this secret for over a week. She wouldn't pry it from him now, no matter how vividly blue her eyes were. No matter how enticing her pink lips.

He shrugged, nonchalant. "Perhaps."

"Is it someone I know?" Her hands bunched in his shirt, atop his chest.

"I can't say for certain," he said vaguely.

"You *do* know." She pinched his arm. "Tell me!"

"I can't. I promised," he teased. "But perhaps you should...go downstairs to welcome them."

"*Them?*" Her eyes widened and her lips parted as, clearly, she considered the possibilities.

She darted away—

He caught her by the arm and pulled her back for a kiss—a fervent blur of soft lips and minted breath. His heart beat faster, as it always did when he kissed her, his vibrant, alluring wife. The woman he loved more deeply as each day passed. How could he have ever known her *before* and not loved her? She was such a part of him now, like the other half of his heart. Being without her seemed so unimaginable now.

She stepped away.

"You're coming with me, aren't you?" She held his hand in both of hers, and pulled him alongside her, cheeks flushed with excitement.

He paused only a moment at the nursery door to rap on the wooden frame. "We've guests."

His mother bolted from her chair. "Stade, they've arrived. Hurry."

She grabbed hold of His Lordship's elbow and tugged him up. Colin reached for Abigail, hoisting her into his arms.

Dominick held Clarissa's hand tightly as she descended the stairs, she always a step below him, concerned that she would take a tumble in her excitement, although he knew she was as sure-footed as he. Darthaven's front doors were already open and the footmen outside. Below stood a large traveling carriage that bore a large gold ducal insignia on the door. Several occupants already were on the grass, having disembarked. Gusts of wind pitched their skirts and threatened to dislodge their hats.

"*Mother!*" cried Clarissa.

She rushed down the front steps and threw her arms around the woman who stood there, dressed in yellow. Dominick followed at a slower pace, watching the melee of feminine excitement that ensued. How quickly Clarissa had forgotten him, and for good reason—for the first time since Abigail's birth, her mother had come for a visit, and this time, she had not come alone.

"Sophia! Daphne!" Clarissa exclaimed, stunned by her family's arrival. "Where's Christian? And where's Michael?"

The duke and duchess's son, Christian, was seven months older than her Abigail, and Michael, the oldest of the family children, was now nearly six years old.

"They're with Claxton and Raikes," Daphne answered, kissing her sister's cheek.

"You left them behind?" Clarissa's voice cracked with disappointment.

"Of course not," replied the smiling duchess as she moved past, headed straight for the children who had arrived in the arms of Colin and Lady Stade. "They'll be along in a moment."

Daphne broke free of Clarissa's embrace to follow her.

Just then, a second and a third coach rumbled through the gates. Then a fourth.

Clarissa leapt off the earth, clapping her hands.

"Everyone's here!" She seized her mother's arm. "Is everyone here? Even Wolverton?"

"Wolverton refused to stay behind. Otherwise, we'd have been here two days earlier. We've been traveling slowly to ensure his comfort," her mother answered.

Daphne returned with Samuel in her arms. "He's beautiful, Clarissa."

Lady Margaretta peered down at the baby and touched his cheek. "Hello, Samuel. Oh, give him to his grandmother."

Tears welled in Clarissa's eyes, and emotion tightened her throat. There had been dark days, not so long ago, when she couldn't have imagined this happy moment. Her gaze found Dominick's. He stood on the steps beside his family, his arms crossed over his chest, smiling at her.

Sophia returned, with Abigail in her arms. "She's not a baby anymore, is she? She's a picture of you, Clarissa."

Daphne reached for the little girl's hand and squeezed it affectionately, teasing "I think she looks more like me."

Lady Margaretta looked up from the baby in her arms, her eyes shining on her youngest daughter—and then on her son-in-law. "I'm so happy for you both."

"We are happy as well, Mother. So happy." Clarissa joined arms with her mother and sisters—with Abigail and Samuel perched in the center—and for a moment they formed a circle. "I can't believe you are all here. It's a dream come true."

"Dreams *do* come true," said Daphne.

"And more will come true. Just wait and see."

The other coaches and their horses scrabbled to a stop behind the first.

"Go see Wolverton," her mother urged softly.

Clarissa left their circle, pausing at the first carriage, waving through the windows at Claxton and Raikes and two little faces as they peered out. The third carriage, conveying servants who traveled with the family, moved around them and disappeared toward the back of the house.

The gentlemen and two rather grumpy-faced children in rumpled clothes disembarked, and Clarissa exchanged kisses and greetings with all of them.

"Is Wolverton there, inside?" she asked.

"Yes, he is, and he's waiting to see you," replied Claxton.

"In the meantime, I'll get his chair." Raikes set off toward the back of the carriage, but footmen, at Dominick's direction, had already lowered the chair to the ground. The two men shook hands.

Clarissa climbed the steps into the carriage, where shadows and the scent of soap and tobacco met her. Wolverton sat on the bench, smartly dressed in a traveling suit. He leaned forward, reaching for her. "There you are, my granddaughter."

He framed her face in his hands and kissed her cheek.

"I'm so happy that you've come, my lord," she murmured.

"These old bones don't travel well anymore." He let out a rusty chuckle. "I may decide never to leave."

A deeper voice answered from the door—Dominick stood there, peering inside. "You're welcome to remain at Darthaven as long as you wish."

"Normally I don't travel anymore, but I had to come to see you because I wanted to tell you myself."

"Tell us what?" answered Clarissa, taking a seat beside him.

"Come," he said, reaching for Dominick, who complied by entering and kneeling beside the earl.

He held both of their hands, his face flushed with excitement. "We're all free."

"Free?" said Clarissa.

"St. Guerlain and his Black Violins. They are...no more. We and our children can all now live our lives as they should be led. Without fear. Without further harm."

"How did it happen?" asked Dominick, his gaze intense.

"Well, that story will take quite a bit of telling. Perhaps tonight at dinner." Wolverton smiled, his eyebrows raised. "Let me just say for now, we owe everything to Lords Havering and Haden and...others." His smile broadened. "Such brave young men. They are the new lions of the empire, and England is greater for them."

Clarissa reached for Dominick's hand. "Do I dare believe it?"

Wolverton nodded. "Believe it, and know it would not have been possible if not for your own husband's bravery in leading us all to the truth before it was too late."

Clarissa's chest constricted, filled with love for Dominick.

"I'm so proud of him," she answered, looking between them.

"As am I. Now give your grandfather a kiss for forcing you to marry him in the first place." He grinned, his aged eyes crinkling at the corners, and tapped his cheek with his finger. "Aren't I an astute judge of character?"

"You certainly are." She leaned forward and kissed him.

Dominick chuckled. "I think I have to kiss you as well, then, for forcing me to marry Clarissa."

"A handshake will do." The earl laughed.

A moment later, two burly footmen carried Wolverton up the front steps of Darthaven in his chair. Clarissa and Dominick followed, hand in hand. At the top of the stairs, their families waited in a loud, moving jumble, laughing and chattering. A cool wind rustled the leaves of the trees.

"Just look at that," said Dominick. "Did you ever think to see them all here together at Darthaven?"

"It looks like home, doesn't it?"

"It makes me very happy to hear you say that." Dominick drew Clarissa to a stop beside him and looked into her face.

"You *are* a hero, you know," she murmured.

"I'm honored to be recognized by your grandfather as such, but I'm just a man who did as any man would have done."

"But you aren't just *any* man. You're my husband, and my hero, every day. I love you."

"I love you too." He bent and murmured, "It's *you* and our children who make Darthaven home for me."

He lifted her chin with his hand and kissed her. She sighed, brimming over with happiness. The crowd on the steps above them grew instantly hushed.

"Everyone is watching," he murmured against her lips.

"I don't care," she murmured against his.

She *didn't* care. She wanted the whole world to know how much she loved him.

Laughing, she threw her arms around his shoulders and kissed him again.

The sound of horses' hooves striking earth sounded

again, along with carriage wheels. She and Dominick turned to observe an approaching conveyance.

Clarissa looked to the top of the steps. "More visitors? Who is it?"

"It's Havering," called Claxton. "And my brother, Lord Haden."

"Aren't they lucky?" smiled Clarissa. "They got a whole carriage to themselves?"

"Oh, no. They aren't alone," replied her mother.

"Who else is with them?" she asked.

Wolverton winked. "You'll just have to wait and find out."

Please turn this page
for a preview of

Book One
of the
One Scandalous Season
series,

*Never Desire
a Duke*

he scent of gingerbread in the air!" exclaimed Sir Keyes, his aged blue eyes sparkling with mischief. Winter wind swept through open doors behind him, carrying the sound of carriages from the street. "And there's mistletoe to be had from the peddler's stall on the corner."

Though his pantaloons drooped off his slight frame to an almost comical degree, the military orders and decorations emblazoned across his chest attested to a life of valor years before. Leaning heavily on his cane, the old man produced a knotty green cluster from behind his back, strung from a red ribbon, and held it aloft between himself and Sophia.

"Such happy delights can mean only one thing." He grinned roguishly—or as roguishly as a man of his advanced years could manage. "It is once again the most magical time of year."

He tapped his gloved finger against his rosy cheek with expectant delight.

"Indeed!" The diminutive Dowager Countess of Dundalk stepped between them, smiling up from beneath a fur-trimmed turban. She swatted the mistletoe, sending the sphere swinging to and fro. "The time of year when old men resort to silly provincial traditions to coax kisses from ladies young enough to be their granddaughters."

At the side of her turban a diamond aigrette held several large purple feathers. The plumes bobbed wildly as she spoke. "Well, it *is* almost Christmastide." Sophia winked at Sir Keyes, and with a gentle hand to his shoulder, she warmly bussed his cheek. "I'm so glad you've come."

A widower of two years, he had recently begun accompanying Lady Dundalk about town, something that made Sophia exceedingly happy, since both had long been dear to her heart.

Sir Keyes plucked a white berry from the cluster, glowing with satisfaction at having claimed his holiday kiss.

"I see that only a handful remain," Sophia observed. "Best use them wisely."

His eyebrows rose up on his forehead, as white and unruly as uncombed wool. "I shall have to find your sisters, then, and posthaste."

"Libertine!" muttered the dowager countess, with a fond roll of her eyes.

Behind them, two footmen with holly sprigs adorning their coat buttonholes secured the doors. Another presented a silver tray to Sir Keyes, upon which he deposited the price of Sophia's kiss and proceeded toward the ballroom, the mistletoe cluster swinging from the lions' head handle of his cane. Together, Sophia and the dowager countess followed arm in arm, through columns entwined in greenery, toward the sounds of music and voices raised in jollity.

With Parliament having recessed mid-December for Christmas, the districts of St. James's, Mayfair, and Piccadilly were largely deserted by that fashionable portion of London's population oft defined as the *ton*. Like most of their peers, Sophia's family's Christmases were usually spent in the country, but her grandfather's recent frailties had precluded any travel. So his immediate family, consisting of a devoted daughter-in-law and three granddaughters, had resolved to spend the season in London.

But today was Lord Wolverton's eighty-seventh birthday, and by Sophia's tally, no fewer than two hundred of the elusive *ton* had crept out from the proverbial winter woodwork to wish her grandfather well. By all accounts, the party was a success.

In the ballroom, candlelight reflected off the crystal teardrops of chandeliers high above their heads, as well as the numerous candelabras and lusters positioned about the room, creating beauty in everything its golden glow touched. The fragrance of fresh-cut laurel and fir, brought in from the country just that afternoon, mingled pleasantly with the perfume of the hothouse gardenias, tuberose, and stephanotis arranged in Chinese vases about the room.

Though there would be no dancing tonight, a piano quintet provided an elegant musical accompaniment to the hum of laughter and conversation.

"Lovely!" declared Lady Dundalk. "Your mother told me you planned everything, to the last detail."

"I'm pleased by how splendidly everything has turned out." The dowager countess slipped an arm around Sophia's shoulders and squeezed with affection. "The only thing missing, of course, is the Duke of Claxton."

The warm smile on Sophia's lips froze like ice, and it

felt as if the walls of the room suddenly converged at the mere mention of her husband. It didn't seem to matter how long he had been away, her emotions were still so raw.

Lady Dundalk peered up at her, concern in her eyes. "I know you wish the duke could be here tonight, and certainly for Christmas. No word on when our esteemed diplomat will return to England?"

Sophia shook her head, hoping the woman would perceive none of the heartache she feared was written all over her face. "Perhaps in the spring."

A vague response at best, but the truth was she did not know when Claxton would return. His infrequent, impersonal correspondence made no such predictions, and she had not lowered herself to ask.

They came to stand near the fire, where a delicious heat warmed the air.

"Eighty-seven years old?" bellowed Sir Keyes. "Upon my word, Wolverton, you can't be a day over seventy, else that would make me—" Lifting a hand, he counted through its knobby fingers, grinning. "Older than dirt!"

"We *are* older than dirt, and thankful to be so." Her grandfather beamed up from where he sat in his bath chair, his cheeks pink from excitement. His party had been a surprise for the most part, with him believing until just an hour ago the event would be only a small family affair. He appeared truly astounded and deeply touched. "Thank you all for coming."

Small, gaily beribboned parcels of Virginian tobacco, chocolate, and his favorite souchong tea lay upon his lap. Sophia gathered them and placed them beneath the lowest boughs of the potted tabletop yew behind them, one that would remain unadorned until Christmas Eve, when the family would gather to decorate the tree in the custom of her late grandmother's German forebears.

Her family. Their worried glances and gentle questions let her know they were aware that her marriage had become strained. But she loved them so much! Which was why she'd shielded them from the full magnitude of the truth—the truth being that when Claxton had accepted his foreign appointment in May, he had all but abandoned her and their marriage. The man she'd once loved to distraction had become nothing more than a cold and distant stranger.

But for Sophia, Christmas had always been a time of self-contemplation, and the New Year, a time for renewal. Like so many others, she made a habit of making resolutions. By nature, she craved happiness, and if she could not have happiness with Claxton, she would have it some other way.

She had given herself until the New Year to suitably resolve her marital difficulties. The day after Christmas she would go to Camellia House, located just across the Thames in the small village of Lacenfleet, and sequester herself away from curious eyes and the opinions of her family, so that she alone could pen the necessary letter.

She was going to ask Claxton for a legal separation. Then he could go on living his life just as he pleased, with all the freedoms and indulgences he clearly desired. But she wanted something in return—a baby—and even if that meant joining him for a time in Vienna, she intended to have her way.

Just the thought of seeing Claxton again sent her spiraling into an exquisitely painful sort of misery. She had no wish to see him—and yet he never left her thoughts.

No doubt her presence would throw the private life His

Grace had been living into chaos, and she would find herself an unwanted outsider. No doubt he had a mistress—or two—as so many husbands abroad did. Even now, the merest fleeting thought of him in the arms of another woman made her stomach clench. He had betrayed her so appallingly she could hardly imagine allowing him to touch her again. But a temporary return to intimacies with her estranged husband was the only way she could have the child she so desperately wanted.

Sophia bent to adjust the green tartan blanket over Wolverton's legs, ensuring that His Lordship would be protected not only from any chill but also the bump and jostle of the throng gathered about him.

"May I bring you something, Grandfather? Perhaps some punch?"

His blue eyes brightened.

"Yes, dear." He winked and gestured for her to come closer. When she complied, he lowered his voice. "With a dash of my favorite maraschino added, if you please, in honor of the occasion. Only don't tell your mother. You know just as well as I that she and my physician are in collusion to deprive me of all the joys of life."

Sophia knew he didn't believe any such thing, but still, it was great fun to continue the conspiratorial banter between them. Each moment with him, she knew, was precious. His joy this evening would be a memory she would always treasure.

"I'd be honored to keep your secret, my lord," Sophia said, pressing a kiss to his cheek.

"What secret?" Lady Harwick, Sophia's dark-haired mother, approached from behind.

A picture of well-bred elegance, Margaretta conveyed

warmth and good humor in every glance and gesture. Tonight she wore violet silk, one of the few colors she had allowed into her wardrobe since the tragic loss of her eldest son, Vinson, at sea four years ago—followed all too soon by the death of Sophia's father, the direct heir to the Wolverton title.

"If we told you, then it wouldn't be a secret," Sophia answered jovially, sidestepping her. "His Lordship has requested a glass of punch, and since I'm his undisputed favorite, at least for this evening, I will fetch it for him."

Wolverton winked at Sophia. "I shall have the secret pried out of him before you return." With that, Margaretta bent to straighten the same portion of Lord Wolverton's blanket her daughter had straightened only moments before.

Still a beautiful, vibrant woman, Margaretta drew the gazes of a number of the more mature gentlemen in the room. Not for the first time, Sophia wondered if her mother might entertain the idea of marrying again.

Sophia crossed the floor to the punch bowl, pausing several times to speak to friends and acquaintances along the way. Though most of the guests were older friends of Lord Wolverton, the presence of Sophia's pretty younger sisters, Daphne and Clarissa, had assured the attendance of numerous ladies and gentlemen from the younger set. Her fair-haired siblings, born just a year apart and assumed by many to be twins, would make their debut in the upcoming season. That is, if favored suitors did not snatch them off the market before Easter.

At the punch bowl, Sophia dipped the ladle and filled a crystal cup. With the ladle's return to the bowl, another hand retrieved it—a gloved hand upon which glimmered an enormous sapphire ring.

"Your Grace?" a woman's voice inquired.

Sophia looked up into a beautiful, heart-shaped face, framed by stylish blond curls, one she instantly recognized but did not recall greeting in the reception line. The gown worn by the young woman, fashioned of luxurious peacock-blue silk and trimmed with gold and scarlet cording, displayed her generous décolletage to a degree one would not normally choose for the occasion of an off-season birthday party for an eighty-seven-year-old lord.

"Good evening, Lady..."

"Meltenbourne," the young woman supplied, with a delicate laugh. "You might recall me as Annabelle Ellesmere? We debuted the same season."

Yes, of course. Annabelle, Lady Meltenbourne, née Ellesmere. Voluptuous, lush, and ambitious, she had once carried quite the flaming torch for Claxton, and upon learning of the duke's betrothal to Sophia, she had not been shy about expressing her displeasure to the entire *ton* over not being chosen as his duchess. Not long after, Annabelle had married a very rich but very old earl.

"Such a lovely party." The countess sidled around the table to stand beside her, so close Sophia could smell her exotic perfume, a distinctive fragrance of ripe fruit and oriental spice. "Your grandfather must be a wonderful man to be so resoundingly adored."

"Thank you, Lady Meltenbourne. Indeed, he is."

Good breeding prevented Sophia from asking Annabelle why she was present at the party at all. She had addressed each invitation herself, and without a doubt, Lord and Lady Meltenbourne had not been on the guest list.

"I don't believe I've been introduced to Lord Melten-bourne." Sophia perused the room, but saw no more unfa-miliar faces.

"Perhaps another time," the countess answered vaguely, offering nothing more but a shrug. Plucking a red sugar drop from a candy dish, she gazed adoringly upon the confection and giggled. "I shouldn't give in to such tempta-tions, but I admit to being a shamefully impulsive woman." She pushed the sweet into her mouth and reacted with an almost sensual ecstasy, closing her eyes and smiling. "Mmmmm."

Meanwhile a gentleman had approached to refill his punch glass and gaped at the countess as she savored the sugar drop, and in doing so, he missed his cup altogether. Punch splashed over his hand and onto the table. Lady Meltenbourne selected another sweet from the dish, obliv-ious to his response. Or perhaps not. Within moments, servants appeared to tidy the mess and the red-faced fellow rushed away.

Sophia let out a slow, calming breath and smothered her first instinct, which was to order the countess to *spit out the sugar drop* and immediately quit the party. After all, time had passed. They had all matured. Christmas was a time for forgiveness. For bygones to be bygones.

Besides, London in winter could be rather dreary. This one in particular had been uncommonly foggy and cold. Perhaps Annabelle simply sought human companionship and had come along with another guest. Sophia certainly understood loneliness. Whatever the reason for the woman's attendance, her presence was of no real concern. Lady Meltenbourne and her now candy-sugared lips were just as welcome tonight as anyone else. The party would be over soon, and Sophia wished to spend the remainder with her grandfather.

"Well, it was lovely seeing you again, but I've promised this glass of punch to our guest of honor. Enjoy your evening."

Sophia turned, but a sudden hand to her arm stayed her.

"What of Claxton?" the countess blurted.

The punch sloshed. Instinctively Sophia extended the glass far from her body, to prevent the liquid from spilling down her skirts, but inside her head, the intimate familiarity with which Lady Annabelle spoke her husband's name tolled like an inharmonious bell.

"Pardon me?" She glanced sharply at the hand on her arm. "What did you say?"

Annabelle, wide-eyed and smiling, snatched her hand away, clasping it against the pale globe of her breast. "Will His Grace make an appearance here tonight?"

Sophia had suffered much during her marriage, but this affront—at her grandfather's party—was too much.

Good breeding tempered her response. She'd been raised a lady. As a girl, she'd learned her lessons and conducted herself with perfect grace and honor. As a young woman, she'd maneuvered the dangerous waters of her first season, where a single misstep could ruin her prospects of a respectable future. She had made her family and herself proud.

Sophia refused to succumb to the impulse of rage. Instead she summoned every bit of her self-control, and with the greatest of efforts, forbade herself from flinging the glass and its scarlet contents against the front of the woman's gown.

With her gaze fixed directly on Lady Meltenbourne, she answered calmly, "I would assume not."

The countess's smile transformed into what was most certainly a false moue of sympathy. "Oh, dear. You *do* know he's in town, don't you, Your Grace?"

Sophia's vision went black. Claxton in London? Could that be true? If he had returned without even the courtesy of sending word—

A tremor of anger shot down her spine, but with great effort she maintained her outward calm. However, that calm withered in the face of Lady Meltenbourne's blatant satisfaction. Her bright eyes and parted, half-smiling lips proclaimed the malicious intent behind her words, negating any obligation by Sophia for a decorous response. Yet before she could present the countess with a dismissive view of her train, the woman, in a hiss of silk, flounced into the crowd.

Only to be replaced by Sophia's sisters, who fell upon her like street thieves, spiriting her into the deeper shadows of a nearby corner. Unlike Sophia, who could wear the more dramatically hued Geneva velvet as a married woman, Daphne and Clarissa wore diaphanous, long-sleeved white muslin trimmed with lace and ribbon.

"Who invited that woman?" Daphne, the elder of the two, demanded.

Sophia answered, "She wasn't invited."

"Did you see her *bosoms*?" Clarissa marveled.

"How could you not?" Daphne said. "They are enormous, like cannonballs. It's indecent. Everyone is staring, even Clarissa and I. We simply couldn't help ourselves."

"That dress! It's beyond fashion," Clarissa gritted. "It's the dead of winter. Isn't she cold? She might as well have worn nothing at all."

"*Daphne*," Sophia warned. "*Clarissa.*"

Daphne's eyes narrowed. "What exactly did she say to you?"

Sophia banished all emotion from her voice. "Nothing of import."

"That's not true," Clarissa retorted. She leaned close and hissed, "She asked you if Claxton would be in attendance tonight."

Stung at hearing her latest shame spoken aloud, Sophia responded more sharply than intended. "If you heard her ask me about Claxton, then why did you ask me what she said?"

Her hands trembled so greatly that she could no longer hold the punch glass without fear of spilling its contents. She deposited the glass on the nearby butler's tray. Within seconds, a servant appeared and whisked it away.

Clarissa's nostrils flared. "I didn't hear her. Not exactly. It's just that she's—"

"Clarissa!" Daphne interjected sharply, silencing whatever revelation her sister had intended to share.

"No, you must tell me," Sophia demanded. "Lady Meltenbourne has what?"

Clarissa glared at Daphne. "She deserves to know."

Daphne, clearly miserable, nodded in assent. "Very well."

Clarissa uttered, "She's already asked the question of nearly everyone else in the room."

Despite the chill in the air, heat rose into Sophia's cheeks, along with a dizzying pressure inside her head. The conversation between herself and Lady Meltenbourne had been shocking enough. With Clarissa's revelation, Sophia was left nothing short of humiliated. She'd tried so desperately to keep rumors of Claxton's indiscretions from

her family so as not to complicate any possible future rec-
onciliation, but now her secrets were spilling out on the
ballroom floor for anyone's ears to hear.

"Trollop," whispered Daphne. "It's none of her concern where Claxton is. It is only your concern, Sophia.
And *our* concern as well, of course, because we are your
sisters. Someone should tell her so." Though her sister
had been blessed with the face of an angel, a distinctly
devilish glint gleamed in her blue eyes. "Do you wish for
me to be the one to say it? Please say yes, because I'm
aching to—"

"Erase that smug look from her face," interjected
Clarissa, fists clenched at her sides, looking very much the
female pugilist.

"You'll do nothing of the sort," Sophia answered vehemently. "You'll conduct yourselves as ladies, not as
ruffians off the street. This is my private affair. Mine
and Claxton's. Do you understand? Do not mention any
of what has occurred to Mother, and especially not to
our grandfather. I won't have you ruining his birthday or
Christmas."

"Understood," they answered in unison. Her sisters'
dual gazes offered sympathy, and worse—pity.

Though Sophia would readily offer the same to any
woman in her circumstances, she had no wish to be the
recipient of such unfortunate sentiments. The whole ugly
incident further proved the insupportability of her marriage
and her husband's tendency to stray. Though Lady Meltenbourne's presence stung, it made Sophia only more certain
that Claxton would agree to her terms. Certainly he would
prefer to have his freedom—and he would have it, just as
soon as he gave her a child. Seventeen months ago when

she spoke her vows, she'd been naïve. She'd had such big dreams of a life with Claxton and had given her heart completely, only to have it thrown back in her face when she needed him the most. Claxton would never be a husband in the loyal, devoted sense of the word. He would never love her completely, the way she needed to be loved.

Admittedly, in the beginning, that aloofness—his very mysteriousness—had captivated her. The year of her debut, the duke had appeared in London out of nowhere, newly possessed of an ancient title. His rare appearances at balls were cause for delirium among the ranks of the hopeful young misses and their mammas.

Then—oh, then—she'd craved his brooding silences, believing with a certainty that once they married, Claxton would give her his trust. He would give her his heart.

For a time, she'd believed that he had. She closed her eyes against a dizzying rush of memories. *His smile. His laughter. Skin. Mouths. Heat. Completion.*

It had been enough. At least she thought it had been.

"Well?" said Daphne.

"Well, what?"

"Will Claxton make an appearance tonight?"

"I don't know," whispered Sophia.

Clarissa sighed. "Lord Tunsley told me he saw Claxton at White's this afternoon, with Lord Haden and Mr. Grisham."

Sophia nodded mutely. So it was confirmed. After seven months abroad, her husband had returned to London, and everyone seemed to know but her. The revelation left her numb and sadder than she expected. She ought to be angry—*no!*—furious at being treated with such disregard. Either that or she ought to do like so many other wives of the *ton* and forget the injustice of it all in the arms of a lover. She'd certainly had the opportunity.

Just then her gaze met that of a tall gentleman who stood near the fireplace, staring at her intently over the heads of the three animatedly gesturing Aimsley sisters. Lord Havering, or "Fox" as he had been known in the informal environs of their country childhood, always teased that she ought to have waited for him—and more than once had implied that he still waited for her.

With a tilt of his blond head, he mouthed: *Are you well?*

Of course, Lady Meltenbourne's indiscreet inquiries about Claxton would not have escaped Fox's hearing. No doubt the gossipy Aimsley sisters were dissecting the particulars at this very moment. Sophia flushed in mortification, but at the same time was exceedingly grateful Fox cared for her feelings at all. It was more than she could say for her own husband.

Yet she had no heart for adultery. To Fox she responded with a nod and a polite smile, and returned her attention to her sisters. While she held no illusions about the pleasure-seeking society in which she lived, she'd grown up in the household of happily married parents who loved one another deeply. Magnificently. Had she been wrong to believe she deserved nothing short of the same?

Clarissa touched her arm and inquired softly, "Is it true, Sophia, what everyone is saying, that you and Claxton are officially estranged?"

In that moment, the candlelight flickered. A rush of frigid air pushed through the room, as if the front doors of the house had been thrown open. The chill assaulted her bare skin, and the hairs on the back of her neck stood on end. All conversation in the ballroom grew hushed, but a silent, indefinable energy exploded exponentially.

Both pairs of her sisters' eyes fixed at the same point over her shoulders.

"Oh, my," whispered Daphne.

Clarissa's face lost its color. "Sophia—"

She looked over her shoulder. In that moment, her gaze locked with the bold, blue-eyed stare of a darkly handsome stranger.

Only, of course, he wasn't a stranger, not in the truest sense of the word. But he might as well have been. It was Claxton.

Her heart swelled with a thousand memories of him, only to subside, just as quickly, into frigid calm. Without hesitation, she responded as her good breeding required. She crossed the marble floor, aware that all eyes in the room were trained on her, and with a kiss welcomed her faithless husband home.

Fall in Love with Forever Romance

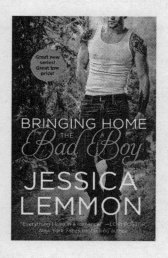

BRINGING HOME THE BAD BOY
by Jessica Lemmon

The boys are back in town! Welcome to Evergreen Cove and the first book in Jessica Lemmon's Second Chance series, sure to appeal to fans of Jaci Burton. These bad boys will leave you weak in the knees and begging for more.

HOT AND BOTHERED
by Kate Meader

Just when you thought it couldn't get any hotter! Best friends Tad and Jules have vowed not to ruin their perfect friendship with romance, but fate has other plans...Fans of Jill Shalvis won't be able to resist the attraction of Kate Meader's Hot in the Kitchen series.

Fall in Love with Forever Romance

FOR KEEPS
by Rachel Lacey

Merry Atwater would do anything to save her dog rescue—even work with the stubborn and sexy TJ Jameson. But can he turn their sparks into something more? Fans of Jill Shalvis and Kristan Higgins will fall in love with the next book in the Love to the Rescue series!

BLIND FAITH
by Rebecca Zanetti

The third book in *New York Times* bestseller Rebecca Zanetti's sexy romantic suspense series features a ruthless, genetically engineered soldier with an expiration date who's determined to save himself and his brothers. But there's only one person who can help them: the very woman who broke his heart years ago...

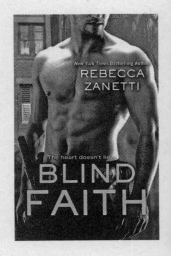

Fall in Love with Forever Romance

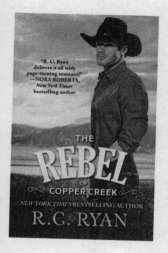

THE REBEL OF COPPER CREEK
by R. C. Ryan

Fans of *New York Times* best-selling authors Linda Lael Miller and Diana Palmer will love this second book in R. C. Ryan's western trilogy about a young widow whose hands are full until she meets a sexy and rebellious cowboy. If there's anything she's learned, it's that love only leads to heartbreak, but can she resist him?

NEVER SURRENDER
TO A SCOUNDREL
by Lily Dalton

Fans of *New York Times* best-sellers Sabrina Jeffries, Nicole Jordan, and Jillian Hunter will want to check out the newest from Lily Dalton, a novel about a lady who has engaged in a reckless indiscretion leaving her with two choices: ruin her family with the scandal of the season, or marry the notorious scoundrel mistaken as her lover.

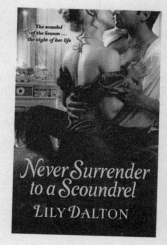